Four Brothers Into the Light

Book III

JEL JONES

(Sequel to Four Brothers In Love)

America Star Books
Frederick, Maryland

Softcover 9781681762760

PUBLISHED BY AMERICA STAR BOOKS, LLLP

www.americastarbooks.pub

Frederick, Maryland

Chapter One

Veronica sat comfortably on the living room sofa with her back resting against the cushions with both legs propped on an ottoman as Catherine strolled into the room. Catherine was professionally dressed with her tan Coach purse swinging on her shoulder. Veronica glanced up from the Newsweek Magazine but quickly focused back on the article she was reading. Catherine glanced about the room as if she hadn't seen it before or wouldn't see it again. But Veronica was busy reading and didn't pay her any attention as Catherine walked across the room to one of the windows, pulled the curtains a part and looked out toward Julian Bartlett new residence. She thought how she had enjoyed her three dates with him on Friday, Saturday and Sunday. She wondered why she couldn't have met him and gotten over Antonio before Antonio sailed back into town? Then as she stood there looking out at the clear day, a cold chill of uncertainty made her trembled. It was Monday, the twenty-fourth of March and the outside seemed calm as her thoughts were a storm brewing inside of her reflecting heavily on the conversation with Veronica the night before:

"Raymond Ross can breathe a little easier since he won't be hit with a murder charge," Veronica casually mentioned the night before as they were getting ready for bed. "He was apprehended and not charged with the murder of Antonio, but he still doesn't get a chance to breathe easy, since he'll still have his day in court for attempted murder of both his wife and Antonio."

"It's surprising that Raymond Ross was cleared. He was their number one suspect," Catherine was stunned to hear he was innocence. "So, if Raymond isn't the one who murdered Antonio, who did?" Catherine asked.

"I'm sure they will find the responsible party. They always do. Therefore, some poor soul will be hauled in for first degree cold blooded murder soon or later," Veronica said.

"But Raymond had a motive. Who else wanted him dead?"

"Who knows, that man was not always that considerate. It could be one of a hundred that he wronged throughout his life along the way," Veronica pointed out. "If you ask me, it was probably some female who decided not to let him off the hook for treating her badly."

"Why do you say that?" Catherine asked.

"I say it because that's probably what happened and I know it wouldn't surprise you if it turns out to be some female that he mistreated the same way he mistreated you all those years ago," Veronica reminded her.

Catherine was forced to snap out of her daydream when Veronica looked across the room at her and made an observation.

"I guess you're looking out at your new boyfriend's house," Veronica said in a teasing manner.

Catherine didn't answer as she was still stuck in thought about their conversation of the night before about Raymond Ross not being the person who murdered Antonio. That new evidence made her realize and face a tough truth that she had to do what she had decided to do from the moment she had gotten out of bed.

"Did you hear me?" Veronica asked. "What are you doing anyway? You are about to head to the library?"

"No, I'm not headed to the library," Catherine mumbled solemnly as she glanced at her watch. It was 10:30 in the morning.

"Well, do you mind me asking where you are headed? I like that brown suit. Is that a new outfit?"

"The suit is not new and if you don't mind, I would prefer not to say where I'm headed," Catherine respectfully uttered, still stationed at the window looking out.

"Whatever, Catherine, I wasn't trying to pry. I just asked," Veronica stared at Catherine for a moment, wondering what was going on with her.

Stepping across the room toward the sofa, Catherine said. "If I didn't thank you for introducing me to Julian, I would like to thank you now. I really do thank you for thinking of me and setting me up with him," Catherine said a bit too formally.

Veronica glanced up over her reading glass. She detected that something wasn't quite right with Catherine, but she didn't comment on her behavior.

"Yes, I'm mighty thankful for Julian."

"How is that going?"

"Well, it's like my mother used to tell me, and she was right. I always end up a day late and a dollar short; and it's no different this time with Julian. So, to answer your question, I'm not going to kid around with you. It's not going anywhere."

"What you mean it's not going anywhere? You could have fooled me. The man has rung our doorbell for three nights in a row. It doesn't sound like there's a problem based on his actions; but I'll ask you anyway, what seems to be the problem?"

"I'm the problem and I know it."

"Why do you think you're the problem? If the man wants to spend time with you back to back, he must doesn't see you as a problem. Really, Catherine, the two of you have gone out three nights in a row, which should count for something. I don't think Julian Bartlett is the kind of man who would hang around and take a woman out three nights in a row if he wasn't interested in her," Veronica stressed seriously, smiling and shaking her head in amusement. "I told him he would like you if he just asked you out and spent some time with you. Apparently he likes you, so what's the issue?"

"The issue is me and not being able to give my heart to Julian because of Antonio," Catherine said as she took a seat on the sofa next to Veronica.

"You don't have to give the man your heart, just date him for goodness sake. You just started going out. Just enjoy getting to know each other and worry about the rest later," Veronica strongly suggested.

"I hear you talking but it's not doing any good. I have gone out with Julian for three nights in a row and each evening he told me how much he enjoyed my company. But he also told me in a discreet way that he was tired of me talking his ear off about Antonio."

"My goodness, Catherine, the man actually had to tell you to put a lid on it where Antonio was concerned?"

"Yes, he did. He politely asked if we could change the subject and talk about something other than what I went through with Antonio."

"So, did you cease your gabbing and yapping about Antonio?"

"Yes, I did, and my company became quite boring really fast, since I don't seem to have any other conversation except about Antonio," Catherine said in a defeated voice.

"Well, can you blame the man for not wanting conversation about your ex-husband to monopoly your time together while he's trying to get to know you?"

"I just wanted to tell him all about my past so he could get to know me better."

"It sounds like you were basically telling him all about Antonio, over and over." Veronica waved her hand toward Catherine. "You need to get a grip and realize that Julian Bartlett is a decent guy and you are super lucky that he's interested in you."

"I know that, I just thanked you for introducing us."

"Well, you need to drop Antonio from your brain when you're out with Julian. He doesn't want to spend his time with you conversing about how awful you had it with your ex-husband."

"I get it and I won't allow the subject of Antonio to monopoly my conversation the next time we are out together, if there's a next time."

"What do you mean, if there's a next time?"

"I sort of ended things with him."

"Catherine, you are a fool," Veronica snapped. "You have been alone for twenty years pining over a man who wasn't worth your tears. You meet a nice guy who likes you and you dump him for no good reason." Veronica held up both hands. "You deserve to be alone and if you don't mind, I don't care to discuss this any further."

"Veronica, it's not what you think."

"What do you think I'm thinking? It sounds like you ended it with the man because you felt if you didn't, he would?" Veronica said irritated. "Does that sum it up?"

Catherine didn't comment as she sat there with a lost look in her eyes.

"I'm sure it does sum it up. You know why? It's because you have no damn confidence in yourself, all because the jerk you can't stop talking about destroyed it."

Catherine shook her head. "No, it wasn't like that." "I didn't officially end things with Julian."

"You just told me that you sort of ended things with the man. What the heck does that mean, if it doesn't mean you break up with the man?"

"It means I have broken off with him in my mind."

"The more you talk the less sense you make," Veronica said, annoyed with her pessimistic outlook.

"Frankly, Veronica, it doesn't matter now. Whatever future I could have had with Julian Bartlett doesn't matter anymore," Catherine wiped a tear from her right eye. "It doesn't matter because our relationship isn't going to get off the ground."

"Why is that? What happened?" Veronica placed her Newsweek Magazine aside and removed her reading glasses and placed them on the coffee table. "Julian Bartlett is a decent guy with a lot going for himself right now. I know he doesn't have any old money, but what's the difference? He seems to be set pretty well," Veronica pointed out. "Where's that outspoken, stronger Catherine that I know who wouldn't let nothing or no one have the last word?" She touched Catherine's arm. "Lighten up and try to give Julian a chance. As I pointed out, he's a decent guy with a lot going for himself."

"I know he's a decent man and doing quite well for himself," Catherine said and looked at Veronica. "The way I feel has nothing to do with how nice he is or whether his money is old or new. I could care less about that." Catherine held a serious stare in Veronica's eyes.

"I guess not since you are used to your men not having a dime so they can rob you of yours," Veronica snapped.

Veronica was irritated and annoyed that Catherine wasn't interested in a decent guy, but spent her entire life daydreaming about a loser like Antonio.

"That remark was uncalled for," Catherine mumbled with no bite in her voice.

"Maybe it was uncalled for but what you are doing is uncalled for as well. You're throwing away a chance with a decent man, and I don't have to guess why. I'm sure it's all about Antonio Armani. The man is dead and buried and you are still hopelessly devoted to him," Veronica said with a voice filled with frustration.

"You are right. It is about Antonio, but it has nothing to do with devotion. It's about guilt," Catherine admitted and touched her chest. "It's about the guilt I feel right here in the depth of my heart."

"Catherine, what are you talking about? You have nothing to feel guilty about as far as that man is concerned. I know you loved him and I don't like to speak ill of the dead, but the truth is the truth and we both know how detestable and awful that man treated you!" Veronica reminded her. "Please, come on and open your eyes. You have moped around about this man long enough. He took your livelihood and now you are going to let him take your drive and strong will about life. You need to shake him off your back and fast because you are becoming some mousy female that I don't even recognize. You have never laid down to be a doormat for anyone, not even Antonio. He may have treated you bad but you always came back swinging. God knows you have never allowed me to get in the last word, so get over this defeated attitude of yours. It's making me sick! I didn't come down on you for the first few days because as awful as that man was to you; I felt empathy for you and your loss. But it's time for you to get over that man so you can move on with your life, preferably with Julian Bartlett and the quickest way to do that is just to concentrate on how bad Antonio treated you," Veronica suggested.

Catherine stared down toward the carpet. "He treated me badly, that is true. But I did something to him that he never would have done to me."

"If you think what you did to him was so much worse than his horrible treatment of you, tell me what you did to him and let me be the judge of whether it was so much worse than his treatment of you."

Catherine turned to face Veronica. "You are damn right about everything you are saying!" Catherine said with a voice filled with frustration and defeat. "I detest this unsure frighten person that I have become."

"When have you ever been unsure and frightened about anything, Catherine? But I can believe it, because Antonio's death has changed you. It has you behaving in a way that I have never seen before."

"That's because I'm in a jam and it has drained me of most of my strength and today I have decided to do something about it. Because I put two and two together and I know it's all the guilt I'm feeling about Antonio."

"Okay, I asked you to tell me what you are so guilty about so I can compare it to the insufferable things that man has done to you."

Catherine turned to face Veronica again, wiping a tear from her right eye with the back of her palm. "I think I took his life from him," Catherine mumbled sadly and then looked toward the floor.

"You think you took his life from him? What does that mean, Catherine? You are feeling guilty for kicking him to the curb and divorcing him? It was the only thing you could do after he had clearly abandoned you. He left because he was only with you to get his hands on your family money and when it wasn't forthcoming, he took off. It's just that simple. So, if anybody took anybody's life, that taker took yours! He took years from you and he is still taking because you keep giving him the power to do so. The man is dead and you still can't shake him!"

"That's why I can't shake him. His death has made that impossible."

"Catherine, could you please look at me and tell me what the heck you are talking about? Are you blaming yourself for the man's death also? Do you actually think there should have been some way for you to have prevented it?"

"That's right; that's exactly how I feel."

"Well, that's non-sense and if you keep talking like this, I might call you a psychiatric," Veronica shouted irritably at Catherine. "It's not like you could have stopped a killer from stabbing the man to death."

"But I could have if I'm that killer who walked into his room and stabbed him to death," Catherine said seriously.

"What did you just say?" Veronica touched her arm.

Catherine took her fingers and dried her tears and then opened her purse that sat on her lap and pulled out a facial issue and continued drying her eyes. Then she looked at Veronica and nodded. "I know you are shocked. But it's true. I'm the one who took Antonio's life. I killed him!" Catherine said firmly. "I had to come clean because I can't take this guilt any longer," she stressed with sad eyes. "Therefore, after we are done talking I plan to head to the Barrington Hills Police Station and turn myself in for my crime."

Veronica grabbed her stomach as she almost choked from the thin air after listening to Catherine's confession. She strung from the sofa immediately but was speechless as she looked at Catherine. She couldn't believe what Catherine had just said. She took a deep breath and collected herself. "Catherine, you are sitting there admitting to cold blooded murder. If I heard you correctly, you are admitting to being the perpetrator who went into that hospital room and stabbed Antonio while he was asleep in his bed?"

Catherine nodded but she didn't look toward Veronica. "Yes, I'm admitting to it and I plan to turn myself in. I'm heading to the Police Station as soon as I walk out that door." Catherine's defeated sad face looked up at Veronica and then pointed toward the front door. "Yes, I'm going straight to the authorities!"

Veronica stood before Catherine with both hands on her hips, nodding and tapping her left foot on the floor. She was beside herself with all kinds of emotions from Catherine's stunning unexpected admission. "Before I allow you to walk out of this house to throw your life away by confessing to a cold blooded murder, you need to convince me that you did this horrible crime!" Veronica shouted angrily. "I'm not convinced at the moment since all I have heard from you is a bunch of nothing! For one, you may be many different annoying things, but a cold-blooded killer isn't one of them! Therefore, I'm not going to take your word that you have committed this gruesome ghastly crime without some proof. Just because you say you did it, doesn't make it so! Besides, you have been behaving a bit strange and right now you don't seem to know your head from a hole in the ground!" Veronica boiled inside with frustration. "My goodness, Catherine, what has gotten into you that you are willing to spend the rest of your life in prison for something you didn't do? I know you have suffered since Antonio's death, but taking the wrap for his murder is not going to make you feel any better."

"You need to listen to me, Veronica. I'm not talking off the top of my head. I'm in a real jam here! I'm not taking the wrap to feel better; I'm turning myself in because I'm the one who killed Antonio in cold blood when he was lying there helpless!" Catherine grabbed her face and cried. "I loved Antonio so much. I didn't mean to kill him. I was just so crushed and upset after I heard the news that he and Mildred Ross were planning to leave town together."

Suddenly a cold chill dashed through Veronica's stomach as it dawned on her that Catherine confession was real. A thousand things flashed in Veronica's mind and none of them were good. She thought how a murder trial would contaminate her sons' reputation. She thought how Catherine would spend the rest of her life behind bars. She thought how Charles Taylor would most likely step away from her and that he would encourage his daughters to step away from a family scattered all over the news in such a hideous murder trial. She stood there boiling with emotions and she knew that even though Catherine's confession had pushed her into a corner she would do whatever necessary to keep her sons unscathed by such negative scandalous press.

"Catherine, if you actually murdered Antonio, you have to promise me that you will keep quiet about it. I know it's a lot to ask, but what's the alternative?"

"I know the alternative and I have come to terms with it and I'm ready to take my punishment," Catherine assured her.

"You might be ready to take your punishment, but this family shouldn't have to face punishment along with you. Therefore, Catherine, I'm pleading with you to keep this to yourself. Nobody suspects you, so why throw the rest of your life away for a man who already destroyed your youth? Don't allow that man to destroy the rest of your life. You have a chance to be happy with a decent guy who bought the estate next door. Maybe the two of you could eventually marry and you and I would be next door neighbors," Veronica anxiously stated, trying to get through to Catherine. "I beg of you, please don't turn yourself in," Veronica pleaded as she took a seat back on the sofa next to Catherine.

"But I can't live with myself knowing what I did to him," Catherine said in tears as she turned to face Veronica. "When I thought Raymond Ross did it, I could rest a little easier. But now if he didn't do it, I know I'm the guilty one."

"Wait just a minute. You either killed the man, and know you killed him or you didn't do it at all."

"That's the problem. I know I did it, but I have blocked it out and I can't remember doing it."

"You don't remember because you didn't do it."

"But I did, because he died from a butcher knife and of all weapons why would anyone else who wanted him dead use a butcher knife? I stole a butcher knife from the kitchen that morning and went to the hospital with the sole purpose of stabbing Antonio. I wasn't in my right mind, because I would have never hurt him if I were. When I arrived at the hospital I went into the building the first time with the knife in my coat pocket and when I returned to my car the knife was no longer in my pocket. I must have thrown it somewhere."

"So you went inside with the knife and continued up to his room?"

"I don't remember going up to his room the first time I went inside, but that's when I killed him. Because the second time I went inside and up to his room, the police guard at his hospital door told me that he had been murdered with a butcher knife."

Veronica shook her head. "Catherine this is a very big mess! I never thought I would live to see the day that you would end up in a mess like this, that you claim is of your own making. You want to go and confess to a murder that you most likely didn't commit! But you want to confess to it because you think you are the perpetrator."

"You tell me, do you think the average killer out there is usually walking around with a butcher knife on them? I believe it was me without a doubt and I need to do the right thing and turn myself in," Catherine stood up from the sofa, grabbed her purse, threw it on her shoulder and headed toward the front door.

Veronica strung from the sofa as if it was on fire. She rushed to the fireplace mantle and opened a golden box. She quickly removed a small black gun and then rushed over and stopped Catherine halfway to the front door.

"Stop right there, you inconsiderate, selfish bitch! I pleaded to you for my son's sake and begged you not to go to the authorities, but all you can think about is your own damn skin and freeing your conscience! Freeing your damn conscience means more to you than keeping quiet for my son's best interest! So if you feel going to the authorities is what you have to do! Then I guess you'll understand when I blow a hole in you to stop you is what I have to do!" Veronica roared as tears rolled down her face.

Catherine mouth fell open and her heart pounded with fear. "Veronica, what are you doing? You have to understand that going to the authorities is not what I want to do; it's what I have to do! I can't live with this guilt any longer! My conscience will not let me!" Catherine tearfully explained.

"I love you Catherine and I think you know that. I took you in and made you apart of the family because it's what Ryan would have wanted. But when it comes to my kids everyone else comes in second! I will blow off your leg before I allow you to harm a single hair on their heads! Going to the damn authorities will turn their lives upside down! I would rather cut out my own heart before I see their lives destroyed by the sins of you and that damn Antonio Armani! Your parents said that man was going to be the death of you and it's looking more and more like your folks were on to something! They knew you better than you knew yourself!"

"What do you want me to do, Veronica? I can't live with this lie knowing that I took another person's life, especially Antonio!"

"But that's just it, Catherine. You don't know if you killed the man or not! You are guessing and assuming it was you because you had the motive and you left home prepared to do the crime! But damn, you don't remember doing it! He had conned and lied to too many women and maybe he had other enemies out there! Maybe one of them walked into his hospital room and stabbed him?"

Catherine slightly trembled as she wiped her tears with her fingers. "I know you are trying to give me doubt that I didn't do it, but the butcher knife lets me know that it was me!" Catherine threw up both arms. "So, there's no doubt in my mind that I'm the one who took

Antonio's life from him! He may not have been a good person in your eyes and many others, but I loved him more than anything and I can't live with myself knowing I took the life of the man I loved! By turning myself in, I'll be able to look myself in the mirror every day! It may end up being the mirror of a jail cell, but at least I'll be able to look myself in the mirror, knowing I did the right thing!"

"That's debatable because what's right in your eyes causes my sons to suffer the fallout! Therefore, it's not right in my eyes! Therefore, you better think again if you think I'll ever allow that to happen!"

"Veronica, I will walk out that door and head straight to the authorities because I have no other choice but to turn myself in! You have the gun and I guess you'll have to use it to stop me!" Catherine said, crying.

"Catherine, don't miscalculate this vital moment and think for a minute that I'm bluffing you! I won't hesitate to use this gun if I have too! When it comes to protecting my sons you know I'm almost capable of anything! Nobody else in this world knows that better than you! I will pull this trigger to stop you from walking out of that door! So you either live with your conscience or not live at all!"

Chapter Two

Catherine heard Veronica's words and her instincts told her that Veronica was dead serious. Therefore, Catherine stood there shaking. Her shiny black Givenchy low heel shoes felt like they were stuck in cement as she was suddenly glued in her tracks. She wanted to call Veronica's bluff, but her impulse and inclination sounded loud in her head and told her to stay put. Suddenly Veronica held a power over her like a magnet. Cold frightful thrills ran up and down Catherine's spine as she stood motionless in that spot aware that Veronica was pointing a loaded gun straight at her back. And what felt like eternity to Catherine was only thirty seconds before the welcoming clicking sound of someone turning a key in the front door lock. Catherine swallowed hard but she still didn't move as she continued to stand motionless in shock, looking directly at the front doorknob. She was rapidly breathing, anxious for that person to unlock the door and step inside. Meanwhile, angry and shaken, but with nowhere to hide her weapon, Veronica swiftly stashed the small silver gun in her dress pocket.

Laughter and voices at the door lightened the mood as Catherine slowly glanced over her shoulder and noticed that Veronica was no longer holding the gun at her back. Her nerves calmed as she took a deep breath and grabbed her face with both hands. She glanced up at the ceiling shaking her head. She knew Veronica well, but never imagined that Veronica would have pulled a gun on her. Breathless and shaken, Catherine fell against the living room wall trying to catch her breath just as Rome walked through the front door with Amber by his side. The newlyweds were too preoccupied with Amber's homecoming to notice that Catherine was beside herself with breathless relief. Dillion was also trailing behind them with both of his hands and one arm filled with bags and luggage. However, Dillion just headed straight toward the staircase in route to Rome and Amber's room.

"Aunt Catherine, Mother, look who's back home," Rome said excitedly as he smiled at Catherine and his mother.

Catherine and Veronica walked up to Amber and they both hugged her and then followed Rome and Amber into the living room. They both felt out of place but knew they had to push aside their quarrel and pretend they were not just in a dispute so Rome and Amber would not pick up on the tension between the two of them.

It wasn't an easy task for Catherine and Veronica but they managed to visit with the newlyweds until Rome took Amber upstairs and the newlyweds didn't surface again until dinner was served. In the meantime, Veronica sat on the living room sofa and guarded Catherine all afternoon. She made sure Catherine didn't set foot outside of the property for any reason. Catherine didn't say anything to Veronica but she darned to make any kind of an attempt to leave home. She believed Veronica would stop her attempts at a confession to the authorities at all cost to protect the four brothers. She wasn't sure where Veronica had stashed the little gun but she knew it wasn't far from her person. She didn't want to do anything to upset Veronica in that manner again. Therefore, after dinner, Catherine retired to her room and didn't surface from her room until the next morning for breakfast.

Catherine walked into the living room that Tuesday shortly after most of the house residences had scattered throughout or left for work. She strolled right past Veronica who was seated on one of the sofas paging through an issue of Fortune Magazine. Veronica slightly glanced at Catherine as she continued looking through the magazine as Catherine strutted straight toward the living room house phone that was stationed on a table in the corner of the room. Catherine picked up the ivory princess style phone and dialed the phone number to the Barrington Hills local library. Veronica could clearly hear Catherine when she informed the head librarian that she would not be in to volunteer. Therefore, when Catherine hung up the phone, Veronica curiously looked toward her.

"I guess you don't feel up to going into the library today," Veronica said as she leaned forward and placed the Fortune Magazine on the coffee table.

"I don't feel like dealing with inquiring people today," Catherine mumbled with no pep to her voice as she headed across the room toward the sofa.

Veronica nodded as she noticed that Catherine appeared more at ease than the day before. "Well, I can't say that I can blame you."

"Wow, finally something I did meets with your approval," Catherine snapped as she took a seat on the opposite sofa facing Veronica.

Veronica drew an attitude as she reached out and lifted the magazine from the coffee table. "Catherine, you might as well take that damn cranky chip off your shoulder or keep stepping into another area of the house!" Veronica sharply advised her. "I can't stomach another round with you and your crabby non sense," Veronica firmly stated, pointing her out of the room. "This is a very large house with 40 plus rooms. Therefore, Catherine Franklin! If you came in here to be grouchy and dampen my day, please find yourself another spot and stay out of mine! Do I make myself clear?"

"Please just hold your horses," Catherine humbly uttered. "I have no intentions of walking around grumpy and testy, dampening your day. I just didn't feel up to dealing with anyone today and felt it would be best to call in."

Veronica nodded. "I'm sure you are not up to dealing with people today. However, you didn't have to walk in here and snap my head off just because I agreed with you! Catherine, really. If that's not being grouchy and crabby, what is?"

Catherine nodded with apologetic eyes. "I know you're right." She raised both hands. "But you need to bear with me and my nerves for a while until I can pull myself together. I'm so raw with emotions right now."

Veronica didn't immediately comment. But after a short while, she looked at Catherine and nodded. "I want to thank you for dropping that crazy idea you had about going to the authorities about something that you can't even prove."

"You're right, I can't prove that I did the crime but my gut tells me that I did it."

"I'm not getting into this conversation with you. But you know what, Catherine?"

"What?"

"You are your own worst enemy."

"Why do you say that?"

"I say it because most people try to save their own neck even when they're guilty as sin. But you are willing to risk yours on the premise that you might be guilty. How much sense does that make?"

"It makes a lot of sense to me since I want to be able to look myself in the mirror everyday. But you have convinced me that it would be a waste and stupid for me to confess to something on a hunch. But most of all, I don't want to put my nephews in the middle of a media circus and a scandal attached to their names."

Veronica smiled and nodded. "Now, that's what I want to hear. As long as you put those young men first, you and I will get along just fine."

"You have my word that I will not go back on my word," Catherine assured her. "But can you do me a little favor?"

"What favor do you need from me, Catherine?"

"I need you to cut me a little slack."

"Cut you a little slack in what regard?"

"In the regards to my situation."

"And what situation is that, Catherine?"

"The situation that I'm going to be uptight and moody or downright hard to put up with from time to time."

"And why should I cut you slack to put up with your bitching?"

"Because although, I will drop the idea that I could be guilty of murder. I still have to live with that burden on my shoulders just the same," Catherine humbly pointed out.

"I guess you do, at that," Veronica mumbled as she paged through the magazine.

"You guess I do, so does that mean you'll overlook my less than perfect moods? And stop threatening to kick me out of Franklin House every time I get on your nerves?"

Veronica stared at Catherine and didn't immediately comment. But as Catherine stood from her seat and waited for a response. Veronica glanced back at the pages of the magazine and uttered seriously. "I'll consider your plight."

"Thank you, I appreciate your consideration. This will be a long road to hoe, but with the grace of God I'll get through it," Catherine said, stood from the sofa and headed toward the kitchen.

"Where are you off to?"

"Since I have a free day, I might as well try to enjoy it." Catherine stopped in her tracks and looked around at Veronica.

"I like the way you are talking, what did you have in mind?"

"I'm headed to the kitchen to fetch you and me a serving of hot tea. I figured now would be a perfect time to sneak in the kitchen and take charge of Natalie's space since I just saw her headed up the staircase with a tray."

"She's probably taking a snack up to Amber. Rome feels she'll probably join us for dinner later since she didn't feel up to coming down for breakfast. My heart goes out to her and how she has to somehow get over losing those two beautiful kids."

Catherine nodded. "Yes, it's ashamed that she lost her kids. But the bright side is the fact that she's still very young and can have more children. Her future is not lost to her," Catherine said sadly. "She still has a life ahead of her."

"I agree and I'm sure that in time, she and Rome will have a houseful of beautiful children for both of us to spoil. Just the same, my heart goes out to her because I dare to imagine what she has been through and what she's going through," Veronica said warmly.

"It's sad how bad things happen to good people. But as I said, Amber is still very young and she's a very good looking young lady with the love of a man who actually love her back," Catherine sadly uttered.

"Don't get started with your sad story," Veronica snapped. "You can't seem to discuss anything lately without feeling sorry for yourself."

"That's not what I was doing," Catherine quickly mumbled.

"It is what you were doing. Saying how young and beautiful Amber is, thinking about how you are not so young and not so beautiful anymore. Besides, I'm sure you were referring to how you don't have the love of the man that you loved," Veronica stated firmly. "So I dare you to stand there and say I'm lying, that you were not feeling sorry for yourself."

"Maybe you're right and I do feel sorry for myself. But it's all true. I'm not so young and so beautiful anymore. And I don't have the love of the man that I love."

"And you are better off. No disrespect to the dead, but Antonio Armani wasn't worth your love. He didn't deserve your love and kindness."

Catherine didn't want to feel the pain that conversing about Antonio would cause her. Therefore, she changed the subject back to Amber. "She really looks good and I hope she does join us for dinner this evening."

"Me too. God blessed my son with a beautiful wife. I'll be so happy when she's upon her feet and can be a wife to him."

"Let's pray it will be soon. God knows it's a blessing to have her back home with Rome. I know they say how Shady Grove is a world class place for someone who is going through what Amber is going through, but I'm old fashioned and feel being with her husband is the best medicine," Catherine said.

Veronica nodded. "I'm incline to agree with you on that. I never thought Shady Grove was the best place for her. But they felt so and if it helped her, that's what counts."

"Yes, if it helped her that is what counts. But the way I see it, heartbreak and all, this is where she belongs right here at Franklin House with her husband. Therefore, he can be the one to help nurse her back into the fold of everyday life of coping with the loss of her children," Catherine said, still standing there looking toward Veronica.

"Now that she's back home, that will give Rome the opportunity to do just that," Veronica commented with her face in the magazine.

"You are right, and the two of them will be just fine," Catherine mumbled, and when Veronica didn't comment or look toward her,

Catherine pointed in the direction of the kitchen. "I better head to the kitchen and fetch our tea before Natalie gets back in there."

Veronica glanced up at her. "That's right. She'll never allow you to serve us if she gets back to the kitchen first," Veronica said laughingly as she waved her hand toward the kitchen. "So run along and get the tea."

Catherine smiled. "I figured we could sit and chat about something exciting for a change instead of all these depressing pages from my life," Catherine suggested as a small smile curled her mouth. Feeling somewhat more at ease, she turned on her shoe heels and headed across the room in the direction of the kitchen.

However, when Catherine stepped back into the living room with the serving tray in her hands, she had a dismal gloomy look on her face. Veronica kept her eyes on Catherine curious as to what had changed her mood from upbeat to downbeat in a matter of minutes.

"Why do you have such a miserable look on your face?"

"I don't have a miserable look on my face," Catherine denied as she headed across the room toward the sofa.

"Take a look in the mirror and see for yourself," Veronica said. "So what happened? When you headed for the kitchen a few minutes ago, you were smiling. Now what?"

"How can you ask me now what?" Catherine snapped as she placed the serving tray on the coffee table. "It's obvious I'm having a rough time trying to separate my life from the horrible thoughts that are dancing around in my head. That's why I asked you to cut me some slack and you promised to do so."

"Yes, I promised to do so, but do I have to put up with your dismal snappy moods all day long? You just said before you left for the kitchen that we would discuss some upbeat topics over tea. Now, I guess I can scratch that idea."

"No, I still want to discuss some upbeat topics," Catherine said. "But please bear with me. It's just hard as hell to get through this nightmare I'm living wide awake. I loved Antonio and now I have to live with the thought that I'm the one who most likely took his life," Catherine mumbled sadly. "Maybe he wasn't perfect; and God knows he didn't love me. But he didn't deserve to die such a horrible death."

"Snap out of it, Catherine!" Veronica said sharply.

"If I don't snap out of it, do you plan to grab your gun and kill me the way you threatened to do yesterday?"

"I didn't threatened to kill you, I was going to shoot you," Veronica quietly admitted.

"You had the gun pointed at my back. You were livid and determined to stop me from leaving here to see the authorities! It felt like you planned to pull that trigger."

"Catherine, you are right. I was fighting mad and determined and I was going to pull that trigger to stop you from leaving this house. My goal was to stop you from making the biggest mistake of your life. I would have blown a hole in your leg and that would have stopped you. But my intentions were stop you. And yes, if I have to grab my gun again to stop you from making a crazy mistake, I'll do the same. But we need to stop this conversation right here before it goes any further," Veronica stressed strongly. "Because frankly, I don't plan to ever go through what I went through with you yesterday. So, snap out of your damn despair and misery right now!" Veronica sharply insisted. "We'll talk about something that's more exciting and uplifting. Those subjects that you suggested before you headed toward the kitchen to fetch the tea. Is that clear?"

Catherine glanced down at the carpet and mumbled in a low humble voice. "So, you expect me to sit here and have tea as if my life is normal?"

"That's exact what I expect. Besides, it was your idea to fetch the tea. I was having a relaxing morning just reading my magazine. But you happened in here and suggested we share some tea and discuss some upbeat topics. So I need to ask you."

"What do you need to ask me?" Catherine asked.

"I need to ask you do you have a problem with sitting here and discussing upbeat topics as we had planned?"

Catherine didn't immediately answer the question as she sat there in deep thought.

Veronica leaned forward, lifted the silver teapot and poured tea into her cup. "Are you going to answer my question?"

Catherine scooted to the edge of the sofa, leaned forward and lifted the teapot and poured tea into her cup. Then she dropped two cubes of sugar into her tea and leaned back against the cushions of the sofa, looking toward Veronica. "No problem with discussing upbeat topics, but a big problem with the controllling." She placed the cup to her mouth and took a sip of tea. "I'm going through this nightmare and I'm trying to deal with it. But you can't dictate how I should feel and act."

"Catherine, with all due respect. I want you to know that I'm not trying to control you. You are a grown woman and your life is your own."

"Thanks for letting me know since it sure feels like you're trying to control my life."

"I'm not trying to control your life, but on the other hand, due to your situation." Veronica stared in Catherine's eyes. "That's exactly what I'm doing, and expect from you, in order to keep you out of a jail cell. Do I make myself clear?"

"Yes, Veronica, you made yourself crystal clear."

Veronica nodded. "Okay, if I made myself clear. I need to know that we're on the same page in regards to what I'm referring to. Therefore, I need you to tell me what you think I expect from you," Veronica seriously inquired.

Catherine waved her hand. "I know what you expect."

"Well, if you know what I expect, just verbally tell me so I'll know that you know and there'll be no misunderstanding between us," Veronica urged.

"You expect for me to live and act as if I didn't murder Antonio?"

"That's exactly right since you don't know for sure if you did it."

"I think we both know I did it."

"We don't both know anything; and I think you're a fool to keep insisting on making a theory into a fact."

"Veronica, I know you don't want to keep discussing this, but it's too obvious not to be the truth. I'm supposed to believe that someone other than myself walked into Antonio's hospital room and killed him with the same weapon I had planned to use. If it was any other weapon than a butcher knife, I might would have some doubt about doing it. But think about it, it adds up. The weapon I left home with and had in my pocket when I entered the hospital is the kind of weapon he was murdered with. Although, the knife was missing from my pocket when I returned to my car after my first visit to Antonio's room."

"The fact that it was missing should tell you something."

"Yes, it does tell me something. It tells me that apparently I had sneaked in his hospital room and stabbed him on my first visit to his room when I first arrived at the hospital. Because I clearly recall going into the hospital twice that morning."

"Catherine, I don't want to discuss this any further or ever again!"

"What do you mean? I think we need to discuss it to figure out how I'm supposed to live with myself."

"I don't want to discuss it because every time you open your mouth and mention that horrible ordeal, there's a good chance for someone to overhear and I do not want the staff or the boys to ever hear of this. Do I make myself clear? I love having you here, but if you feel you cannot keep your mouth shut, constantly exposing my sons to your guilt, you'll have to move out."

"What did you just say?"

"You heard me, Catherine, and I'm not kidding around. This is serious and I need you to take it serious and put this mess out of your mind," Veronica warned her. "I get you're upset and torn a part over this. But it is what it is and there's nothing you can do to make it any better. Your senseless idea to turn yourself in, is just that. It's stupid and it would help no one. The only good would be to clear your conscience of something that you may not have done. In the meantime, my sons' whole world would be destroyed by a murderous scandal of their aunt splattered all over the media!" Veronica sharply stated in a low voice. "If you know anything about me, you know I do not play around with my children's liveilhood and future. Yesterday when I pulled that gun on you, Catherine, it wasn't a prank. I would have used it as my last recourse to stop you from destroying my sons' life. Therefore, if you insist on going down that road of confession and constantly bringing up this subject. You will definitely have to move out of my home."

"You would actually make me move out of my family home?"

"What do you think, Catherine?"

"I think you probably would, since you would see me as a liability to your family."

"That's damn right, and if you insist on keeping this non sense talk at the tip of your tongue and at the forefront of your thoughts to the point of turning yourself into the authorities, you'll give me no other choice but to kick you out!" Veronica snapped, irritated about their dismal conversation. "By kicking you out of here, at least the media couldn't broadcast how a lovesick murderous lunatic were living here at Franklin House. That kind of press would ruin this family's name and throw my children in turmoil, causing dishonor and gossip to follow them," Veronica assured her.

Catherine nodded with wet sad eyes, looking toward the floor. "If I'm not living here at least the scandal wouldn't cause as many problems for the boys," Catherine sadly agreed.

"That's right, but don't get any big ideas about moving out, and then turning yourself into authorities. It's not a better option and the idea shouldn't be on your radar as an option. Just bear in mind that your last name is Franklin. You are forever connected to the famous Ryan Franklin, your dead brother and my children's father. Therefore, any negative media about you involved in something as hideous as this, will definitely tarnish your brother's good name as well as his children's no matter what's your residence."

"Being a Franklin is a blessing and a curse. It's wonderful as long as everything is going good, but if you have trouble, then the entire world will know it as well."

"Yes, Catherine, that's the down side of being able to live high on the hog, which you love as much as the rest of us. So, keep your nose clean and your mouth shut and all should work out fine," Veronica assured her. "However, if you don't keep your mouth shut about this ridiculous guilt that's riding your back, you are going to force my hand. I swear to you on Ryan's grave that I will not allow you to shame this family and ruin my children's future. I don't know how I'll stop you, but believe me, if I have to, I'll stop you from bringing disgrace and shame to this family's name," Veronica warned her.

Catherine nodded as she sat there with her head lowered, listening to Veronica lay down the law. She didn't want to bring humiliation and disgrace to the family, but she didn't know how to deal with her burning conscience. In her heart, she wasn't a murderer and she didn't know how to deal with the thought of being one.

"I plan to take your advice." Catherine held up both hands. "I love those young men and I couldn't live with myself if I brought disgrace to their lives and shamed Ryan's memory in a horrible spectacular," she said looking toward Veronica. "I know you're pretty upset that I brought this up, but I promise you that I'm trying to deal with it and I will deal with it. I know a scandal as gruesome as that would pretty much destroy our social status."

Veronica gave her a sharp look. "You mean mines and your nephew's social status." Veronica shook her head. "You might as well face it, Catherine, either way, you don't have any social standing in this community. Everybody sees you as the weak pushover who got cut from the family fortune. But because you have been living in misery all your life doesn't mean you have to throw it on our backs!" Veronica stressed strongly in a low voice.

"I get the point and I do not want disgrace for those young men. I agree with you, why should they have to suffer because their fanatical aunt life hasn't been worth a dime since before I could drive a car. If I were to move out, it would be difficult for the media to throw my sins on their heads when I'm not living under the same roof. Nevertheless, I know what you mentioned, and realize it doesn't matter where I live. If the truth came out, it would still destroy this family. So, I just want you to know that I don't want to or have any intentions of relocating from Franklin House. This is my home and I love it here. I will take your advice and try to push it out of my mind," Catherine said with conviction.

However, still irritated with Catherine, Veronica looked toward Catherine and shook her head and then looked the opposite way.

Catherine understood Veronica's frustration with her and knew Veronica was making a good point and agreed with her. "I know your patience is wearing thin with me. However, I know you are right and I need to find a way to put this out of my mind and just live with it. This is the only home I have and I wouldn't want to live anywhere else, and it has nothing to do with the privileges."

Veronica looked questionably and surprised toward Catherine after she made that statement and held her stare as Catherine continued.

"That's right, it has nothing to do with the privileges. It's all about the warmth and love I get from those young men and the staff, and also you, Veronica. Plus, we have a new bride in the house; and I'm excited about Rome and Amber starting their life here. Besides, I'm smart enough to know that you're just looking out for those young men. I wouldn't expect anything less of you," Catherine said sincerely and continued. "I know I brought it up, and I apologize, but can we start over and have our tea in peace?" Catherine looked toward the teapot. "Thanks goodness for the warmer beneath the pot, otherwise we would be drinking cold tea. So, what do you say? Can we have the rest of the tea and talk about something upbeat as we originally planned."

"You are the one who had the bright idea to sit and discuss something upbeat. Whatever that might be?" Veronica held out both hands. "But frankly, Catherine, I cannot think of anything I would want to discuss with you right now." Veronica pointed her out of the room. "I don't want to see your face. I was in such a good mood until you brought your damn miserable chatter into my space. So, just leave the room so I can collect myself."

"I'm sorry, you are so pissed. But you have asked me to get those gruesome thoughts out of my system and I think that talk helped me to do just that. Therefore, unlike you think, the talk wasn't a waste of time. It was a talk that we needed to have. Now, we can move on and I promise not to spill my guts or mention anything about guilty feelings or making confessions to authorities. You have my word," Catherine promised.

Chapter Three

Catherine and Veronica sat there in silence sipping their tea, when Veronica closed the Fortune Magazine and placed it on her lap. She looked over at Catherine and could see that Catherine seemed contrite and humble as she sat there looking down toward the floor. She could also see that Catherine appeared to be in deep thought as she sat there on the opposite sofa holding her teacup with both hands. Suddenly, a pinch of sadness dashed through Veronica's stomach as she looked at Catherine. She had never known anyone who had faced more disappointment than Catherine. Quickly her heart went out to her sister-in-law and she wanted to ease Catherine's mind and take away some of her sadness.

Veronica allowed the frustration to roll off her back as she smiled toward Catherine and softly uttered. "Catherine, a penny for your thoughts."

Catherine glanced up and looked at Veronica with surprise eyes as if she was slightly startled that Veronica had said something to her. "What did you just say?" she asked.

"You looked so far away until I couldn't resist to say penny for your thoughts, but of course, I was just kidding," Veronica softly said. "Plus, I didn't mean to startle you. But listen, after giving it some thought, I guess we can move on with our tea party and try to be civil with each other and discuss some happier times," Veronica suggested.

Catherine glanced back toward the floor and nodded. "That's fine."

Veronica smiled, still looking toward Catherine. "So, do you have any suggestions on what would be an upbeat topic to discuss? I know Britain and Sabrina are getting closer everyday. I'm so blissful about that until I could just float away," Veronica excitedly stated.

Catherine lifted her teacup and took a sip. Then she smiled and quickly commented with the cup up to her mouth. "I'm also very happy for Britain and Sabrina that they have found their way back to each other,"she said smiling. "I wouldn't be surprised if another wedding is right around the corner," Catherine predicted.

"That's music to my ears and one of my prayers for those two Sweethearts," Veronica said excitedly. "Sabrina will make such a beautiful bride. Samantha and Starlet as well. They are all beautiful, but Sabrina is such a radiant beauty," Veronica smiled.

Cathrine discreetly nodded as she looked at Veronica. She could see that their current topic was making Veronica quite happy and talkative.

"Yes, Catherine, I'm sure you have noticed just as I have that Paris and Samantha are getting closer and so are Sydney and Starlet. The young ladies are a Godsend and I'm so happy that they are in my son's lives. However, Britain and Sabrina is particularly special to me." Veronica held up one finger. "I'll tell you why. They are connected in a special way as if they were born to be together."

"The others seem just as connected. Paris and Samantha and Sydney and Starlet seem devoted to each other," Catherine pointed out. "They are always together and both couples seem joined at the hip. So what do you see so different about Sabrina and Britain's relationship that stands out from the other two?" Catherine asked.

Veronica smiled. "To be honest, their connection remind me of your brother and me. Therefore, remember that prediction you made?"

"The one I made about another wedding on the horizon with Sabrina and Britain?"

"Yes, Catherine, and I think you are on to something. I believe with complete certainty that your prediction will come to past."

"I agree hundred percent. Those two are quite stunning together and I can agree that they do look like they were made for each other. Now that I think about it, I have noticed on occasion that they sometime even finish each other sentences," Catherine recalled with a big smile on her face as if their continued conversation on the topic of Britain and Sabrina was lifting her spirits.

Veronica noticed the gleem in Catherine's eyes and the smile on her face. "I can tell that you are getting a kick out of this conversation; and that's good. Something pleasant to take your mind off of less uplifting things," Veronica said.

Catherine nodded and leaned forward to place her teacup on the coffee table. "It is exciting just thinking about their happiness and the beautiful life they have ahead of them. I can tell you now, when those two walk down the aisle that will be one happy day for me," Catherine smiled excitedly, looking toward Veronica. "I know they are your sons, but they are my children too and I'm invested in all of their lives." Catherine grabbed her face and just looked at Veronica for a moment as if she was overwhelmed by her love for her nephews. "Their happiness makes my happiness complete," Catherine said sincerely.

"You said that so movingly. It touched me. Plus it mirrors my very soul. Your words are my sentiments exactly," Veronica smiled. "Since my happiness comes from their happiness and without their happiness I could never be happy," Veronica eloquently stated.

"Yes, we can both agree that we are exceedingly happy that Sabrina and Britain are back together. However, I wasn't thinking that we would discuss the two of them," Catherine said. "I was actually thinking about more of a distant past discussion."

"Wha's a distant past discussion, Catherine? I'm afraid I don't follow you."

"I just mean something from the past, but not recent past."

"How far back in the past?"

"Not that far back, just far back enough to tell me how you snagged my brother?"

"How I snagged Ryan?"

"Yes, I would just like to know, because I know you didn't snag him by making the mistake of going out with his brother first," Catherine chuckled.

Veronica waved her hand in a playful way. "I know you are trying to be funny since your brother didn't have another brother for me to go out with."

"Of course, we didn't have another brother. But I was trying to make a point. And my point is, you seem gun shy with Charles instead of just being straightforward with him the way you are with everyone else," Catherine suggested as she lifted the silver teapot from the coffee table and poured hot tea into each of their cups.

"Why do you think I'm not being straightforward with Charles?"

"Accepting a date with his brother for one, as a way to push Charles into making up his mind. Something like that could backfire on you and you could end up losing Charles interest while you try to empathize with his brother."

"I see your point, going out with his brother is not the best way to snag Charles."

Catherine grinned. "I would agree with that. Therefore, that's why I'm asking how did you snag my brother?"

"Catherine, maybe we should change the subject. What brought on this interest, which is ancient history interest. Besides, shouldn't you be more interested in your own lovelife than to be inquisitive about my current and past lovelife?"

"I just thought it would liven up my spirits since you and Ryan were the only couple I knew to stay happy from the moment you met until the moment he passed away. You two were incredibly happy with each other all the time. Besides, it's enough to boggle the mind since my brother was so straight-laced and you were you."

"What are you getting at, Catherine?"

"You know what I'm getting at. You and Ryan were so different. He was an angel and you were always mischievous," Catherine admitted. "You were my best friend and I was over the moon when he started dating you and married you, but before he fell for you, I had always figured that my brother would end up with a good girl."

"Thanks for telling me," Veronica snapped. "In other words, you didn't think I was a good girl?"

"Well, do you think you were a good girl?"

"Maybe I wasn't a good girl, but where in the world did you come up with the idea that I was mischievous? That's not the word I would call myself."

"Maybe it isn't, but that's how you were and still are, Veronica," Catherine grinned, staring at Veronica. "The reason I call you mischievous is because I looked it up and the Merriam dictionary definition describes you. The dictionary states that being mischievous, is someone causing or tending to cause annoyance or minor harm or damage, showing a playful desire to cause trouble," Catherine explained. "That's you exactly. You will push the envelope only so far, never doing anything that could land you in an embarrassing situation or trouble with the law."

"Whatever, what's your point?"

"My point is, you were so different from my brother, but yet you became his wife. He loved you enormously. I could see it in his eyes, even at the end when I spoke to him for the last time in his hospital bed. In his eyes, you were an angel," Catherine admitted.

"Thanks for sharing that, but let me tell you something, Catherine. It was my impulse or natural inclination to be caring, faithful, devoted and good to Ryan. I wasn't an angel and you and I both know that. But I wanted to be an angel in his eyes and I treated him as if he was the only man in the world because to me that's what he was. Your brother didn't love me because he thought I was good. He loved me because he knew exactly who I was and he loved me unconditionally in spite of myself. He knew I wasn't a delicate flower who would get blown away by the wind. He loved the strong force in me and saw me as a strong willed, outspoken, go after what I wanted kind of person."

"That's you exactly," Catherine remarked and nodded.

"Of course, it's me exactly, and Ryan loved me not because I was so wonderful and good but because he knew I was wonderful and good to him and that I always beyond a shadow of a doubt put him first in my life. Just as I always beyond a shadow of a doubt put my children first. I have only one regret from my marriage other than the obvious of wishing Ryan was still alive. Ryan and I wanted to have more children. He told me once that he especially wanted to fill the world with respectful, caring individuals. He and I both felt that we could have our children and bring them up to be compassionate, respectful citizens and all around caring human being. We would talk and Ryan would say how he wanted our children to grow up to be good citizens who helped others and the community; and he wanted them to possibly help change the laws to reflect more fairness for all people," Veronica recalled, looking into space for a moment. Then she looked toward Catherine. "I know it seems unbelieveable because we were different in so many ways, but it's true. Ryan and I were blissfully happy."

Catherine nodded. "Everyone could see that, but you haven't told me how you met."

Veronica smiled. "That's right, you wanted to know how Ryan and I met. But you already know how we met. We had crushes on each other during our junior year and we started going steady and officially dating at the start of our senior year in high school. But as I just said, you already know that, Catherine. So what else do you want to know about how Ryan and I met? You probably know it all."

Catherine shook her head. "I don't know it all. But I do know about the junior year crushes and that you two started dating during your senior year," Catherine admitted as she dropped two lumps of sugar into each cup and passed Veronica a cup of tea and took a seat on the opposite end of the sofa. She looked toward Veronica as she sipped her tea.

"Well, you should know it. You were right there with me the whole time," Veronica said as she lifted her cup to her mouth and took a sip of tea.

Catherine nodded. "I also remember how you used to go on and on talking about Ryan before he finally asked you out. It was a big surprise to me when I looked around and the two of you were boyfriend and girlfriend."

"What do you mean it was a big surprise to you?" Veronica asked, smiling. "You knew how much we liked each other."

"Yes, I knew that. But it still surprised me. I guess you don't get what I'm getting at."

"I guess I don't, so what are you getting at?" Veronica asked.

"Okay, here's the thing and I want you to focus on what I'm saying," Catherine smiled, trying to make a point. "One semester you were sitting in class daydreaming and talking about how much you liked my brother, and then at the start of senior classes, the two of you were glued together, going steady like Romeo and Juliet. What I'm missing is the getting to know me segment for the two of you." Catherine threw up her hands.

Veronica thought for a moment. "Catherine, you were my best friend. I'm sure I told you about my first date with Ryan and when we started dating."

Catherine shook her head. "You didn't tell me any of that. All I remember is that you went from wanting to date my brother, to just plain dating him," Catherine recalled.

Sitting there staring at Catherine and wondering about the past, suddenly it dawned on Veronica that Catherine was absolutely correct in her recollection as all her fun memories of her early days with Ryan floored her thoughts. She treasured every single memory of Ryan, and every single memory of him flashed clear in her mind as if it had just happened yesterday. She smiled and nodded toward Catherine. "You have an excellent memory because you're positively correct of how I went from daydreaming about Ryan to straightout dating him."

"I can't wait to hear how that happened," Catherine smiled. "I guess he showed up at your doorstep and asked you out and you just forgot to tell me."

Veronica smiled. "It didn't happen quite like that. But lucky for you, I have a photographic memory and can remember everything about the way Ryan and I met and fell in love. Nothing was never as easy as the two of us falling in love. It was so easy for us because we loved each other from the beginning," Veronica softly explained as her eyes sparkled with happines as she spoke of her past memories of Ryan. "In all fairness to Ryan's history with me, and to be completely on the level, I think I was crazy in love with your brother before he was crazy in love with me."

Catherine shook her head. "I'm not so sure about your theory."

"About my theory about what?"

"About your theory that you were crazy in love with Ryan before he fell in love with you," Catherine quickly countered her remark. "I'm not sure about that because before the two of you started dating, he seemed more than mildly curious about you. Remember, I lived with the guy; and he would sometime come to my room and bring up your name in a discreet way. He was definitely interested in you, otherwise he wouldn't have been so inquiring," Catherine smiled at Veronica. "Remember I told you during that math quiz that I thought Ryan liked you?"

Veronica pointed her finger, shaking it at Catherine. "You are absolutely correct, and by you telling me how you assumed he felt, it gave me confidence and encouragement that there could be something between Ryan and I," Veronica recalled.

In the background the house phone was ringing. They both stared toward the phone and listened to see if maybe Helen, Dillion or another staff member would answer, but on the third ring, Catherine sprung from her seat and rushed across the room toward the phone to answer it.

Chapter Four

Catherine smiled on her way back toward the sofa, the caller had been a wrong number and she was excited about hearing about how her brother and Veronica met and fell in love. "I think your relationship started when the two of you kissed for the first time at your family barbecue," Catherine said as she took her seat. "Remember when Ryan came home from Los Angeles? It was a big deal and everybody thought of him as a star already?"

Veronica nodded. "I see you are not going to let this go."

"Why do you say it like that? I thought you would be thrilled to spill your guts about your one true love."

"I guess I'm just not in the mood, but I can see that you are determined to talk about the unforgettable fascination of the love I shared with your brother."

"Yes, I'm determined to hear about the good side of love and maybe that will help to buildup my confidence so I won't constantly dwell on the humiliations, debacles, fiascos and shambles of my past love," Catherine stressed sincerely.

"I see, and you are right," Veronica agreed.

"What am I right about?"

"You're right about the date. It was that hot Fourth of July in 1973. The day we were all gathered at my family backyard barbecue," She recalled with a joyful glow in her eyes. "That summer changed my life into something that seemed better than heaven, if that's possible," Veronica smiled as she reflected on those happy memories.

Catherine eyes had a distant look in them as she stared into space. "Those were fun memories and a happier time for me. It was before I got drugged through the mud by Antonio and every other boy that I looked twice at."

"Why do you say every other boy? As far as I know, you were only interested in Antonio and Jack," Veronica reminded her, slightly frowning. "I'm not sure which one of boys were the worst. Therefore, again I ask, why do you say every other boy?"

"That's because every other boy at school that I thought was cute and I wanted to go out with, never asked me out."

"I can answer that for you, Catherine."

"You can answer what? I didn't ask you to answer anything."

"I know you didn't ask me to answer anything, but I'm going to answer your question about every other boy that you had a crush on."

Catherine rolled her eyes toward the ceiling, ready for the remark that was coming her way. "Okay, sure, what's your theory?"

"The way I see it and remember it, you were always interested in boys that treated you badly that wasn't interested in you."

"That's no answer. That's old news that we both know," Catherine interrupted.

"I wasn't finished. So just listen and I'll tell you my theory of why you went after one bad choice after the other."

Catherine folded her lips as she stared curiously at Veronica. "Okay, what's your theory? Not that it really matters now."

"I chalked it up to your childhood feelings of feeling inferior to Ryan."

"You what?" Catherine slightly snapped, but caught herself and calmed her reply. "Where did you get that idea?"

"I got it from the way your folks treated you compared to your brother," Veronica seriously stated. "It was your life but I was right there by your side witnessing it all. Therefore, whether you want to admit it or not. I believe somewhere deep inside of you, bad treatment feels normal to you and you feel you deserve bad treatment."

Catherine laughed as if what Veronica was saying was completely off the mark. "Along with everything else, I guess you consider yourself a shrink as well."

"Catherine, you can joke if you like, but I'm serious," Veronica said firmly. "And I'm sure you know that I'm probably right. Why else would you have put up with such bad treatment from both Antonio and Jack?"

Catherine waved her hand. "That's water under the bridge. Besides, how in the world did we get off track from you sharing some fun memories of how you met my brother? You were telling me about that, then suddenly we have gotten off the fascinating subject of you and Ryan to the gloomy topic of my dark romance?"

"I know we got sidetracked, but I was just giving you my theory."

"I know it's your theory, but that's all it is, just your assumption. Because just as I said, you are not a shrink and you cannot size up my rationale. So let's just stick with your happy story and dig my miserable one," Catherine firmly suggested. "Let's stick with that wonderful summer of 1973. We started the school term as seniors. You bragged about it and told every student that would listen, that the senior class owned the campus that year," Catherine reminded her.

Veronica nodded and smiled as she thought of the fun memories. "I remember so well what it felt like to be a senior that year. And what else is crystal clear in my mind is that hot day of my family backyard barbecue. The butterflies that ripped through my stomach when Ryan drove up and parked his new car at the edge of our driveway. It was a crowd of guest gathered on the front lawn and they all paused from the festivities and looked down the driveway at him. They were not just amazed with the fact that he was the most handsome boy in the community, they were also impressed over the fact that an eighteen year old boy was stepping out of a brand new black Corvette that he had purchased with his prize money," Veronica said, smiling.

Catherine nodded. "That's right, he won that huge amount of money for receiving that best actor award for his performance on stage in that school play. I remember how it was so incredible that the prize ended up being that much money. The award got so much attention that it ended up in the paper, on the radio and television," Catherine recalled.

"He always treasured that award and felt it started the ball rolling with putting his name in the spotlight," Veronica recalled. "The only thing that wasn't exciting about Ryan winning that award was the fact that he had to leave home and stay in Los Angeles for two months."

"I know, but that trip to California was apart of the prize, and to touch on how you said he treasured the award. Our parents felt the same way, and felt the high school award started his popularity, especially since the prize he ended up with was so much money," Catherine said smiling as she lifted her teacup and took a sip of tea. She glanced at Veronica. "$100,000 dollars back in 1974 was a boatload of money."

Veronica smiled and nodded. "It's still a boatload of money in 2014."

Catherine waved her hand in agreement. "Of course it is! Therefore, when Ryan won that award for all that money which included a trip to Los Angeles for two months to shoot an Ivory Soap commercial, in my mind I already considered my brother a star."

Veronica nodded. "He really was from that moment on."

"You're right, because after that, the moment he set foot in college his career shot to orbit and never headed back until the day he passed."

"That's true, but if you'll listen. I'll tell you how your brother and I went from not talking to full mode dating at the start of senior classes."

Catherine nodded. "By all means talk away."

Veronica took a sip of tea, looking toward Catherine. "It's amazing how all of those wonderful memories are never far from my thoughts. However, I'll start from the beginning," she took a deep breath and then began. "Well, he had been away for the summer enjoying his two months in sunny California, seeing the sights and learning the ropes of show business. The incredible opportunity to perform in a commercial and the incredible opportunity to learn all about what goes into shooting a commercial."

"I'm not trying to interrupt," Catherine quickly cut in. "But I just want to say how Ryan's award, and the fact that he was in California shooting a commercial, made him an instant star in the community and all over Chicago. He started getting calls to appear in other commercials."

"You are absolutely correct. Ryan hadn't even finished high school but he was already famous in the eyes of the community and the entire Chicago metropolitan area," Veronica agreed.

Catherine nodded. "Yes, he was and our folks couldn't praise him enough about his instant overnight rise to stardom and achievements. He was their golden boy and I was their disappointment."

"I think that's just in your head. Your folks loved you just as much as they loved Ryan. They just didn't care for some of the choices you were making, Catherine."

"You can't convince me otherwise by sugar coating it, Veronica. I have accepted the fact that my parents thought of me as their second best. Besides, you already know this. You have pointed it out in the past, that if you were dissatisfied with the conduct or choices of one of your sons, never would you cut them off from their inheritance. You said you would rather cut out your heart before you would do something so hurtful to one of your children," Catherine reminded her.

"That is correct. Therefore, I see your point. It's sad and it pains me to admit, but you're most likely right in your assumptions about your folks in regards to their favoritism and preferential treatment toward Ryan. After all, they made it obvious that they shared more affection for Ryan than you," Veronica admitted, noticing the immediate frown on Catherine's face and the sad look in her eyes.

Veronica waved her hand. "Don't get caught up in unpleasant memories. Let's get back to the happier ones instead."

Catherine took a deep breath and collected herself as she shook off the cobwebs of old hurtful memories of her teenage years when she felt unloved and misunderstood by her parents. She looked at Veronica and nodded. "I'm fine. Those memories roll off my back like water. So, go ahead with your story. You were at the point where Ryan had come home for the weekend, after spending one month of the two that he was scheduled to stay in Los Angeles for his commercial," Catherine said. "I was at the barbecue, but I don't recall you and Ryan hanging out with each other. I don't even recall seeing the two of you talk to each other. But I know you and he found each other at the barbecue, but I never knew how you two connected."

"I had my reasons for not filling you in at that time," Veronica admitted, smiling.

"You definitely didn't fill me in at the time. After the barbecue, Ryan went straight back to Los Angeles and didn't come back home until the weekend before classes started; and the first day of class, you excitedly told me that you and Ryan had started dating. Therefore, it's safe to say that the two of you had put your heads together and connected at the barbecue or sometime over that weekend before school started."

"That's true, but let me get on with it and you'll soon know it all," Veronica calmly uttered as she glanced at her watch. "I want to have this story wrapped up before the boys get home and Natalie call us in to dinner."

"Okay, get to it. I'm listening."

"I was so glad Ryan was home visiting for the weekend. But I also knew he would be heading back to California for the rest of the summer; and as much as I hate to mention his name, its utterly impossible to tell this story without mentioning his high school shadow."

Catherine pointed her finger at Veronica and smiled. "That would be Jack."

"Yes, during that time Jack Coleman was glued to your brother's coattail. He was always hanging out, going places and doing things with Ryan. However, in all fairness to Jack Coleman, Ryan had complete faith and confidence in that boy for some reason," Veronica admitted with a happy distant look in her eyes. "Yes, Catherine, your brother was not an ordinary guy. He was a complete package of perfection. I can recall just sitting in class daydreaming about Ryan," Veronica said and held up one finger. "Before you say I'm off track from the story again. I know I am, but it just dawned on me how handsome he was. So much so that all the students at school started calling him, Mr. Gorgeous. Do you remember that incredible nickname that they gave him at school?" Veronica asked, smiling.

Catherine nodded. "Oh, yes, how can I forget that special nickname they gave my brother? He was Mr. Gorgeous and I felt awkward as if the students thought of me as chopped liver. Nevertheless, I know now that I was just allowing my insecurities to get the better of me."

"Okay, enough of that, back to the story," Veronica smiled with subdued excitement in her voice to be conversing about her deceased husband. "Ryan pulled into our driveway about an hour into the festivities. It was such a hot sticky July day and all the smoke from the barbecue grill smelled as if it had landed in my hair. I stood on the front porch anxious to see him step out of his new car. But before Ryan could even open his car door, all the teenagers in attendance at the barbecue, mobbed him. I watched as he stepped out of his car barely able to step forward or to either side for the crowd gathered around him. But as they stood back to give him breathing space, I noticed that he was wearing a Saint Laurent outfit, a striking red silk short sleeve shirt and a pair of black silk pants with a red stripe on each side. His black Christian Louboutin shoes sparkled and shined from the sunlight as if he had just stepped out of a shoeshine shop. His medium length black hair was styled back off his face, cut low on the sides with soft waves hanging on his shoulders.

"My word, Veronica. You have a damn good memory to recall exactly what he was wearing all those years ago."

Veronica nodded, leaned forward and lifted her teacup from the coffee table. "Yes, I do and I remember everything there is to remember about Ryan. He was unforgettable and that's for sure. But the moment he stepped out of his car that day, I frowned when Mildred Latham, who is Mildred Ross now, threw her arms around him, pulling his face down to hers. He didn't resist as she forced her lips all over his smiling face. He stood there collected and polite and allowed her to kiss both sides of his face. She was in tears when she released him and went giggling with a group of teenagers toward the backyard. They were all giggling excitedly and I heard Mildred say to the group of girls that she had kissed Ryan and he was a shooting star headed for a great career."

"You didn't get jealous over that did you?" Catherine asked. "Of course, you knew why Mildred kissed Ryan. She kissed him because he performed opposite of her in the high school play, "Romeo and Juliet. The play Ryan won that mega award for."

"That's right, Mildred was Juliet," Veronica recalled.

"That's right, she was; and that's why she was so excited that day. She was just thrilled about his success that she had contributed to," Catherine said assurely. "However, with that being said, I'm still puzzled after all these years about one simple fact."

Veronica stared at Catherine curiously. "What are you puzzled about?"

"It just boggles my mind that Mildred was able to land the role of Juliet. She was very pretty back then and quite slender as well, but it was a common fact that she couldn't act and perform well in school plays. Therefore, everybody at school was surprised and scratching their heads when she landed the part opposite my very talented brother."

"I can answer that, it was rumored that the drama instructor clearly knew that Mildred was incompetence and couldn't act, but chose her for the part mainly because they wanted someone with her particular look and her long natural golden hair," Veronica said.

"I never knew that was how she ended up with the part. Ryan never mentioned that. But I do remember Mildred's thick golden curls hanging down near her waist at the time," Catherine said and continued, "But I'm just trying to make a point of why she kissed Ryan at the barbecue. She did that because she was happy for him. Get it, since she had played opposite of him in the role that won him that best actor's award."

"Maybe so, but it gave her no right to bombard and kiss him on the face like that in front of everybody," Veronica recalled.

"Maybe you're right; and I don't plan to take up for Mildred since she was a thorn in my side then and she's still a thorn in my side. That woman will probably be the death of me if I can't find away to get over how Antonio loved her in the end."

"If I don't stay on track with this story the boys will be home and we'll be sitting down to dinner and I won't even be a quarter through. Since we both keep getting off track on to other topics about how I didn't like Mildred kissing him and you didn't like Mildred period. So, this time I'll try telling the story without getting sidetracked."

"Okay, go ahead." Catherine waved her hand.

"Back to the story, I can remember how Ryan didn't seem put off by everybody questions about his stay in Los Angeles and shooting the Ivory Soap commercial. However, after about an hour of monopolizing his time everyone drifted back into the festivities, drinking fruit punch and eating hotdogs, barbecue ribs and chicken."

"Can you recall if Ryan said anything at all that day about how he felt about staying in Los Angeles? Plus, did he mention anything about how it felt for him being in front of the cameras while the cameramen were shooting the commercial?"

Veronica shook her head. "Not at that time because he hadn't started talking to me yet. I'm getting to that."

"Hi, Mr. Jordan," Ryan spoke to my father as Dad stood over the grill turning the meat over the low fire: Ribs, chicken, hamburgers and hotdogs. I was sitting a distant away on the backsteps with my eyes glued to Ryan. I hadn't taken my eyes off of him for one second. He probably hadn't even noticed me and in my mind at the time, I was sure he wouldn't notice me. I remember how I was discreet about my staring and didn't make it appear obvious that I was eyeing him. But I just kept sitting there on the backsteps looking out across the yard at him and my father, watching them converse as Ryan visited with my father. Dad offered him a glass of fruit punch and pointed toward the back door where I was seated. I clearly heard him tell Ryan that he could find a gallon bowl of punch on the table in the kitchen. Therefore, Ryan had to walk right past me to enter the back door and step inside to the kitchen. I hadn't noticed, but the way I was seated on the backsteps, I was halfway blocking the pathway to the back door."

"Hi, Veronica. How are you?" he said and gave me a ten second stare that melted my heart. "I think Catherine is out front looking for you," he said, smiling as I scooted aside and he rushed up the backsteps, opened the door and stepped inside.

"When he smiled at me, I couldn't manage a word. It was crazy but it seemed as if looking in his eyes left me speechless. Back then, when it came to love I was so idealistic about the whole idea of falling in love. In my mind, he was already my Prince Charming and he hadn't even asked me out or shown any real interest in me. But as I said, I couldn't take my eyes off of your brother. But when he stepped into the kitchen, my mother was standing at the kitchen counter putting out more snacks, napkins and paper cups."

"Hi Mrs. Naomi," Ryan said to my mother as she passed him a tall paper cup filled with ice.

He placed the cup on the counter and dipped a dipper into the punch bowl and filled his cup with pink punch.

"Help yourself, Ryan," Mom said. "There's also some cherry punch in the refrigerator."

"Thanks, Mrs. Naomi, but this will do the trick," he said as he rushed back outside with his cup of punch in his hand, onto the backyard among the festivities.

"You were just like his shadow that day. I know it was from a distant, but where ever he ended up, you were not too far from him. But I guess he didn't say anything to you?" Catherine asked.

Veronica shook her head and then narrowed her eyes toward Catherine. "Not really, until later. However, I wasn't his only shadow. You were his shadow as well. You sort of stuck with him because he was getting a lot of attention and you wanted to be apart of the attention and praise he was getting; and with his compassionate heart he wanted to make you feel included."

"How do you know that?" Catherine asked.

"I know because I noticed how he went out of his way that afternoon to keep you by his side. He didn't want you to feel left out, even though all the attention wasn't about you. It was about him and the rising star he was becoming."

Catherine nodded. "You're right. My brother was almost a saint how he was always thinking of others."

Veronica smiled and nodded. "That was my Ryan, always thinking of others, but back to the story. Shortly after you and Ryan walked around to the front yard, I was curious about how the two of you seemed to be in such a serious discussion."

"I don't recall having a serious discussion with my brother that day."

"Well, it appeared that way to me from where I was standing. But maybe you two were just talking in general."

"I'll bite," Catherine said. "What difference did it make?"

"It made a difference to me that day, because I was jumping out of my skin anxious."

"I guess you were anxious about Ryan being at your house?"

"That is correct, and I thought you were talking to him about me and how I had a crush on him. I thought you were going to tell him what I had told you. That's why I started to follow you and Ryan when you headed around to the front yard. But if you can remember, I didn't follow you guys," Veronica explained. "I really wanted to, but I just didn't want to make my behavior and staring seem too obvious. But I'll tell you now, it took all my willpower to stay in the backyard and not spy on you two in the front yard. Therefore, after you and Ryan left the backyard, I walked over to the picnic table and grabbed a hamburger and then walked inside. But the moment I quickly strolled into the living room I rushed over to the living room window to see if you two were still standing in the front yard having that discussion that seemed so intense. But when I peeped out the window you had stepped away from Ryan and you were mingling with some other friends. But as I scanned the yard and spotted him at the edge of the driveway near his car, I also spotted Mildred Latham standing there talking to him. I wasn't pleased that she was in his face again. So I kept peeping out of the living room window at them but I knew they couldn't see me staring out since the sun shadowed my view from them. After awhile, as I stood there frowning with my eyes glued toward Ryan and Mildred wondering what she was saying to him, suddenly you walked over and grabbed Ryan's arm and pulled him to the side. The two of you were momentarily engaged in some intense conversation as you both smiled at each other. Then Ryan looked toward Mildred who stood a few feet away and nodded at her. Then he walked quickly across the lawn toward his car. When he reached his car and grabbed the door handle of the driver's side, before he could hop in, Mildred pulled the door open on the passenger's side and slid in on the front seat. She had her face glued toward Ryan and she was smiling and laughing. She seemed especially excited and in a cheerful mood. I was boiling inside to see her in such a cheerful mood hanging out with Ryan. For a moment, I thought I would choke from frustration as I grabbed my mouth with both hands when she leaned toward Ryan, whispering in his ear."

Catherine waved her hand. "I don't know what she whispered in his ear, but it couldn't have been that much."

"How can you say that for certain? You just said you don't know what she whispered in his ear."

"That's correct, but we both know that Ryan wouldn't have tolerated her saying anything out of the way to him," Catherine pointed out.

Veronica nodded. "I'll have to agree with you there."

"Listen, I'm no fan of Mildred's, but to be completely frank, she had only taken a seat in Ryan's car because she was fascinated by it. Actually, every teenager in your yard that day was fascinated by Ryan's car. After all, he was the only eighteen year old high school boy in the area who owned a brand new sporty Corvette. Mildred was no different and she was impressed by his car. She just wanted to see what it felt like to sit inside," Catherine admitted.

"How do you know that was all it was to her fresh behavior that day?"

"Let's just agree that we saw it differently. You can think what you like. Nevertheless, I didn't see her as being fresh. But I know she wasn't coming on to Ryan."

"But how do you know that?"

"I know because I was there and that's what she said to Ryan. She told him she was fascinated by his car and that she would be honored to take a seat inside. Besides, you saw her when she hopped in and then minutes later she hopped right out. Besides, she was crazy in love with Antonio at that time," Catherine pointed out.

"I always wondered about that incident and why she had hopped in Ryan's car. I wasn't sure if she had a crush on Ryan or what? I do recall that she had a boyfriend at the time and was dating Antonio."

"Yes, she was dating Antonio. The boy I wanted to date, but why remind me?" Catherine snapped.

Veronica smiled. "I figured Ryan wasn't interested in Mildred back then. She was too skinny but cute as a button as you so quickly pointed out before. Nevertheless, she wasn't as cute as I thought I was during our senior term," Veronica said arrogantly. "Besides, I had my eyes on Ryan and had decided and promised myself that he would be my boyfriend at the beginning of the school term."

"You had decided and promised yourself that he would be your boyfriend?"

Veronica nodded. "Yes, I decided he was the only boy for me. Nevertheless, I was so upset with Mildred for kissing him in front of everybody and throwing herself on him in such a bold manner," Veronica recalled and laughed.

"What's funny about it?" Catherine asked.

"What's funny is what happened later that evening when I sneaked over to Mildred's house and pulled up all her flowers from her precious flower garden. Remember the flower garden that she was bragging about at school?"

Catherine stared at Veronica for a moment as if she was trying to recall what she had just asked her. Then she nodded and braced herself for more surprises from that incident that she felt was coming her way. "I remember that garden. It was really a big deal to Mildred back then. I recall how she was always talking about her special garden."

Veronicia shook her head. "Yes, she talked about it so much until the senior class hated to see her coming. Everybody knew her conversation would be about her precious little garden. She really annoyed me how she talked about those flowers all the way through lunch period. She wasn't at our table but everybody could clearly hear her at the next table over going on and on about how she could plant flowers."

"She did talk about it too much, but it was exciting to her since her garden was the only one that turned out great. Plus, she ended up with an A+ for that garden project in science class. The rest of us failed the project," Catherine reminded her.

"I know, but I wasn't interested in getting my hands dirty trying to plant some flower seeds; and most of the class felt the same way including you, Miss Catherine, remember?"

Catherine nodded. "You're right, not many wanted to tackle that project. But we were all being stupid since we needed the grade to build our grade average."

"Maybe we did, but we all graduated and I haven't had a need to know how to plant any flowers, have you?" Veronica arrogantly stated.

"That's because we are blessed to have a gardener, but everybody isn't so lucky and if they want a flower garden they have to get outside and plant the seeds themselves."

"I guess so, Catherine. But why are we discussing something that doesn't matter to me at this point?" Veronica asked impatiently.

"You brought it up about how you pulled Mildred's flowers from her garden."

"Oh, yes, that's right," Veronica slightly laughed. "It makes me laugh whenever I think about how I destroyed her garden and none of the students including you ever suspected I had a hand in it."

"That's because they all thought I had a hand in it," Catherine reminded her. "However, back to the point. Mildred was so happy about her garden and talked about it so much because she had planted all those flower seeds and they had all grew like crazy and turned out so well that summer for her. Remember how our science teacher sent a picture of Mildred's flower garden to the local paper and then threw Mildred a party during class after the picture ended up on the front page of the Daily Herald?"

Veronica discreetly smiled. "Of course, I remember. I reminded you."

Catherine narrowed her eyes toward Veronica and shook her head. "Now you admit to the dirty deed. When Mildred was crying in class wondering who hated her so much that they would destroy her garden you didn't say a word. It was a great mystery to all of us with no clues of who sneaked over to her house in the dark to destroy her garden. It never dawned on me that it was you."

"Well, I had to teach Miss America a lesson for kissing Ryan like that in front of all the other students that were at my house. Besides, she ended up with another garden just as nice that next summer and it wasn't for a school project. I guess she's just one of those people with a green tumb."

Catherine smiled. "Yes, it was a big mystery to the whole senior class. You were getting back at Mildred but the fallout fell on my head."

"What do you mean?" Veronica asked.

"Remember how all the juniors and seniors including Mildred was pointing their fingers at me. I stop coming to lunch in the cafeteria for awhile because I was getting so much harrassment. Everybody thought it was pretty low to sneak over and destroy someone flowers. I know I had done nothing wrong but I was a good scapegoat since they all thought my jealousy over Antonio had gotten the best of me. That made me an easy target to blame as someone who could have sneaked over to Mildred's house and ripped up her flowers from her garden."

Veronica nodded as she stared into space for a moment. "I do recall how hey were all pointing the finger at you and it caused you some headaches," Veronica said solemnly and then looked toward Catherine with a slight smile. "I was having fun with Mildred's grief, but I want you to know I wasn't at all happy about everyone blaming you. A few times I almost told off Raymond Ross. He had a big mouth and wouldn't stop teasing and harrassing you over the incident. Nevertheless, I kept my lips sealed since my hands were tied. I realized that I couldn't stand up for you because I didn't want to shed light on myself. I was the culprit and that science teacher had put holy fear in me when she stood before class with a determined look in her eyes. She promised the class that if any of us were proven guilty of destroying that garden she would personally see to the guilty person being kicked out of senior class. I couldn't take a chance on that happening. Therefore, I never confessed to my crime of being the one to destroy Mildred's garden."

"It was surprising how the incident ended up pictured in an article in the paper."

"I remember. It called me a plant hater."

"You're right, it did. It stated that some mysterious plant hater had secretly torn the garden a part, ripping up all the lovely pink and yellow flowers by their roots. The outstanding little garden had just won an award in a high school science class," Catherine said looking toward Veronica. "However, your name wasn't mentioned in that article since nobody knew it was you."

"It only got all that attention because that science teacher pushed it. That's how Mildred's garden ended up in the local paper. If the teacher hadn't contacted the paper in the first place about Mildred's garden and sent them that picture, a destroyed flower garden by some student at a high school would not have been news," Veronica pointed out.

"You're probably right. However, if anyone had gotten wind that you were the perpetrator back then, that would have made news I bet."

Veronica smiled. "It felt good to rip up her special flowers after she had threw her lips all over Ryan," Veronica admitted.

"Veronica it was a congradulations kiss and I don't know why you can't get that. Maybe you didn't get it then, but you should get it now."

"I get it now, but that was then and I thought she wanted Ryan."

"But she didn't. Otherwise, I would have had a chance with Antonio. Your jealousy and revenge was all for nothing; and that was a cold hearted thing to do at the time to Mildred Latham. It wasn't like she was trying to date Ryan or anything. She was just excited like all the other students because he had won that best actor award and ended up being in a commercial," Catherine explained.

"I know, but I needed to retaliate against her for kissing him. Besides, I was quite spiteful and vindictive back then."

Catherine gave Veronica a hard stare and narrowed her eyes. "You were spiteful and vindictive back then?"

"Catherine, I know you are being funny, calling me spiteful and vindictive now," Veronica waved her hand. "Nevertheless, why give me grief for chastising Mildred after all those years ago. You said she's still a thorn in your side," Veronica reminded her.

"That's true, but at that time Mildred hadn't hurt you the way you thought she had. She was never interested in Ryan."

"Maybe not, but I destroyed her flowers and I would have destroyed her hairdo if so many people hadn't been around. It really didn't matter at the time why she did what she did. It just mattered that she had put her hands on Ryan, who I had high hopes to be my boyfriend. My mind was in a different place and I saw Mildred as a threat since Ryan and I wasn't really together," Veronica explained. "Besides, why are you surprised that I did that to Mildred's garden. I was no angel back then," Veronica reminded her.

"If the truth be told, you are still no angel," Catherine mumbled in a low voice.

"I heard what you said and I'm not offended because I never claimed to be an angel. Ryan was the angel in our household, but he loved me just the same, flaws and all," Veronica strongly stated."

"We both know that's the truth, but you also hid your mischievous ways from my brother. He only saw the good side of you and never that underhanded, scheming side."

"Lay it on thick if you will, but you can't get under my skin right now because it feels good to relive these fun memories of my perfect Ryan."

"Did you ever confide in him about what you did to Mildred?"

"No, I never mentioned that to anyone at the time. Right now is the first time I have ever admitted or mentioned anything about that."

"That was probably the best that you didn't mention it," Catherine grinned. "Knowing my straight-laced brother so well. He probably would have insisted on you confronting Mildred and confessing your crime; and then he probably would have paid Mildred for the flowers that you destroyed. That's how he was, you know."

"Yes, I know he was too good for his own good. But back to the story. Where did I leave off?"

"How you sneaked over Mildred's house and destroyed her flowers," Catherine reminded her.

"Okay, I was upset that she kissed Ryan but I couldn't ask her to leave my house."

"I guess you didn't want to make a scene with her in front of Ryan."

"No, Catherine, that's not it. Just listen, okay? Besides, I would have found away to pull her to the side for that honor, but I couldn't ask her to leave because she was at the barbecue at my parent's request."

"So, your folks invited Mildred to your family barbecue?"

"Yes, why wouldn't they? Afterall, they invited all my classmates; and I think they mostly did that because they knew how excited everyone were about Ryan's big break. Therefore, they sent a special invitation to Ryan and also Mildred since she had played opposite of him in that play. That's why mildred received a special invite along with her entire family," Veronica explained.

"I see." Catherine nodded. "I was wondering how Mildred ended up at your family picnic. Since at that time, the two of you were not close. Besides, you knew I didn't want her at the barbecue."

"You are right, I knew you didn't want her there; and I was never close with Mildred and I slowly began to really dislike her when she started being Ryan's sidekick in his drama class," Veronica admitted. "However, I had no choice over my parents' invites."

"I'm sure you didn't, but now that you mention it, I can remember how Ryan and Mildred were always staying after school to rehearse together," Catherine reminded her. "I would call and tell you and it would always upset you."

"It did always upset me that she was the only girl in his drama class that always co-starred with him in all those plays."

"But you two were never friends, right?" Catherine asked.

"Hell no, at no time were Mildred and I close," Veronica stressed. "Catherine why would you ask me that stupid question? You know I was never friends with Mildred Latham. You were always glued to my side back then. Did you ever once see Mildred at my side? For real, Catherine, sometime I wonder about your memory."

"It's not so far-fetched that Mildred Latham could have been one of your friends during high school. God knows you had many and I wasn't aware of every friend you knew," Catherine pointed out.

"You have a point, but no, Mildred and I never hung out together on the school grounds or off. She was a nice girl and somewhat silly in my opinion; and although we had some classes together, we were never friends," Veronica lifted her cup to her mouth and took a sip of tea as she looked at Catherine.

Catherine held up both hands. "Why are you looking at me? Mildred Latham definitely wasn't my best buddy. She was the apple of Antonio's eyes and that made me not want to be around her at all," Catherine explained. "We had one class together and I changed classes because I couldn't stomach being in the same classroom with her. The girl Antonio worshipped. I used to cry inside to myself how Antonio would give her all of his attention when I was so crazy about him and she didn't seem that into him. I know she liked him but it just didn't seem like she liked him as much as me. Although, I guess that was a lie, since she almost got herself killed for the man 40 years later."

"I was upset enough to tear Mildred's hair out at the barbecue because she kissed Ryan: all thirty inches of it. Other than that, I really didn't have a beef with Mildred during high school," Veronica admitted. "All during senior year, I basically stayed clear of her because I knew Antonio liked her and you liked him. So truthfully, I stayed away from her because I knew she liked the boy you liked. We were friends and I knew you wouldn't like it if I were friends with a girl that you had a beef with."

"That's the story of my life. I always wanted Antonio but he always wanted someone else," Catherine said and stared into space for a moment.

Veronica looked at Catherine. "So what was that serious discussion about?"

"What serious discussion?"

"The serious discussion you were having with Ryan in my front yard that day?"

Catherine smiled and shook her head. "I don't think you want to know."

"Spit it out, what was that discussion about? You seemed intense about something and I never asked you about it before now."

"I was actually begging Ryan to call Antonio and invite him to the barbecue."

"Well, did he?"

"No, he did not. He made it clear to me that it wasn't his place to invite Antonio or anyone else to your family barbecue if they hadn't already been invited by your family."

Chapter Five

In the middle of their conversation, the doorbell sounded and Veronica and Catherine both looked in the direction of the front door. Moments later, Dillion hurried across the room toward the door. Catherine and Veronica sat motionless as they could hear low voices, Dillion's voice and two other voices coming from the foyer. They were curious and exchanged looks as they paused their conversation. Then they heard the door shut and they both stared curiously at Dillion as he headed across the room toward them.

"These are for you, Miss Veronica." Dillion held out the small white paper bag he was carrying. "These are the Girl Scout cookies that you ordered. Should I take them into the kitchen and tell Natalie to put them in the cookie jar?" Dillion asked.

Veronica nodded and seemed slightly annoyed that the interruption at the door was just a delivery of Girl Scout cookies. "Sure, please do. Thank you, Dillion," she said and quickly turned toward Catherine as Dillion walked away in route to the kitchen.

"Okay, back to the story." She rubbed her hands together. "Where were we?"

"I think you were standing in the living room window looking out at Ryan."

"That's right, and after awhile I finally stepped out of the house and into the front yard to mingle with our guests. I remember feeling so nervous and anxious, but I discreetly kept my eyes on Ryan. Nevertheless, my excitement of his presence would end quickly, since shortly after I build up my nerves and stepped outside, he made his way across the lawn to his car and left the barbecue. I remember so clearly how my heart sunk when he drove off. I stood in the yard and watched his car fade into the distance. He had been at my house without even approaching me. That made me feel that our feelings for each other were onesided. I knew how I felt about him. But all the encouragement that I had given myself that maybe he felt the same, all went down the drain when I watched him drive away that sunny hot day. Suddenly I felt breathless and felt like crying as I rushed back inside the house. But the moment I stepped through the front door and before I could pull my emotions together, I remember very clearly how startled I was when I glanced across the room and spotted you standing in the living room. I never will forget how you seemed ticked off with me. You were standing near the fireplace with your right hand on your hip. You were also patting your right foot on the floor, frowning with a disappointed look on your face. Seeing you caught me off guard and I had to collect myself quickly since I was all geared up to cry before I spotted you in the room. You stared at me and asked me a question that didn't make any sense."

"I want to know what you have done to my friend?"

"What are you talking about, Catherine?" I asked.

"I want to know where is the real Veronica Parker?" You strutted across the room near the window where I stood and waved both hands in front of my face. "Earth to Veronica; are you in there? I surely do not recognize the girl who's standing before me?"

"I'm waiting to hear you explain what in the world you are talking about?"

"I'm talking about your distant behavior toward Ryan while he was here. You are always saying how crazy you are about my brother, but all while he was here at your house, you seemed to be avoiding him. You were sneaking about as if you didn't want him to notice you. I know I'm right because I saw you doing it."

"I was still lost for words and caught off guard as I slightly shook anxiously in wonder and confusion about what you had said to me."

"Catherine, please tell me what you are talking about? What do you mean by that? Why would you think I was trying to avoid Ryan?" I asked curiously.

"It appeared that way. You gave him the cold shoulder all while he was here."

"Why would you say or think that?"

"I can say and think it, because it's true. I was curious to know if you two had found time to talk so I asked Ryan. That's when he informed me that the two of you didn't really hold any conversations with each other. So, what's going on with you anyway? You couldn't wait for him to get back in town. But when he does, you freeze up and don't talk to him at all. I'm surprise of you to miss out on such a perfect opportunity to talk to Ryan."

"We just didn't get a chance to say anything to each other."

"Why didn't you? I know you didn't think anything was going on with him and Mildred, did you?" You asked curiously.

"Catherine, stop badgering me. I don't know what I thought."

"We both know you can be arrogant sometime, Veronica. So maybe, just maybe you thought you were too good to walk up to him and start the conversation."

"That's not it at all."

"I bet that is it. You wanted him to approach you. I almost forgot. Miss Veronica Parker is too good to just be normal and talk to the boy she likes," you teased me.

"Get real, Catherine and stop having a tantrum. Besides, why would you say something so stupid as that in the first place. For your information I don't think I'm too good for Ryan. If you want to go down that road, why don't you wake up and smell the coffee. Maybe it's the other way around."

"What do you mean?"

"Ryan is the one who's the rising star of the community or did that slip your mind? Maybe you're chastising the wrong person," I quickly snapped. "For goodness sake, Ryan is the one who just won that best actor award and was featured in a commercial. So just maybe your brother thinks he's too good for me. Therefore, why should I make a fool out of myself by throwing myself all over him the way Mildred did?" I said firmly.

"You would have been throwing yourself all over him if you had held a conversation with the boy that you can't stop talking about in class?" You asked in a heated voice.

"I think so. He found time to talk to others. He could have seeked me out if he wanted to," I said in a pouty way.

"Just give me a break, Veronica. It wasn't going to be any skin off your nose to walk up to Ryan and strike a conversation with him."

"Maybe not, but he could have done the same. He could have walked up to me and started a conversation with me."

"You're saying he should have come to you?"

"No, I'm not saying anything. This is all your assumptions," I snapped at you. By now I was so angry with you for thinking I was trying to act stuck up with Ryan until I shouted in your face before I realized what I was saying. "Think whatever you want to think, Catherine! But you have no right to stand here in my living room and chew me out for not holding a conversation with your brother, because that's not the way it was."

"Calm down, Veronica. I was teasing you mostly. Just lightened up already."

"I could tell you were confused with me for being so ticked off with you, when you were mostly just playing around with me and sort of teasing me about Ryan. But I was uptight and blowing off steam since he hadn't approached me during the barbecue."

"Veronica, please, there is no need to shout in my face. Just forget the whole thing. Maybe you're right, I'm sure! Ryan probably wouldn't give you the time of day! You're too idealistic and too darn childish!" You said firmly, giving me a sharp look before strutting into the kitchen, shaking your head.

"I knew I had ticked you off when I really didn't mean to, but what you didn't know was how deeply I had fallen for Ryan. I cared for Ryan intensely by then, but I felt I had no chance with him so I tried to hide my feelings. However, you were right, I could have shown some backbone and held a conversation with him. Afterall, he was at my family Fourth of July, barbecue picnic. There were no excuses for my behavior, but I guess I was so overwhelmed that he was back in town and at my house. I didn't know how to handle it. Needless to say, I followed you into the kitchen where you placed a piece of barbecue chicken on a paper plate. You took a seat at the kitchen table, looking over at me as I stood in the doorway. You frowned at me."

"What now, Veronica? Can I please enjoy my drumstick in peace without getting into another discussion about my brother?"

"I couldn't hold my tears any longer as I walked over to the kitchen sink with my back to you. I somewhat envied you and felt you were lucky to have Ryan as a brother. Then I thought about Jack Coleman and thought if only Ryan would want my company as much as he wanted to be around Jack Coleman. Then after a moment, I apologized to you."

"I'm sorry, Catherine. You were right. I should have attempted to hold a conversation with Ryan," I wiped my tears with my fingers.

"Don't worry about it, Veronica. I guess I was a little hard on you. But it sort of seemed like you were trying to avoid Ryan, which didn't make any sense. So, the next time you see him just tell him you weren't trying to give him the cold shoulder just in case that crossed his mind."

"Did he say that?" I walked over to the kitchen table pulled out a chair to be seated.

"Yes, he sure did, but I want you to know that he said it in a teasing way," You answered, looking me in the face.

"What was his exact words?"

"He said to me, I didn't see much of Veronica. Do you think she was avoiding me? But in all fairness, he said it in a teasing way as if he was kidding about you avoiding him, but he still said it."

"No way did I want to give him that impression."

"What with the tears?"

"I broke down and held my head on the table and told you for the first time, that I was in love with Ryan."

"Catherine, I'm in love with Ryan. I have felt this way about him for a long time now. But I feel I don't have much of a chance with him now. I feel like there are hundreds who probably feel the same way about him since he's so famous now."

"It's funny because when you were wondering how Ryan felt about you, he was also wondering how you felt about him. The two of you were crazy about each other and either of you knew that about the other. But I knew it about you both," Catherine confessed.

"I didn't know it," Veronica said as she continued the story. "I ran out of the back door before you could respond. I walked out into the backyard, past the flower garden and down the hillside to the clear water pond. I sat there in the grass, throwing sticks into the radiance little pond while the sun glittered on the waves. Then I stood up and just stared into the water. I always enjoyed standing on the banks admiring the clear sparkling water and the beautiful white stones beneath. But on this afternoon, my heart was so lonely for Ryan. I couldn't stop thinking about Mildred kiss and seeing the picture of her lips on his face. I wondered if he liked her, but figured he would never ask me out. I wondered what did I have that other girls didn't have and what could I give him that other girls couldn't give him and what made me more special than any other girl? I was thinking that in my mind and trying to think of some way that would make me appear more special to your brother. I was determined to be with Ryan," Veronica said. "But it seemed impossible."

"Why did you say that. You already knew that Ryan liked you too."

"I was hoping and you were always saying so, but I wasn't for sure. He was always friendly and polite but he had not asked me out."

"Now that you have paused with your story. I could use another cup of tea and I'll fill your cup as well," Catherine said as she got out of her seat and lifted the silver tea pot and poured them both a fresh hot cup of tea.

Veronica sipped her tea and smiled. "The sun was shining bright that afternoon as I sadly dropped back down on the grass and fell over with both arms beneath my head. The fresh scent from the outdoors and the little pond filled the air as I laid there looking up at the endless sky and the tall trees overhead. Tears poured down the sides of my eyes and I told myself how foolish I was to be all bent out of shape for a boy who had only shown limited interest in me. Nevertheless, after lying in the cool soft grass awhile, something warm touched my neck. It startled me. I opened my eyes and there stood Ryan, smiling down at me! I thought I was dreaming. I couldn't move or speak."

"Hi, Miss Veronica Parker. You're lying there looking beautiful soaking up the sun," he said in a whisper and slightly shook his head. "I must repeat. You do look very beautiful lying there," Ryan smiled down at me.

"I still couldn't speak and as I went to sit up, his quick smooth hand rested on my chest and stopped my rise, as he dropped down to his knees and looked me straight in the eyes. I knew I had to be dreaming and I was hoping I wouldn't wake up because my face was just inches from the most handsom boy in town."

He looked directly in my eyes and smiled in a warm way. "Catherine told me what you said. I wish I had known before now," Ryan whispered as he smiled sexily, bringing his smooth, handsome face closer to mine, kissing the side of my face and neck.

"But I still hadn't managed a word as I laid there in the sunlight smoldering out of control from the mere thought of him, and as I struggled to breathe, he covered my lips completely with the softness of his smooth lips. He stretched out beside me, lying in the grass wearing his expensive designer outfit. He wrapped his arms around my head and made me literally explode with passion as he smoothed his lips over mine and kissed me in a tender demanding passionate way. I was like a feather in his firm arms. It took all my strength to breathe. I couldn't move an inch or utter a word. I could only shed silent tears as he held my neck between his smooth hands and kissed my throat, traveling side to side to my shoulders, which he held and kissed through my blouse. His hands were soft and warm as they burned me through and through. He gently and slowly pulled my blouse out of my skirt and touched my stomach. He smoothed his hands across my stomach as his touch warmed me through and through. I had never felt anything so thrilling." He smiled and before I could catch my breath, he leaned down and gave me a quick kiss on the stomach and then smoothed my blouse over my stomach.

"Veronica, you are more radiant than anything I know. Looking in your eyes makes me feel more and more alive," Ryan whispered.

"I guess my brother was quite the romantic type," Catherine smiled.

"Yes, Catherine, he was very romantic and especially that afternoon. His words were spoken in a soft, passionate manner as I felt the heat building in me. His touch was too unbearably invigorating when he rubbed his hand across my stomach. After awhile he brought both hands up to my shoulders and gripped them as he brought his handsome face down to cover my lips with an urgent tender kiss. That's when I screamed.

"Ryan, I love you. I can't take anymore," I said breathless as I managed to push him away. I jumped up and straighten out my long white skirt, tucking my blouse in. A few tears were falling from my eyes. I couldn't look at him. I saw him out of the corner of my eye as he raked the grass and bits of leaves off his clothes. Then he faced me, lifting up my face. He had a confused expression on his face. His hands were still warm as he held up my face toward his. My body tingled and ached from his touch. I wanted him to place me back on the ground and ravish me, but I couldn't let my hopeless love blind me of my good sense. I knew he wasn't in love with me, and even less than that I felt he wasn't interested in dating me, since he hadn't asked me out or bothered to talk to me at the barbecue. All kinds of thoughts were going through my mind and I was wondering if he was trying to go all the way with me because he figured he could. Afterall, I knew you had told him that I liked him. I figured that's why he was trying to be so romantic and fresh because he figured he could get somewhere with me."

"Wow, you thought straight-laced Ryan was trying to take advantage of you?"

"That's how it seemed. It appeared as if he were trying to go all the way with me. But I wasn't hundred percent sure if that's what he was doing. I just knew in my heart that if he was trying to sleep with me, I didn't want to be a meaningless affair to him. I had my heart set on being his girlfriend."

"Yes, I know. You told every student that would listen when school turned out that at the beginning of the new school term, Ryan Franklin would be your boyfriend; and at the time, I'm sorry to tell you. But I felt the chances of you getting together with my brother was pretty much a pipe dream since Ryan had so much going on with his new career. Besides, you two weren't even talking to each other. Nevertheless, you said he would be your boyfriend at the beginning of school and you were right."

"I told everyone because it helped my determination. Besides, I felt if it didn't happen before school started that my chances would be slimmer since he would be starting senior year at such a famous star level. But nevermind that, let me go on with the story:

"Sure, go ahead. I'm anxiously listening to every word," Catherine said.

"Okay, after I tried chewing him out and pushing him away. Your brother looked deep into my eyes long and hard and I'm sure he could feel my passion."

He slightly smiled, as he moved his face closer to mine. "Kiss me again, Veronica."

"With those words from him, I was back under his spell again as he pushed his mouth tenderly against mine, swallowing me up, placing me against the trunk of a tall tree, pressing his solid frame against mine, sliding his hands up and down my hips and with every bit of strength I could manage, I tore from his arms."

"No, Ryan, I won't do this."

He held up both arms. "I'm sorry, Veronica, if I have offended you. I didn't mean to."

"You haven't offended me, Ryan."

"If I haven't offended you, why did you push me away?"

"I can't go all the way with you. I love you but I can't do this. This is a big step. A very big step for me. I haven't gone to bed with a boy yet and I don't plan for it to be some quick roll in the hay with the most popular boy in town no matter how much I care for you. Besides, I promised myself back in tenth grade that the boy I go all the way with would have to be in love with me too," I nervously and anxiously explained to him while looking him straight in the eyes. "I know you are not in love with me, Ryan. I'm really confused about all of this. I can't even believe you are actually here with me in the first place."

"I'm not sure if I get what you just said," he said while smiling.

"I'm trying to say how you haven't shown me much interest before. So it shouldn't be a surprise that I said I can't believe you are here right now. Think about it, you are here being very romantic with me and you haven't even asked me out," I managed to say to him.

He nodded. "I guess you do have a point at that."

"Yes, I have a point. So, how did you know I was down here by the pond? And why did you come looking for me, Ryan?" I asked.

His eyes widened and he looked away, turning his back to me momentarily and then he faced me with a serious expression. "Well, after I left the barbecue, Jack called and said he was going to drop by your house for a while. He said he received an invite. Therefore, I told him that I would drop back over for a while as well. But when I got back to your house I didn't see Jack. I waited awhile and then decided I would leave. Before leaving I wanted to say goodbye to you. But I scanned the front yard and didn't spot you among any of the groups that were gathered about mingling and eating. I also walked around a little to see if I could spot you anywhere in the backyard. All I could see were the people that had been invited, still hanging out enjoying the barbecue festivities. Therefore, when I wasn't able to spot you anywhere, I had just decided to leave when I looked across the backyard and spotted your father talking to what's his name."

"Who is what's his name?" I asked him.

"You know who I'm talking about. He's a little on the heavy side. That kid who's always rubbing the history teacher the wrong way."

"Who never turns in his book reports on time," I smiled.

Ryan smiled. "Yes, he's the one."

I nodded and kept smiling. "I know who you mean. You're talking about that know it all, opinionated Raymond."

"Of course, that's his name, Raymond Ross. Anyway, back to my point. I spotted your father talking to Raymond and I wasn't trying to eavesdrop, but I could hear their conversation clear enough to know that Raymond hadn't been invited."

I abruptly interrupted Ryan because I knew that was not true. "I can tell you now, that was an oversight if Raymond didn't get an invitation. I know firsthand that my folks sent out an email stating that all my classmates were welcome at the barbecue," I quickly said. "I furnished my mother the email addresses and Raymonds' were on the list."

"I guess you're right because your father told Raymond that he was welcomed to stay," Ryan paused and grinned.

"I asked him what was funny?"

"Nothing is really funny, but I was just thinking how the moment your father told him that he was welcomed to stay, Raymond smiled and hurried across the yard in the direction of Mildred Latham. But she was busy talking to a group of girls from school."

I nodded. "Raymond is crazy about Mildred but she has a boyfriend."

"I didn't know," Ryan acknowledged.

"I thought you knew. Mildred is dating Antonio. They are always glued to the hip."

"Maybe, but I didn't see him at your house, did you?"

"No, I don't think he was there. But I know he's crazy about Mildred and that's why he's not with Catherine," I told him.

"You have lost me now," Ryan asked curiously with great interest. "What do you mean that's why he's not with Catherine?" Ryan wanted to know.

"I shouldn't have said anything," I quickly mumbled.

"Maybe not but you did. So, what's going on with Catherine and Antonio? She can do what she wants. However, I'm not too comfortable with some of the rumors I have heard about Antonio's fast life."

"Antonio is okay," I quickly told him. "He's just as good as your friend Jack. The way you feel about Antonio is the same way some of the students feel about your friend Jack."

Ryan nodded and smiled, looking me in the eyes. "You are right, Veronica. I shouldn't judge Antonio because it's not right to judge others. Therefore, I take back what I just said about Antonio and the rumors that are floating around about him," Ryan took a deep breath and nodded. "I'm not going to be that person who judges others and when I have children one day, I'm going to raise them the same," he said with conviction.

"That's wonderful, Ryan," I said heartfelt and smiled at him. "I'm sure you will be a wonderful father one day. However, at this moment, you still haven't answered my question," I reminded him as we stood there talking about everything that I didn't want to talk about. I wanted to talk about whether he had feelings for me or not.

He smiled and held up one finger. "That's right. I was getting to that point when I ended up bringing up Raymond and Antonio and everything else. But I didn't forget. You wanted to know how I was able to find you down here by the pond?"

"Yes, I would like to know that."

"Okay, I'll tell you now. It was right after Raymond walked away from your father. I could see your father wasn't engaged with anyone, so I quickly headed across the yard toward the barbecue grill in the direction he was headed. I reached him before he reached the grill and asked Mr. Jordan where were you. However, he glanced about the yard and shook his head, not sure of your whereabouts. Your mother was nearby busy at the grill putting chicken on a platter. So your father walked up and tapped Mrs. Naomi on the shoulder to get her attention and asked her about your whereabouts. She glanced around holding a platter of chicken and told your father that Catherine had told her that you ran down the hillside toward the pond. Your father glanced over his shoulder and nodded at me, since he knew I had heard what Mrs. Naomi had just said. So, I found Catherine in the front yard and we had a short conversation. She confided in me about your feelings for me. Then she told me I could find you down by the pond."

"I can't believe Catherine would tell you what I said. How could she do that knowing you couldn't possibly have any feelings for me?" I mumbled, slightly dropping my head.

"Veronica, that's a strong statement to say I couldn't possibly have feelings for you." He touched my face. "Why would you say something like that? Don't you know how special and beautiful you are?"

"Ryan, are you saying that I'm special and beautiful to you?"

"I don't have to say you're special and beautiful. Regardless to how it's worded. You are a very special young lady and a very beautiful young woman. Therefore, why would you say I couldn't possibly have any feelings for you? I don't think I get that, not at all."

"You should get it, Ryan. Because I'm just calling it the way I see it. You haven't given me any reason to believe that you have feelings for me."

He smiled at me warmly. "Well, I guess I need to do a better job and get busy."

"What are you saying, Ryan? Do you have feelings for me?"

He smiled at me, but did not answer.

"Silence doesn't tell me anything and I don't really know what get busy mean. I don't know if you are saying you need to get busy and show me that you have feelings for me or if it means, you don't have feelings and need to get busy trying to have some." I waved my hand at him and turned my back to him. "Anyway, you probably don't have any feelings for me. But I'm sure its not a surprise to you that I."

He reached out and touched my shoulder and guided me to face him. "What's not a surprise to me, Veronica?" he asked with deep warmth in his eyes.

"It's probably no surprise to you that I love you."

"After a long silence of Ryan just looking at me with warm serious eyes and me looking back at him. He shook his head but did not answer. I wasn't sure why he was shaking his head. It seemed more like a warm gesture than a flat out no to my question. But since he wasn't talking, I continued to talk nervously."

"You know, Ryan, I cannot count the number of letters that I actually took the time to write to you." I held up both hands. "Nobody really takes the time to write anymore. Everybody is busy sending emails and text messages. Nevertheless, I have taken the time to write you letters every week while you have been stationed in Los Angeles for that commercial. But when I check the mailbox there's never a letter from you. I just figured with your popular future on the horizon, you probably see my letters as fan mail."

"Look, Veronica, lighten up," he said.

"Ryan, tenderly grabbed my shoulders and brought his mouth closer and closer to my neck as I stood there actually trembling from his touch. My whole, entire being wanted his touch as if I needed his touch to be complete. It was the most magically feeling I had ever experienced. I wanted to be in your brother's presence every moment of every day. I loved him so deep until it consumed me. It's clear as day how I felt that day. I desperately wanted him to kiss me again. But most of all I wanted him to say he loved me."

"Miss Veronica Parker. Standing here looking in your beautiful eyes. You just amaze me, you know that. You think you have all the answers, and for some particular reason that particular fact happens to amuse me as well. I want you to know, you are one extraordinary young lady," he whispered in my ear.

"Thanks, but I'm asking if you have real feelings for me? I know it's putting you on the spot, but I need to know how you feel about me, Ryan."

"I'm sure you probably already know how I feel about you."

"I don't know, but I want to know. So, is that something you can tell me? Do you love me, Ryan? Do you have any feelings for me?" I asked and then stopped myself and said, "I guess I shouldn't ask you that question since I already know the answer."

"So you already know the answer?" he asked curiously.

"Yes, I do. It's obvious that you are not in love with me. If you loved me, I'm sure you would have answered one of my letters or returned my phone call," I said humbly and continued as he listened. "Plus, you most likely would have asked me out. So that's my answer right there," I mumbled, pouting in his arms.

"Veronica, you are not giving me any breaks are you? How can you speak for me? I don't think you are a mindreader, are you?" he teased.

"No, I'm not a mindreader, but I don't have to be. All I have to be is a realist and it's clear you're not in love with me. Most people show interest by going after what they love."

"Therefore, you are basing your hypothesis on the fact that in your mind I haven't shown interest nor chased you?" he said in a whisper against my neck.

"Can you say I'm incorrect?"

"What I can say is that you are a strong willed girl who speaks her mind and I like that. But you are also big on assuming and I'm not a fan of that. We are living in a world that is not always black and white. Things are not always what they appear. You feel I do not have feelings for you, but it's all an assumption on your part, is it not?" he asked.

"Yes, I guess it is an assumption, but two and two always equals four," I said.

"That is correct, two and two will always equal four, but that is a factual. On the other hand, your assumptions on how I feel about you is just that, a theory which could or could not be true. I'm a realist and deal in facts and you hit me as somewhat of a realist yourself; and that's why you asked me my feelings, but after you asked, you decided to forgo my answer and just assume."

"I know; my assumption just seem to make sense when you look at the big picture."

"Okay, but I wish you wouldn't assume since you really don't know how I feel or what I'm feeling for you," he whispered in my ear. "Is this conversation really necessary right now? I would prefer if we really didn't talk," he said teasingly.

"Ryan, don't tease me right now. I'm serious about knowing your feelings for me."

"I gathered that much, but as I said before, you don't know what I'm thinking or how I'm feelings or what I'm feeling for you."

"Maybe you're right, that's why I asked you," I cried.

"What would you say if I told you I love your clear brown eyes and your beautiful laugh, and not to mention your mesmerizing smile."

With those words, he pulled me in tighter, as his breathing became rapid and I could feel a compelling connection from him.

"Can you just please answer my question? You either do or you don't? Yes or no?"

"I guess my brother wasn't as much as a gentleman as he seemed to be all over you like that and the two of you weren't even together," Catherine quickly remarked.

"Don't say something like that about Ryan. He was a complete gentleman," Veronica snapped irritated at Catherine's remark. "You know he was an angel of a guy, but he wasn't a saint in that department. He wasn't about to walk away if I was willing. Granted, he put the brakes on to make sure I was willing and I was. That afternoon love session sealed our fate. I knew then that I loved him more than anything," Veronica warmly stated.

Catherine interrupted and asked. "I get it; so, did Ryan tell you he loved you?"

"I'm getting to that. He actually went on about other things about me that he loved."

"I love your stunning figure that feels incredible wrapped in my arms. I love your perfect shaped nose and your perfect lips and not to mention your thick, black curls sweeping beneath your shoulders. I love touching your hair like this and holding a handful as I kiss your neck. I also love the feel of your hair against my face," he whispered in my ear as he continued to touch and caress my hair. He gently pulled my head back and placed his lips against the side of my neck, and by now there was no turning back. My body had become weak and I was ready to surrender my love to Ryan. Buildup after buildup of deep love and passion for him had robbed me of all strength as I managed to utter once more as he lowered me down to the grass. "Are you in love with me, Ryan?" I muttered, breathless.

He laid me back on the grass and placed one finger on my lips. "Shhh, no more talking. I just want to kiss you," he said and stared lovingly in my eyes. "But to answer your question and to be completely honest and on the level with you. The answer to your question is no. I'm not in love with you, Veronica. But I love the feelings you are stirring in me and I love being with you,"he whispered sexily. "Any other answer wouldn't be realistic since we don't really know each other that well and we have never dated."

"That's my brother for you, Ryan was nothing if not completely honest at all times," Catherine quickly remarked. "But I'm sure that's not what you wanted to hear."

Catherine held up one finger as she stood from the sofa. "I think this is a good stopping point. I need to make a quick business call."

Veronica suspicious radar went off. "You need to make a business call?"

Catherine nodded. "Yes, please excuse me, but I have a business call to make."

"I'm assumming it's not police business," Veronica said lightheartedly.

Catherine glanced at her and smiled. "No, it's not. I'll only take a minute."

"Okay, Catherine, hurry back so I can wrap this up before the boys get home."

"Of course, I'll hurry back. I want to hear what happened after my brother so boldly admitted to not being in love with you," Catherine swiftly headed out of the room.

Chapter Six

Five minutes later Catherine strolled into the living room and took her seat. "Okay, you can continue now. You left off where Ryan had told you he wasn't in love with you. And as I said before I left the room, I'm sure that's not what you wanted to hear."

"No, it wasn't but after he told me that, I opened my eyes as I laid back on the grass, but I quickly closed them and inhaled sharply. The fact that he wasn't in love with me didn't change an ounce of how I felt about him. I still wanted Ryan to be my first," Veronica paused and stared at Catherine for a moment. "Before I go any further with this story, you are about to find out something about me and your brother that you didn't know."

Catherine raised one eyebrow and smiled. "So, you didn't wait until marriage with my brother, who cares?" Catherine joked.

"I think my sons would care. They have this image of their father in their minds and I don't think they would picture their father as a young man who would have taken me to bed before we were married. But in all fairness, he put on the brakes and I didn't want him to stop."

"Get real, Veronica. You need to give your grown sons more credit than you do. Of course, they would not think less of their father if they learned that bit of information about him. It just makes him human that he had sex with you before he married you."

"That may be so, but my sons still don't need to know that their parents had sex out of wedlock."

"Okay, I don't think you have to worry about them ever finding that out," Catherine laughed. "I'm sorry but its funny to see you so concerned about your grown sons finding out something so insignificant. "But what's even funnier is the fact that you think they would find out."

"Why is that so funny? It's not impossible that they could find out," Veronica stated.

"No, it's not impossible, it's just outrageously impossible!" Catherine continued to laugh. "Think about it, Veronica. Who's going to tell them? Only three people know of the incident," she said and stared at Veronica in silence for a moment. "One of the three happen to be deceased, leaving you and me," Catherine pointed out. "You are not going to tell them, Ryan can't tell them, and I'm definitely not going to tell them."

"Well, see that you don't let it slip," Veronica warned her.

"Get real, can you see me striking up a conversation with those boys out of blue where I tell them, Oh did you hear the news about your mother and father having sex before they were married." Catherine shook her head. "If I were to walk up to those young men and say that, they would think I'm loony; and they would have a right to think that since it's none of my business what you and Ryan did before you were married, and even less my business to blab about."

"Okay, I get your point."

"I'm glad you do, and now maybe you can get back to the story."

"Okay, sure. My point is that, even though Ryan and I were not dating. I loved him deeply and felt I was ready to take that big step with him."

"I'm surprised you were not turned off when he said he wasn't in love with you."

"I was disappointed but I wasn't turned off because I could tell that he liked me; and with Ryan being a realist he just wanted to be completely on the level with me. He wasn't in love with me but as I said, I believed that he cared for me. Besides, it was no use to try to leave his side. I felt like a flower floating in the wind with no control of my own hands to push him away. Plus, I didn't want to push him away. And as he pulled me closer and held me tightly in his arms, I felt myself fading into a special existence unknown to me. It was an existence of absolute happiness."

"Veronica," he whispered breathless against my lips. "Now that I have answered your question, and you know I'm not in love with you, do you still feel comfortable taking this step with me? Just say the word and we won't go any further," he promised.

"I slightly pushed him in the chest and he rolled off of me, stood to his feet and reached for my hand and assisted me up off the ground. I smiled at him and then glanced toward our guesshouse down by the pond. "Yes, I'm still comfortable and I'm ready to be with you in that way, but not here in the grass for all of nature, the birds and any small animal walking by to see," I said laughingly. "Let's go to my family guesthouse right over there past the pond." I pointed toward the pale green cottage with white shutters.

"I remember that little guesthouse," Catherine smiled. "We used to sleep there lots when I would stay over night many times. But remember how we thought the cozy little house was kind of creepy because it was a good distant from the mainhouse and so close to that pond."

"I do remember that I thought it was creepy, but that was only when we stayed there overnight. Otherwise, I loved it; and what I loved about it most was all the flowers my parents would have planted in all those flowerbeds surrounding the little house."

"I remember the flowers, but could you please try to stay focused and stick to the story," Catherine suggested.

"Okay, but you are the one who interrupted and said you remember how creepy the place was. Anyway, back to the story. Ryan grabbed both of my hands and smiled down at me. "Veronica, I'm not in love with you, but I do care about you and I have a lot of respect for you and I don't want to rush you into anything that you are not ready for. Are you sure about this?" he asked with concern in his eyes.

"Of course, I'm sure. You don't have to wonder if I'm sure about what I'm about to do. Because I'm hundred percent sure. Besides, we are not kids. We are both eighteen and seniors when school starts back next month."

"I know, and as much as I'm honored to be with you in this way, Veronica, I feel as if I have pressured you in some way."

"Ryan, you have not pressured me. You have been completely honest with me and I wouldn't expect anything less from you. You are such an honorable person."

"Thank you, but somehow I do not feel too honorable right now."

"Why not?" I asked.

"He didn't immediately answer me as we held hands and headed down the narrow path past the sparkling water pond to the guesthouse. When we reached the guesthouse I lifted the flower pot to the left of the door and removed the spare key and opened the door. Ryan and I went inside and took a seat on the short red sofa. For a moment we just looked at each other in silence. Now that we were behind closed doors some of my courage left me. Although we were the same age I felt somewhat awkward as if I was incompetence in that department since I hadn't crossed that bridge before with a boy. Ryan would be my first, but I wasn't sure if he knew that. Although I had mentioned it to him while I was lying on the grass, I wasn't sure if he had paid me much attention when I told him. Therefore, I knew I needed to mention it again and I was sort of nervous. However, it was easier to conjure up the courage to tell him that I was still a virgin since I knew how honest he was. I felt he had been on the level with me and I also wanted to be totally on the level with him. I needed to find away to let him know that being with him was going to be my first time."

"Are you going to tell me why you don't feel honorable?" I asked him.

"It's because I don't feel I deserve the right to be with you in that way, at this time."

"I don't understand what you mean by that Ryan."

"I feel I haven't earned the right to be given something of yours that is so special in my eyes. It's not just the fact that I'm not in love at this time. We haven't gone on one date and I don't want you to feel used."

"Ryan, I will not feel used, but there is something I would like to tell you first."

"Okay, what would you like to tell me?"

I looked at him awhile and we stared at each other in silence for a moment before I uttered in a low voice. "I thought you should know," I said and stopped talking.

He looked at me with smiling eyes as he caressed the side of my face with his right hand. "What is it that you want me to know?"

I looked in his handsome face and wanted to melt from the anticipation of what awaited us. "This will be my first time and I just wanted you to know." I said as I kept my eyes on his. "Ryan, you are so caring, forthright and honest. You make me want to be just as wonderful as you are."

Ryan touched my face again and looked warmly into my eyes with what appeared to be love in his eyes for me. "Veronica, I don't make you want to be wonderful. You are already wonderful beyond imagination."

"You think that way about me?"

"I think that way about you and more; and couldn't imagine that you would want to go all the way with me, while knowing I'm not in love with you. Therefore, I'm not going to take advantage of this situation. I have too much respect for you to make love to you, knowing your heart and soul is not in it. So it's up to you. I would love to spend the rest of this day lying on that big bed in there." He pointed toward the bed in the connecting room. "Being here in your guesthouse with you, enjoying your warmth, but it's your decision whether I stay or go. What do you want me to do, Veronica? Should I leave or do you want me to stay?"

"I found the strength to touch his handsome face and his long, soft hair. I had to reach out and touch him to bring myself back to reality. It just seemed too good to be true. I felt so blessed to be in the arms of Ryan Franklin. He was everything to me; and by far the most popular, famous and goodlooking boy in school. I was so filled with happiness that afternoon until all that mattered was the fact that I was in his arms. The reality that he wasn't in love with me didn't change the fact that I desperately wanted to be with the boy I loved just one time if nothing more. I managed to mumble, "My answer is yes, Ryan. I want you to stay. I love you in spite of you not being able to say the same to me."

"Sorry to interrupt again, but I'm surprised Ryan didn't confess his love to you. Because at that time, although, he hadn't asked you out, he was crazy about you."

"I might would believe you, if he had approached me or asked me out back then before that afternoon."

"You don't have to believe me. I lived with the guy. He was my brother and I knew him a little better than you at the time."

"Okay, but its water under the bridge now. But thanks for telling me. Nevertheless, after I told Ryan that he could stay, all his energy took over full force. He grabbed me up in his arms and carried me into the connecting bedroom. He placed me on the edge of the bed but I stood up and wrapped my arms around him and held on to him as if I was hanging on for my life. His mouth and his hands were all over my neck and face, unlike anything I could ever have imagined. Then we fell over on the bed while in each other's arms. His smooth hands trailed over my skin as he kissed me. He wrapped me in his arms and rolled me over on top of him, looking up at me with those clear brown eyes. I could barely keep my balance from the bigger than life feeling his touch gave me. He held my face and pulled my face down to his. He kissed me gently, long and deep, rolling me back over on my back as he gripped me tightly with his entire force, taking my virginity forever."

Catherine smiled. "Wow, Veronica. Who knew that Veronica Parker, the popular cheerleader and homecoming queen of our senior class wasn't a virgin like the rest of us."

"Shut up and listen, Catherine."

"I'm listening, so go ahead. I can't wait to hear what the two of you said afterward."

"When it was all said and done, we both rolled off the bed and got dressed and went back into the small sitting room and sat arm-in-arm on the short sofa. The sunlight poured through the windows and warmed us. Somehow it seemed especially glittering through the windows, probably because I felt so happy inside. I had never felt so refreshed, so alive, so happy, and it was not a dream. I was sitting there side by side with the man of my dreams. My one true love. I knew I would love Ryan forever, even if he never confessed his love to me. But needless to say, I didn't want our time together to end, as I looked over at him I noticed some trash in his gorgeous head. I hadn't noticed it before but now that I was more collected and relaxed, I could see that his beautiful hair was filled with bits of grass and leaves from earlier when you were lying in the grass. I picked the grass out of his hair as I kissed the side of his face. For a moment as we sat there on the sofa together, I was living in a fantasy world in my mind. I was thinking of your gorgeous brother that had just made love to me as my boyfriend. That was what I wanted more than anything in the entire world, but that was not a reality. Therefore, I had to start thinking more like a realist than an idealistic love sick girl and face the situation for what it was. Therefore, I whispered in Ryan's ear, "Ryan, would you like to have dinner with us tonight?"

"I noticed a slight smile to his mouth as he straighten his back on the cushions of the sofa and glanced at his solid gold diamond watch. "What time is it anyway?" He asked. "Oh, my goodness, Veronica, it's almost 3:30, I ready need to leave. I have stayed too long already," he said with his eyes on mine. "Are you going to walk with me back up to the mainhouse?" he said as he stood to his feet.

I didn't comment since I was caught off guard that he needed to leave so abruptly.

He smiled at me romantically. "I guess you plan to stay here for a while longer and enjoy the rest of the sun pouring through these windows?"

"Then suddenly, a cold chill rushed through me as he seemed a bit anxious to leave my company, now that he had gotten what he wanted. Deep down I knew that wasn't what he was all about, but I still felt that way when he had to leave so abruptly."

"I asked you a question, Ryan," I said as I stood from the sofa.

"Yeah, I heard you, but I can't make it to dinner tonight. I'm sorry, Veronica, but I promised my folks I would have dinner with them at home tonight. You understand how they want to have dinner with me since I have been away from home for an entire month. I'm sorry, but I promised, so you know how that goes," he apologetically explained as he reached out and touched my face. "I'll try to see you before I leave."

"That's right, you have to head back to Los Angeles."

He nodded. "That's right for another three weeks. I'll be back the weekend before school starts. So, listen, today was too special for words. So if I don't see you anymore before I head back to California, I hope you enjoy the rest of your summer," he said, smiling as he gave me a quick kiss on the lips and then hurried toward the door to leave the little guesthouse.

"I quickly stepped over to the window and watched him as he walked swiftly up the hill toward my house. I felt so lonely when he left and tears just started falling from my eyes. I felt like such a fool, but I could only blame myself. I had given my virginity away to a boy who wasn't in love with me. I had always promised to give myself to someone who loved me as much as I loved him. I cried harder with each minute. I loved him so much until it was almost unbearable to think of never being that intimately close with him again."

"So, did you see Ryan again before he left for Los Angeles?"

"No, I didn't see him again until the Sunday night before school would start."

"So, did he come over to see you?"

"What happened is, Jack Coleman dropped over which I wasn't too pleased to see since he had treated you and I so awful before school let out. However, he told me that he was sorry about the way he treated us. Then he went on to ask me to do him a favor. He wanted to borrow my curling irons. And seriously, you knew I couldn't stand Jack after how he treated us, but Ryan saw him in a different light and thought he walked on water. Therefore, I learned to tolerate him. Besides, if I'm completely honest, I didn't really mind Jack coming to my house," Veronica admitted.

"What are you saying, Veronica? I know you couldn't stomach that creep after how he treated us in his house."

"You're right, I couldn't stomach Jack. Nevertheless, since he was Ryan's best friend, in some weird way I was excited when he showed up at my house. His presence made me feel that I had a better chance of seeing Ryan when he was around."

"Back then, you were probably right," Catherine agreed. "But you know what, it's crazy how I wasn't aware that you already knew Jack when I introduced him to you after I developed that huge crush on that bastard."

"Well, I knew you had a secret crush on some boy at school. I just had no idea it was Jack Coleman until you introduced him to me at his house party. At that time, I knew he was Ryan's friend but I just didn't know his name until you told me that day."

"Jack and I were in the family room chatting for a bit after I gave him the curling irons. He was seated on the sofa and I was standing."

"So, Jack, I guess Ryan left for California."

"Yeah, he did after visiting for the fourth festivities, but that was three weeks ago. He's back now," he told me. "You didn't know?"

I shook my head and lowered my eyes toward the floor. "I didn't know he was back home. He didn't call and Catherine didn't tell me."

"Maybe they didn't let you know, but he's back home," he assured me.

"Thanks for telling me. But can I ask you something personal?"

"Sure, what is it?"

"Did Ryan say anything to you about me the last time you saw him? I don't care how insignificant. Did he mention me at all?"

"Veronica, what do you mean?"

"I'm just asking you did he say anything about me."

Jack seemed surprised and uncomfortable about my question. He was loyal to Ryan and didn't want to say anything behind his back. "Veronica, I don't know what you are trying to find out." He held up both hands.

"Nevermind, it's not that big of a deal. I just asked did he mention me or say anything about me."

"Did he say anything like what?" Jack asked curiously. "Are you looking to hear anything in particular that he said? Was he supposed to say anything?"

"No, I just wondered. So I guess you are saying that he didn't mention me?"

"Jack looked at me with a curious look on his face and slightly smiled, "He didn't say anything to me about you. On the other hand, I said something to him about you. I told him how you felt about him." Jack grinned. "It's clearly obvious that you have fallen hard for Mr. Franklin. Everybody at school knows about your crush. Ryan probably knows it also."

"What did he say when you told him how you thought I felt about him?" I asked eagerly.

"Well, he really didn't say anything. He just smiled, but to answer your question, he didn't mention you the last time we were together before he left town," Jack said.

"My heart skipped a beat and my face warmed as I thought I would die from misery. He hadn't even mentioned me to his best friend. And even though Ryan gave me no sign that he cared, other than that one unforgettable moment in our guesthouse, I wrote to him every week. The letters were usually just a few lines, just to say hello. I was so in love until I had no other choice but to write him. I put on paper all the things I wanted to say to him. I also sent him cards and pictures, but he never wrote me one letter or sent me one card the whole time he was staying out in Los Angeles for the summer. Even though we had made love, it didn't seem to matter to him."

Catherine waved her hand. "That's when you should have forgotten my brother and just started dating someone else."

Veronica stared at Catherine as if she had said something forbidden. "You got to be kidding me with what you just said. Ryan was perfect but I just didn't know it at that time. Besides, I didn't have the mind to go out with any other boy. I only wanted to be with Ryan. After having his perfection, no other boy I knew came close to capturing my attention."

"Okay, I get it. We all know my brother was perfect."

"You sound a little jealous, but yes, Ryan was perfect in my eyes."

Catherine inhaled sharply. "Now that we have crowned my brother a saint, do
you think it would be too much to continue with the story?"

"Okay, I'll continue on with the story. I was at the part where Jack looked at me and nodded. "Veronica, you might want to know the reason I walked the three blocks to your house to borrow your curling irons. Other than you being the only classmate within walking distant other than Ryan's house, but I didn't want to stop there and borrow the irons from Catherine. I think she still has a crush on me and I don't want to encourage her."

"You never told me that Jack said that about me," Catherine quickly remarked.

"I never told you because when he said that about you, I thought he was being full of himself to think you still had a crush on him after the way he had treated us. However, I didn't let on to him that I thought he was out of his mind to think that about you. But anyway, back to what Jack said. He told me that Ryan was back in town and he knew because he had just heard my father mention it to my mother when they had opened the door for him and he was waiting for me to come to the door."

"Needless to say, I almost jumped out of my skin when he said he heard my parents discussing Ryan. I hurried out of the family room toward the kitchen to find my parents, and Jack followed behind me. But when I spotted my parents in the kitchen, Jack waved goodbye and said he would show himself out. I walked up and interrrupted my parents' conversation, pulling at my father's arm, causing him to almost spill his glass of red wine.

"Is Ryan in town?" I asked excitedly.

"Wait a minute, Veronica. Sweetheart, don't knock my glass out of my hand," my father said as he sit his glass of wine on the kitchen counter. He leaned up against the counter and gave me a curious look, and then looked at my mother.

"Your daughter is out of her head in love for the first time, you know," my mother shared my feelings for Ryan with my father after I opened up to her and told her how much I cared for Ryan."

"Jordan, she is reaching out to the young man with weekly letters, but the young uprising star has never written back to her."

"Naomi," my father exchanged looks with my mother and then looked at me. "Veronica, Sweetheart, I wasn't going to mention this, but I think I should because that young Ryan is such a levelheaded honest young man. He called me a couple weeks ago and asked me to ask you to stop writing to him, Sweetheart."

"Father, why would Ryan get in touch with you and ask you to ask me not to write him? I don't understand why he would do something like that."

"I think he's trying to be honorable and let you down easy. He doesn't want to lead you on if he doesn't feel for you what you feel for him."

"But to call you instead of me?"

My mother eyes were sad. "Sweetheart, he felt it would be easier to talk to Jordan and ask him to talk to you. I'm sure he was trying to spare himself and you an uncomfortable situation," my mother explained.

"I stood there shaking. I couldn't say a word. My father's words blew me out of the water and I was greatly surprised. Those words were so painful until they made me wish I had never been born. Seconds later, tears were falling from my eyes. I grabbed my stomach and cried."

"Oh, Father, you and Mother just don't know how much I love Ryan Franklin. This love I feel for him will never fade. I will love Ryan for the rest of my life." I stood there crying and my father stepped near me and patted my back.

"Here, here, it's not the end of the world. You'll be just fine in time once you get over the young man," my father tried to comfort me.

"There is no getting over Ryan. We were born to be together," I cried.

"Sweetheart, you are not facing facts. If the young man doesn't feel the same, you can't will him to feel a certain way," my mother solemnly stated.

"I just know how I feel and I know what I saw in his eyes the last time I saw him."

"When was that?" my mother asked. "When you saw him at the barbecue?"

Suddenly it dawned on me that I couldn't say too much since I didn't want my folks to know that I had slept with Ryan. "Yes, when he came here for the barbebue."

"That's strange," my mother said.

"What's strange?" my father asked.

"I was keeping my eyes on you, Sweetheart because I knew how much you wanted to visit with Ryan, and I didn't see the two of you talking to each other at all. But I guess the two of you found time to talk, if you were able to see something special in his eyes," my mother said hopefully. She knew how much my heart was breaking. But my father didn't know that much about Ryan. He just knew you were my best friend and that Ryan was your brother. Plus, he knew Ryan was a classmate that had struck it famous."

"Besides, Naomi, do we know anything about this young man that our daughter just said she plans to love forever, other than he seems to be a good kid who just hit paydirt with his high school acting?" my father asked.

"He's a good kid, Jordan. You know he's Catherine's brother, but you might not know, Ryan and Catherine are Samuel and Ellen's kids," my mother told my father.

"I never will forget the look on my father's face as he swallowed hard and tried to keep his composure. But hearing that bit of information changed his attitude since he knew your parents were the riches family in town. It seemed my father was more inclined for me to be patient and give it time than just to throw in the towel.

"So Ryan and Catherine are Ellen and Samuel Franklin kids?" my father grinned. "That is really something. The young lady is Veronica's best friend, and the young man is who she plans to love forever." He looked at my mother and smiled. "I don't think we could ask for anything more," my father said jokingly and then patted my back again.

"So this young Ryan, who now I know is as rich as they come, gave you the wrong impression and made you think he was ready to date you, but he reneged. Is that it?" my father asked.

I stood there against the kitchen counter still drying my tears with my fingers. I was crushed and felt my life had ended. My mother answered for me.

"Jordan, it wasn't like that. Don't change your good viewpoint of Ryan Franklin. Because as much as Veronica is hurting right now. We can't blame Ryan for the way Veronica feels. She's standing there and can tell you herself that the boy never led her on. He has never even asked her out," my mother pointed out.

My father looked at me with confused eyes. "Veronica, you are standing here crying when you haven't even been out with the boy? I was under the impression that you two had dated for a while and it didn't work out, so he wanted to let you down easy."

"No, Father, Ryan and I haven't gone on a date."

"So, Sweetheart, why are you crying like that if your relationship with the young man never got off the ground?" He lifted his glass of wine from the kitchen counter and took a sip and then placed the glass back on the counter. "However, I'm not going to tell you to try to move on from that young man or encourage you toward meeting and falling in love with another boy. You said you're going to love the young man forever, therefore, I believe you. All you can do now is just to be patient. The two of you are still young. You attend the same school so who knows what can happen down the line. However, we also need to keep in mind how much is on Ryan's plate right now; and just because a girlfriend may not be on his radar at the moment, I say, just be patient and give him time," my father encouraged me.

My mother didn't seem too pleased with my father encouragement. She didn't want me to keep my hopes up for something that may not happen. "Listen, Veronica. I think you should just dry your eyes and face what's actually happening here. Ryan is a wonderful young man, but if he's not ready for a relationship as much as it's breaking your heart, you need to respect his wishes," my mother exchanged looks with my father and he didn't seem pleased with her pessimisted viewpoint.

"Noami, I'm sure the kids will figure it out. She saw something in his eyes, so maybe the boy does like her and just have cold feet," my father said. "I think the best me can do for the two of them is just to stay out of it."

"Jordan, maybe you are right," my mother patted me on the back. "Sweetheart, I just got this to say. We know how nice Ryan is, but if the two of you are looking for different things. You have to respect his wishes and maybe the two of you can be friends. Maybe he's not looking for a girlfriend right now, but will welcome your friendship," my mother said. "However, just as your father mentioned. If you have your heart set on him, which we know you do, just give it some time."

"I nodded and politely walked out of the kitchen, but when I stepped into the hallway, I ran down the hall to my room. Knowing that Ryan had asked my father to ask me to stop writing him, stabbed at me and had forced me to face reality."

"That was sort of out of character for Ryan to ask someone else to relay a message for him. He was always forthcoming no matter what. I'm puzzled to why he would call your father and ask him to ask you to stop writing him. I think that meant something big," Catherine curiously uttered.

"Yes, it meant something alright," Veronica quickly stated. "It meant he wanted we to stop writing him."

"I think it meant he knew he had fallen in love with you and it scared him," Catherine grinned. "But go on with the story."

"I was still in my room lying across my bed feeling crushed when I heard Ryan come to the front door around 8:00 o'clock and knocked. He asked for my father and the two of them talked awhile and then Ryan left. I heard your brother's soft, sexy voice as he talked briefly in the living room with my father. I'm not sure what they talked about but I could hear them vaguely and Ryan didn't ask if I was home. I just figured that maybe he was at my house checking up on the message that he had given to my father. And after Ryan left, I thought my father would come down the hallway and knock on my door to tell me why he had visited, but my father didn't come knock on my door and I was too devastated to go to my father. I was afraid to hear more unpleasant news. So I just laid there in my bed feeling like my world had ended. Then to my shocking surprise, Ryan's car pulled up in the driveway again around 9:00 that evening. He had only been gone for one hour. Therefore, I hopped off the bed and sat there at the foot of the bed. All sorts of thoughts came to my mind. I wondered if he had collected all my letters and were delivering them back to me. I sat there quietly in my room imagining the worse possible scenario. But I was hoping to hear his voice as I wondered why he had returned to talk to my father again. My father answered the door and I heard them both chatting in the living room. Then I heard them laughing in low voices; and figured that was a good sign. Then as I listened closely, I heard my father's voice when he said, "That way, Ryan."

"My heart was in my throat when it dawned on me that he was headed down the hallway toward my room. My heart sunk deep inside of me with anticipated sadness as I heard his shoe heels walking quickly on the hardwood floor, arriving closer and closer to my bedroom door. Then suddenly I heard a knock on my door and I thought I would jump out of my skin. My heart started beating so fast. It was hard enough that my father had shared his message to stop writing him. Now, I had convinced myself that he had shown up to tell me personally, since he was so forthright. Therefore, I held my breath for a moment as I gripped the doorknob. Then I swung the door open and lost my composure when I looked in his eyes. I grabbed my face with both hands and ran across the room and propped my back against my dresser. I didn't want to hear what he had to say to me. Nevertheless, he closed my bedroom door and stepped inside, slowing making his way across the room near me. He touched my arm as I stood there holding my face looking down toward the floor as tears dripped from my eyes. "Veronica, are you okay, darling?" He asked with great concern in his voice.

"I wasn't okay when your brother asked me that question, and from the mere thought of him calling me darling, didn't help matters. My entire essence warmed and I could barely breathe. But my strong willed thoughts told me to collect myself and dry my eyes. Therefore, after a few minutes, I dried my eyes and pulled myself together and smiled at him. "Please, excuse my manners, Ryan. I don't know what came over me."

"You seemed quite emotional, Veronica." He touched my arm again. "Are you sure you're okay? Maybe you're not pleased with me but just don't want to tell me."

I pretended I didn't know what he meant. "Why wouldn't I be pleased with you?"

"For one, that message I gave your father to give you," he spoke solemnly.

"I got your message, but I'm fine," I assured him, smiling.

He stood there with serious eyes, dressed in a gorgeous blue Givenchy outfit. I was trying to keep my composure but the magnetism scent of his expensive cologne enticed me overwhelmingly. Knowing he was there to bid me farewell, I couldn't think of anything else to say. I was praying that his visit wasn't to bring more gloom to my heart, but in light of things, I couldn't imagine no other reason that he would be in my room other than to say he was feed up with the attention I had been showering on him with my cards and letters, all of which he hadn't answered. I was quite certain that those words would come from his mouth. Then he took my hand and led me over to the settee in my room. I took a seat first and after a moment of just standing there looking at me, he then sat down next to me on the settee, looking me straight in the eyes without saying a word. After awhile, he lifted my right hand and held it between his hands. And holding my hand in that manner woke up every nerve and muscle within my body."

"Is it okay if I kiss you, Veronica? I would like nothing more than to feel your lips against mine. I have dreamed about kissing you," he whispered.

"I was stunned and confused by his words and before I could answer him, my tears were falling again. I was too fragile and too much in love for him to tease me like that, but before I could say a word, he had covered my mouth, holding the back of my head with one hand, caressing my hair with the other. I had no willpower and surrendered in his arms, as he tenderly pressed his lips against mine and passionately gave me a long lingering kiss; and just as I threw my arms around his back, he pulled away. I looked at him in silence. I knew he was trying to find the proper words to tell me goodbye since he wasn't ready for a relationship. But yet, he was silent as he held my hand, caressing my fingers as he leaned in and gave me another urgent kiss, which he pulled away from quickly."

Then he looked at me with serious eyes. "Veronica, I want you to know something."

When he said that my heart skipped a beat, but I kept my composure ready to heard what he had to say to me. "I'm listening, go ahead.

"You are the most beautiful female alive," he whispered with a smile, and then reached out and held my face as he continued to gaze lovingly in my eyes. "Veronica, I have something I would like to say to you."

"Yes, I know," I mumbled.

"Okay, here we go again," he teased. "You and your assumptions. I thought you were going to keep the assumptions to yourself since they seem to get you in trouble everytime," he said in a joking manner. "Besides, if you already know what I'm about to say, why don't you just tell me what it is and save me the trouble of telling you?" He laughed. "How does that sound?" he said teasingly.

"You are teasing about it, but I'm serious and can just tell you what you came to say to me. You're building up your nerves to tell me to stop writing you those personal letters. I heard from my father that you no longer want me to send you letters," I said with a cracked voice and held up both hands. "I promise I'll stop mailing you letters. Besides, you are back home and there's no need to write to you."

He grinned at me. "That's why you should leave your assumptions in your head. Because you know what? You are totally off base with this one."

"When your brother told me that I was totally off base with my assumption, that gave me some hope that maybe he wasn't at my house to bid me farewell. However, I had subdued joy as I stared in his eyes waiting to hear his next words."

He smiled at me and then kissed the side of my face. "Now are you ready to listen to what I came here to tell you?" He placed one finger on my lips. "Veronica, you can stop assuming and wondering about how I feel about you. I came here tonight to tell you how I feel," he said in a soft humble voice.

"I came here earlier when I was running an arrand for my parents. I dropped by and asked your father if it was okay to visit you around nine. I know tomorrow is the first day of school and I needed to make sure it was okay with your folks for me to show up here at nine o'clock on a school night," he stared at me for a moment before he said. "Luckily for me, your father was great. He told me that it would be just fine to show up here at nine o'clock and assured me that he would look out for my car pulling in so he could come downstairs and let me in since you couldn't always hear knocks on the front door from your room. I'm not sure what it is, but your father seem to have taking a liking to me."

"My folks are proud of you just like the entire community," I told him.

"Maybe that's it. But he didn't seem as warm to me at the barbecue. He was nice and kind then, but now he just seems to like me a little more. I'm just pleased he does. But anyway, back to my important news and why I'm here."

"Why are you here, Ryan?" I asked.

"To tell you one thing," he said in a whisper. "I love you, Veronica. I have been going crazy trying to hide and dismiss how I feel about you. That's what was going on with me. I was in denial, denying my feelings for you," he humbly stated. "But there's no denying anymore because when we were lying in the grass that day, and then ended up being one with each other in your guesthouse, you gave me your love, proving that you loved me more than anything," he said with love pouring from every word. "Frankly, Sweetheart, I have never been the same since the day I left you at that guesthouse. You are it for me, Miss Veronica Parker. There is just something about you that is unique from any girl I have ever known. The bottom line is that I like who and what you are. You are simply beautiful through and through. A forthright, courageous, never give up, strong young lady, and before I fell for you, I didn't think I was ready for a girlfriend. Then I fell for you and my life changed in a wonderful way. Therefore, will you do me the honor of being my girlfriend? I know last year, during our junior year, you had a crush on me and of course, I also had a crush on you. But our crushes never got off the ground. We are both older and I want to start our senior classes knowing that you are officially my girlfriend." He smiled and winked. "Once you say yes, I'll know it's okay to kiss you again," he whispered.

"I nodded yes as one tear rolled down my face as he held me in his arms and covered my lips with his in a passionate loving kiss."

"Veronica, what a story and what a memory," Catherine said, smiling. "You and my brother were an inspiration to me. The two of you had what I always wanted, someone there who loved you no matter what, unconditionally. I have lived my whole life without that. Now, I have a man in my life who seems genuinely interested in me and I'm too uneasy to give myself to him because I don't feel worthy of him or anyone else."

"Catherine, please, let's not head down your road of misery again. Do as you said and get a grip on your life. Make your life what you want it to be and don't settle for the hand you were dealt if it's not to your liking. Besides, I just told you a beautiful love story about your brother and me, and I don't want to lose the feeling of those wonderful memories so fast by indulging in your demoralizing business," Veronica softly but firmly uttered and held up both hands. "I'm happy right now and I would like to keep it that way for more than two seconds, do I make myself clear?"

Chapter Seven

Dillion Bradley, the Franklins 63-year-old grounds man had incorrectly informed Natalie that Sydney was out in the kitchen having a snack with Starlet. However, that had been an hour and a half earlier when Dillion had spotted the two in the kitchen area. At that time he was in the kitchen explaining a project to Veronica. He had noticed Sydney and Starlet seated at the kitchen table eating red grapes and sampling six bottles of vintage wine. Between the samples from all six bottles either one had drank one full glass of wine. Therefore, when Natalie entered the large kitchen she found no sign of Sydney or Starlet. She buzzed Dillion again on his phone and he informed her that he saw Sydney in the kitchen area over an hour ago and that he saw Sydney drive Starlet home within the past thirty minutes.

After Dillion gave her that information she instantly knew that Sydney would most likely be in the den. Therefore she hurried through the big house to the den and spotted Sydney a room length away through the glass French doors. She strolled over to the double doors and softly opened them as she quietly stepped into the room. She noticed that Sydney was seated on one of the mauve sofas with his lap top in his lap. He seemed preoccupied into what he was doing on the computer and hadn't noticed that Natalie was standing near the doors hoping he would glance up across the room and see her. She didn't want to disturb him but since he wasn't looking up, she softly strolled across the room. However, he looked up and noticed her after she had stepped halfway across the room. He kept his eyes on her, curiously waiting to see what she needed him for.

"Mr. Sydney, I'm sorry to interrupt your work," she apologized.

He smiled at Natalie. "That's okay. You didn't interrupt me from anything. Did you need me for something?" he asked politely.

"Yes, there's someone here to see you."

"There's someone here to see me?" he repeated what she said as she looked at Natalie with surprise in his eyes.

"Yes, Mr. Sydney, I would have turned him away at this late hour, but it's a policeman; and he asked to see you," Natalie said anxiously.

"A policeman is at the front door to see me?"

Natalie nodded. "Yes, he said his name is Officer Pete Fields," Natalie said as she stood in front of the sofa where he was seated.

Sydney glanced at his watch and noticed it was almost ten o'clock in the evening. He wondered why an officer would be calling on him so late in the evening. Then it dawned on him that Officer Fields was one of the officers that worked on his kidnapping case. However, before he could speak, Natalie asked. "Should I send him away and tell Officer Fields that you're not taking any visitors at this time of the evening?" Natalie asked politely.

Sydney discreetly shook his head. He felt it was an indecent time to pay him a visit by an officer, but he closed the lid of his lap top and placed it on the sofa beside him. "I'll see Officer Fields. Please show him to the den. Thanks, Natalie."

Natalie nodded and headed out of the den, down the hallway toward the living room where she had left the officer standing near the front door. Veronica and Catherine as well as Rome and Amber were out at a fundraiser event while Britain and Paris were out on dates with Sabrina and Samantha.

Sydney and Starlet had just spent a quiet evening together before he dropped her off at home for the evening. Now before heading upstairs to his room for the evening. When Natalie stepped into the den he was busy on his lap top conducing some Franklin Gas business.

Natalie showed the officer to the den and then softly closed the double French doors as she left the room. Then she stuck her head back in the room and said politely. "Can I get you any refreshments, Mr. Sydney?"

Sydney immediately stood up from the sofa and stepped over near the officer and shook his hand. "Would you care for a bottle of water or anything at all?" Sydney asked the officer.

He shook his head and then Sydney shook his head toward Natalie; and then Natalie closed the doors softly and quietly left the area.

"Thanks for seeing me at this late hour," Officer Fields said. "I know it's not really late but it's too late for a house call."

Sudden it dawned on Sydney that it must be a serious matter that was regarding Jack Coleman. His heart raced anxiously as he stood there waiting to hear what the officer visit entailed.

"Have a seat if you like," Sydney pointed toward the two sofas. The officer shook his head. "Thank you, but I'm pressed for time and need to get to another appointment. I just dropped by to deliver this." Officer Fields handed him a business size envelope. "We finally completed our investigation on the kidnapping and disappearance of Jack Coleman. The case is still open," Officer Fields nodded.

Sydney looked at the envelope. "Is this a copy of your report?" Sydney asked with a curious impression on his face.

Officer Fields nodded. "I thought you would be interested in our findings."

"Yes, of course, I'm very interested. However, I didn't expect that the department would share a copy of the report with me."

"This is highly irregular to furnish a victim with a report of our findings. But you made an impression on me and Officer Hal Ford. Therefore, we both decided that we would keep you abreast. You're the first victim that we have ran into after 30 years on the job to be just as concerned about your abductor as yourself."

Sydney looked at the officer with sincere eyes. "What he did was unthinkable, but he was a very troubled man. And a best friend to my father for all of my father adult life," Sydney said warmly.

Officer Fields glanced at his watch and nodded. "I think I'll have a seat after all. I still have a little time before the meeting that I need to attend," he said.

"Please be seated," Sydney said and watched as Officer Fields took a seat on one of the sofas; and then Sydney took a seat across from him.

Officer Fields looked at Sydney with serious eyes. "To be frank, I wanted to stay until after you read that report you're holding."

The officer's words alarmed Sydney and he wondered what he would read in the report as he sat staring at the envelope in his hand. Then he slowly begin to open the envelope. He pulled out the two page report and begin to read out loud:

Police Report on Jack Coleman
Filed: March 26, 2014 (Wednesday)

Based on the evidence obtained from Jack Coleman's business office, he could have easily escaped the crime scene on Sunday, December 29, 2013. According to the blue prints of the little cottage where the victim were being held hostage, the little house had an escape shoot in the roof. It is believed that Jack Coleman masterminded his escape by hoodwinking the authorities into believing he perished in the fire. He had made preparations to live on the run in a foreign country. His original plan fell through to take Sydney Franklin along, but he executed his plan to travel alone. He is believed to be living somewhere in another country under an assumed name. His production company, Coleman Productions is now owned and operated by another production company that merged Coleman Productions with Unlimited Productions. The new owner informed the authorities that the sell went through a few days before Jack Coleman's disappearance.

Jack Coleman rental and live-in properties were also sold within a few days before he kidnapped Sydney Franklin. He also drained all his bank accounts and there has been no phone or paper trail left by Jack Coleman. None of his relatives or associates have spoken to or seen Jack Coleman since his disappearance. Jack Coleman is considered armed and dangerous with the means to attempt abduction of the victim, Sydney Franklin or other members of the Franklin family. However, the department believes that Jack

Coleman will not attempt to abduct the victim or any member of his family due to the unusual circumstances surrounding the kidnapping. However, there's good reason to believe Jack Coleman is not mentally stable. Therefore, there's a possibility that he could attempt to contact the victim, Sydney Franklin. However, it's highly possible that he will not since he put himself at great danger of being apprehended by the authorities when freely of his own free will released the said victim from his captivity into the safe hands of police custody.

After Sydney read the report he nodded. He thought to himself awhile, reflecting on what his Aunt Catherine had told him and his family during breakfast the morning after his kidnapping. She had shared with them about the shaft in the roof of the little cottage and suggested that it was a possibility that Jack Coleman could have saved himself from the fire through that hole in the roof of the little house. He also recalled how he and none of the family gave much attention to the possibility that Jack Coleman had used that escape route when his Aunt Catherine shared the secret escape chute. Now, months later, Officer Fields delivers the same information that proves Jack Coleman masterminded and faked his death to escape the law.

"I shouldn't be relieved but I am. That image of Mr. Coleman perishing in that fire never left my mind. But now it can. It's clear that he's alive out there somewhere in the world," Sydney said humbly.

"So, how do you feel about the possibility of Mr. Coleman trying to contact you or anyone in your family?" Officer Fields curiously asked.

"I feel that he'll never contact any of us. I feel he has gone off to make a new life for himself," Sydney said with empathy.

"For a victim, you almost sound as if you're pleased that Mr. Coleman has escaped the authorities, but I'm sure a fine upstanding young man like you wouldn't want a criminal on the loose," Officer Fields said.

"Officer Fields, you can hear it in my voice that I'm relieved that Mr. Coleman is alive. I didn't want him to lose his life and especially I didn't want him to lose his life in that way. However, in a perfect world, I would have hoped that he could have faced his punishment. What he did to me and my family was unspeakable and it's an unpleasant experience that I will carry with me always. Nevertheless, I don't think he'll ever pay for his crime. He took the law into his own hands and decided to reap torture on me and my family; and he will not be brought to justice for his crime. However, the thought brings me some closure when my instincts tells me that in a way he is being punished."

"How so, because he had to give up his livelihood?" Officer Fields asked and shook his head. "He's rich enough that he won't miss one mansion for the next. I'm sure he won't live underground. He'll live just as lavish under some assume name."

"I agree with you, Officer Fields, but when I said I think he's being punished, I mean I think he's being punished because of how he feels," Sydney explained.

"I'm not sure if I follow you," Officer Fields said.

"What I'm trying to point out is, I feel Mr. Coleman is being punished because I don't think he has ever been happy since the death of my father. He was my father's best friend for all of my father's adult life until my father passed away," Sydney said warmly. "You see, while being held captive by Mr. Coleman he shared with me a lot of stuff and I have mix emotions about some of the things he told me. But when he shared with me about how much my father loved him. I knew he was telling me the truth."

Officer Fields looked at Sydney with confused eyes as Sydney continued. "My point is I know he was telling the truth because my father showed that kind of love to the world. Therefore when Mr. Coleman shared with me that my father was the only person who had ever loved him unconditionally, I knew it was the truth," Sydney candidly stated.

Officer Fields nodded because he then understood what Sydney was trying to say as Sydney looked at the officer with sincere eyes. "I truly believe that Mr. Coleman was trying to find and recapture that love that my father showed him and made him feel. However, I feel sorry for Mr. Coleman because I know he can search the world over and he'll never be truly happy because he is trying to find something that is not out there."

"Mr. Franklin that may have been his only truth. Sociopaths have a way of bending the truth to the point that it ends up being anything else but the truth. However, in this case regarding your father, maybe it is the truth," Officer Fields said as he headed out of the room with Sydney by his side. "I do hope that this information brings you and your family a bit of closure. Although, he hasn't been apprehended he'll slip up and fall into our trap. Meantime, rest assured and relay this information to your family as well, that we will have surveillance not too far from your home at all time," Officer Fields said with conviction, not pleased that Jack Coleman was still on the loose.

Still enroot to the front door, Sydney said, "Thank you Officer Fields for the good job that you and the Barrington Hills Police Department is doing," he said humbly. "I definitely appreciate your visit and the information you delivered to bring us into the light about Jack Coleman's case," Sydney said as he opened the front door for the officer.

Officer Fields stepped across the porch and down the steps and headed down the driveway toward his black squad car. He had parked at the end of the driveway. Sydney closed and locked the front door, but stood in the living room window and watched until the officer entered his car and drove away from Franklin House. He was stunned by the information, but headed across the living room floor toward the staircase to head to his room feeling lighter. He was pleased that Jack Coleman's life had been spared. Nevertheless, he felt bittersweet that justice had failed him and his family since his instincts told him that the authorities would most likely never apprehend Jack Coleman and bring him to justice. Now, at such a late hour in the evening, he would not settle into bed until sending out a mass message to all his family members, Starlet's family, and all the staff members, about Officer Fields home visit and the news he delivered along with a police report that confirmed that Jack Coleman did not perish in the fire.

Chapter Eight

Sydney arrived home from work that Thursday afternoon with an at ease look on his face, but Natalie was biting her fingernails waiting in the foyer for his arrival. She inquired and found his afternoon schedule, knowing he would be arriving home around 4:00 o'clock. She had left the kitchen area where she was busy chopping fresh vegetables for dinner and waited in the living room, looking out of the window from a quarter to four until she saw his car pull into the driveway at 4:05. She inhaled sharply, relieved to see him pull into the driveway. Her heart raced as he killed the engine and stepped out of his car. When he unlocked the front door and stepped inside Natalie greeted him with a shaky smile as she anxiously stood there in the corner of the foyer holding an envelope in her right hand.

Sydney looked at her and smiled but his smile quickly faded when he noticed the concerned look in her eyes. "Natalie, is anything the matter?" he asked.

She nodded with sad eyes. "Yes, Mr. Sydney, I believe so."

"Okay, what's going on?" he asked as he stepped into the living room with his suit jacket across his arm and his briefcase in his hand.

She followed him into the living room and held up the envelope in her hand. "I'm worried because I found this envelope taped to the front door. It doesn't have a return address but it's addressed to you," she solemnly said and passed him the envelope.

"Thanks, Natalie. But why have this bothered you?"

"It was taped to the door and nobody around here does that."

"You don't think anyone around here would tape anything to the door?" he asked, still not sure why she was upset.

"No, Mr. Sydney, I don't think they would."

"And you're upset because this letter was taped to the door?" he asked.

She nodded. "Yes, Mr. Sydney, I'm bothered by it."

He smiled. "I don't think it's anything to be concerned about. I'm sure whoever taped it there didn't mean any harm," he said casually. "You definitely didn't have to wait here to give me this. You could have placed it on the table in the library with the rest of the mail," he said respectfully. "I hope you didn't trouble yourself to look out for me."

She nodded as she followed him across the room where he placed his suit jacket across the arm of the sofa. "I looked out for you because it struck me a little odd that the envelope would be taped to the front door without a return address," she explained. "We don't usual get that type of mail here. But I guess you're right. It could be just an invitation from someone or something like that. I'll make sure to place it in the library with the other mail if anymore arrive taped to the door," Natalie assured him.

He smiled and nodded. "Natalie, whatever you do is fine," he said. "I just don't want you to trouble yourself unnecessarily for me. You have plenty to keep you busy and I don't want to add to it." He took a seat on the sofa and placed his briefcase in his lap. He opened his briefcase and placed the envelope inside. He looked at Natalie. "I thought Fred assorted all the mail or is it Mrs. Bradley or Helen who does that?" Sydney asked.

Natalie nodded. "I know it's not my job. But I didn't mind. Besides, Mr. Sydney, it sort of made me anxious to see a letter taped to the front door like that."

"I'm sorry it shook you," he said compassionately. "But why would that make you anxious, Natalie?" he asked as he stood to his feet. He had his suit coat across his left arm and his briefcase in his right hand.

She looked at him with serious eyes. "I guess for a while it reminded me of that evil Jack Coleman. That man has been on my mind a lot since you sent out those text messages and told all of us about that police report last night. Knowing he's still on the loose out there really makes me anxious," Natalie explained. "I was worried out of my mind when that maniac grabbed you the way he did." Natalie wiped a tear from her eye with the back of her left hand. "You are the baby of the family. I feel close to all of you young men but I especially feel close to you. I raised you from a baby and I couldn't stand to go through something like that again," Natalie went on and on and realized that she shouldn't be talking so much. "Mr. Sydney, now that we know he didn't perish in that fire. I just worry," Natalie admitted.

Sydney patted Natalie's shoulder. "We can't have you worrying yourself about stuff like that," Sydney said warmly with great concern in his voice. "You need to promise me right now that you will try not to let what happened to me back then worry you."

Natalie nodded. "Sure, Mr. Sydney, I promise," she said and headed in the direction of the kitchen.

Sydney strolled across the room and headed directly toward the staircase. He glanced at his watch and knew he had exactly one hour and thirty minutes before dinner would be served. He needed to get upstairs to his room and read the note and then call Starlet about their date plans for later. Then he had a business conference call coming in at 5:20 to last until 5:50. Therefore, when he stepped into his bedroom, he closed the door and immediately placed his briefcase on the bed and opened the lid. He removed the envelope and then closed the lid and sat his black leather briefcase on the floor near his comfortable chair that faced the fireplace. He took a seat in his comfortable chair and placed one foot on the footstool. He then settled his back against the soft cushions and without hesitation opened the envelope and removed the one page typed letter.

Dear Sydney,

I hope this letter makes it to your hands and no one else's. It wasn't the easiest task to get this letter to you. But it was a lot easier than you could imagine. But hell, you probably thought you had heard the last from your old pal Jack. By now, this letter is probably no big surprise! I'm sure you have most likely heard the good news that I didn't perish in that damn shameful fire last winter.

After Sydney read that line, he dropped the letter to the floor. Natalie had her suspicions about the note but he didn't have an inkling of suspicion that the letter could have been from Jack Coleman. After a moment, he inhaled sharply and reached down and picked up the letter from the carpet. He was stunned that Jack Coleman had left a letter for him. If he had any doubts about whether he actually survived the fire, receiving the letter was his proof that jack was indeed alive. He pondered if he should continue reading the letter or if he should just notify the authorities or someone in the household. He knew he was the only brother home from work because he had left work early. He also knew that his mother, Aunt Catherine and Amber were all out of the house at a fundraiser. However, he breathed a sigh of relief knowing that they would all be home soon to gather around the dinner table at six o'clock. Therefore, he decided to continue reading the letter and deal with the message afterward and share with his family during dinner.

Please accept my apology for what I put you through to witness my demise of being burned alive. But it was my only option. I didn't want to be apprehended by those incompetent bungling fools that they have dressed in law enforcement clothes at the BHPD. And if you doubt what I'm saying, if they had anyone with half a brain in charge of things there, maybe I wouldn't be on the loose. Good for me but sick for the community. But as I mentioned, I'm apologetic for your pain and nightmares. The authorities are so inapt until I probably could have come up with something that could have been less horrifying for you.

This note is just to let you know that I'm doing fine and I came up with a full proof plan to keep the authorities off my trail. I know by now that they probably figured out that the little house had an escape shaft in the roof. However, I'm not speaking of that, I'm speaking of the fact that I'm living my life right here in Barrington

Hills under their noses and they will never in this life time figure out my secret. Therefore, knock yourself out if you have the need to inform them of this letter. I'm sure you will probably rat me out. You're too damn straight-laced not to.

Sydney your good character will cause you to miss out on a lot of stuff in life. For instance, if I could trust you, I would give you my whereabouts and we could be friends and see each other sometime. I would also tell you my secret as to how I'm able to evade the law and why they will never stiff me out and bring me to justice for my crime against you and your family. This is a moot point since I don't trust you to be on my side and not theirs. I'm your friend but you think I'm your enemy. I loved Ryan too much to ever be an enemy to his kids.

If you are wondering about the fact that I wanted to marry you, I want you to know that I no longer have that urge to get married. I don't need to marry you to be happy, I just need to be near you to be happy. I really love you. You are my Ryan now and forever! And if I could trust you I would share a treasure with you. It's not a treasure of diamonds or gold. It's a treasure that I ended up with from your father.

Your father kept a journal when we were in high school. He kept it from 9th grade through our senior year and as a graduation gift to me, he gave me his private black diary journal. It's a little small six by five book that contains a portion of your father's life. It records your father's life from the tender age of fourteen until he was eighteen years old. This book is my gift to you if you ever throw your "have to do the right thing trait" out of the window. Think about it, a gift like this would be a priceless treasure to you and your brothers and the generations to come. You have the opportunity to find out things about your father that you ever thought possible to find out. Therefore, if you need to reach me, leave a note taped to your front door after midnight. If you alert the police, I'll know and your note will not be picked up and delivered to me. Besides, I'm smarter than you and the rest give me credit for. I'm smart enough not to risk my freedom. If they put a surveillance camera outside Franklin house, it would never see me or anyone who knows me. My messages go through a few twists and turns to get to me or you. Think about it.

Signed by: He who loves you, Jack Coleman.

Sydney grabbed his neck with both hands and gracefully laid his head back on the headrest of the chair. He thought about Jack's letter awhile then he got out of his seat and stepped across the room to his dresser. He picked up his cell phone and dialed Starlet's number. He stood with his back propped against the dresser as he waited for her to answer the phone. He glanced at his watch and noticed he had ten minutes before he needed to be downstairs for dinner.

"Hello, you," she answered laughingly.

"Hello, you back," he said softly with no pep to his voice.

"Is everything okay?" Starlet asked after noticing that he didn't sound quite himself.

"Sure, I'm fine, why do you ask?"

"You don't sound quite like yourself," she said.

"Well, I did just read a letter from Jack Coleman, if you can believe that," he announced.

"Tell me you are kidding," Starlet spoke in a panicky low voice.

"I cannot tell you I'm kidding because I'm not. I just received and read a letter from that would be dead criminal," Sydney said in a frustrated voice.

"This is incredible after you just told me yesterday about that police report and the fact that he had escaped the fire. Not in my wildest dream would I have thought you would be informing me today that you just received a letter from that deranged man," Starlet said with panic in her voice.

"I'm with you there, not in my wildest imaginings would I have pondered the thought of Mr. Coleman contacting me in any manner, but to receive a letter in such a direct way. I'm stunned and beside myself to say the least," Sydney admitted.

"So you just received this letter in the mail today?" Starlet asked.

"No, it didn't come through regular mail. Our Cook found it taped to the front door. She's pretty smart because when she handed me the letter, she was quite uneasy with an instinct that the letter could be from Mr. Coleman."

"Sydney, this is horrible news," Starlet cried. "I thought that horrible man was gone and out of our lives for good," she sadly mumbled. "I know you told me that the authorities believed he didn't die in the fire, but in my mind I had accepted him as dead. Now he has resurfaced to cause more mayhem in your life again," she said tearfully.

"No, I don't think he will."

"You didn't think he would have done what he did the first time. How can you say you don't think he will?" Starlet cried.

"Please, do not cry over this news. I know it's unexpected and stunning. But he has taken enough joy from us and I don't want you to shed any tears over this man," Sydney stressed. "Besides, let's not bother trouble since it's not out of hand. I got the letter and I'll turn it over to the authorities. "

"But I'm afraid of what this man might try to do to you. He kidnapped you once."

"That is true. Nevertheless, I don't think he wrote the letter to warn or threaten me in any way. He just wanted me to know that he survived the fire. He didn't want me to keep that disturbing image in my mind of him dying in that fire in such a horrifying way," Sydney explained calmly.

"I'm glad you can be calm, but I'm scared to death just knowing he's roaming around out there free," Starlet said.

"Starlet, this man is on the run from the authorities and he's not going to do anything foolish to risk his freedom," Sydney said assuringly to try to calm her down. "I'll pick you up after dinner."

"Okay, I'll be ready."

"Are you okay?" he asked.

"Not really. Just hearing Jack Coleman's name has really gotten to me. But I'll be okay after I see you," Starlet told him.

"Okay, beautiful. Everything will be okay. I'll see you later," Sydney said and hung up the phone.

Chapter Nine

The tall grandfather clock in the corner of the living room read straight up six o'clock when Sydney walked into the dining room. He cut it close after his conference call since he wanted to wash his face and hands and change into another dinner jacket before dinner. Therefore, as he hurried down the staircase he thought he was arriving a little behind everyone else and would walk into the room to found everyone else already seated. But as he casually walked into the room he was at ease to see that he had arrived for dinner on time. He could see that everyone else was just pouring into the large elegant room and being seated as well. He greeted and exchanged hellos with everyone as they all were taking their seats. He kept his composure and was conscience in his effort not to show any ill signs of the major disturbing news about Jack Coleman that had crushed him inside.

Sydney had the letter in his hand as he took a seat at his place. Natalie who was just entering into the room noticed the letter in his hand as he was being seated. It made her warm with anxiousness when she spotted the letter as she rolled in the serving cart that held seven Garden Green Salads to be placed at each of their seats. Her first thought when she spotted the envelope in his hand was the envelope that she had given him when he first arrived home from work. Therefore, as she pushed the cart with both hands, her hands noticeably trembled on the handle of the serving cart. She stopped in her tracks for a moment to collect herself as she took a deep breath and checked the salad plates as if she hadn't stopped to compose herself. Therefore, after checking the salad plates, she discreetly glanced about the dining room table at everyone and was pleased that no one noticed her anxiousness. Spotting the envelope lying next to Sydney's glass of iced tea had rattled her in a panicky way. She wasn't sure it was the same envelope but felt it most likely wasn't a coincident that Sydney had an envelope at the table after she had just handed him an odd enveloped taped to the front door. He didn't want her to worry about certain things but she had qualms about it because she was fearful and considered Jack Coleman extremely dangerous. Therefore, she felt anxious and uneasy as she pondered in her mind if it was the same letter that she had taken from the front of the door. She had the urge to walk over to Sydney and discreetly ask him if the letter was from Jack Coleman. However, she knew it would be inappropriate for her to approach him with that question. He had asked her firmly not to worry about such things. She couldn't drop the thought since it must have been of importance for him to have brought the letter to the dining room. She pushed the negative thoughts out of her mind and focused on the fact that maybe it was something of importance and good cheer that he wanted to share with the family. Nevertheless, she would make sure she kept her ear close to find out what the letter was about. She had an instinct that it was about Jack Coleman and she wouldn't be able to stop fretting until she knew for sure.

After Natalie served the salads she hung around at the serving corner hoping to hear Sydney mention the letter. She felt uneasy about eavesdropping but she felt desperate and scare for Sydney and the family if her hunch was right. But she couldn't continue to hang around the serving corner since she had to stay on schedule with serving their dinner. And the exact moment she left the room, Sydney held up the letter and slightly waved it about.

"This letter comes on the heels of the police report from Officer Fields yesterday. If you're wondering if it's from Jack Coleman, you guessed correct. Natalie found it taped to the front door sometime this afternoon," Sydney announced.

Veronica grabbed her stomach with her right hand. "Did he threatened you? What did he say? We need to call the authorities right away," Veronica firmly stated, exchanging looks with Catherine. "When they informed you yesterday that he was alive out there somewhere, it didn't dawn on me that he would be so bold considering the consequences to bother this family again," she stated with disbelief. "However, sending a letter means he's on a rampage again with his criminal shenanigans. Apparently he still has qualms about something and looking to retaliate."

"Excuse my French," Catherine angrily blurted out. "But he's a real sick bastard. His ulterior motive for all his shenanigans against this family is that you stole Ryan from him." Catherine nodded toward Veronica. "Like he ever had a chance with Ryan whether my brother had married you or not." Catherine hand shook anxiously as she forked salad into her mouth. She chewed her food and all eyes were still on her to continue. She placed the fork on the dish and pushed the salad aside. "Why can't that maniac go on a rampage with his shenanigans somewhere else?"

"Catherine, we all agree, but just calm down and let Sydney continue telling us what he was saying about the letter," Veronica respectfully suggested.

Catherine nodded. "Of course, but it's not like it's going to be any good news where that crook is concerned." Catherine looked toward Sydney.

Sydney nodded with a solemn look on his face. "Aunt Catherine is correct. This letter has no indication that it's good news."

"Did that weasel of a human being threaten you in some way?" Veronica asked.

"Mother, he didn't threaten me or anything like that. It sounds as if he just wanted me to know that he survived the fire," Sydney said unsure.

"Why would Jack Coleman bother and risk his freedom to send you a note just to say that?" Veronica asked. "He didn't go through all that trouble to get this letter to you just to say that. I think he's on the rampage looking to cause trouble for this family again," Veronica said sharply and glanced across the table at Amber. She didn't want their discussion to get too deep or negative. "Maybe we should table this discussion until after dinner," she said calmly, looking toward Sydney. "Sweetheart, I'm glad you brought it to our attention. However, none of us will enjoy our meals that much if we continue this line of discussion about Jack Coleman."

Paris took a sip of iced tea and looked toward his mother. "Mother, I respectfully disagree. I know it's hard to listen to and all our stomachs are in knots but this letter that Jack Coleman managed to tape to our front door, is highly serious and potentially dangerous information."

Rome nodded and glanced toward Paris. "I agree hundred percent that this is a discussion that we need to continue. We need to get to the bottom of why he sent that letter."

"It just makes no good sense that he would risk being caught just to leave a note to tell Sydney that he didn't die in the fire when he probably knows that Sydney already found that out," Veronica stressed.

Sydney looked toward his mother as he lifted his glass of iced tea to his mouth taking small sips as he spoke. "That's not all he said. He also touched on other subjects. But my point is, I don't think he means us any harm," Sydney said as he placed his glass of iced tea on the table. "I know he's a fanatic and whatever else he's being called; and I know Mr. Coleman cannot be trusted. Nevertheless, after reading the letter, I don't get the sense that he's on a rampage to cause more turmoil and mayhem in our lives," Sydney said as he took his fork and placed a cherry tomato in his mouth.

Catherine looked toward Sydney with a worried look on her face. "How can you assume that man isn't out to harm any of us? I have zero confidence in that crook. If he can flip out and kidnap you, he can do anything. None of us are safe until that man is captured and brought to justice," Catherine stressed strongly.

"I didn't debate about showing this letter," Sydney quickly said. "I knew I had to share it with the family and the authorities. However, I'm profoundly sadden that sharing this note has brought so much gloom and despair into this house." Sydney exchanged looks with his mother and Catherine. "However, Mother, Amber and Aunt Catherine, I don't want the three of you worrying over this letter and the possibilities of what all this means. Besides, as I said before and I'm pretty convinced in my mind that Mr. Coleman has no intentions of jeopardizing his freedom by coming near this house or any of us." Sydney held up both hands. "Frankly, that's not what his letter was about," Sydney told them.

Rome reached over and touched Sydney's wrist. "I think if you'll give a full disclosure of the letter it will make us all breathe a little easier," Rome politely said. "Because surely, he sent you the note for a reason. And we're all sure it had more to do with than Mr. Coleman wanting you to know he made it out of the fire," Rome politely said and then reached over and touched the top of Amber's hand.

Amber seemed a bit uneasy as they discussed Jack Coleman. Rome had just shared with her yesterday the news that he didn't perish in the fire. Yet, she sat there feeling quite fragile and vulnerable to the depressing and alarming news given her recent struggles with the death of her two daughters and her ex-mother-in-law. Plus, the thought that she had to be institutionalized for a month to deal with coping with her loss. Any kind of upsetting news seemed heightened to her.

Rome touched her hand again when he observed that she wasn't eating her salad. "Are you okay, Sweetheart?" he asked with concern in his voice. "You're not eating any of your salad. You haven't even touched it."

"I know I haven't," she looked at him with concerned eyes. "I can't eat anything right now. When you told me yesterday that he escaped the fire. I thought that awful man had vanished to never surface in public again," Amber humbly said.

"Sweetheart, he hasn't surfaced in public and I'm sure he won't," Rome assured her.

"It surely sounds like he has surfaced if he's leaving letters taped to the front door," Amber uttered softly as she finally forked some salad into her mouth.

"He left the letter on the door for a reason, but Sydney is quite convinced it wasn't to terrify any of us," Rome looked toward Sydney. "Sydney is going to share what Mr. Coleman mentioned in his letter and we'll all know what he left the letter for."

Sydney looked toward Amber and nodded. "Don't let this letter bother you. He's not on the warpath or trying to terrify us. He stated in the letter that he wish I could throw my do the right thing trait out of the window so he and I could be friends," Sydney explained.

Paris lifted his iced tea glass and took a sip of iced tea. "Mr. Coleman is quite sure of himself and quite bold to even suggest possible friendship with you," Paris discreetly shook his head. "Hopefully the authorities will finally apprehend Mr. Coleman and bring that man to justice. He's clearly unstable."

Britain nodded as he forked his last bite of salad into his mouth. "I agree wholeheartedly that the sooner he's Mr. Coleman is captured, the better. He doesn't need to be free to roam the streets in his unbalanced state. He's a complete danger to the community as long as he's on the loose," Britain said, looking toward his mother. "After dinner we need to jump right on this and call the authorities and inform them about this letter," Britain firmly suggested.

Sydney nodded. "I agree and hopefully they can trace the letter from the typewriter or anything to get a lead on Mr. Coleman. I don't think he's after us or represent another threat to us. Nevertheless, he's a criminal and he need be captured and brought to justice for the crimes he has already committed."

"I think we would all be able to sleep better if the authorities were to apprehend Mr. Coleman," Amber said as she pushed her half eaten salad dish aside.

"Listen up everyone," Sydney said. "I have just decided I will do everything in my power to see that Mr. Coleman is brought to justice."

"Sweetheart, what do you mean by that?" Veronica curiously asked.

"I will give them the letter and if they want to use me as bait to catch Mr. Coleman, I provide myself for the task. Anything to help the authorities capture him."

Veronica held up both hands. "Sweetheart, I don't think that's a good idea." She exchanged looks with her other sons and they all agreed with her. "It's very honorable, but too dangerous. Besides, it's not your place to help the authorities do their job," Veronica firmly stated.

"But Mother, without my help they will probably never catch Mr. Coleman," Sydney seriously stressed.

"If that's the case then I guess that awful man will stay on the loose," Veronica stated firmly, giving Sydney a serious stare. "He's unbalanced and way too dangerous for you to take a chance at risking yourself to give the authorities a better chance at capturing that unhinged deranged lunatic?"

Chapter Ten

Friday morning around eleven thirty five while Sydney were busy on a business call, Starlet knocked on his ajar office door and when he didn't answer she peeked her head inside of his door and noticed he was swirled around in his big comfortable maroon leather chair facing the wall while engaged in conversation. She observed that he appeared to be in a deep business discussion talking on the phone. She smiled as she softly stepped inside of his office and closed the door. She didn't want to disturb his phone call. Therefore, she softly made her way across the room into his office bathroom. She had a bag of lunch from Upscale Corner and decided to surprise him with lunch since she had an early day at Taylor Investments her job downtown. She attended an 8:30 office meeting and then she was done for the day. She hadn't informed Sydney of her schedule and he wasn't expecting her for lunch. Nevertheless, she was there to surprise him and she left the bag of lunch on the edge of the round table in the corner of the room off from the bathroom.

The instant Sydney hung up the phone from his business call, as he swirled around to face his desk in his office chair, he glanced up from the document in his hand at a soft knock on his office door. Still seated he had just lifted the receiver to make another call. But lowered the receiver to his desk as he held it in his hand. He wasn't expecting anyone but was accustomed to staff and employees knocking on his door at any time.

"Please come in," Sydney casually said.

A tall person dressed in all black opened the door and stood in the doorway awhile then stepped backward and glanced both ways down the hallway before entering Sydney's office and shutting the door behind him.

"May I help you?" Sydney asked, then glanced at his watch knowing he needed to make his business call before noon.

"I'm here about the bookkeeping position," the stranger said. The person was dressed in black clothing and their face was covered as well. The only thing visible was the person's eyes. Sydney wasn't alarmed by the person's attire. He knew that some individuals covered their entire body for religious purposes. Therefore, he quickly pulled open his top desk drawer and pulled out an application. He smiled and nodded as he slid the application to the edge of his big Mahoney desk. He and all his brothers had top of the line matching office furniture that made their offices look upscale and elite.

"Help yourself," Sydney said as he pointed to the round table with four chairs to the right. "You can complete the application there. Afterward, I'll look over your application and interview you for the position at that time. Did you bring a copy of your resume?"

The stranger shook his head as he stepped across the room and removed the application from Sydney's desk. "I don't have a copy of my resume with me."

"A copy of your resume would have been helpful." Sydney nodded. "But that's fine," Sydney said. "After you complete the application I will still interview you for the position. However, if you'll be so kind to excuse me awhile. I need to make a call," Sydney said as he began to dial the numbers on his desk phone.

"Please put the phone down," a familiar voice demanded.

Sydney looked up from his desk and his hand went limp as he dropped the receiver to the floor. He was stunned to see that the person who had entered his office in search of the bookkeeper position was Jack Coleman. He had removed the black scarf from his face as he stood there holding a gun on Sydney.

"Oh my goodness! Mr. Coleman, I can't believe you are here in my office," Sydney said with stunning surprise. "Coming here was a mistake. Every law enforcement in town is looking for you. Nevertheless, you completely fooled me. Walking in here wearing all black clothing with even your face covered with a black scarf did the trick. I had no idea it was you when you walked in here," he inhaled sharply.

"This wasn't planned," Jack said calmly. "I kept thinking about you and I knew I had to risk everything just to see your face again. And this will play out okay if you keep your cool and just do as I say. I'm not here to harm you or anyone else. I'm not looking for a scuffle or any kind of tussle with anyone. If you cooperate none of that will be necessary!"

"Mr. Coleman, you are not thinking clearly and have most certain lost your grip on reality. If you were thinking clearly you would know that you are a wanted man. A fugitive from justice and here at my place of employment is the last place you should have shown your face. How do you expect to come into my place of business and leave without being noticed or spotted? This visit will not end well for you," Sydney warned him.

"I think it will end just fine if you cooperate and do as I say."

Sydney held up both hands. "What do you want from me this time? I guess you realize this place is crawling with staff, workers and customers. Anyone could knock on my door at any time." He pointed toward his door. "Anyone could just walk in as well."

"We'll fix that problem." He beckoned for Sydney to go toward the door. "Lock the door so nobody will be able to just walk in here," Jack demanded.

Sydney walked across the office to the door and locked the door and as he headed back toward his desk he glanced toward the round table and did a double take when he noticed the lunch bag that read Upscale Corner sitting on the edge of the table. He wondered if Jack had brought the bag in and sat it there. He wasn't aware that Starlet had entered his office while he was on a phone call; and now she was in his office private bathroom. She could hear their conversation and she was beside herself with panic and fear. She wanted to use her phone and dial 911 but she was too afraid to move and didn't want her phone to make too much noise that it would grab Jack Coleman's attention.

"I want to spend the afternoon with you and if you grant me that treat I will disappear out of your life and you will never see me again. Plus, if you'll do me that favor I will give you your father's diary. I have the diary and will leave it with you," Jack promised.

"Do you want to spend the afternoon here in my office?" Sydney asked.

"No, I have another place in mind. I want you to leave with me and I'll take you to a private place where we can spend time with each other. I have never spent the kind of time with you that I dreamed about. I have never even held your hand or touched your face. Therefore, I have a place in mind for just the two of us; and I promise you do not have to be afraid of me, Sydney. I just want to be alone with you. Can you grant me that?" Jack asked.

Sydney shook his head. "Mr. Coleman, you have the audacity to ask me to grant you something from the kindness of my heart after your rampage of torture and malice. I'm offended that you would even ask me for any kind of favor," Sydney said sharply. "I'm highly offended that you have shown your face here. By doing so, you didn't honor your word that you gave stating to leave me and my family alone. I honestly believed you had done so. I tried to give you the benefit of the doubt, but here you are on the warpath of destruction again! You are here in my office holding a gun on me." Sydney looked toward the ceiling awhile and then looked at Jack. "You claim to care about me, but you're here to torment me again after you held me against my will and faked your death and then lead me to believe that you had perished in a fire. I'm still bothered by those images in my head. You claim to care for me and my father and if that's true you need to leave me and my family in peace. You need to turn yourself into the authorities and seek medical attention for your mental condition. You are clearly unstable," Sydney stressed strongly. "You are holding a gun on me and I do not wish to be harmed but I also know that nothing could make me leave this building with you."

"Don't make me mad," Jack said sharply. "I'm trying to reason with you. I love you. But when it comes to saving my own skin, I don't plan to get caught by the authorities. Therefore, I need you to leave this building with me! You can't have it your way. You can come with me dead or alive, but one way or another you'll leave here with me," Jack said.

"I thought you just wanted to spend the afternoon with me and then disappear out of our lives. Therefore, why are you saying that you need me to come with you dead or alive? Why would you say that?"

"I said it because what I originally said was a lie. I don't want you to spend the afternoon with me. I want you to spend forever with me. I have come for you. I have decided that if I can't have you then my life isn't worth the effort."

Sydney inhaled sharply and then swallowed hard. He was stunned by Jack's confession. He honestly felt that Jack Coleman wouldn't bother him again. Now he was faced with reliving the same nightmare all over again.

"Listen, Sydney, I want you to know that I meant what I said. I don't need to marry you. I just need to be with you. I can't live without you. It's too much torture trying to live without you. I have tried and failed," Jack explained.

"Mr. Coleman, this is not a good situation. I don't know what to tell you. I feel for you because I believe you are hurting. But I also realize that you are not dealing with reality as it is. You are living a fantasy in your head. You feel your fantasy can become reality if you force it upon me at gun point. But I beg of you to let me help you," Sydney pleaded in a low voice. "You are a marked man and a fugitive from justice and you could be shot down trying to hide from the law."

"I'll take my chances and I need you to cooperate so we can both get out of here undetected. I have a car and driver in front of the building across the street. It's a black limousine. I need you to walk a head of me. My face will be covered but I'll have my gun pointed right at your back inside of my jacket pocket. As busy as this place is around this time of the day with everyone trying to grab lunch, I'm sure no one will notice us."

"I think we'll be noticed," Sydney held up one hand. "What's your plan? You've decided you want to drag me on the run with you. You want to ruin my life unlike before when you said you cared too much for me and my father to turn my life upside down."

"I changed my damn mind! I rather have you with me. You're my whole life. I know that more clearly now than I have ever." Jack glanced at the clock on Sydney's wall above his desk. It was 12:15. "We need to leave here in the middle of lunch to make sure everybody is too busy heading to lunch to notice us," Jack suggested.

"Mr. Coleman, I have no intentions of leaving this building with you."

"You have no other choice. I will use this gun to make you leave. So head out now! If you try anything to bring attention to us, I will shoot you, Sydney. I promise."

Sydney stepped over to his office door and unlocked the door and stepped out as Jack walked right behind him. The hallway outside of his office was clear of traffic nobody was walking about. Jack and Sydney got on the elevator and headed down to the first floor. The moment Starlet heard them leave the office, she ran out of the bathroom barely able to catch her breath. She had heard everything Jack said to Sydney. Therefore, she dialed 911 and notified the authorities that Jack Coleman was at Franklin Gas disguised in all black with his face covered attempting to snatch Sydney Franklin.

When Starlet hung up the phone with the Barrington Hills Police Department she grabbed her face with both hands. She was frightened and overwhelmed beyond anything she had ever experienced. With her back propped against Sydney's desk, while still holding her face, it dawned on her that she needed to let his brothers know what was going on as well as call his mother. But as she removed both hands from her face and inhaled sharply, she grabbed her stomach with both hands and remained propped against his desk. After a moment, she felt calm and began to head out of Sydney's office. But halfway to his office door, Starlet fainted on the floor in front of his desk.

By the time Jack and Sydney made it outside, standing to cross the street to head to Jack's limousine on the other side of the street, police cars pulled up with their siren going. Within seconds the eight police cars had surrounded Jack Coleman and Sydney.

"Drop your weapon and put your arms in the air," Officer Fields demanded over the loud speakers.

Jack made no attempts to drop his weapon or raise his arms. Sydney heart raced with relief that law enforcement had showed up before

Jack could force him into the car to be driven to an unknown location. But he wasn't sure how everything was going to end. He still felt solemn, anxious and shock. Then Jack suddenly ripped the covering from his face and the long black cape from his shoulders. Beneath he wore a pair of Fendi black slacks and a Niemen Marcus black pullover turtleneck top. He grabbed Sydney by the arm and held him close with the gun pointed in Sydney's back.

"I will shoot if you don't get out of my way and let us leave together. You will have this man's blood on your hands if you make me shoot him. So here's what I plan to do without any interfering from you!" he shouted angrily. "Do I make myself clear? I plan to get in my car and I'm taking Sydney Franklin with me! So back off now and let us leave."

When Sydney and Jack reached Jack's limousine, Jack made Sydney open the door. And as Sydney grabbed the door handle, two shots were fired both at Jack Coleman but he wasn't hit. Two more shots were fired as Jack tried to push Sydney into the car. Sydney was determined to get away from Jack and figured Jack probably wouldn't shoot him. Therefore, Sydney took a huge risk and broke away from Jack; and with no hostage to protect him, Jack quickly hopped inside of the limousine and ducked his head down to the floor of the car. Meanwhile, Sydney didn't look back as he ran breathless across the street toward Franklin Gas. Officer Ford grabbed him and tucked him inside of his squad car.

Ten minutes into the chaotic dangerous event, every employee of Franklin Gas had gathered outside with frightened confused faces. They were all stunned by the incident. Reporters from all the news networks had consumed the area. It had made the breaking news on TV that alerted Veronica, Catherine, Amber and all the staff. They were horrified by the headlines that stated a dangerous criminal was on the loose at Franklin Gas. Therefore, Catherine, Veronica, Amber and all the staff arrived one by one in separate vehicles at the horrific scene taking place at Franklin Gas.

Jack Coleman ordered his driver to leave the area but the short stout Chinese driver refused to start the car. Besides, they were surrounded by policemen. Fourteen officers gathered around the limousine with their guns pointed at the car.

"Get out of the car and surrender yourself now! If you do not exit the car within the next two minutes, we will start firing," the voice over the loud speaker demanded.

Jack pushed opened the passenger's door and at the same time the Chinses driver pushed open the driver's door. They both stepped out of the car with their arms in the air. "I will cooperate with you hundred percent if I can just see Sydney," Jack promised as he slowly lowered his right arm and dropped the gun to the ground.

The moment Jack gun hit the ground a swarm of police officers surrounded Jack on one side of the car and a group of officers surrounded the Chinese driver on the opposite side of the car. They handcuffed the Chinese driver and read him his rights while several officers were tussling with Jack. He resisted arrest as he pleaded to see Sydney.

"I love Sydney and I demand to see him. This was my time to be happy. You nitwits spoiled my joy," he cried as tears dripped from his eyes. "This was my only chance and now it's gone. Where is Sydney? He tricked me and broke away. He wasn't supposed to leave me." Jack glanced about and spotted Sydney siting in one of the squad cars. His suddenly broke a loose from the officers and headed toward the squad car where Sydney was seated.

"Mr. Coleman, stay where you are! Don't go near the victim," Officer Fields yelled.

Jack started walking toward the squad car where he spotted Sydney. He had no intentions of missing an opportunity to see Sydney. However, on his fourth step toward Sydney a single shot was fired and hit Jack in the shoulder. Jack grabbed his shoulder and continued to walk toward the squad car. "Don't come any farther!" Officer Ford demanded.

Jack kept walking toward the car and by now Sydney had stepped out of the car and raised both arms in the air. "Mr. Coleman, here I am. Now, you see me. But please stand back if you don't want to lose your life," Sydney suggested.

The warning from Sydney or Office Fields did not stop Jack from trying to get to Sydney. Sydney stood against the car bracing himself for the next shot that he figured would be fired from Officer Ford's gun. The shot was aimed at Jack's lower extremities and landed right above his left ankle. Jack went down and his hands grabbed the hood of Officer Ford's car. Jack struggled and pulled himself up while facing horrendous pain.

"I love you, Sydney. Why did you trick me? I was going to give you your father's diary. You have deprived me of your love. But I need to shake your hand so I can leave this bitch of a world in peace. Please come shake my hand. Can't you see I'm dying?"

Sydney was compelled to walk near Jack who was were down on his knees. But the two officers that stood on either side of Sydney to protect him, asked Sydney to stay put until after Jack had been cuffed and secured inside of a squad car. Therefore, when Sydney gave the officers a silent glance showing his unspoken desire to at least be allowed to shake Jack's hand, both of the tall, stout officers shook their heads.

Seconds later, Jack fell over on his back as blood poured from his shoulder and lower leg. The paramedical team quickly attended to his wounds as he was cuffed and rushed to Barrington Hills Memorial Hospital in serious condition. The news later updated his condition to stable and that he was expected to make a full recovery.

Chapter Eleven

Seated in the Waiting Lounge of Barrington Hills Memorial Hospital six hours after the showdown in front of Franklin Gas, Sydney was in deep thought about the chaotic day. He kept his composure while sitting on the comfortable long green leather bench with the company and support of Starlet there by his side. They held each other's hand as they sat there in silence. They were at the hospital at the request of the Barrington Hills Police Department. Officer Fields had phoned Franklin house and relayed a message to Dillon for Sydney to meet him in the Waiting Lounge of the hospital. He wanted Sydney to sign for a personal letter written by Jack Coleman. Jack Coleman had left instructions for the letter to be hand delivered to Sydney Franklin.

Meanwhile, Sydney sat there relieved that all the pain and suffering for Jack Coleman was over. And all the danger and uncertainty of looking over his shoulder was over for him and his family. Yet, somehow his heart felt heavy with sadness for Jack Coleman, especially since his father loved the man unconditionally. Sydney grieved that his efforts to help Jack had failed. He also grieved that no one else had been able to reach Jack and give him professional help. Yet, good thoughts of what could have been if Jack hadn't been unbalanced flashed in his mind. He silently thought of a Jack Coleman that he wished would have been a normal healthy person that could have shared so much about his father. Sad thoughts also floated in his head about a Jack Coleman that had the world on a silver platter but was never happy with his blessings because he was lost and could not see the treasures that were laid out at his feet.

Sydney squeezed Starlet's hand, looked at her with solemn eyes and smiled. Then he kissed her on the side of the face as they didn't exchange any words. They sat there anxiously awaiting Officer Fields to walk into the lounge and approach them. As he held Starlet's hand firmly, he silently thought about what started out as a routine busy Friday morning at Franklin Gas and how it turned into a ball of confusion, ending with unexpected disaster that no one saw coming. Jack Coleman was rushed into surgery at Barrington Hills Memorial Hospital at 1:30 PM and spent two hours in surgery for the removal of the two bullets, one from his shoulder and one from his lower leg. Two hours later his eyes fluttered opened while in the recovery room and at 5:30 PM he was moved into a private room. Shortly after the nurse left the room after bringing him a pitcher of ice water and a drinking glass, Jack Coleman passed away from a self-inflicted wound. He broke the glass and cut his own throat. The nurse had originally given him a plastic cup but he convinced her that he could only drink from glassware. Therefore, the nurse went out and brought him back an eight ounce drinking glass and then left the room.

When the nurse stepped back into his room approximately ten minutes later to check on him, she was shocked to discover his lifeless body lying on top of the covers saturated in blood that had poured from his neck all over his chest. The nurse grabbed her face with both hands and screamed as she stood there eyeing Jack Coleman lifeless body. She noticed that the broken glass was still in his hand buried in his throat. The two guards posted at his door, heard her scream and rushed into the room. They were stunned to see that he had taken his own life. They ushered the nurse out of the room and told her not to touch anything. However, she collected herself and pointed toward the bedside table. Propped against the water pitcher was a letter. One of the officers placed on a pair of plastic gloves that he pulled from his back pocket, and then stepped over to the bedside table and retrieved the letter. It was addressed with two names on the outside of the envelope that read: Sydney Franklin.

March 28, 2014, Friday night

Dear Sydney,

By the time you read this letter you will already know that I took my own life. It wasn't worth saving. I know you feel sad and think of it as a big mess that was uncalled for. However, I lost the battle and I wasn't willing to face my punishment. I lost because I took a page from your book. I trusted you. I knew you didn't love me back, but I believed you cared about me and my well-being. But you couldn't care about me in the way that I needed you to care about me. You turned out to mirror your father. He had no special loving feelings for me. But the difference with your father. He did genuinely care about me. He was the only person in my life who truly cared about me. I wanted you to care about me in that way. I thought I deserved some love. I believed that love would come to me in my life before death. You had that piece of love but you deprived me of it. I couldn't stay in this world without you being by my side. I realized that after the kidnapping and that's why I risked everything to return for you.

Sydney, I want you to especially know that I wanted to be good and honorable. I wanted to be those things because that's the way you wanted me to be. I broke my own heart when I reluctantly decided to set you free from my bondage. All this time I have suffered and thought of you. My life was the worse torture being without you. I knew when I risked everything and showed up at your office that you would either end up with me or I would end up captured and sent to prison. But living in a penitentiary without you would be worse than living anywhere without you. Therefore, I decided to end my torture of a life. Maybe on the other side I'll travel into the light.

I lived a privileged very unhappy life. I had everything given to me on a silver platter. I had everything I could possibly want. But things never mattered that much to me. What I wanted was a touch or a hug from my parents. Neither of them ever embraced me. We were all in the same household but they were invisible to me. The only time I knew they existed were the times they showered me with possessions. But the two things I wanted most that meant more to me than any of my possessions were you and Ryan. I know Ryan cared about me and deep down I believe you cared about me too.

Look on the bright side, at least you know I haven't faked my death. I'm out of your life for good. You and your family no longer have to look over your shoulders wondering about me and what I'm up to. And last, but not least, I know your family wealth is enough to last you six life times. But all my worldly possessions which were all liquidated into cash has been willed to you and your three brothers. My holdings and cash is worth one and a half billion dollars.

I know I terrified you and your family and this is my way of trying to make up for that. Besides, I wasn't a good man but my money was made honestly by hard work. Granted, my folks left me sitting pretty high on the hog when they left the Coleman mansion which I sold for a boatload of money. However, besides from my parents' wealth, I made my own fortune from the ground up with sheer determination that I could be the best at whatever I took on. Your father and I finished college with that kind of attitude. That's why his fortune grew on top of the fortune left by his folks.

I believe that the four brothers will go all the way into the light to surpass all the financial goals that Ryan and I set for ourselves. Therefore, take the money and do as you please. I have family on my mother and father's side that I had the option of leaving my wealth to. However, my two Aunts and five first cousins on my mother's side never once called or contacted me in any way after my mother's funeral. My two uncles and cousins on my father's side never called or contacted me after my father's death. None of them ever seemed interested in me. You showed me more kindness than any of my family members. You had more compassion for me when I was holding you captive than anyone has ever shown me. Have a good life.

Signed: Jack Coleman

Shortly after the officer showed up for Sydney to sign for the letter, Starlet and an emotionally drained Sydney left the hospital and walked across the street to the hospital parking lot. They were both shaken and couldn't think of much else other than what had taken place earlier at Franklin Gas. Therefore, they didn't exchange any conversation enroot to his car. After they were seated inside of his car, Starlet looked at Sydney and touched his arm to break his deep thoughts.

"Are you okay? I'll understand if you want to cancel our plans," she said compassionately. "You have gone through a lot today and tonight."

He started up the engine and looked at her with solemn eyes. "You're such a beautiful sight to look at among all the chaos that took place today," he humbly stated as he touched the side of her face and smoothed her hair back from her neck. "Looking at you and your quiet beauty makes what I have just gone through seem like it happened in another world." He leaned over and kissed the side of her face and then gracefully dropped his head on the steering wheel awhile.

They sat in silence awhile as Starlet didn't say anything, allowing him to collect himself and take in all that had happened to him. However, after about three minutes of silence she touched his arm.

"You have been through so much. You probably should just go home and relax."

He lifted his head from the steering wheel and looked at her and smiled. "You're right. It's been a lot to process."

"So, do you want to just drop me off at home so you can relax with some alone time?" she softly asked.

He shook his head. "We might as well stick with our plans. You're on the schedule to have dinner with us. Mother would be disappointed if you didn't show up."

"Okay, sure, if that's what you want. I would love to stick with having dinner at your house," she assured him. "However, after dinner, we can cancel the musical. I think you need to just have some time to yourself to take all this in. What happened to you was very dramatic," Starlet grabbed her face. "Now that man is dead. I know you feel just awful. It's probably hard to know how you feel right now."

"That's true. I have very conflicting feelings going on right now. Mr. Coleman was dangerous and needed to be locked up. However, he was also quite ill. My father's friend, but I couldn't help him. I wasn't able to sway him toward help," Sydney solemnly admitted.

Starlet leaned over and kissed the side of his face. "Maybe you couldn't help Mr. Coleman, but I'm sure you tried because that's who you are."

"Thank you for that, but I couldn't get through to him." He glanced at his watch. "I need to get moving so we won't be late for dinner." He pulled out of the hospital parking lot and headed down the street toward Franklin house.

"I'm so sorry you went through this," Starlet warmly said.

He threw her a quick glance and then focused back on the road. "Thank you, Sweetheart, I know you are. However, I should tell you, there's one thing you're not quite right about," he said as he leaned over and gave her a kiss on the side of the face again.

"What's that I'm not quite right about?" she asked, smiling.

"You're not quite right about alone time. The last thing I want right now is to be alone. I don't want to talk about what happened today. I want it all to fade out of my head."

"I'm sure you want it to all fade out of your head. But Sweetheart, that's going to be hard to do when the person you want to forget just willed you his billion dollar fortune."

Chapter Twelve

The outrageous incident instigated by Jack Coleman rattled and dismayed everyone in the Franklin household as well as all the Franklin Gas employees. Then came the shocking news of his demise implemented by himself. Nevertheless, showing great courage and composure, the four brothers comforted their mother and Aunt Catherine and gave the staff an uplifting talk in hope that no one would allow the incident to cause them too much stress. Rome was especially concerned for Amber fragile state as he showered her with attention and stuck by her side. But she held up extremely well and helped to comfort Veronica and Catherine. After going through the worst nightmare of her life, losing her two daughters, somehow the incident with Jack Coleman didn't disturb Amber as strongly as she and Rome had anticipated. Yet, the horrific event of the day had troubled her mind. Nevertheless, after everything settled down with Jack Coleman in custody and then the unexpected news of his demise, Rome called a family and staff meeting in the library where he gave a pep talk. By the end of his fifteen minute talk, everyone had agreed to move forward and not allow the devastating incident that had taken place to disrupt their lives. Rome had encouraged everyone to stick to their evening plans.

Britain left home overwhelmed by the events of the day but shook it all off his back as happy thoughts of spending the evening with

Sabrina filled his mind. He arrived at the Taylor mansion at ten to seven to pick her up for dinner at his house. Dinners were normally served earlier but due to the chaos of the day, the time had been pushed back to accommodate everyone's unexpected schedules.

Britain was in good spirits and dressed divinely in a blue two piece casual designer outfit by Michael Kors as he waited at the bottom of the staircase for her to come down. Their plans were to spend a quiet evening at Franklin House after dinner. The time had passed rapidly for the couple after their unexpected night out where they enjoyed dinner together at the Upscale Corner. While waiting for Sabrina to come down the staircase, Britain warmly reflected on how one month had passed since Sabrina started working at Franklin Gas and two weeks had sailed by since the two of them had reunited.

Sabina looked lovely coming down the long staircase with a smile on her face. Her eyes were glued to Britain's face as he looked up in awe of her beauty as if seeing her was the first time. In his eyes, she was floating toward him heavenly dressed in a maroon casual two piece dress outfit designed by Saint Laurent that only enhanced her beauty to him. As she floated down the staircase toward him she was filled with content of how their happiness felt complete and solid again. However, she had a dark flash in her mind that told her they still had a shadow of darkness hanging over them. In her mind's eye, it was Courtney's feelings for Britain that was hanging over their heads. Her instincts told her that Courtney's feelings for Britain was as strong as ever. Nevertheless, Sabrina continued to smile at Britain since she was desperately trying to convince herself that Courtney was no longer interested in Britain. Yet, no matter the effort, she was still suspicious of Courtney and realized that she went against her better judgment when she allowed Courtney to penetrate her inner circle, entrusting Courtney into her life as a friend.

Later in the evening, Britain and Sabrina found themselves seated on the living room floor in front of the fireplace looking through old photo albums of the Franklin family. They were amazed to see so many pictures of Britain's grandparents and great-grandparents. They shared a bowl of popcorn as they both had a strawberry milkshake sitting beside them as the low flames in the fireplace gave the room a romantic ambiance. The rest of the house was quiet since no one else was home as Britain and Sabrina enjoyed the soft romantic background music of Kenny G.

Sabrina smiled and pointed at two young men photos that resembled Sydney and Britain. "These pictures are dated 1882 and 1905. Therefore, I know it's not you or Sydney. But wow, look at the striking resembles," she said, amazed at the likeness.

Britain looked at the pictures and smiled. "Where did these two come from? I never spotted them in this album. That one does look a lot like me, and that one looks like Sydney." He pulled the pictures from the plastic sleeve and read the back of each photo: Born 1882, Ryan Samuel Franklin, age on photograph 16; and Born 1905, Samuel Ryan Franklin, age on photograph 17. He put the photographs back in their plastic sleeve. "This one that looks like Sydney is my great-great-grandfather, Ryan Samuel Franklin, and this one that resembles me is my great-grandfather, Samuel Ryan Franklin," he said, smiling.

"Your great-great-grandfather and your great-grandfather were both exceedingly good looking young men," Sabrina said with amazement as she lifted her milkshake and pulled two sucks through the straw.

"If you think those are close resembles, there's a snapshot of my grandfather in that green album to your left." He pointed to the album and she reached for the book and passed it to him. "In the picture, my grandfather is a split image of Paris." He reached into the popcorn bowl, gathered a hand of kernels and placed in his mouth.

Sabrina sat there smiling with her legs folded beneath her, holding her milkshake with both hands as he flipped the pages in the picture album. Middle ways through the book he stopped and pointed at a picture of a young man propped against a white fence. "That's a picture of my grandfather, Samuel, but if you didn't know better you would think it was a photo of Paris." Britain grabbed another fist of popcorn and placed in his mouth, and then lifted his milkshake that had mostly melted, removed the lid from the cup and took a big swallow.

"You are exactly right, even from the way his hair is slightly long, pulled back in a ponytail," Sabrina agreed. "These pictures are incredible. Starlet and Samantha need to see these family pictures. Your entire family has a long line of beauty genes," she said and playfully hit his shoulder.

"So I have been told," he said and smiled at her.

"I'm sure you have been told," she said seriously.

"No, I was just kidding; nobody has told me that."

"Maybe not, but it's true." She smiled looking in his eyes. "Just think, even your great-great grandfather who lived over a hundred and thirty years ago was an exceptionally handsome man. I can only imagine how gorgeous his father was," she said still looking at the pictures. "Is your great-great-grand father, Ryan Samuel Franklin, as far back as the Franklin tree goes on your father side?" She asked, and then corrected herself. "I know your family history goes farther back, but what I meant to say, is this as far back as your family picture collection goes?"

Britain nodded. "Yes, this is as far back as the collection goes," he said, lifted his milkshake and took two pulls through the straw.

Sabrina was still paging through the photo album when Britain placed his milkshake on the floor beside him and scooted closer to her. Then he collected the four photo albums that were scattered about on the floor and placed them to the side. Sabrina looked at him and smiled. "Do you want to put this one aside as well?" She passed him the album that she had been pages through.

Britain stacked it on top of the others and then leaned in and gave her a long lingering passionate kiss. They were both breathless by the time the kiss ended.

"Wow, that was some kiss," he whispered against her neck and then looked lovingly in her eyes. "We have been back together for how long now?" Britain asked.

She held up two fingers. "Exactly two weeks and counting," she smiled.

He smiled. "Okay, we have been back together for two weeks now," Britain said, as he sat next to Sabrina, overjoyed by her presence and the fact that they had found their way back to each other. "However, if we count our very first date when we first met, it would mean we have actually been seeing each other for seven months."

"You are right. I can't believe it's been that long."

"Yes, beautiful girl. It has been that long. Time rushes by when you're young and in love and happy."

She smiled. "All of which we are, of course," she said laughingly. "But seven months really?"

"Yes, really," he said smiling. "If we count all the time that we have known each other since we first met, it adds up to seven months." He leaned next to her neck and tenderly kissed her on the neck and then on the side of the face.

"I just had a thought," he looked at her with excitement in his eyes.

"Okay, what are you thinking?" she asked curiously. "I can see that look in your eyes that means you're excited about something."

"I am somewhat enthused, I'll admit. But frankly, it has nothing to do with the spontaneous thought that crossed my mind. Moreover, this pleasant disposition is my constant state of emotion from just being in your enchanting presence, Miss Sabrina Taylor. You do this to me, you know."

"Do what to you?"

"You make me this crazy in love happy fellow." He smiled at her lovingly. "I'm sure you are fully aware of this incredible effect that your distinct essence have on me." He reached for his milkshake, removed the lid and lifted it to his mouth, finishing the last swallow.

"You make me insanely happy as well." She smiled.

"Therefore, I guess we are both just two insanely happy individuals," he said playfully, touching her cheek with the back of his palm.

She gave him a quick kiss on the side of his face. "You are so right, and I speak for myself. You make me so incredibly happy inside until sometime I feel as if I could just burst with bliss," she said warmly and then touched his shoulder.

He touched her cheek again as he looked into her eyes lovingly. "When I thought I might lose you forever it was a thought too disturbing to bear."

"You have no idea what it means to have you back in my life, and the agony I suffered when I thought you could be lost to me forever," she said heartfelt. "Therefore, don't remind me of how not together I was to push you away. It rips me up inside just to think about the thought of almost allowing you to slip through my fingers," she said seriously, looking into his eyes.

"We are both blessed that our prayers were answered. "We have both found our way back to each other," he said lovingly.

Sabrina smiled. "We have and I'm so happy it feels like I'm dreaming." Then she paused for a moment as she looked at him and it dawned on her that he had something to tell her. "You have something to tell me, remember? Some thought of yours. That's right, it was some bold thought; and I'm still waiting for you to share that very bold non-traditional thought you mentioned. I don't want you to forget to tell me."

"Just hold on, it's coming." He stood to his feet and placed the empty milkshake cup on the coffee table, and then he reached down and grabbed the photo albums off the floor and placed them on the coffee table.

Sabrina stood up from the floor and then reached down and grabbed her empty milkshake cup and placed it on the coffee table. "I'll take our trash and throw it in the kitchen garbage," she said over her shoulder as she headed toward the kitchen with the empty milkshake cups.

While she headed across the huge stretch of floor in the direction of the kitchen, Britain grabbed the half eaten bowl of popcorn from the floor and headed toward the kitchen right behind her, and when she reached the kitchen she glanced over her shoulder and smiled at Britain. "I didn't know you were coming this way to."

"Yes, I'm following in the footsteps of beauty," he said, smiling.

"Okay, if you're following in the footsteps of beauty when you're following me, who am I following when I follow you?" she said playfully as she dumped the two plastic milkshake cups in the trashcan.

"That answer is simple, you're just following in the footsteps of a man," he said, smiling as he stepped over to the trashcan.

She laughed. "Following in my footsteps are beauty, but as stunning as you are, you're just a plain man," she said playfully.

Britain gave her a serious look after she spoke and she sensed that he wasn't pleased with something that she had said. Nevertheless, he asked.

"Hold the lid open while I dump this popcorn."

Sabrina held the trashcan lid open as Britain dumped the remaining popcorn into the garbage can; and after which, he grabbed her hand and lead her back into the living room. They were both smiling as they took a seat on one of the twin sofas, seated next to each other.

He glanced at his watch and shook his head. "That old saying is true. Time flies when you're having fun."

"Just as you said a few minutes ago that time flies when you're young and in love," Sabrina reminded him.

He glanced at his watch again. "It's flying right now. It's almost 10:00 o'clock in the evening, but it feels like our evening just begun."

"I know, but I'm still waiting to hear some topic that you wanted to discuss," she reminded him.

"Oh, that thought," he said and paused.

"Do you have cold feet and not sure if we should discuss it or not?" she touched his arm in a playfully manner.

He smiled and narrowed his eyes at her. "Why do you ask that?"

"Well, let me see why I would ask that? For one, you don't seem as eager as you acted when you first mentioned it."

"Okay, that's good observation." He nodded.

"So, I'm right and you're having second thoughts about discussing whatever you were planning to discuss with me."

He nodded. "Yes, Sweetheart, that is true since after further thought, I'm not sure it's really worth discussing. Besides, it would just be a hypothetical discussion. However, what I would like to mention is the statement I made in the kitchen about following beauty."

"Why would you say that?" she smiled.

"I say it because you are more beautiful than anything that I have ever seen. Your beauty is beyond description or expression. It's like infinity," he said lovingly. "That's how I see you."

She grabbed her face with both hands. "What a beautiful compliment. You have a beautiful way with words, but all I can say is that you are the most handsome man and I just adore everything about you."

"Hold that thought until after you hear our hypothetical discussion," he said, smiling.

She narrowed her eyes at him. "What are you up to? Hearing you say that just makes me more curious to know what it is that you are referring to, especially since you also said you think we shouldn't discuss it."

"You're right, I think it's not worth discussing anymore. However, you are all geared up to hear about it." He held up both hands. "Now, I'm cornered and have to mention it."

"I'm very curious now," she kept smiling.

"Okay, here goes. It seems ever since Rome and Amber walked down the aisle and said their vows to each other, I have been thinking a lot about the subject of matrimony," Britain said in a soft romantic whisper while looking straight in her eyes.

Sabrina heart raced excitedly as she braced her back against the cushions of the sofa. It felt to Sabrina as if Britain was about to propose to her. It would be like a dream come true but she had not expected it at this time in their relationship. Therefore, she sat motionless listening to him, waiting to hear what he was about to say.

"Sabrina, you are too beautiful for words and looking at you sometime makes me lose my focus."

She smiled as their faces met and kissed each other. When they pulled away from each other, she asked, smiling. "Is that what you needed to tell me?"

"That's not what I needed to tell you. It's what I wanted to tell you. But has nothing to do with what we are about to discuss." He grabbed both of her hands and held them. "I hope you are not offended by this hypothetical discussion."

Sabrina became more and more anxious and unsure of what he was referring to. It made her somewhat apprehensive.

"Just start the discussion already," she said laughingly. "I'm starting to feel too anxious by what you could be referring to be."

"Don't be anxious. Just keep in mind that it's just a hypothetical question. So here it goes. What's your viewpoint on couples residing together before marriage?" he asked and paused as if he knew he had said something she didn't want to hear.

Sabrina narrowed her eyes at him and smiled. "Are you asking me this question for a particular reason?" she curiously asked.

He nodded and held up one finger. "It's just hypothetically speaking. I would like to know how you feel hypothetically about moving out of your home and into this one?" he asked.

Sabrina stared at him with stunned eyes. She was silent for a moment as she collected herself and took in what he had just asked her in a hypothetically manner. "Move in here?" She asked with great surprise in her voice.

He nodded. "Yes, that's what I said. But bear in mind, this is just a hypothetical discussion. So tell me, how would you feel about something like that?"

"You said it's just hypothetical, but you seem serious," she said, smiling.

"I'm only serious about knowing your thoughts, but not about the idea. I'm just teasing you a little to hear how you feel about the whole idea."

Sabrina grabbed her face with both hands. "I'm not sure how I feel since it's not something I expected you to ever ask me. I guess if I feel anything I feel hesitant about it. I'm not at all comfortable discussing it. Because although, you say it hypothetical and I believe you. I just don't feel comfortable on the topic because it makes me feel as if you are actually asking me to consider living under the same roof with you out of wedlock," Sabrina said sincerely. "So, there you have it. That's my viewpoint about couples living together out of wedlock. I'm against it," she said firmly.

He nodded. "Okay, Sweetheart, I just wondered about your viewpoint on the topic."

"But why would you care about my opinion on that topic if it's hypothetical and really doesn't involve us. Usually two people have this kind of discussion if they are considering such a step," she said with a disappointed voice.

Britain agreed. "You are right and I shouldn't have asked you that question sense I definitely doesn't want to give you the idea that I would expect that of you. However, I did want your views on the topic. And hypothetically speaking, I would love to have you here at Franklin house to see your beautiful face first thing in the morning and the last beautiful sight at night," he humbly stated.

Sabrina grabbed her face with both hands. "So, you really are serious."

He shook his head. "No, I'm not anticipating ever asking you to coexist with me out of wedlock. However, hypothetically speaking I'm serious about cohabitation with you. You know how I feel about you and I think you feel the same about me. So what's stopping us with imagining a fantasy world where we are coexisting together?" He leaned over and kissed her on the lips. "In my mind's eye I can see the two of us living under the same roof. Therefore, I have cohabitation on the brain right now."

"Maybe you do, but Britain, I think we need to change the subject because it makes me feel uneasy," Sabrina admitted.

"You're right, if it's making you uncomfortable then we need to table this discussion. "I was just throwing it out there as a hypothetical dream world where we could do whatever she wished," he said sincerely. "Frankly, I'm just climbing the walls needing to be near you and around you at all times." He touched the side of her face.

"I feel the same. I miss you like crazy when we're not together," she said.

"Plus, when outrageous things happen like that dangerous incident at work today when Jack Coleman tried to kidnap Sydney again, it just reminds us of how fragile life and time is. When really we don't know from one moment to the next what will occur. All we have is right now and this moment." He grabbed her right hand and held it between both of his hands. "I feel it was a million to one that you came into my life and that we met when we did. It was like fate was on our side to meet. I truly believe that you are my soulmate and that if somehow we didn't end up together, I would never feel exactly what I feel about you with anyone else. You are the female that I have always thought I would fall in love with. You and your essence was of course, almost like that impossible dream for me. I knew in my mind what you looked like because in my mind I had met you. Therefore, when I saw you standing there in those beautiful red shoes, I knew you were the one that I had always imagined in all my thoughts," he said lovingly. "You may not get what I'm trying to say because I may not be saying it in a way that is clear to you. Nevertheless, I get it, and what I'm really trying to say is that you are the one for me always."

Sabrina nodded and smiled. "Of course, I get it. That was a lovely thing to say. You just mirrored how I feel about you. It's great to be happy and in love and I just want to be with you all the time as much as possible."

"Not a fragment of the desire that I have for you," he smiled. "That's why hypothetical dream worlds are on my mind. However, hypothetical speaking, in this dream world that I have conjured up. If you are concerned about your father, and I'm sure you are, just as I'm concerned about my mother, we can arrange a time to sit down and talk to your father as well as Mother," he suggested, smiling.

"Britain, I thought we were going to drop this topic? I don't like this hypothetical discussion. It sounds too real, especially when you mention my father and your mother."

"I'm just having fun with you," he teased. "Can you imagine the look on their faces if we were to suggest such a turn of events?"

Sabrina grinned. "It's really not that funny, Sweetheart. However, Mr. Wonderful, I'm starting to wonder why we are having this hypothetical discussion?"

"It's something to change the mood. I don't know about you, but I'm drained from all the outrageous commotion and danger that took place at work today. Focusing on what took place today, just confirms how fragile life is. I guess, in a way I just wanted to discuss something that would take our minds off of the horrific events of today," he smiled.

She nodded and touched his shoulder in a playful way. "You picked the right topic to take my mind off of the events of today, because now I'm wondering about the events of tonight and why we are having this discussion."

He put one finger against her lips. "It's just hypothetical, Sweetheart," Britain said sincerely as he caressed the top of her right hand. "You know, Jack Coleman was a troubled man with deep mental issues and he tormented Sydney, not once but twice. He definitely needed professional help. He was alive earlier today to wreak havoc on our lives, but within a matter of a few hours later, his life ended at his own hands," he said compassionately. "All of that was just too horrific to focus on. Therefore, I wanted to discuss something out of the ordinary to saturate our attention."

She shook her head, looking in his eyes smiling. "I can understand why you wanted to bring up such a topic to overshadow the chaos and sadness of the day, but I just don't want to saturate my thoughts with something that's never goes to apply to you and me. So, let's talk about something else other than couples living together out of wedlock," she said firmly. "I realize that we are dealing with a lot of emotions right now. It was just awful what your family dealt with today. I wouldn't have been surprised if you had called and cancelled our evening. But here you are strong and loving as ever," she softly uttered.

"It wasn't so strong and loving of me to come up with an off base hypothetical topic that you don't approve of," he said.

"That's okay, it's allowed for a Franklin brother to say something off base at least once a year. You and your brothers don't have to be perfect all the time. You are allowed to be flawed like the rest of us every once in a while," Sabrina said, jokingly.

He gave her a long stare. "Are you being funny, Miss Taylor? If you are, you are mighty cute when you're funny. But seriously, you know I was teasing you and just having fun with the subject." He grabbed her face in his hands for a moment, released her cheeks and then leaned in and kissed her on the lips, smiling as he pulled away.

They were both silent until he touched her knee. "Sabrina, your father seems to like me quite well. Don't you think?"

"Yes, Father does like you. You didn't think differently did you?"

"I thought he just might. We have a good rapport."

"Father actually likes you very much."

"Very much," he said, smiling. "I was pleased to hear he liked me. To be liked very much by Mr. Charles Taylor is a bonus," he seriously stated.

Sabrina nodded. "Yes, it is a bonus. However, Sweetheart." She hit his shoulder in a playful way. "I don't think he'll be so fond of you if you mention that hypothetical topic we were just discussing." She smiled.

Britain smiled. "I'm sure he wouldn't. But that discussion is over and dead in the water," Britain assured her. "However, I think you're irritated with me for bringing it up?"

Sabrina didn't answer him. She went on talking about her father. "I was just telling you how Father thinks and wouldn't go for that subject in any manner, hypothetical or not. Besides, this shouldn't come to you as a surprise about how my father feels about two people living together out of wedlock."

"It doesn't come as a surprise," Britain agreed.

"I guess because you already know that my father is quite old fashioned and doesn't believe in couples coexisting together out of wedlock," she explained. "He feels two people who lives with each other before marriage isn't doing the honorable thing. It's the way he was raised and the way he thinks."

Britain looked at her and smiled. "Yes, I know this already, beautiful girl." He held out both hands. "Why are we still on this subject that you don't want to talk about?"

Sabrina wasn't letting it go since the subject matter had made her more uneasy than she thought. She ignored his question and continued talking. "Besides, you have pointed out that your mother feels the same way as my father."

Britain nodded. "Yes, Mother does feel the same way." He held up both hands. "And I understand your father's stance. My father felt the same," he quickly said, looking in her eyes and then gave her a quick kiss. "In case you didn't know this and would like to have my viewpoint on the topic, I mirror those traditional thoughts just as your father and my father and my mother. I don't believe in coexisting with a woman if she's not my wife."

"Okay, why did you bring it up?" she asked.

"I thought I explained why." He kissed her again. "Beautiful girl, I think we should just let it go," he suggested.

Hypothetical or not, Sabrina wasn't pleased with the subject of cohabitation in any other manner other than marriage. Britain could sense that she wasn't comfortable that it had been discussed.

"Please excuse me for a moment as I head to the bathroom," she said.

"Sure, you can use the one to the left outside of this entranceway." He pointed toward the left of the hallway. His heart became heavy knowing she had excused herself to digest their conversation.

Chapter Thirteen

Sabrina had a smile on her face as she headed out of the guest bathroom down the hallway back to the living room. She entered the living room and headed across the floor toward Britain. Smiling as well, he kept his eyes on her as she dropped down to the living room floor beside him. He felt rather disappointed with himself in regards to their previous subject matter that he had been so carefree and bold to discuss and tease about something that really didn't set well with her.

During her short time in the bathroom he reflected on how uncomfortable he had made her, which made him want to turn back the hands of time and delete their previous conversation. Therefore, he softly touched the top of her hand. "I know why you rushed off to the bathroom. You wanted to get away from our discussion." He nodded. "I don't blame you. You were right to be offended," he said caringly. "I wasn't really being considerate and thoughtful of your feelings. You asked me to drop the discussion and I should have dropped it the moment you asked."

She touched the side of his face. "It's okay," she mumbled.

"It's not okay since I can see that I have genuinely made you feel uneasy. I can sense that it bothered you more than just a little." He grabbed the back of his neck.

"Britain, I said its okay. I know you were just teasing me. It's not your fault if I took a hypothetical story personal, thinking you wanted to live with me but not marry me."

"Yes, I was teasing and I hope you can excuse my lapse in judgement for making that topic a part of our discussion," he humbly said. "While you were in the restroom it dawned on me how inappropriate it was to discuss with you. Granted, it was hypothetical and to tease you a bit; and to overshadow the dreadful event of the day," he explained.

"It's okay, but it did make me feel uneasy and a little offended. But I'm okay now."

"Look, Sabrina," he warmly uttered. "You have a right to feel uneasy and offended," he acknowledged. "I should have been more sensitive."

"Really, it's okay. We can move on past this and finish enjoying our evening."

"Sweetheart, I know you say you're okay, but I can see it in your eyes that you are disappointed. I beg your pardon and would appreciate it very much if you would just erase it all right out of your mind. I shouldn't have teased around about such a serious life changing event," he said, gazing into her eyes. "My beautiful Sabrina, it does drive me crazy when you are not with me and I guess I lost my head in a fantasy, caught up in my feelings and the events of the day," he said as he gave her a tender kiss on the lips.

"Britain, I feel the same and I'm only completely happy when we're together." She held her chest with both hands. "Plus, I know you already know that I'm traditional all the way. Father and Mother raised us that way. Besides, I know you were raised the same."

Britain smiled. "You are absolutely correct," he looked at her with apologetic eyes.

She slapped his knee in a playful manner. "We're good if you promise me no more hypothetical stories," she teased. "I love you more than anything."

He smiled and removed a long curl that had fallen over her left eye. "I love you even more than that," he softly whispered. "Seeing my brother walk down the aisle with the woman of his dreams opened my eyes to reflect on just how important and how blessed we are to meet that special someone that we want to spend the rest of our lives with." He leaned in and kissed her as she laid her head back on the arm of the sofa. He kissed her passionately for nearly five minutes. When their kiss ended and they both sat up the sofa. They glanced about the large room. He looked at her and smiled. "We need to behave ourselves or head to the library, den or family room," he whispered.

They both nodded in each other's eyes and then he said. "I'll watch myself." Then he reached out and held her face with both hands and smiled. "But the way you make me feel makes me lose my head sometime," he softly whispered. "You live inside of me so deep until I know you will live there forever. I'm so deep into you, Miss Sabrina Taylor. When we were a part, nothing around me felt right. I was dreadfully miserable."

"I was miserable too. More miserable than I have ever known in my life. It was a double whammy for me, since I was miserable for you and my mother."

He nodded. "I have empathy for how you felt. My work was my medicine. I was sort of just going through the motions of my daily life and routines without any enthusiasm," he warmly admitted. "That's exactly what I did during those days and weeks that we were a part. Nothing felt right or good in my life until we were back together."

Britain smiled at her. "Sitting here talking about who missed whom the most during our breakup, we are working up an appetite." He glanced at his diamond Rolex watch. "That is about right. We had dinner at seven and its half pass nine. But we're in luck, Natalie told me before she left that she left a tray of cheese and fruit in the refrigerator for us if we wanted a snack later. She prepared the tray after she overheard me mention to Mother that you and I would be spending the evening here. So what do you think, do you have any room for fruit and cheese before I head to the kitchen to retrieve it," he asked her.

Sabrina nodded. "Fruit and cheese sounds ideal. The popcorn and milkshake wasn't to my liking. Plus, it seems I'm always hungry soon after enjoying a nice Chinese meal."

He agreed. "It's funny how it works that way with my stomach as well. I enjoy most Chinese dishes, but they do not keep me filled for long, especially the fried rice dishes."

"I have to compliment your cook. The food tasted as if it was being served in some exclusive Chinese restaurant," Sabrina told him. "I thought it was catered in until you shared that your cook prepared the dinner.

"Natalie has worked for us as long as I can remember. She makes all the meals from scratch. Sometimes, depending on the menu, I prefer to dine in than out. Natalie meals are just that delicious. That's one of the reasons my family always have dinner together."

"I can understand why," Sabrina smiled. "She's an amazing cook."

Britain nodded smiling. "Yes, Natalie is an amazing cook. But you are just amazing."

"You are also amazing," Sabrina smiled and tapped his shoulder in a playful manner. "I'm in awe of just the thought of you and being with you."

He touched his chest with his right hand and held his hand there. "My feelings mirror yours! It's a powerful incredible connection that we share. You also live right here." He padded his chest. "It blows me away how I fell for you." He nodded with a distant look in his eyes. "Probably because you're actually the first woman I have felt this way about," he said with conviction. "Sitting here with you like this, being alone with you and actually doing nothing but just hanging out together is enough for me. It fills me up."

Britain spoke seriously from his heart. Sabrina sat there looking at him with a permanent smile on her face as she took her right hand and softly caressed the top of his left hand that rested on the sofa beside him.

"Nothing comes close to making me happier than how I feel when we're together." He looked in her eyes and softly whispered. "Miss Sabrina Taylor, I have fallen deeply in love with you and I want to spend the rest of my life with you," he whispered lovingly.

Sabrina slightly shifted in her seat as her heart raced excitedly, since all during their relationship; he had never confessed that he loved her. "Britain," she softly uttered, looking in his eyes as she touched his face. "Did you just propose to me?"

He stared warmly in her eyes and after a bit of silence of looking at each other, he nodded and smiled at her. "I guess I did just propose to you. Therefore, I might as well make it official and ask you properly." He took both of her hands and held them in his. "Miss Sabrina Taylor, will you marry me?"

Chapter Fourteen

Sabrina sat in awe and speechless for a few minutes as Britain sat beside her holding both of her hands and looking into her eyes. But she couldn't speak or move. Suddenly in her mind it seemed that time had stood still. The whole room went quiet and the only sound noticeable was the tick tock of the old grandfather clock in the corner of the living room. Sabrina heart pounded in her chest with excitement and Britain swallowed hard at the realization of what had just occurred. Then he reached out and touched the side of her face. "Are you going to give me an answer?" he softly whispered. "I know this is a surprise to you, and it's a surprise to me. It wasn't planned, but I couldn't mean it more if we were in a room filled with roses and champagne. I have fallen deeply in love with you, Miss Sabrina Taylor, and I want you to be my wife. So, do I get a yes?"

Sabrina kept staring in Britain's face as she took both hands and held her smiling face. "Britain, I can't believe this is happening. Did you really just ask me to marry you?"

He nodded. "Yes, I want you to be my wife," he said lovingly.

"Of course, you get a yes! One hundred times yes! I'll marry you," she said excitedly, wiping a tear from her left eye. "I'm so in love with you," she said joyfully. "Who knew this evening would bring us so much happiness? You started out teasing me and going on and on about cohabitation out of wedlock to lead up to this beautiful moment where you ask me to marry you! I can't believe we are engaged. Just a month and a half ago at Amber and Rome's wedding; I sat next to you and dared to hope that we would someday walk down the aisle together as they had. On that evening, we were seated next to each other but we barely said two words between each other."

"That is true, but that was then and this is now. And although, we felt so far apart at Rome's wedding. We couldn't feel closer to each other if we were one body," Britain said, smiling as he stood up from the sofa and headed for the kitchen.

"Stay right where you are." He glanced over his shoulder. "I'm headed to get that tray of cheese and fruit."

She nodded, smiling, sitting on the sofa in awe of their engagement. Five minutes later, Britain returned with the cheese and fruit. He placed the tray on the coffee table. And before he could be seated, she smiled at him. "I think we'll need a couple plates, a couple napkins and some silverware."

He looked at her and smiled. "Of course, we will and it's coming right up." He turned right around on the heels of his shiny black Givenchy Maximiliano Tuxedo shoes and headed across the large room toward the hallway and to the entrance to the kitchen.

Shortly he returned with plates, napkins and silverware that he placed on the coffee table. She stood from the sofa and proceeded to help him place fruit and cheese on their plates. Then they couldn't stop smiling, with plates in hand and nibbling on the fruit and cheese, Britain placed a single grape into Sabrina's mouth."

"Now, that we are engaged, what do you have in mind for a wedding date? I thought it was romantic how Rome and Amber chose Valentine Day. That's the most romantic wedding date on the calendar as far as I'm concern. Therefore, we cannot top that."

"I was thinking about Independence Day, July 4th. The day of our dependence with each other to live in love and harmony for the rest of our lives," she said excitedly, smiling.

"Okay," he agreed.

"Let's see what day the fourth fall on. He grabbed his phone from the end table and clicked to the calendar. "It falls on a Friday. That's perfect, don't you think?"

"Yes, it's perfect. So now when we announce our engagement on Sunday, we can also announce our wedding date," she said excitedly. "I'll tie the colors red, white and blue into the wedding somehow. It will be fabulous and just the way we want it."

"Be ready for Mother to take the lead of our wedding plans."

She looked at Britain awhile without commenting. She wasn't upset, but surprised.

"Are you okay with that?" he asked.

"How do you feel about your mother taking an active role in our wedding and basically taking it over?" she asked.

"It's our wedding and I want what will make you happy," he assured her. "Although, I say this because Mother was very let down that she didn't have more input toward Rome's wedding. She was crushed about that. Therefore, I already know she's going to want to take an active role and basically take control of ours," Britain said seriously.

Sabrina smiled and slapped his knee in a playful manner. "I get it. She has four sons and want to be a part of their wedding plans since she doesn't have a daughter to automatically plan a wedding for," Sabrina explained. "I'm okay with the input your mother might have. Besides, your mother has excellent taste."

"Sabrina, you need to realize that it won't just be input from Mother. She will want to take complete control from the guest list to the menu, right down to the flowers and music. She will want to own the wedding," Britain seriously explained, and then placed his plate on the coffee table and popped a grape in his mouth. "I'm okay with it just to please and make Mother happy. However, it's your wedding too, and my main priority is making you happy. I won't allow her to take control if her doing so bothers you."

"Your mother and I can compromise. I'll let her be in charge of the guest list and the menu and the location of the wedding and reception. But I would prefer for you and I to be in charge of everything else. Do you think that will please your mother?""

Britain shook his head. "It's sad to say but Mother actual cried when she couldn't be in charge of Rome's wedding."

"Your mother actually cried?"

"Yes, she did. I doubt if she'll admit it, but we all know she cried over that and if possible, I would like to accommodate her and allow her the opportunity to be in charge of my wedding. However, at the same time I realize you have the final say."

"So, if I understand you correctly, your mother will take control of our wedding plans, and I'll have minimum input except for my wedding gown and the attendants' gifts."

He nodded seriously. "That is correct, she'll of course ask for your choice of flowers and colors and then she'll run with it. She'll be ecstatic with enthusiasm."

"Let me think about it. I want to make your mother happy and based on what you have relayed to me, having a major part in handling our wedding will make her very happy. Plus, it's also important to you that she takes on the task. But, it is my wedding and I have visualized in my mind the way I would like for my special day to be," Sabrina softly said.

Britain took a small cube of Swiss cheese from the tray and put it into his mouth then he lifted his wine glass from the coffee table and took a sip.

"I understand how you feel completely and as much as I want to present this task to Mother, I will only do so if you are completely on board with the idea." He sipped his wine. "You are my bride to be and your happiness toward your wedding comes first."

Sabrina was quiet, as he lifted her wine glass from the coffee table and passed it to her. She took the glass and slowly lifted it to her lips and took a sip, in deep thought.

"Sweetheart, snap out of it. There's no rush on deciding about whether you're going to allow Mother to handle our wedding plans," he whispered softly against her neck and then looked at her and nodded as he leaned in and gave her a tender kiss on the lips.

She smiled. "I know there's no rush but it's going to be sort of a difficult decision for me to make. Besides, I want to make my decision before the dinner party on Sunday. This way, we'll be able to inform your mother after our announcement," she said and became quiet. Britain noticed that she wasn't talking.

"What's the matter? You're too quiet all of a sudden. Are you still thinking about the possible issue of Mother wanting to control our wedding?"

She nodded and mumbled regretfully. "I thought about it and I want to accommodate your mother, but my heart is not in it," Sabrina sadly uttered. "I hope I don't sound too selfish but I have always dreamed of my wedding and how I would like everything to be. If your mother takes full control, I wouldn't be comfortable or pleased giving her complete control over my wedding."

Britain nodded. "That's fine with me. Whatever you want is what you'll have," Britain assured her and touched the side of her neck in a lingering caress.

Her eyes filled with water as she reflected on their time a part.

"Are those tears in your eyes?" Britain noticed.

She looked at him solemnly but didn't comment as she wiped tears from her eyes.

"Sweetheart, are you that bothered over the conversation we had about my mother and her control issues regarding our wedding?"

She smiled and shook her head. "No, I'm not thinking of that right now. I was just sitting here reflecting and thinking about how close we came to losing each other," she took a deep breath. "All that time we lost and all the misery I went through missing you, not knowing how to let you in when I was grieving for my mother." She looked at him with serious eyes. "It baffles me that I pushed you away like that?"

"Don't be so hard on yourself. You were going through something bigger than anything you have ever faced. There's no way under the sun you could have been prepared to lose your mother. The body and mind is never ready to accept the loss of a love one. It took a huge toll on you and you couldn't think of being with me since you were consumed with your grief of losing your mother," he stressed strongly. "Believe me, I get it."

"I know you are right. I was grieving for my mother, but when I think of how close I came to losing you it just rips at my heart. I'm just so grateful to God that I came to my senses and we found each other again." She touched her chest. "You live right here inside of my heart; and as much as I miss my mother, I can't imagine not having you in my life."

He smiled at her. "You won't have to imagine. You're going to be my wife."

Suddenly the large room seemed quiet again as they sat facing each other, lingering in their blissful time together. It wasn't a typical Friday night for them. Usually, they would go out to a nice dinner and then to a movie or a play. But after getting back together, Sabrina preferred to stay away from crowds and gathering because it still sort of reminded her of dining out and family gatherings with her mother. Therefore, they were spending a lot of time at her home or his; and this evening seemed perfect to the both of them as the dimmed lights and the low flicking flame in the fireplace added to their romantic ambiance.

He smiled, touching her face. "Mrs. Sabrina Franklin has a special ring to it."

She nodded and laughed. "I think it has a lovely ring to it."

"A lovely ring to it, indeed," he laughed. "But we both know that this wasn't planned." He grabbed the back of his neck with both hands and stared up at the tall ceiling. "I just proposed to you! We are engaged!" he looked at her and smiled. "How amazingly incredible this night has turned out to be, but I don't even have you a ring."

"I don't need a ring," Sabrina quickly said.

"Of course, you need a ring. It's not official without something on that finger to constitute that we are engaged." He touched her ring finger.

"What do you mean it's not official?" She laughed excitedly and hit his shoulder in a playful manner. "You can't take it back."

"I don't want to take it back. I want to make it official." He glanced about the room. "We need to find something to put on your finger until I can stop in Neiman Marcus or Bloomingdales and find the perfect ring for you."

"We are not superstitious are we?" Sabina smiled. "Who said an engagement isn't official without the ring being on the lady's finger?"

"I don't know who said it, but I'm sure it's written somewhere," he said, laughing blissfully content and happy inside. "Frankly, it doesn't matter who said it, I just would feel more like a gentleman if I had placed a ring on your finger when I asked you to be my wife."

"I know, sweetheart, because of your flawless impeccable manners. However, I have a news flash for you," Sabrina said jokingly.

Britain narrowed his eyes, smiling. "What news flash is that, do tell?"

Sabrina held up her left hand and touched her ring finger with her right hand. "This finger will be just fine until you place the perfect ring on it, and I say perfect, because any ring from you will be perfect," she assured him. "Just as you said, this magical evening wasn't planned. It just happened and I'm blissfully happy with or without a ring."

"Okay, I know you want to shout it to the world, and when I say world, I mean your two sisters. However, we both need to let this be our little secret until tomorrow."

Sabrina stared at him and grinned and then threw both hands over her mouth. "You are asking me to keep our engagement a secret?" She shook her head. "I'm bursting to tell my family right now. I'm not sure if I can wait until tomorrow."

"Can you try, Sweetheart?" He smiled. "It would make me feel better to know I have planted that perfect ring on your beautiful finger before you tell our good news," he explained. "I'll go shopping early tomorrow and buy your ring. I have the perfect ring in mind that fits your unique beauty. Anyway, I would like for it to be on your finger when we announce our engagement," he suggested.

She stared at him and could understand his request. Yet, she knew how anxious she was to share her news the moment she stepped into the Taylor mansion.

"Listen, Sweetheart. I know you want to run home and tell your sisters; and they may think nothing of the fact that your ring will come a day later. However, I don't want to risk the chance of you going home and sharing our engagement with Samantha and Starlet and have them think I'm not much of a gentleman or a romantic to ask for your hand in marriage without shopping for a ring first," Britain said seriously.

Sabrina touched his face. "I know you take this seriously, but I don't think my sisters will care about where's the ring. They'll just be over the moon excited for us! This is wonderful and definitely no negative reflection on you as the perfect gentleman that you are. Although, most guys who plan to propose already have the ring, but your proposal wasn't planned. It just happened out of the blue to make me the happiest I can ever recall being in my entire life," she warmly expressed. "I never knew I could feel this complete and happy inside." She grabbed her cheeks with both hands. "I'm ecstatically over the moon happy and I want to shout it the world. But listen, no worries, okay. I understand how you feel and what it means to you as the perfect gentleman that you are to do things a certain proper way. Therefore, it will be hard to keep my mouth glued about this wonderful news until the ring is on my finger. But I promise you, I won't mention a word to anyone until that perfect ring you have promised, is right here." She tapped her ring finger.

He smiled and nodded. "That's great. But I promise you my Princess. You will not have to wait that long. I will be at Neiman Marcus the hour they open their doors tomorrow morning." He leaned in and kissed her on the lips. "So, how do you feel about making our engagement announcement here at Franklin House at a Sunday evening dinner party?" Britain suggested. "We'll keep it as a surprise by telling Mother and the others that the dinner party is for a special occasion that we will disclosed at the party." He glanced over at the flicking low flames and smiled, and then looked at Sabrina. "Of course, they'll probably put two and two together and figure out our secret before we make the announcement, especially Mother, but the dinner party will still be enjoyable."

Sabrina nodded. "You can bet they'll put two and two together, especially Samantha and Starlet. If I mention to them that the dinner party is for a special occasion in our honor, they will figure it out," Sabrina said. "Therefore, I won't mention that part; I'll just tell them and Father that we are invited to a dinner party at Franklin House."

"Therefore, Sunday, March 30th you and I will announce to our family that we plan to be married on Friday, July 4, 2014 and spend the rest of our lives with each other in marital bliss," Britain said, smiling.

"The rest of our lives together sound heavenly," Sabrina said excitedly. "I know I want you in my life for the rest of it. I knew that the first night I met you. When you walked over to me and asked me to dance, I thought I was dreaming and I prayed I wouldn't wake up. To me on that night, you were the most gorgeous man alive and you were asking me for a dance. Dancing with you and spending that time with you made me happier than I could ever remember. I went to bed that night pleased and content that I had spent that special time with you. I dared to think that we would actually get together and start dating. But it happened and now here we are engaged. When something like this happens that brings so much joy and light into our lives, we forget about the possible darkness that can rain on any parade," she softly uttered. "I was so hurt when all the darkness surrounded us during the time I lost my mother. Now, with all this joyful light pouring in on us, I feel that everything will be coming up roses for you and me from here on in," she excitedly predicted.

"I mirror your thoughts and your affection. Becoming engaged to you, the woman of my dreams is so incredible until it's unreal. It's almost as if we have stepped into another dimension of everyday life. A dimension that feels perfect." He touched her face. "I knew you were the one when I first looked in your eyes. But I wasn't sure if you and I would make it to this point. It was what I wanted. But I must be honest, and say at times I had my doubts that we would get past all the roadblocks, mainly the sadness you went through losing your mother. But we made it through the darkness into the light and here we are."

"Britain Franklin, you have no idea just how honored I am to be the one that you have chosen to be your wife," she said beaming with blissfulness. "You couldn't be more right about the feeling of being in another dimension surrounded by love. It feels like a dream that I do not want to awaken from." She looked lovingly at him, feeling anxious and excited. Then slowly tears dripped from her eyes from the thought of becoming his wife. "I love you, Britain. I love you so much and I feel so blessed to have found you."

"I'm the one who's blessed," he whispered and stood from the sofa.

He stepped across the room to the fireplace, grabbed the fire poker and poked into the hot ashes of the low burning flame. He stirred the fire and it burnt at a higher pace.

"Britain, thanks for that sentiment. But I'm the one who feels blessed to have you in my life," she said, watching him walk back toward the sofa to be seated beside her.

He kissed the side of her face as he took his seat. "You won't convince me that you're more blessed than I am. So we might as well change the subject." Britain said, jokingly.

"No, listen to me," she softly uttered. "I feel especially blessed since I'm the one who could have destroyed our future together. I came so close to messing up the best thing that has ever happened to me." She took both hands and touched her chest. "Your love is my blessing and I get cold chills every time I think about how I lost my head and pushed you aside for all that time." She kissed the side of his face. "Nobody would think I'm exaggerating when I say you are super smart and exceptionally handsome. You completely have your act together with impeccable manners that are completely above reproach; and besides all that, you could have any woman of your choice," Sabrina said with conviction.

"Okay." He nodded, smiling. "I could say the same about you, Sweetheart. You are very smart and exceptionally beautiful and definitely have your act together." He held up one finger and smiled. "As great as all that is, it's even better that you are, Miss Sabrina Taylor, my choice," he said warmly, looking in her eyes.

"I'm your choice?" Sabrina asked.

"Yes you are," he whispered warmly. "You just said I could have any woman of my choice, did you not?" he teased.

"Yes, I sure said that," Sabrina said, smiling.

"I'm just relaying that you are that choice," he said, smiling. "I would be crushed if I couldn't have you."

"No worries there." Sabrina smiled. "You have me for sure. I'm going to soon be Mrs. Britain Franklin."

"I like the sound of that name," Britain said as he reflected back on their first meeting again. "It was nothing but fate when I walked into your home at the end of August last year for that house warming party your family was throwing. It was fate because I had planned not to attend. I had other plans for the evening. However, Mother made it clear that any other engagement we had needed to be cancelled. She wasn't about to take no for an answer. She was dead set on all of us attending your party as a family. Therefore, we dropped everything to come to your house that night to accommodate Mother," he shared.

She nodded. "You're right. I believe it was fate that we were destined to meet on that night as well. You attended a party that you hadn't planned to attend and you didn't want to attend, but you only attended since you had no other choice in order to accommodate your Mother," she explained.

"I had no idea I would meet you and see you actually alive and walking." He smoothed his hand down her hair and caressed the side of her neck.

She smiled and narrowed her eyes at him for clarity of what he meant.

"You see, before I met you I saw you just as you are in a beautiful lighted image in my mind. Just like a designer sketch out a design of a perfect dress. My mind drafted out and designed the woman of my dreams. But to be honest, I never thought I would actually lay eyes on that unique stretch in my mind. Then there you were and at that moment that I laid eyes on you. I knew it was love at first sight. I knew you would end up being that one special lady that would steal my heart completely." He folded his lips and nodded. "You, Sabrina Taylor is the love of my life."

"Britain, now that we are engaged and about to become husband and wife. I want to share everything with you. I'm so overwhelmed with happiness right now until I can't really think straight. However, I just recalled how awful I felt that night we met."

"You felt awful that night?" he asked with surprise in his eyes. "You looked so perfectly beautiful that night. You didn't appear to feel bad," he said.

"When we met and were dancing and talking, I felt fine. I'm referring to the part of the evening before you and your family showed up. I had a splitting headache that wouldn't fade away. I had taken two aspirins and my mother had urged me to go up to my room and lie down, but it was an opportunity to dress up and I wanted to stick around to make an appearance. I felt it was important for our entire family to be present for the party," she shared. "Especially since it was a party to welcome us to the community. Therefore, I drank some ginger ale to settle my stomach and stuck it out with my discomforting headache. Then you and your brothers walked into the room and when I saw you, I was beautifully stunned until either my headache left or my anticipation and excitement over meeting you overshadowed it. By the time we were on the dance floor, I felt heavenly with no sign of a headache."

"Did it ever occur to you that maybe the two aspirins stopped your headache? And not the magical wonder of love at first sight," he said, jokingly. "I'm just kidding, of course. Since it was definitely love at first sight for me as well. When I spotted you and looked in your eyes, I knew you were it for me. I didn't even know anything about you, but

152

deep down I felt like I already knew you and that you would become the woman in my life. Afterall, you were that live sketch in my mind of my dream girl. Someway, somehow I was going to ask you out and make that happen." He got out of his seat and walked over to the wine bar in the corner of the room. He took the wine opener and popped the cork of one of the forty bottles of Romanée-Conti wine that lined the wine rack. He looked around and beckoned for Sabrina to come to the wine bar.

"I think this evening calls for a special celebration among ourselves, to celebrate our new status of being engaged." He reached above the wine counter and removed two wine glasses from the overhead shelf.

He handed Sabrina a glass and placed the other glass on the counter. Then he lifted the bottle of red wine and poured Sabrina's glass half full. She held her glass steady as he poured wine into his glass that sat on the counter. "Take a sip and tell me what you think. This bottle is one of only seven bottles from a 1990 vintage of Romanée-Conti wines."

Britain tapped the rim of his crystal glass against hers. "Here's to the beautiful life we will share together." He took a sip of wine and so did she.

They both nodded in agreement and took a sip from their wine glasses. "This wine is sweet and smooth. I like it," Sabrina said, smiling.

"It is good, but believe it or not, Mother told us that my father purchased ten of these bottles in 1991 for a ridiculous expensive price. Granted my family does stock fine wines on the pricey side." He held out the glass and looked at it. "But according to Mother and Aunt Catherine, the cost for this one bottle of wine was more than some people earn in a year."

"That's insanely costly. Maybe we shouldn't be drinking this one." She touched his arm and laughed. "I hope your mother doesn't mind we opened a bottle," Sabrina took another sip of wine.

Britain smiled at her and shook his head. "She doesn't mind, my father was a wine collector, not my mother. She doesn't care about those kinds of collectibles. Besides, there's about forty more bottles of Romanée-Conti wines left on the wine rack," Britain said and took a quick sip of wine, and then took her hand and led her back over to the sofa.

They both placed their glasses on the coffee table and then he looked down in her eyes and smiled at her as they stood in front of the sofa holding hands. "Here we are. You and I are engaged and nobody knows it but us. "Mother loves you and she's going to be almost as ecstatic as we both are," he said and wrapped her in his arms and kissed her passionately. Then they took their seats, still kissing as her head fell over on the arm of the sofa. "Having the house to ourselves tonight is like a God sent miracle," he said as their kiss ended and they sat up on the sofa and faced each other. He grabbed her hands in his. "As I mentioned, spotting you and meeting you at your house party was fate and like a miracle itself. Then you went through your depression after losing your mother and I was deeply worried that we wouldn't find our way back to each other. Then to my astonishing unexpected surprise Sydney walked into my office and announced that he had just hired you at the company. That piece of unexpected good news brought you back into my orbit and into my life. My approach had to be right and I didn't want to pressure or chase you. Therefore, when I managed to approach you and asked you out, I was beside myself with bliss that you accepted to go out with me to give us a second chance. The rest is history and now you have just accepted my proposal to be my wife."

"It's funny now, looking back," she said softly. "You actually had me worried for a few days after Sydney hired me."

"Why were you worried?" he asked.

She slapped his arm playfully. "I think you know what I mean. I was worried when you didn't ask me out right away. You still haven't told me what took you so long to do so?"

"I thought I had explained why. Are you sure I didn't tell you why?"

She shook her head. "No, you never told me why it took you so long to ask me out after Sydney hired me."

"For sure, I had intentions of asking you out all along. But Sweetheart, you have to put yourself in my shoes. I was so happy you were there nearby and I just didn't want to move too quickly. Remember, I told you that I didn't want to make you feel uncomfortable. But believe me; I had intentions of trying my luck at getting you back from your first day of employment at Franklin Gas. You were a sight for sore eyes and I had missed you terribly. I can even recall what you were wearing. It was a long sapphire skirt and navy blouse."

"Wow, you remember what I was wearing?"

"How could I forget? I had missed you beyond description. I kept my composure and did my work. But it was incredibly hard to get through each day without you being a part of my life. Seeing you at the company on the day that Sydney hired you were just like seeing you for the first time. I didn't want to stare, but that's what I did when I arrived at work and spotted you behind the counter. It threw me for a loop since I had no idea you even wanted to or had considered working for us," he softly explained. "Therefore, even though I saw you behind the counter I still wasn't sure you were working at the company until I reached my office and Sydney walked into my office and told me the good news. But as I said, it was hard not to stare at the beautiful woman that I had missed day and night."

"I know, because I didn't want to stare at you either," Sabrina admitted. "But when I looked up and saw you coming through the entrance door, I couldn't help myself. My eyes were glued to you and I had to force myself to tear my eyes away from you. It was very hard because you know what Mr. Franklin?" she said, teasingly. "You are definite the kind of man that makes people do a double-take. Therefore, when you stepped up to the counter and said hello, I couldn't wait on any customers because I was star struck staring at you until you finally stepped away from the counter," Sabrina explained.

"That's really cute coming from you," he said, smiling.

"But, Britain, you do make people do double-takes. Just look in the mirror."

"That should have been my line to you," he nodded, touching the side of her face. "Besides, I'm not convinced I would turn anybody's head," Britain said, jokingly.

"Maybe not anybody's, but you turned mine."

He nodded. "Point taken, since yours is the one that counts. But if anyone could hear us talking about turning heads, they would think we're a couple of smitten teenagers. But I'm serious." He touched her cheek. "You definitely turned my head like no other ever has. You didn't just turn my head you turned my entire life and made it more than I could have ever dreamed it could be just by you being a part of it," he whispered. "It's surreal how I was content and not actually looking to get into a serious relationship. Then out of the blue there you were at a party that I didn't want to attend," he admitted.

"Plus, I wasn't feeling well and had only planned to stay awhile and then head upstairs to room. But I spotted you and my world changed," Sabrina softly whispered.

He shook his head. "It was so unexpected but from the moment I spotted you there, I was blown away by you. It wasn't just your physical beauty. After all, you were standing there with your two exceptionally beautiful sisters. So, I want you to know, it was something more about you that attracted me to you. Something deep inside of you that my soul desires. The essence of you hit me like a gush of wind against my face." He reached out both arms and lifted their wine glasses from the coffee table, passed her a glass as they each took a sip of wine and continued to hold their glasses.

He kissed the side of her face. "You were standing there with your sisters, but it was almost as if they were invisible. All I could see were you. You smiled at me and the look in your eyes froze me for a moment," he warmly explained. "You were my dream sketch of that perfect woman that I thought would only live in my mind. Then it was like a bolt of lightning through me when it hit me that I was standing there looking right at someone that was the equivalency of the perfect vision in my mind," he seriously stated."

"When I looked at you and noticed you were looking at me, I smiled because I was tongue tied and didn't know what to say," Sabrina admitted. "I actually thought I had gone upstairs and taken that nap that my mother had suggested earlier. Standing there looking at you, it took a moment before it dawned on me that I wasn't dreaming," Sabrina recalled.

He smiled. "I guess for a moment we both thought we were dreaming, but it was no dream. I was wide awake standing there in awe of you. Mother taught me and my brothers when we were just boys that it was impolite to stare, but I'm sure I did more than a little of that when I spotted you. "He whispered, took their drinks and placed them on the coffee table as he pulled her in his arms, held her firmly, giving her a passionate lingering kiss.

Chapter Fifteen

Monday, the 31st of March, Vickie Simpson summoned her brother, Wally to meet her at the local Casual Cafe for lunch. The restaurant was within walking distant of her job, just one block from Franklin Gas. She had promised her brother that lunch would be her treat. He had agreed to meet her during his lunch hour from his school with the thought in the back of his mind that maybe their discussion would be about the new teaching job he had just hired her for.

"I see you came home late again last night," Vickie said the moment they were seated at their table. "Don't tell me you were hanging out at Courtney's again?" Vickie said seriously to her brother as they both got comfortable, pulling off their jackets at the table.

Wally stood up and removed his suit coat and hung it on his chair. "Okay, I won't tell you," he said, smiling as he looked across the table at her.

"You won't tell me what?" She asked, placing the napkin in her lap.

"You just said don't tell you if I were hanging out at Courtney's, so I was just doing what you asked," he said in a joking manner.

"Wally, don't kid around about that messed up female," Vickie stressed strongly. "I'm serious and that's why I asked you to lunch. You need to seriously consider just cutting all your ties with Courtney Ross."

"My goodness, Vickie, what's the urgency?" He smiled. "It's not like Courtney is going to be walking down the aisle with me anytime soon," he said in a joking manner.

"Of course, not, but you need to completely take her off your list. You are too much of a decent guy for that female."

"What's going on here? Why are you suddenly so against Courtney? Granted, Courtney and I can't seem to see eye to eye about connecting again, but that never bothered you before. What's going on?"

"It's all the talk at work." Vickie shook her head and pointed her thumb downward. "It's all bad and it's all about Courtney. I'm sorry to tell you."

"Don't be sorry, just tell me what's all the racket is about."

"It's about her fallout with the Franklins. Her two bosses, remember? She dated them both and it's a mess; and it's not them, it's her. She just doesn't know how to leave well enough alone. They gave her back her job and she's still causing problems."

The waiter stepped up to their table and handed them each a menu and then stepped away.

Wally leaned forward with his elbows on the table but before he said a word he glanced about the restaurant to see if he knew any of the customers that were dining at the small cozy restaurant. Plus, he wanted to make sure no one could hear their conversation.

"What kind of problems are she causing?" he asked with concernly.

"She's chasing up behind Britain and it's obvious that she's still trying to get her hooks in the guy. Everytime he comes downstairs to the service counter whenever she's at work, she tries to monopolize his time. If she keeps it up, they'll fire her again," Vickie said. "That's ashame if it happens since we both know how much her folks depend on her pay."

Wally nodded. "Yes, especially now since her mother doesn't have the support of their father, who's locked up and serving time for attempted murder." Wally shook his head. "What a tragedy surrounds her now."

"You're right, it's a tragedy going on with her parents and how her father went off the rails and almost killed her mother over some secret affair. But Wally, that's not her biggest problem!"

He nodded. "Okay, you got my attention. I'm listening."

"Her biggest problem is that Courtney is spinning out of control independently of what's going on with her folks."

"What do you mean about that?" he asked just as the waiter stepped back over to their table with a pad in his hand, ready to take their orders, but they both looked toward the tall, pencil thin, dark haired waiter and shook their heads, and then the waiter turned and headed toward another table.

Wally leaned in with both elbows on the table. He was somewhat shaken since Vickie seemed quite concerned about what was going on with Courtney. "So, tell me what do you mean about what you just said, her biggest problem is that she's spinning out of control independently of what's going on with her folks. I don't even know what that is supposed to mean."

"It's means what I just said and you need to get over her because she's not worth your time at this time," Vickie stressed strongly.

"Make me understand the point you are trying to make. I understand how you said she's acting up at work, and getting in Britain Franklin's face and trying to get his attention. You are afraid she'll get fired if she doesn't tone it down. But other than being a thorn in Britain's side, and although I'm not pleased to hear it, that doesn't sound like earthshaking news to cause me to write Courtney off and run for the hills from her," Wally explained.

"It's not just that. It's that and everything else. But mostly it's the change in her. She's just different and a pain to be around. You should hear how she talks to everybody at work now. She is just plain nasty and rude to everybody as if everybody is the reason why Rome break up with her, and Britain rejected her. I tell you, Wally, she's pathetic right now and I don't see her improving anytime soon. I know you have always had a thing for her, but she's not the same woman that you fell for back in college," Vickie seriously stressed.

Wally lifted his left eyebrow at his sister. "Don't you think you are coming down a bit hard on Courtney? You think I should stop purusing her because she's not good enough for me, when in the past you always thought that she felt I wasn't good enough for her."

"I know, that's the way I felt back in college. But this is a new day and Courtney Ross is a far stretch from the respectful, soft spoken young lady that she was back in college." Vickie raised both hands.

"She's a far cry from the person she was last summer. She changed for the worse after what happened with the Franklins."

"So, you think I should write Courtney off and just not pursue her anymore because you don't feel she's the right person for me?"

Vickie shook her head. "You have it wrong…"

Wally cut her off and continued talking. "You think I should just write Courtney off because you feel she isn't good enough for me. You know, Vickie, I could say the same to you about Kenny."

"You have it wrong, Wally. I don't think you should stop pursuing her because she's not good enough for you, I think you should stop pursuing her because the behavior and conduct that she has displaying at work has me greatly worried about her state of mind," Vickie stressed and then glanced about the restaurant to make sure nobody was listening. Then she leaned in toward her brother with both elbows on the table. "Personally I think she has suffered a mental breakdown."

"Come on, Vickie. You think that about, Courtney?"

"Yes, Wally, I do. Courtney Ross was always a soft spoken respectful young lady. But you should see her outrageous conduct at work. I tell you, she doesn't even resemble the person she used to be, if you ask me."

"Well, I have spent the past three nights visiting her at her home and she didn't seem as over the top as you are saying. She seemed a little different, but frankly, I didn't get much of a chance to talk to her over the past three nights that I visited. We were stuck in the living room with the rest of her family, watching a movie. I plan to see her again tonight and supposedly we will have the house to ourselves."

"Well, if that's the case, you'll get to see the new Courtney Ross for yourself. Besides, you know me. I'm honest and on the level and would never say these things about Courtney if they weren't true or if I didn't strongly think she signified a problem for you."

Wally nodded. "I know that, but you have always been a bit anti Courtney."

"Yes, in the past I was always upset about how you chased her and she never acted interested. That was my original beef with her, but now it's a whole new ballgame. I'm just plain worried about the direction she's headed and I don't want you mixed up with her."

"I appreciate your concern but I think I can handle myself with Courtney and whatever is going on with her."

"I hope so. I know you are a grown man and what you do is your business, but you have always had a soft spot for her and I just don't want that soft spot to blind you to be objective about her."

"It won't blind me. I appreciate your concern, but I'll handle Courtney just fine."

"Wally, I hope so. You are my brother and I love you and want the best for you. And right now, Courtney is not the best for you. I hesitated about telling you these things about her and about her behavior and conduct at work, but I decided to have lunch with you and bring this up since it appears you're getting closer to her."

He smiled and shook his head. "What makes you think Courtney and I are any closer than what we were, which is not that close at all in terms of a romantic link."

"I just assumed you two were getting closer, since you came home quite late three nights in a row. The first thing that came to my mind was that you were probably visiting Courtney on those nights. Besides, you just admitted it, therefore, I was right."

Wally stared at his sister with a surprise expression on his face. "Vickie, are you serious? You summoned me to lunch and offered to pay the tab so you could tell me to end my affiliation with Courtney?"

She nodded. "Yes, that's it exactly. I hope you don't feel that I'm out of line. It's just as I told you, the fact that I work with Courtney and see how she has changed." Vickie paused and shook her head. "Courtney is headed down the wrong road toward trouble."

Wally shook his head. "Vickie, I don't think you are out of line. I just think you are being overly protective of me where Courtney is concerned. Just let me worry about what's going on with Courtney. I'm a big boy. But I do appreciate your concerns. Besides, you are my sister and rent a room from me. You are not in my apartment to spy on me and worry about how many nights in a row that I stay out pass a certain time," he said in a joking like manner. "Besides, if I wanted to be technical about it, when it boils down, it's really none of your business what time I get home and who I'm hanging out with," he firmly stated.

"You're right, but it bothers me that you can't see through Courtney Ross. She has changed big time. I'm trying to tell you she's not the same, Wally," Vickie stressed strongly.

"We have all changed since college; therefore, who is the same?" He paid no attention to his sister's warning as he got out of his seat and headed toward the salad bar. "I'm heading to the salad bar for a salad. What about you?"

"That sounds good. I guess I'll have the same." Vickie got out of her seat and followed him toward the salad bar.

"I think it's kind of neat," she said as she placed lettuce on her salad dish. "I didn't know they had a salad bar in here."

Standing behind her with his six foot frame towering over her five four frame, he tapped her shoulder lightly so she could step aside from the lettuce bind. "The salad bar here is a new addition. I just found out about it the other day in the newspaper; and I also read something about it on the Internet."

The moment they left the salad bar and took their seats back at the table, Vickie started right in trying to discourage her brother from his feelings toward Courtney. "You need to wake up and see her for who she is now. Being with the Franklins changed her into some wacked out bitter headcase. If you could hear what people are saying about her at work it would give you cause to rethink how you feel about her."

"Well, we all know how straight-laced the Franklin brothers are, so if Rome, Britain, Paris nor Sydney hasn't seen a major reason to let her go, then maybe she's not as bad as everybody on your jobs is saying."

"I can't answer that. I don't know what the brothers know about her behavior and conduct at this point. I just know I'm surprised she hasn't gotten fired again already," Vickie uttered, frustrated that Wally didn't seem that alarmed by the things she was telling him about Courtney.

Wally glanced at his watch. "Could we please change the topic to something other than Courtney? I thought you wanted to meet me for lunch to discuss your new job I just hired you for. I expect you to start in two weeks. Did you give your notice at work yet?"

"No, I didn't give it yet, but I plan to give it as soon as I return to work from lunch."

"Okay, good. I'm glad to get you aboard. I need good dedicated teachers for my students and I'm sure you're be excellent. I was hoping to hire Courtney, but she doesn't seem to want to part ways with the service counter at Franklin Gas," Wally said confused.

"Wally, that's my point exactly. If Courtney was thinking straight, of course, she would accept a good paying teaching job over working at a service counter at Franklin Gas. I know I'm glad to finally get the kind of job that I went to college for. Plus, it was my understanding and the understanding of Franklin Gas that Courtney was just temporary until she landed a teaching job. Well, the word is out that she has turned down two teaching job offers just so she can stay at Franklin Gas."

"I didn't hear about that," Wally seemed upset to hear.

"Of course, Courtney wouldn't mention something like that to you and allow you to call her out on why."

"How did you find out?" he asked.

"The rumor at work is that another worker overheard her tell Britain that she had turned down two teaching job offers so she could stay at Franklin Gas to be near him. And the same employee who overheard that, also overheard Britain tell her that if she keep displaying that kind of conduct toward him that he would be forced to let her go."

Wally shook his head. "That's hard to believe that she turned down two teaching job just to stay at Franklin Gas."

"It's not hard for me to believe since I get to see how wacky she has become. I tell you, just as I told you before, she chases up behind Britain whenever he comes to the service counter or walks into the cafeteria," Vickie stressed. "So if you think I'm butting in or being too nosy regarding you and Courtney, and you want me to move out, I can."

"Did I say you needed to move out?"

"No, you didn't say it, but you seem annoyed by the things I'm telling you. But I'm just trying to open your eyes about her, that's why I said I would move out if you wanted me too," Vickie said respectfully as she picked a cucumber out of her salad and placed in her mouth. "Besides, with the decent teaching salary that you're be paying me, I'll be able to afford my own apartment."

The waiter walked over to their table with his pad. "I see you both are having the salad bar? Can I get you some beverages or breadsticks?"

Wally nodded toward the waiter. "Please, a Coke for her and a Pepsi for me. We would also like a basket of your breadsticks," Wally said.

The waiter took their orders and walked away from the table. Wally was busy eating his salad and didn't look toward Vickie to comment on her remark about being able to afford her own apartment from her teaching salary. But she didn't let up.

"I'm just one year older than you, but I still consider you to be my little brother. Therefore, no way will I keep my lips zipped when I see how you have no clue about how wacked out Courtney has become," she assured him.

Wally smiled across the table at his sister. "I'm sure you will not. However, you are right. I will be paying you a decent teaching salary, but you can stay at my apartment for as long as you like. Nevertheless, I really don't appreciate this discussion that we are having. Hearing you talk so negative about Courtney isn't helping my spirit or my appetite."

The waiter arrived at their table and placed a basket of breadsticks in the center of the table and then placed their beverages at their salad plate.

"I understand that nobody wants to hear pessimistic negative talk about someone they care about." She reached out and grabbed a breadstick, broke it in half and took a bite. "But Wally, it's not negative talk for the sake of trying to bash her. It's the truth and I just want to enlighten you so you can see her for who she has become. And as I mentioned before, that's why I asked you to lunch today. The fact that I asked you to lunch for this sole purpose of discussion makes this a very important topic to me. Negative or not, I needed to tell you the things that I have shared with you."

"Vickie, we live in the same apartment. I see you every morning for breakfast and every evening after work, so why was it so urgent for you to ask me to lunch during the middle of the day to tell me these things about Courtney? Why couldn't you have told me these things at home?" Wally wasn't pleased to air unenthusiastic talk about Courtney.

"Yes, you are correct. I could have told you these things at home, during breakfast or in the evening," she paused. "The truth is, I just couldn't bring myself to tell you. Besides, when you get in from work, you always look so stressed dealing with all those teachers and students. I didn't want to add to your stress," Vickie explained.

"But here at lunch, in the middle of my salad, in this crowded restaurant seemed like a good time to bring it up, is that correct?" Wally shook his head, halfway joking as he tried to push away some of the disappointment of hearing about Courtney.

"I know I told you weeks ago about her behavior, but it's even worse now. As I said before, It's obvious she has come unglued how she snaps and talks loud and rude to everybody at work. However, she's not rude to the customers and that's probably why Sydney hasn't fired her. She is so wacked out she doesn't know how to be thankful that she has a job, especially since they fired her once," Vickie reminded him.

"You're not alone in your concern about Courtney." He pointed to his forehead. "I have a few brains and I can see the difference in Courtney. It's not a big difference as you are pointing out, but it's a difference just the same. However, I was hoping it would fade, but you're right, she's just not completely herself anymore," Wally admitted.

"So you see why you need to cut Courtney loose. She's not who you fell for back in college. She's obsessed with Britain Franklin. I know it's easy to say, and you are tired of hearing me say it, but if you could just witness how everybody is pointing and talking about her behavior at work. It doesn't seem to matter to her that Britain is dating Sabrina Taylor. It doesn't stop her from making a fool out of herself trying to get his attention. She's in his face every chance she gets. He's too polite to tell her to get lost! But that's what you have to do. Open your eyes and tell that girl, so long! Good riddens!" Vickie encouraged.

Wally lifted his fork and forked a cherry tomato into his mouth. He nodded at his sister with sad eyes. "It won't be easy to walk away from her. You know I wanted a future with Courtney," he said.

Vickie nodded. "Yes, I know you wanted a future with her at one time, but that was then and this is now, and now she has gone off the deep end."

"Vickie, I just think you are making a little more out of it than it is," he said. "I have noticed a change in her but it doesn't seem as radical as you seem to think."

"How can you think I'm making too much out of it?" Vickie asked. "If you have spent anytime with her over the past couple months, and of course you have since you have spent the past three evenings at her house, you know she has changed in a big way for the worst!"

"I did spend the last three nights visiting Courtney, but she didn't seem extremely different. But then again, as I had mentioned, over the past three nights Courtney and I were limited to the time we got to spend alone with each other. We were not able to have any private conversations with each other. Just as I told you earlier, she was quiet and not that talkative since we were watching movies at her house each time."

"What about after the movie?" Vickie asked.

"When the movie ended on each night, I would leave her house immediately, in a good mood with the thought in the back of my mind that she and I were making progress."

"So, what about tonight? Since it's a week night, it's possible that the two of you could end up with an audience again?"

"That's true, but I'm hoping for a different setting. I'm hoping this evening that she and I will have a private evening together. Although, it's not like she has personally invited me over. I told her I would drop by after work and she said okay, mentioning that she would be home alone tonight. I'm looking forward to getting an opportunity to have a long conversation with her. Therefore, if Courtney has changed the way you insist that she has, I'll get my chance to find out this evening."

"Okay, I guess you will and then you'll see for yourself. Because it really doesn't matter how many times I tell you these things about Courtney, you are not going to really believe me until you find out for yourself." Vickie lifted her glass to her mouth and took a swallow of her beverage.

"Wally, you know I'm not the kind of person to bash or just talk about someone for casual talk. I'm trying to look out for your welfare just like you look out for me."

"How am I looking out for you?" he asked. "I certainly don't but into your personal affairs and tell you who and who not to date."

"You don't do that, but you are still looking out for me in other ways, like allowing me to stay at your apartment," she reminded him. "You are doing me a huge favor by allowing me to stay at your apartment at the faction of the cost of average rent. I appreciate that and I'm not about to mess it up by trying to push Courtney out of your life without a good reason. You're find out for yourself that my concerns are legitimate."

"I hope so, because without my generosity you would still be living in Aunt Minnie's house enduring her ridiculous strict house rules. But you asked to move in with me until you landed a teaching job and I was more than pleased to say yes to give you a break from Aunt Minnie," Wally reminded her.

Vickie nodded. "Yes, I know and I appreciated having a wonderful brother like you. And I'm not trying to push Courtney out of your life just for the sake of not liking her. I know it sounded that way in the past, but it's not about that. I just see her headed down the wrong track and don't want her to pull you down with her. Besides, as I told you, I liked and respected Courtney during college and thought she had a good head on her shoulders and would make you a good wife." Vickie waved her hand. "But no way would I say that now; but Wally, you need to think for a moment, because even if she hadn't changed into this rude, bitter person, Courtney was never really interested in you and make no secret of letting you know."

Wally forked salad into his mouth and nodded. "I have to admit, she was never that warm to me."

"Maybe she wasn't that warm to you, but at least back then she was worth wanting." Vickie took a sip of water. "That's why it shouldn't be so hard to tell her so long. She has lost it, and she's nothing like the person she was before she got Franklin on her brains."

"As I said, I plan to drop by and see her after work," Wally mumbled.

"To break things off with her?" Vickie asked.

"To break what off?" he asked. "How can I break off something that never was? Courtney and I are just friends. Of course, I wanted more than friendship but she never wanted more than that with me. For a time in college, it seemed like it would be more, but our college relationship never really got off the ground good before it was over. And since college and the new principal job, I have pursued her to no avail. But mostly when I was in pursue of her, she was dating a Franklin; and since she has been available we just haven't been able to connect and spend any real private time together," he explained.

Vickie shook her head. "I'm glad you are going to have a talk with her because you'll see where her head is, and you'll know that with her issues, it's not going to work."

Wally nodded. "Okay, that's your theory, but I just hope to have a private conversation with her and see where her head is for myself; and then we can go from there. The problem has been visiting in front of her entire family for the past few evenings that I have dropped over."

"I know, you said each time you visited she wanted to watch movies on their big screen in their living room. She wouldn't spare any private time to talk with you?"

Wally nodded. "That's exactly the way it was."

Vickie smiled and shook her head, holding her Coke glass with both hands as she pulled through the straw. "That should tell you where her head is. You're visiting her but she can't spare a moment to talk to you in privacy." Vickie glanced at her watch. "I have five minutes and then I need to tear out of here and get back to work. "I know you probably still have feelings for her. But seriously, Wally, please think about making yourself scarce from that messed up female. You are a respectful principal and have your reputation to uphold. You don't need to be seen with that wacko," Vickie stressed.

Wally nodded. "It's a pity, and as much as I want to wish it away, I have to agree with you that she does seem somewhat different. I haven't spent a lot of time with her lately, but the little time that we have spent together, she's always uptight and on edge and ready to bite my head off."

"Join the club," Vickie said. "That's how she is around everybody now."

"Have Kenny said anything to you about how Courtney has changed?" Wally asked.

"No, not a thing. But what do you expect? It's his sister and he's not going to say anything negative about her to me. Although, I'm sure he has noticed her conduct and how unbalanced and far-out she

168

behaviors at times. She probably bites off his head and everybody in her household a lot more than she does around others."

"You could be right, but I'm not ready to walk away from Courtney. I'll see her this evening and hopefully the two of us can finally have a private talk. Getting her to agree to go out with me to dinner or a movie, is like pulling teeth. She's never available, so she says."

"Wally, why can't you take a hint or get a clue? She won't go out with you because she has Britain Franklin on her brains; and besides from that she's doing you a favor. You need to cut ties with her. You are known to your co-workers, your family and friends as a smart, leveled headed truthful person; therefore, it's necessary that you part ways with that girl. Besides, your involvement with her has only caused you heartaches and made you question your own integrity when you were tempted to grant one of her selfish wishes against the Franklins."

"I was never going to call Britain and tell him that lie," Wally assured her.

"But she asked you to and you considered it."

"I didn't consider it. I told Courtney I would think about it."

"That's the same thing as considering something."

"Well, you have my word that I was never tempted to call Britain Franklin and tell him he had made a mistake by choosing Sabrina over her. I don't know the man, I just know of him, and it's not in my nature to do something so over the top to please someone who, from the way you are describing her, is clearly over the top," Wally stressed.

"You're right, Courtney is over the top. She's so unstable she's almost deranged."

"I wouldn't go that far." Wally shook his head. "She's not deranged."

"She may not be deranged yet, but she has come unhinged and obviously disturbed and unbalanced to the point that her family should be worried. Because based on the way she talks and carry on at work, I'm sure it can't be much of a difference in her conduct and behavior at home," Vickie said seriously.

"It is so hard to believe that she has displayed herself and changed in the manner that you are saying; but yet I know you're a person of integrity and wouldn't lie about her."

"Of course not, I wouldn't lie. I'm just thinking of you and want you to stay clear of the problems she can cause you."

Wally paused and stared seriously into his sister's dark brown eyes for a moment and then he said, "What happened to Courtney? Just last year, she was so beautiful and smart with a bright future ahead of her?"

"The Franklins happened to her. Her spinning out of control hatred and bitterness for the world, stems from the fallout with the Franklin guys. It mostly boils down to the fact that Britain rejected her for Sabrina Taylor." Vickie glanced at her watch again, hopped out of her seat and grabbed her shoulder bag as Wally stood up from the table and pulled out his wallet, removing a twenty dollar bill that he placed next to their meal ticket.

Wally placed his wallet back into his back pocket and then they both headed out of the restaurant together. They walked quickly toward the the restaurant's parking lot, and when Wally grabbed the doorhandle of his car, Vickie patted his shoulder.

"Think about what I have said," Vickie said seriously, looking in her brother's eyes. "You don't need to get pulled into Courtney's vendetta against Sabrina Taylor and her irrational idiotic thoughts of thinking she can win back Britain Franklin," Vickie said as she rushed away from her brother and headed across the street toward her job.

She left Wally standing next to his car in the Casual Cafe parking lot. He looked at her as she crossed the street and headed up the block toward the Franklin Gas building.

Chapter Sixteen

It had just begun to rain as Vickie stepped through the revolving doors, arriving back at work. Her mind was focused on her appointment at hand when she walked through the door. She headed straight toward the elevator. In passing, she glanced toward the service counter, smiled and waved toward Courtney and Trina who were both behind the counter. Trina smiled and waved back at Vickie, but Courtney frowned and stared at Vickie, and then held out her arm and touched her watch, making a gesture with her mouth, silently telling Vickie that she had arrived from lunch late. Feeling tense in regards to Courtney from her conversation with her brother during lunch, Vickie hesitated slightly but did not stop and made no gesture or comment to Courtney as she strolled past the service counter and continued walking toward the elevator. After Vickie stepped on the elevator and punched the button to the fourth floor to the business offices, she glanced at her Citizen watch and noticed it was nearly 1:30. She had spent nearly thirty minutes over at lunch with Wally. But what came to mind was the fact that Courtney wouldn't be leaving work until 3:30, therefore, she had to tolerate her for the next two hours.

When Vickie went to knock on Paris office door, she noticed it was ajar. She stood there and looked in on him sitting at his desk, hoping he would look up and see her there. She could see that he had just finished a business call, placing the phone back on the hook. He appeared to be in the middle of getting ready to have lunch at his desk. Vickie noticed a can of Pepsi and a pizza box on his desk with a few napkins on top of the box. After a second and he hadn't looked toward the door, she felt uneasy as if she was spying on him. However, she didn't want to knock and figured he would soon glance toward the door and see her. But he was busy removing the napkins from the box when she slightly coughed just to make some noise. He was getting ready to open the lid on the pizza box when he looked toward the door and saw Vickie standing there with a sheet of paper in her hand.

He smiled and his smile was like that of an angel to her. He was the most handsome man in the whole world to Vickie. She almost lost her balance looking in his face.

"Hi Vickie, please come in. What can I do for you?" He asked and then glanced down at the pizza box on his desk. "Please excuse my desk at the moment. I keep trying to grab a moment for lunch, but so far, it's not happening," he said friendly.

She held up one hand. "I can come back if you want to go on and have your lunch. Please, don't let me stop you. I'll even put a don't disturb sign on your door to keep people out until you're done," she said and stopped herself when it dawned on her that she was carrying on too nervous and obviously smitten by him.

"You were just kidding right? Never knew you had such a sense of humor, Vickie," he smiled and folded his arms on his desk.

She discreetly took a deep breath and was pleased that he hadn't taken her seriously about posting a "do not disturb" sign on his door. Actually she would do more than that for him, since she had secretly loved him since the first day she walked into Franklin Gas and Sydney hired her. Paris was the one to show her around and she fell head over heels for Paris. But always looked at her feelings for Paris as a fantasy since she knew they would never amount to anything in his eyes. She wasn't an idealist; she was pragmatist as they come. She didn't daydream and she knew hoping for a life with Paris when he had zero interest in her would be unrealistic, opposite the realist, very practical, down-to-earth person that she was. Therefore, she kept her feelings for him in check and very discreet.

She stepped into his office hesitating. "I would like to see you for a moment."

"Sure, come in and close the door behind you."

Vickie closed the door and Paris smiled and pointed to one of the two chairs that sat in front of his desk. She took a seat and after she was seated she stared at him for a moment before she said a word. Being alone with him in his office affected her in a powerful seductive way that she hadn't expected; and suddenly she had the urge to confess her feelings to him whether he accepted them or not. But that thought faded quickly since she was a sensible young lady. She knew there would never be a time that Paris Franklin would look twice at her. She felt she wasn't in his class. She was a smart in her books young lady with a degree in education and she came from a regular working class family where both of her parents were retired farm workers. Although, for a while her father had served as principal of a high school in Charleston, Mississippi. Now her brother was a high school principal. However, she came from a family of hard workers, other than her Aunt Minnie, who was somewhat well off, none of her relations had any real money that would put them in the same circle with the Franklins.

"So, what is it that I can do for you?" Paris asked again.

"Oh yes, excuse me. I seem to be preoccupied," she said, smiling. "It's about this paper in my hand." She leaned forward and passed the paper to him.

Three minutes after he read the paper, he looked at her and smiled. "Congratulations, Vickie. I'm pleased for you and of course we will miss you around here. I recall that was your intentions when you took the job that it was only temporary until you landed a teaching position." He nodded. "Therefore, sometime in the next two weeks expect a going away party," Paris said, smiling.

"Okay, thank you," Vickie said as she stood.

He got out of his seat and hurried around his desk to open his door for her. "Thanks for coming and giving us the two weeks' notice."

She looked up in his face and quickly turned away. "You're welcome," she said and headed straight down the hallway toward the elevator.

Chapter Seventeen

Monday evening straight from work around half past six, without notice, Wally Simpson knocked on Courtney's front door. After he waited a few seconds and no one answered, he pushed the doorbell. This was his fourth visit in four days. He was hopeful that he and Courtney could start a new affiliation that could lead to a romantic attachment and somehow connect to find the closeness that they once shared in college. He was cautiously hopeful and felt they possibly stood another chance since she was no longer in a committed relationship and he wasn't dating anyone. Yet, each time he had visited during the last three evenings, she had turned down his invites to take her out but had allowed him to visit at her home without privacy. She had basically used him as a sounding board to vent about her troubles and how the Franklins had shut her out. But on his most recent three visits, he and Courtney had not been completely alone in the house. Other members of her family were home and gathered in the living room with them as they were seated side by side on the living room sofa. They had chatted casually with each other between watching a movie on the television set. However, on this visit, Trina, Kenny and their mother were out shopping at the supermarket. Kenny had recently gotten his own apartment but was staying some nights since his father had abandoned home by turning criminal and being imprisoned.

Courtney rushed out of the kitchen where she had just begun to make a cheese sandwich. She knew Wally was coming over but when she got home from work she completely forgot his visit and made no attempts to dress accordingly, since his visit was not important to her. When she pulled open the front door and looked into his face she immediately frowned. Her thoughts were delusional and since her breakup with the Franklins, she felt that one day she would open her front door and Britain would be standing there to confess his love to her. Seeing Wally face was a too familiar reality check that she didn't want to face.

He stood there with a slight smile on his face and a curious look in his eyes as if he was trying to read Courtney's mind or figure her out. Somehow, she seemed different to him and not as warm and inviting as he remembered of her in the past.

She wasn't wearing any makeup and her hair appeared untidy. She was dressed casual as if she wasn't expecting any company. The torn at the knees blue jeans and the big red pullover tunic top appeared to be clothing to clean house in. Therefore, Wally felt over dressed as obvious surprise showed in his eyes at her unkempt appearance. In the past he always remembered her to look well-groomed and neatly dressed.

She walked away from the door, and then glanced over her shoulder, still frowning. "Well, don't just stand there. You're here, so you might as well come in," she said, shaking her head as if he was the last person she wanted to see.

He didn't attempt to head inside as he stood there sandwich between the frame and the door. His eyes watered as a wave of hurt dashed through his stomach from her cold attitude toward him. He had always treated her good and had genuine feelings for her, but her rude treatment had started to rip away at his feelings and they were hanging on my a single thread.

"I don't know, Courtney; maybe I shouldn't come in since you're already in a fighting mood before I sat foot in your house," he said firmly.

"Oh, get in here. You know you're not leaving. You just got here. Besides, I always talk to you this way," she said and then reached down and grabbed her Vodka cocktail from the coffee table.

"I couldn't have said it better. It's exactly the way you have talked to me lately," he said as he stepped into her living room and closed the door. "And that's the problem, Courtney," he said seriously. "Maybe I'm fed up with your rude attitude."

"Of course, you are, that's why you keep coming back for more," she snapped and held up her glass. "Excuse me if I don't offer you a cocktail. I know you frown on my drinking so I won't try to taint you with my vices, although it's not like you don't touch the stuff yourself. I have a good memory and during college you could knock back your share of booze, Wally Simpson!" She lifted the glass to her mouth and took a big swallow and didn't frown from the sting in her throat that she had become accustomed to.

"I have never claimed not to drink, Courtney," Wally said as he looked toward a nearby chair but decided not to be seated.

"No, you never claimed not to drink; you just make it seem like a crime that I do. Did I hit the nail on the head?" she dropped on the sofa and crossed her legs.

"No, you didn't hit the nail on the head," Wally said as he stood next to a big brown recliner chair. "I have never told you that I think it's a crime that you drink."

"Not in those exact words, but I know how you feel about my drinking."

Wally felt uneasy because his evening with Courtney wasn't getting off to a good start. He had come to try to see if they could start anew and she was on the warpath and seemed angry and bitter and he had just arrived. He felt anxious and knew he needed to change the conversation to calm her down.

"Courtney, could we please change the subject if possible. I would just like to have a nice visit with you," he suggested.

"You're here, so visit. You can keep standing there or you can have a seat. It really doesn't matter to me," she snapped and pointed toward the kitchen. "But don't expect me to be your hostess. Those days are over for me, waiting on men who kick me in the teeth."

"Courtney, slow down. What's going on? I just walked in the door so I couldn't possibly have gotten on your last nerve that fast. Therefore, I wish you would reserve your anger for the person you're furious with so the two of us can enjoy our evening," he said and then grabbed a straight back chair from the corner of the room and pulled it across the floor to be seated opposite Courtney.

"How do you know it's not you I'm pissed at? You are all hypocrites, every last one of you," she said bitterly.

"Courtney, I have no idea what you are trying to say," he said irritable, not pleased at her rudeness and extreme impolite behavior. "How many of those have you had anyway?" He pointed to the cocktail glass that she held in her right hand.

She looked at the glass and shook her head. "I haven't had nearly enough! Does that answer your question? When I drink enough of this that makes me forget you and everybody else in this damn town, then I'll be able to say that I have had enough." She looked at him with cold eyes. "Until then, I'll just keep drinking."

"Courtney, maybe you should put that drink down and stop while you're ahead. Remember back in college when they had to pump your stomach?" he reminded her.

She waved her hand. "No need to worry. I'm long past not being able to hold my liquor."

"I'm not so sure of that. It's pretty obvious that you have had too much all ready."

"See what a hypocrite you are," she snapped. "You and all my other friends drinks but just because I love a cocktail more often, I'm the problem drinker, right?" she snapped.

Wally nodded and wondered what and who he had walked in on. Courtney had definitely changed by a huge degree and was talking through a few glasses of Vodka. His last three visits she had been somewhat quiet and withdrawn as if she had been defeated by the world, aiming her focus on the movie they were viewing but now she was carrying on as if she was mad with the world!

"Courtney, I'm not a hypocrite, but you clearly have a drinking problem. You had a serious drinking problem when we were in college together; and I recall you swore off drinking, but I guess you are back at it. I just want you to be careful!" he said with concern in his voice.

"Oh, what do you know? You are a smart guy in your books, landed yourself a big time Principal position, but you can't sit here and assume to preach to me when your bottom line is still peanuts!" she laughed and then grabbed her face for a moment as she noticed his shiny black

Christian Louboutin shoes. Seeing his nice shoes only brought blissful memories of Britain and Rome to her mind. They were the kind of memories that made her feel special and on top of the world. She smiled at his shoes but within a split second those happiness memories turned to dark painful memories as a sharp pain dashed through her stomach. The sudden agonizing memories reminded her of a life and time that would never be hers again. Those bittersweet thoughts only fueled her sour mood. But Wally had come to expect a bitter attitude from her which he tried to ignore, hoping the warmer side of her would surface again. But more and more he was starting to think that the warmer side of Courtney could be lost forever.

"Wow, I like your shoes," she said as she stared down at them for a long while. "I didn't think you could afford shoes like that on a principal salary," she said, placed her cocktail on the coffee table and hopped off the sofa.

"I remember how you were always a saver back in college. I guess you saved your pennies pretty well to have afford a pair shoes like those," she said with a tinge of appreciation in her voice as she headed toward the kitchen.

"I guess you think the Franklin guys are the only ones who can wear Christian Louboutin shoes," he said irritably trailing behind her.

Courtney never took enough interest in Wally to get to know him well enough to know that he liked expensive shoes and had a few pairs. He also was the type who liked to dress well in fine designer clothing, and along with the extra financial support from his Aunt Minnie, he had accumulated a sizeable wardrobe.

Daily he wore two piece suits along with nice shirts and ties, which was simply his work attire. Nevertheless, Courtney hadn't taken the time to notice how well he dressed for his position as principal of Barrington Hills High School. Besides from being a neat dresser, it was a required dress code that he dressed in suit and tie every day for his job.

"Courtney what's going on with you and this mad at the world attitude?" he seriously inquired.

She stopped in her tracks and leaned her back against the doorframe that separated the living room from the dining room and propped both hands on her hips.

"If I'm such rotten company why do you even bother dropping by here? You were here last night and the night before and the night before that! When are you going to get a hint that I just don't care about what you have to say or what you think! I just want to be left alone," she shouted rudely. "If you don't like my mad at the world attitude just stay away from me! It's not like you ever get an invitation to come by. You just keep dropping by as if I have nothing better to do except listen to you tell me how much I have changed," she said firmly and turned on her heels and strutted into the kitchen.

Following behind her, he continued. "Frankly, Courtney, if you had a bag over your head I would think you are a complete different people. That's how much you have changed. So, there you have it!" he said firmly. "It's true, Courtney. You have changed big time."

"If I have changed so much according to you, answer the question I just asked. Why do you keep showing up at my door?"

"I keep showing up, hoping to get a glimpse of the Courtney I fell for back in college," he said as he leaned his back against a kitchen chair.

"Well, you might as well stay away because she died the day the Franklins shut me out; and she won't be returning anytime soon or ever for that matter!" She stood at the kitchen counter where she had a loaf of bread and a pack of American cheese lying on the counter next to a plate and a bottle of mayonnaise.

He nodded. "I can believe that, because ever since around Christmas when Vickie shared with me that you and two of the Franklin brothers had a falling out, you haven't been yourself. But I think it's safe to say, that you were more yourself than you are displaying at the moment."

"So, I'm out of sorts because of the Franklins brothers, is that what you are saying?" She threw him a quick glance but kept her back to him as she stood at the counter and placed two slices on bread on the plate.

"Only you know, Courtney, if that's the root of your distress. I'm just asking."

"Well, don't ask because it's laughable," she took a knife and spread mayonnaise on both sides of the bread. "My life doesn't revolve around a Franklin man or anyone else for that matter! That's

179

why it's so damn laughable to me for you to stand there and indicate that it does revolve around them."

"Why is it laughable? If it's true, and from where I'm standing it's appears to be plausible. Therefore, I want you to get over what happened and get back on track to being yourself. I miss that sweet, soft spoken version of you," he said seriously.

"Well, that's too bad! Because like I said, she's dead to the world! What you see is what you get from here on in!" She took the knife and cut the sandwich in half.

"You are contradicting yourself," Wally crossed his arms at the counter. "You just told me that the Courtney I knew died after the Franklins shut you out! Then I ask you if you have changed because of the Franklins and you said it was laughable. Either you are or you're not an emotional upheaval based on your assumption of what went down between you and the Franklins,"

"Okay, yes, it changed me. But it changed me for the better and made me stronger. I have an iron armor around my heart to protect me from rich snobs and bitches that would take liberty to walk over me and shut me out!" She opened the pickle jar and placed a pickle on the dish next to the sandwich.

"That's what you think happened with the Franklins?"

"You're damn right, they shut me out!" She reached out toward him, handing him one half of the sandwich.

He shook his head. "No thank you. I have lost my appetite."

"Well, excuse me while I eat because I haven't lost mine. Besides, I need something in my stomach to soak up all this alcohol that goes inside of me like a bottomless pit." She lifted one half of the sandwich to her mouth and bit into it. "No amount of any kind of booze, vodka, whiskey, wine or beer seems to drown out how I feel."

"That's pretty sad then," Wally said sadly. "But tell me why, Courtney? Why are you so bitter? Are you really this bitter because of what went down with you and the Franklins?" he asked curiously. "It bothers me that you are so filled with bitterness. You are definitely not yourself, and by no stretch of the imagination do I see anything good in this difference in you!"

"Why would I want to be myself? It only got me a kick in the teeth. From here on in I'm taking charge and shaping my own destiny. You got that?" she said and took another bite from the sandwich.

Wally nodded and then shook his head. "So, you're admitting to me, that this side of you is all because of the Franklin brothers just as I suspected?"

"You damn right it's because of the Franklin brothers."

"You never really told me what happened between you and Rome or Britain. Everything I know I have gotten it second handed. So, can you share with me what happened that has you tied in such knots and carrying on as you are?"

"It's not important what happened with them! What's important is that I'll show them all! I'll do what needs to be done to bring them all down!" she shouted bitterly. "If Britain wants Sabrina Taylor he can have her but he won't want her when I'm done with her! I plan to throw all four of those brothers into such a tailspin they'll never find their way to the light," she said, shaking her head. "I just hate them, which is about the size of my wrath!"

"Hate is a very strong word, why can't you share with me, why you hate them so?" Wally insisted.

"It's not worth knowing why I hate them, but I hate them all including all those Taylor bitches." Courtney took the last bite from the sandwich and then picked up the pickle with her fingers and took a bite.

Since Wally arrival, he had paid close attention to Courtney's impolite talk and anxious manner. He sensed a strong red flag regarding her behavior and felt she was far from being a little different. He sensed that she had an urgent need for counseling to help her ease out of her anger and bitterness toward the Franklins and Taylors.

"If you want details, I can give you details," she said as they headed back into the living room.

"The bottomline is that they didn't treat me right." She grabbed her drink from the coffee table and took a quick sip as she took a seat on the sofa.

Wally took a seat in the straight back chair and then glanced at his watch. He felt the evening was turning out to be a waste and he didn't see any indication that it was going to get any better.

"So, let me get this right," he said, looking across the room at Courtney. "You feel that the Franklins and the Taylors didn't treat you right. In your eyes, they have all wronged you and you want to get even, is that what you are saying?" he asked.

"Yes, that's exactly what I'm saying! I just want Britain and Sabrina to feel some of the pain I'm going through. But I could care less about Rome. Besides, he's married now and honestly regardless to how rich and gorgeous he is, I was never in love with him, it was always Britain." She held her glass in her lap with both hands as she shook one knee.

"But you were dating Rome Franklin."

"Yes, I was dating him, but I couldn't help myself I wanted his brother."

"You wanted Britain Franklin when you were dating Rome Franklin?"

"That is correct, but it wasn't what you're thinking."

"What do you think I'm thinking?"

"You probably think I was in and out of bed with Rome's brother while I was dating Rome. But that's a damn lie and I have heard that rumor too."

Wally nodded. "I'm sure that those on the outside could assumption that. Besides, dating one and fooling around with another, usually means that."

"I know it does, and how I wish that was the case. But it wasn't. It pains me to say I was never anything to Britain Franklin. I might as well have been invisible in his eyes!"

"You are holding grudges against that man for nothing that he actually did to you, but because he couldn't feel for you, what you felt for him?" Wally shook his head realizing that Courtney was being completely irrational.

"I'll make him pay for ripping out my heart. I was invisible to him, so I'll make Miss Sabrina disappear and she'll be invisible in his eyes," she said with a fiery tongue and then laughed as if she found pleasure in thinking about what she had said.

Wally leaned forward and put both elbows on his knees. He was cautiously alarmed by what she had just said. "Courtney, come on, what are you really getting at? What are you really up too? I know you are bitter and your pride has been stepped on, but you're not thinking about going all the way to the dark side are you? I would advise against it. It's not worth it, just forget the Franklin guys and try focusing on someone who'll be there for you."

"I guess you're talking about yourself."

"Of course, I'm talking about myself. I have cared about you for a long time and I want the opportunity to make you happy if you'll just give me that chance," Wally said seriously. "I admit that I'm a little uneasy with your situation at the moment and you appear to need some real professional help to assist you in sorting out all your emotions, but I have no doubt that you can get back on track if you put forth the effort."

"Put forth what effort?"

"Put forth an effort to get yourself back on track. You are so much better than who you have become. Not caring about your appearance, your looks, the way you dress, what you wear, how you talk to people and what you say to them, isn't the real Courtney." He shook his head. "Not the real Courtney Ross I knew in college," he said humbly. "When we first met, I thought you were the prettiest, neatest girl on campus."

"Did you think I was prettier than the Taylor girls?"

"Why is everything about you?" Wally snapped. "Why do you need someone else to be less beautiful for you to feel that you are beautiful? The Taylor girls are beautiful without a doubt, but so are you and many other women," he pointed out.

"So, tell me, what do others see when they look at the Taylor girls that make them put those women up so much higher than me? Is it their money and class that puts them up so much higher than me?"

Wally shook his head. "No, Courtney it's not their money or class that put them up so much higher than you, the only person that puts them up so much higher than you, is yourself," he said respectfully and took a deep breath to try and attempt to get through to Courtney once more. "You know, you didn't answer my question. I asked that we give it another shot and see where things take us," he suggested.

"Seriously Wally, why should I agree to start anything with you? All you want is to criticize the way I am now, and try to change me into the weak flower I was before the Franklins stepped on me!" Courtney shook her head. "Besides, I know you are interested in a romantic affair, but I just don't feel the same about you as you feel about me. I can't make myself feel what is not there," she said seriously.

"That's because you haven't even tried."

"That's not true, Wally. I have tried and I'm just not interested in you in a romantic way." She lifted her cocktail glass and took a quick sip from her drink. "I only think of you as a friend," she snapped. "And it burns me that you are suggesting anything more when you clearly know that I'm still hung up on Britain Franklin."

"I do know that you are hung up on the guy, but I know you are headed down the wrong road and you need to let the thought of him go, and move on with your life."

"Well, it's not going to happen with you since I only think of you as a friend."

"Do you treat all your friends this nice?" He frowned and shook his head.

"I know how rotten I treat you, Wally. But I'm on edge all the time now and I'm just so overwhelmingly unhappy." She stared at him with cold eyes. "And before you judge me, you might want to walk in my shoes for a while. All you can see is someone drinking heavy who seems to be having a rough time coping with the breakup of a relationship. Granted, that is part of it. But if I started counting the reasons for my drinking, it would take all night before I would finish," she said sharply. "Should I keep talking and enlighten you to my nightmarish dreadful existence?"

"I guess you're not just referring to the Franklins right now."

"Your damn right, I'm not talking about the Franklins. I'm referring to my nightmarish of a life. How my father lost his mind and almost killed my mother and her lover. I'm glad he was apprehended and was cleared of murdering Anthony Armani in cold blood while he was asleep in his hospital bed. We are also pleased that he's no longer on the run to end up being shot down by the authorities. However, it's all downhill from there," Courtney sadly explained.

"I'm sorry but I clearly forgot about your father's situation with the law."

"Sure, you forgot. It's not your problem or concern. But it's part of all I can think about. I worry everyday about his health and his well-being. I wondered how he's holding up being locked up in a penitentiary for attempted murder, of all crimes. My own father tried to kill my mother," she said clearly without a crack in her voice but her pain ran deeply. "Then there's my mother. She's getting stronger and stronger each day from her injuries, but she's an emotional mess of late. She was truly in love with Mr. Armani and no longer my father. Now, she doesn't have either one of them. Mr. Armani is dead and my father may as well be dead to her. She said she'll never speak to him again for what he did. She blames him for the death of Anthony Armani because if Mr. Armani hadn't been hospitalized he wouldn't have been killed in his bed. So there you go, Mr. Wally Simpson, my life is a big sad fat mess!"

Wally nodded. "I know that's a lot to deal with. You and your family are dealing with a lot right now. However, that's no excuse to be so impolite and rude to me."

"Maybe it isn't an excuse. But why are you whining? You usually let me treat you this way and you don't complain," she got out of her seat and headed toward the kitchen. "You know I basically don't really mean it when it comes out so crude toward you. You are sort of my outlet for venting." She stepped into the kitchen and grabbed the dish that held the other half of the cheese sandwich from the counter and took a seat at the round kitchen table that seated six; and Wally took a seat at the table as well.

She hopped out of her seat and snatched open a kitchen drawer and pulled out a butter knife. She took the knife and took her seat at the table. "I know you didn't have an appetite earlier, but please share the rest of this with me, suddenly my appetite has left," she mumbled as she took the knife and cut the half sandwich into another half, which was now a quarter of a sandwich and then handed him the quarter piece. He took the piece of sandwich and placed it on a napkin that lay on the table in front of him.

Courtney could see the disappointment on Wally's face and the defeated look in his eyes. She was aware of how disappointed he probably felt from her behavior. Suddenly it hit her that she needed to rope him back in a little and not allow her sour attitude and stomach full of vodka to push him completely out of the door. Therefore, she tried to tone it down and soften her attitude a little toward him, only because she wanted to keep him around for when she needed a favor.

She placed an elbow on the kitchen table and looked at him. "Wally, I know how you feel about me and although I'm not romantically interested in you. I'm quite grateful to have you in my life as the friend that you are. I know that lately I'm not that nice to you, but I hope you don't and won't hold that against me. Seriously, you are by far the best friend I have and the only person that's really in my corner. Your understanding and friendship means a lot to me right now," she said humbly, staring down at the plate and her last bite of sandwich. "Considering what a special friend I regard you as, I hope you can do me a very important favor." She looked at him, and popped the last bite of sandwich into her mouth.

"What kind of favor?" he lifted the piece of sandwich with his right hand and took a bite, and then placed it back on the napkin.

"Will you help me get back at the Franklins for treating me so cold and pushing me aside the way they did as if I didn't matter?"

"You told me that you were dating Rome Franklin, is that correct?" She nodded. "Yes, that's correct."

"So, is that the way he treated you, cold and then pushed you aside?" Wally asked.

"That's right; he treated me cold and then he pushed me aside."

"I heard it differently from Vickie," Wally quickly said.

"Your sister doesn't know how I was treated by Rome Franklin."

"Courtney, she works with you and hears all the gossip that goes on; and according to everybody she knows that knows you, Rome Franklin treated you like you were a precious piece of gold."

"Whatever, but I don't feel like gold now and it's not about how Rome treated me, it's about how Britain treated me. He was cold to me and definitely pushed me aside. But I'll show him and his Miss Sabrina too," she said with a bitter tone. "So, I'm waiting!" she firmly asked. "Can I count on you to help me teach those two a lesson?"

"I'll have to think long and hard about it, Courtney; and it boils down to what you have in mind," he said and paused. "Because I still care a lot for you and want to do whatever I can to make you happy, but the revenge you have in mind toward Britain Franklin and Sabrina Taylor is not really something I want to be apart of or involved in.

186

Besides, I have my reputation to consider. I'm a school principal and it wouldn't look too good for me to get caught up in some future mess that I couldn't explain."

She threw up both arms. "Just say no and be done with it! You don't seem to have any backbone anyway!"

A cold chill rushed through Wally's stomach. He didn't like where their conversation was headed, but he pretended so he could see what she had in mind. Plus, he wanted to try to keep her as calm as she had been for the past ten minutes.

"Calm down, Courtney, and just tell me what do you have in mind in terms of revenge against these people?" he asked as he felt his heart racing with anxiety.

"Don't worry about what I have in mind, if you care so much about me, you'll help me because I have asked you to help me." She grabbed her face with both hands. "Wally please do this for me."

"I'm waiting to hear what is it that you want me to do? If I follow you correctly, you're upset with both the Franklins and the Taylors. Nevertheless, your real beef is with Britain and Sabrina," he said and paused in her eyes. "You want me to help you pay them back for what exactly?"

"For what they did to me, of course!"

"And what was that?"

"They took my liveilhood and my sense of worth, my confidence and my self-esteem. The old me that you loved so much they took that from me. I'm this bitter cold person that I am today because they ripped out my heart and left me with this frame of a being!"

"You blame Britain Franklin and Sabrina Taylor for your bitterness and everything that has ever happened badly to you? Is that correct?"

"Yes, it's correct! Sabrina set it all in motion when she moved to town and caught Britain's eye. He was interested in me before she showed up. After that it was downhill for me all the way."

"What about Rome Franklin? When I asked to take you out for your birthday back then, you told me that you were dating Rome." He reflected on what his sister had told him. "Nevermind, Vickie told me how the incident at Christmas was about you confessing to one brother that you were in love with the other one. So, I guess that other one was Britain?"

"Yes, it was Britain. I poured my heart out to him and he treated me like something to throw out with the trash."

"Courtney, I'm not trying to take up for the Franklin guys, but I hear they are all gentlemen. Is that correct or not?"

"Yes, it's so! They are all gentlemen that are too damn good for their own good! But what does that have to do with anything?"

"It has to do with the fact that you just said he treated you like something to throw out with the trash. That doesn't sound like the treatment of a gentleman."

"He treated me like that alright. He was sneaky with it, and I didn't know I was being played as he lead me on and made me believe that he had feelings for me. He promised to take me to his home to meet his mother," she said angrily. "He laid it on thick and I wasn't the wiser until one day he was having lunch with that Sabrina Taylor bitch."

"Bottomline, you had a crush on Britain Franklin and he never officially asked you out. Now you want to get payback and disrupt his life and that of Sabrina Taylor's because that guy rejected you?"

"It's not just about being rejected." She hopped up from the kitchen table and headed out of the room.

"Then what else can it be about?" Wally asked, hopped out of his seat and followed her out of the room.

Courtney took a seat on the living room sofa and grabbed her face with both hands. She didn't make a sound but Wally got the sense that she was crying.

He stood and did not sit as his heart skipped a beat. He could see that she was really in a bad way over her separation with the Franklins.

"Courtney, are you crying?" he asked.

She looked up at him. "Hell no, I'm not crying. I was just trying to focus and think of a way that I can make those bastards cry!" she laughed. "Get a clue, Wally. You thought I was crying?" She shook her head. "I guess you really don't know me now."

"Maybe I don't, but I know one thing that you need to know," he said seriously.

She waved her hand and shook her head. "This should be good. So tell me, what is that one thing that you know that I need to know?"

"You need to talk to someone about all that anger and hate you have bottled up inside of you for the Franklins and Taylors. I don't want to be the barrier of sour grapes, but if you don't make an appointment with a psychiatric about all your anger and bitterness that bottle up for those people, it's not going to end well," he seriously explained. "I don't know why I didn't notice it before, but you're way out of line and out of control based on your dialogue about those people. My goodness, Courtney, If you don't talk to someone, or see a doctor, you might end up doing something you'll be forever sorry for."

She hopped off the sofa with anger in her eyes and in her voice. "Shut up, Wally Simpson! If you can't be on my side, there's the door!" She pointed toward the front door.

Wally didn't say another word as he headed straight for the door. He twisted the doorknob and stepped through the door. Courtney couldn't believe that he had just left in the middle of their discussion. But she had pointed him out. But as she stood there and listened for the engine of his car, he never started the car. Then she rushed to the window and looked out and noticed that he was still seated in his car. She swallowed her pride, opened the front door and stepped out on the porch. But when she looked toward his car, she could see that he wasn't looking toward her house. He was seated in his car sending a text message on his phone. However, when he lifted his head and saw her standing there on her front porch. She then beckoned for him. But he shook his head and started up his engine. When he switched on the car headlights and started backing out of her driveway, she stepped back inside and closed the door.

Chapter Eighteen

Courtney had just switched off the living room lights and headed toward the kitchen when she heard a knock at the door. She was hopeful that it would be Wally returning. Not that she had feelings for him, but she wanted to keep him at her disposal. Therefore, she immediately strolled across the floor and switched the living room lights back on; and forced a smile as she opened the door and greeted him.

"So, you came back."

"Yes, call me crazy if you like, but I'm here for more punishment."

"It was sort of rude the way you left."

"Yes, it was rude, but I was just obeying your orders. You told me to leave."

"You know, I didn't mean it in that way."

"Maybe you didn't and that's why I decided not to head home until we had a chance to finish our conversation."

Courtney nodded. "Sure, I think we should finish it too." She pointed toward the sofa. "Please be seated if you like."

Wally took a seat on the sofa and wondered why he had returned to her house, knowing the writing was on the wall that it was useless.

"I think we should finish our conversation, but first of all, Wally, I dare you to suggest I need to see a shrink."

He stared at her as he had to recall if he had actually said that to her.

"I know you haven't forgotten that you said that to me, just before you left out of the door. I think you were suggesting that I needed to see a shrink just because I mentioned to you that I want to get even with those rich bastards for slamming the door in my face!"

He nodded. "I know what I said, but Courtney. If you would stop to think, it would dawn on you that those people have been rather generous to you and your entire family."

"How do you know what they have been to me and my family?"

"I know because my sister works with you. Vickie doesn't leave me in the dark."

"In other words, she told you my business?"

"No, it wasn't like that. She shares things with me just as I share things with her. And she happened to mention something that was common news all over your workplace how the Franklins helped your family around Christmas time and paid the mortgage on your family home for six months!" he stressed strongly.

Courtney didn't immediately comment as she listened to Wally.

"For goodness sake, Courtney, who else do you know that would fork out that kind of cash to pay a house note for people who are basically strangers to them? Instead of all your bitterness toward those people, you should be grateful!" He said firmly. "You are twisted in knots and playing the victim, but the way I see it, the Franklins have done everything except cut out a vein for you! So please let go of your resentment and hatred and try to pull some compassion out of your heart," he strongly suggested. "I do care about you, but I'm going to call it the way I see it, and I think your anger boils down to the fact that Britain Franklin rejected you for Sabrina Taylor. Is that the core of your anger?"

"You're damn right it is; and I'm out for blood, Britain and Sabrina's."

Wally held up both hands and shook his head. "You're on your own. I'm guilty of being crazy about you and I guess I always will, but you're messed up big time and the dark direction you're headed, I want no part of it," he said seriously.

"Just get out of my house, Wally! And this time I mean it! So when you walk out of that door, start your motor and leave my driveway. If you knock back on my door, I will not answer it. Because why should

I? You are all talk and no action. You talk about how much you care about me, but I ask you for one little favor and suddenly you're too good to get your hands dirty by helping me best those snobs! But I got news for you poor boy! I don't need your help or you anyway! I'll take care of the Franklins and the Taylors and snag Britain Franklin all on my own without you in the midst to hold me back!" She pointed toward the door as tears rolled down her face. "Who needs a loser like you anyway! I don't want some two-bit principal of some school when I can have a Franklin!"

"What Franklin would that be?" Wally shouted angrily as his anger boiled inside from her insults. "It sure won't be Britain or Rome Franklin; and the last I heard, Paris and Sydney were in serious relationships with the Taylor girls. Therefore, I guess that leaves you out on your ear!" Wally stood from the sofa and rubbed his hands together. "I'm done with you, Miss Courtney Ross. You are clearly delusional if you think you have a snowball chance in hell with another Franklin guy!" He strutted quickly over to the front door, grabbed the doorknob and twisted it.

Standing sandwich between the door, he paused and said calmly. "You are clearly messed up in the head and really in need of a shrink or some kind of doctor." He shook his head. "But at this point, even if you weren't acting like a headcase, I don't need your kind of friendship and putdowns in my life. I have cared about you for a long time and everybody who knows me, know that I have waited and been overly patient and understanding where you are concerned." He nodded with a sore look on his face. "It's a pity that it ends this way when I pretty much would have done anything for you within reason; but you never showed any real interest in me," he said, looking in her eyes. "I don't know what you take me for, but I want to be with someone who wants me for me and not just for their lackey. I'm done being that for you, Courtney!"

"You have some damn nerve to say you pretty much would have done anything for me, when you weren't willing to lift a finger when I asked you for help just minutes ago!" She snapped. "So go on and say what you have to say and get out!"

"Don't worry, I'm leaving and I don't plan to come back. I don't need anymore bricks to fall on my head. My eyes are wide open to you,

Miss Courtney Ross. You never really gave a flying hoot for me, but I guess I can't blame you for that. You can't make yourself feel what you don't feel. But I blame you for your disrespectful rude behavior! And I blame you for your hurtful insults and acid words thrown toward me." He pointed to his heart. "In case you didn't notice, I'm not made of rubber where your nasty insults can just bounce off my chest without injury or roll off my back without ripping at my skin. That's why I'm done with you and your little regard for me," he said regretfully. "I should have listened to my sister weeks ago when she tried to pound into my head how you had changed and how you were obviously obsessed with Britain Franklin! And just earlier today when I had lunch with Vickie, she tried to make me see the light about you."

"Don't make me laugh! Your sister is one to talk. How can she point a finger at me considering how she used to hang onto my brother and buy his booze. So if you want to know, I have also heard people at work talk about how Vickie was paying Kenny's way. So, before you leave here looking down your nose at me, think about your own sister! What worthwhile decent female is going to pay a man's way?" Courtney snapped. "So, how can big mouth, Vickie, tell you I'm obsessed with a guy when she's in the same boat?"

Wally shook his head. "It's not the same and Vickie isn't unbalanced. I'm aware that she paid for some of Kenny's drinks and she also drove him around to keep your brother from hurting himself or someone else. That's what friends do for each other. I think you would know that if you had any friends," he was intentionally hurtful with his remark.

"Say what you please about me, but your sister is no Samantha Taylor. Vickie hasn't been with my brother all these months just to hold his hand; and I know first hand because his bedroom is next to mine. So, don't stand here and try to put your skinny big mouth sister up higher than me," Courtney fussed.

"I don't know why I bother standing here in your doorway bothering to talk to you or hear you out? You have lost sight of reality if you ask me. Saying things about my sister that is not even called for. Regardless to what you think of Vickie, she's a decent, respectful young woman with a lot going for herself. Besides, the subject of my sister paying for your brother's drinks is a moot point, since your brother did the smart thing and got his act together. He did what you need to do, he gave up the booze. And just for the record, Kenny treats Vickie with respect now and you would know that if you took the time to be concerned about someone else for a change other than yourself!" He held up both hands.

"I wasn't referring to my brother. I was referring to the big fat crush that Vickie has on Paris Franklin." Courtney nodded.

Wally eyes widen with surprise and he was speechless.

"Yes, your leveled headed, Miss straight A's, honor row sister has a big fat crush on Paris Franklin and everybody at work knows it except him and my clueless brother."

Wally shook his head. "I'm afraid you have me at a disadvantage. I haven't heard anything about some crush on Paris Franklin that you are accusing Vickie of."

"Of course you haven't heard about it, because it's a pipe dream and she knows it! So, before you get all high and mighty on me, look in your own backyard. Your sister is no better than me if she's daydreaming about a man she can't have while stringing my brother along!" Courtney said sharply and then laughed. "What a riot!" She kept laughing. "Your sister and my brother are both barking up different trees. "He secretly wants to be with Samantha Taylor and your sister secretly wants to be with Paris Franklin. They just need to switch partners and they'll all be happy. They are all living in a fantasy world because they are afraid to go after what they want! Take Kenny for instance, my brother and I butt heads sometimes, but he's a tall, nice looking, decent guy and he has been into Samantha Taylor since college." She held up one finger. "One thing is holding him back from taking a chance with the millionaire princess and I'll tell you what that one thing is. For some foolish reason he's intimidated by her and thinks she's too good for him." Courtney waved her hand, laughing. "Then you have your brainy sister on the other hand, who thinks she's not good enough for Paris. Go figure how their minds work. I think they are both nuts to think that way! But what do I know, right? Everybody is calling me a headcase who drinks too damn much! And sure, I'll admit that I love to drink." She paused with serious eyes. "And what if I drink too much in their eyes, you can still mark my word that there will come a day when you will realize that I hit the nail on the head about Vickie and Kenny being hopelessly in love with other people," she lifted her glass to her mouth and took another sip from her cocktail. "If you ask me, I think Samantha would be better off with my brother than that hunk she's with."

"Why would you say something like that, Courtney? How can she do better than a respectful Franklin guy like Paris?"

"She can do better because she isn't good enough for Paris Franklin." Courtney waved her hand. "Don't get me wrong, she's what you call a good girl according to society's standards, but Samantha Taylor is a want to be wild child. She has a wild side to her character. It's a side of her personality that's beneath the surface but when Paris Franklin finds out, she's out the door! Because of all those straight-laced Franklin hunks, Paris is the epitome of straight-laced in terms of being excessively strict in conduct and morals. He strives for perfection in himself and the female that he chooses to date. He will not tolerate a wild streak in any female he goes out with. His significant other has to be almost perfect to coexist with him," Courtney explained.

"Okay, what's the big deal? He picked the right girl. I have heard that Samantha Taylor pretty much fits that bill."

"She does and she doesn't. Because she has that wild streak that is bound to come out at some point. You can mark my word that when Paris Franklin finds out that his precious Samantha has a wild streak, he's going to drop her like a hot potato."

Wally shook his head, not taking Courtney literally because he figured to himself, how could Courtney know what lies beneath the surface of Samantha Taylor's character. He chalked it up to Courtney's jealousy of the Taylor girls.

"I tell you, Wally, I can see that disbelief in your eyes. But I know what I'm saying about Samantha. That's why she might as well hook up with my brother who loves the ground she walks on and doesn't care that she's a potential wild child," Courtney took another drink and staggered slightly. "Kenny will take Samantha and her wild side and all! I tell you, he thinks she's a goddess."

"Oh, is that right? But he's still dating my sister, remember?" Wally remarked.

"Wally Simpson, I hear that tone in your voice. You're not taking me serious. But you should. It could potentially save your sister a lot of heartbreak if Kenny dumps her for Samantha down the road.

Because I might be drinking, but I'm not too loaded that I don't know what I'm talking about."

"Leave it to you, Courtney, to call someone like the innocent Samantha Taylor a wild child. We all went to college together and the Taylor sisters were all above broad with a shining respectful reputation. They didn't drink, smoke or attend wild parties and stay out late like the rest of us. So how can you stand here and call Samantha Taylor wild?"

"You are dense, Wally, and you just don't get it. She isn't in the streets wild. It's inside of her. She's good but she wants to be bad. She wouldn't have dated Kenny back in college if it wasn't so. Think about it, my brother might be tall and cute but that's all he has going for himself. So, why would a mega rich girl like Samantha go out with him? She did it because she likes that wild side of him and what he represents. She doesn't want to like him, but she does. She only stop seeing him because she felt it would be the proper thing to do. Besides, she knew her family would never approve of my penniless brother!"

"Courtney, I think you are dreaming up all this stuff. You seem to need to chop down others to make yourself look and feel better," Wally suggested.

"Look, Wally, I know what I'm talking about. Have you forgotten everything that happened at college? Just remember back to the time when you and Kenny were members of that popular band called "Peacock." It was the most popular band on campus."

Wally nodded with a curious look on his face. "Okay, but what's your point?"

"My point is Samantha Taylor and how she would always show up to listen to the band. Sabrina and Starlet was never with her. She would always show up at those questionable dance halls that you would never normally see a Taylor girl. But she did that just so she could see Kenny on the drums. I don't think she was really interested in listening to you sing or the performances of the other muscians."

"Let me get this right. Your theory is that Samantha Taylor didn't show up to enjoy the band as a whole, just the drummer?"

"Damn right, that's what I mean; and she would always come solo. A long white limousine would drop her off and wait in front of the

196

dance hall for her until she exited the club. Everyone would see her come and go. Granted, she never stayed that long and would sneak out without meddling with Kenny or anyone else. She still showed up to see Kenny perform in the band. I remember all these little things about Samantha," Courtney laughed.

"That may be the world according to Courtney, but if you look around you'll see that Samantha Taylor is happily committed to Paris Franklin. Therefore, if she was fascinated by Kenny back in college, apparently she got over it. So, snap out of it, Courtney, and stop trying to find fault and stick your nose in other folks business! Just try to fix yourself!"

"That's why we are not together, Wally Simpson, I don't like your superior attitude. I'm not perfect but you're no prize yourself. So, you are a school principal, big deal. It still doesn't put you in the league with the Franklins. So, don't stand here and try to make me feel beneath you!"

"Of course, that's not what I'm doing. But I see I'm wasting my time trying to talk to you. Therefore, I don't plan to stand here and listen to your put downs and anything else you have to say!"

"Why is that, Wally? You can ditch it out but you can't take it! You can call me a drunk, but I can't call it the way I see it. So, I guess you just need to leave!" she shouted.

"That's my thought exactly!" He shook his head. "You are worse off than I thought."

"Okay, you have established that, so just get out and don't come back! I'm so sick of you and everybody else in this whole damn town who think in a hypocritical way like you. You don't want to hear what I have to say, because you always think I'm lying. Yet, I'm supposed to listen to your garbage and accept it as the truth," she shouted angrily.

"No, Courtney, I came here with the best intentions and you bit my head off before I walked through the door. You didn't even have the courtesy to find out why I was here before you snapped and offended me," he said strongly.

"I didn't have to ask why you are here. I knew why you were here. You came here tonight because you thought you had a snowball chance in hell to be with me." She walked over to the coffee table and sat her empty glass there; and then pointed both hands toward her mouth.

"Read my lips, I don't want you, Wally Simpson! If you thought you had another chance with me, let me take away all the misunderstanding and tell you straight out. I'm just not into you anymore. Yes, at one time I thought you were worth my time, but that's been so long ago until I can't even remember it." She stared at him and placed both hands on her hips and laughed. "Why are you looking so surprised? I'm sure I didn't tell you anything you didn't already know. If you thought we had another shot you were living in a dream world." She looked toward her glass and then grabbed it off the coffee table and headed toward the kitchen. She glanced over her shoulder. "You might as well open the door again and get out. Standing next to the door isn't the same as actually leaving out of it," she said as her voice faded down the short hallway toward the kitchen. "I need another drink and I don't want your stuffy company when I get back." She waved her hand toward the door. "So go on, get out!" she said as she disappeared around the corner.

He stared at her back with disbelief. He saw her and he heard her voice but she was like a totally different person from the young lady that he thought he wanted to spend the rest of his life with, chasing all through college and carrying a torch for up until the moment before she opened her front door for him on this evening. She had managed to somehow wipe out all the special feelings he felt for her and now all that were left was his pity for the pathetic person she had become.

When Courtney stepped back into the living room, she had filled her eight ounce glass to the rim with vodka. "So, why are you still here? I asked you to leave," she said with a bitter edge to her voice.

"I know you asked me to leave but I wanted to wait for you to return to the room so I could ask you something," he said calmly.

"You want to ask me what?"

"I just want to know, what the hell happened to you?"

She pointed her finger at Wally. "Nothing happened to me. It's the rest of you bastards that something has happened to! You're all walking around on your high horses, thinking you're better than me!"

"Who and what are you talking about?" He pointed to her head. "It's all in your head and it's all about the Franklins and how they kicked you to the curb for good reason, I'm guessing. But of course, you find away to blame everyone else for your mess except you!"

198

"Now I want you to answer one question for me," she said, lifted her glass to her mouth and took a sip from her drink.

"Okay, what's your question, Courtney?"

She stared at him with red, wet eyes and gritted her teeth as if she was mad enough to spit fire at him. "Why are you still standing at my front door?" She pointed toward the doorknob. "Twist the doorknob and get out! We have talked this thing too death and nothing is going to change."

Wally was speechless for a moment and then he said, "You don't have to ask me twice." He held up both arms and then turned his back to her and grabbed the doorknob.

"But I did ask you twice, so don't let me ask you a third time!"

Wally twisted the doorknob and snatched opened the door. He stood at the opened door but hesitated to walk through it. He knew once he sat foot outside of her door that it would be the end of what had once been an important period in his life.

"What a waste," he said. "But Courtney, it's not too late for you to turn your life around and get yourself back on the right track." He held up both hands. "Of course, I'm no longer interested in someone who's their own worst enemy. But if you love life and want to make the best out of it, you need to drop the booze and the attitude and show some retrain and respect for yourself," Wally suggested calmly.

She placed both hands over her ears. "I don't want to hear anymore of your bullshit! Will you please just get the hell out of my house, Wally Simpson! You are so damn dense until you just don't shut up. I have kicked you out and literally thrown you out my door, but you are still standing there trying to give me some last minute advice as if I want or need it! Why the hell can't you just shut up and leave, now?"

"I'm still standing here because I once cared deeply for you, and now I just care that you be okay. That's why I'm desperately trying to get through to you. But as you pointed out, you do not want or need my advice. So, I'm going to take your advice and do as you said and get the hell out of your house," Wally said sharply. "But before I shut this door to walk out of your life for good. I just want to say this." He paused and glanced down for a moment, and then he looked at her. "Good luck to you and I hope you are happy with the road you have decided to take! But a word to the wise. I don't think the destination will be to your liking!" He pulled the door shut behind him and paused at the door for a moment to collect himself before he headed off her porch.

Although Wally was boiling with anger and disappointment toward Courtney and had lost his desire to be with her, it hurt him deeply to walk away from their friendship and say good bye to someone he had once cared so deeply for since their college years. For a moment, the time over the years that he had spent with Courtney flashed through his mind. In his mind's eye he could see all the sweet and bittersweet times they spent with each other, mostly bitter. As the pages from the past turned in his mind, he slowly walked across her small yard toward his 2014 white Mustang that was parked at the edge of her driveway. He opened his car door, hopped inside and started the engine. He drove out of Courtney's driveway without the knife turning pain that he thought would accompany him. Surprisingly, he felt relieved and at ease about their parting.

On the other hand, Courtney stood in the middle of the living room, motionless facing the front door, listening as Wally's car engine faded down the street. She felt pathetic as she stood in the same spot for nearly five minutes as one single tear rolled down her left cheek. She held both hands tightly as if she was willing herself not to lose control and show emotions as she just stood there staring at the door. She was stunned that Wally Simpson had actually walked out of her life. He had always been there to accept her no matter what or how badly she treated him. Knowing he had written her off, she felt not one tinge of love for Wally, just rage as she grabbed a magazine from the coffee table and threw it flying across the room against the door. "It will be to my liking! You'll see! All of you bastards will see! Britain Franklin will be mine if it's the last thing I do," she said breathless, grabbed her face and cried uncontrollably as she hurried out of the living room and headed upstairs toward her room.

Chapter Nineteen

It was nearly mid-night when Wally arrived home that evening after ending his friendship with Courtney. He had driven around for hours trying to make sense of the last five years and why he had saved his heart for someone who clearly wasn't interested in him or deserving of him. When he unlocked the door of his two bedroom apartment, he noticed that the living room light was on, glanced around the door frame of the small foyer and noticed his sister waiting up for him. Vickie was sitting on the living room sofa dressed in a long blue terrycloth robe and slippers. She was wide awake holding a coffee mug in her hand, sipping hot chocolate as she looked in her brother's eyes and instantly knew his visit with Courtney hadn't gone well.

"I hope you don't mind that I waited up for you, but I figured you might could use a friend. If what I think happened actually happened," Vickie humbly uttered.

He nodded with sad eyes as he slipped out of his suit coat and threw it across the arm of the loveseat. "You are right, it happened and I could use a friend or a cup of whatever you're drinking." He threw his car keys on the coffee table and flopped down on the opposite end of the sofa, propped an elbow on the arm of the sofa and looked toward his sister. "Someone who can tell me how I missed the mark on Courtney Ross?"

"I can't tell you that, but I can step in the kitchen and pour you a cup of hot chocolate," Vickie hopped off the sofa and strolled into the kitchen, leaving Wally sitting on the sofa with his head propped back on the cushion of the sofa. He stared up at the ceiling to keep the water in his eyes from seeping through.

Minutes later, Vickie stepped back into the room and handed him a mug of hot chocolate. But he was in a daze and torn up inside with anguish. She stood there for a few seconds before he noticed her standing there.

"How could I have been so wrong about that girl?" He reached for the mug and held it with both hands, immediately taking a small sip. "I wasted five years, distracted with thoughts of spending my life with her," he said seriously, looking toward Vickie.

"In all fairness, she wasn't off her rocker when you two first met. She was a nice girl at that time; soft-spoken, quiet and friendly; completely opposite of who she has become."

"I realize that, Vickie, but nevertheless, with my strong feelings and all the attention I showered on her, proving how I felt about her. I just assumed or figured she would eventually come around and open her eyes to realize that the two of us belonged together. It never occurred to me ever that I would wake up one day and never want to have anything else to do with her. This is so unreal until I feel as if I'm trying to awaken from a bad dream." He took one last sip, then placed the mug on the coffee table.

"I can imagine how you must feel since I was there for the ride. Courtney Ross is the only female I have known you to actually have feelings for. I know you have dated a few, but none of the girls you dated were considered special as you idolized Miss Ross," Vickie reminded him. "At that time, she was worth idolizing, pretty as a picture and sweet as they come. But, I still didn't want you with her since she never shared any real feelings for you. I felt you were wasting your time chasing after her when you should have chased after the sister that wanted you. Trina is the one who wanted to be with you, remember?"

Wally totally ignored what Vickie had said about Trina and repeated himself. "Yes, Sis, I never thought I would live to see the day that I would think of a future without Courtney Ross being a major part of it," he said seriously as he looked toward Vickie nodding. "But believe me when I say, that's exactly how I feel right now." He rubbed both hands together. "I'm so done with that young lady until it feels as if she was never a significant part of my life. I guess it's not too much of a stretch to say her bitter attitude and heartless ways killed what I once felt for her."

"Little brother, it warms my heart to hear you say that. You are a respectful principal. You don't need a basket case like Courtney Ross mudding up your shining reputation. I'm so proud of you and the family is so proud of you. You are the only person in the family and extended family to land a principal position at such a young age. Therefore, that's saying something."

"Thanks for the compliment, but we're not sure how old Dad was when he landed his principal position," Wally said. "We also don't know how old Father was when he was hired as principal of Barrington Hills High."

"You mean your God father, Mr. Ed Hanes?"

"Yes, I do. For all we know, he could have been younger than me when he landed his principal position all those years ago."

"No, way, Wally, I'm sure Mr. Hanes and Dad were both older than 24 years old when they were hired as a school principal," Vickie assured him.

"Okay, maybe you're right," he agreed. "I guess 24 is quite young to land the position. I know I was pleased and honored when Father offered me the opportunity."

"I'm sure you were and you're doing a great job, Wally."

"Thanks for the compliment and your faith in me," Wally casually said. "However, if we look on the real side of how I landed the principal position, it had very little to do with my abilities and all to do with the fact that Father wanted me to take his spot."

"Maybe you're right," Vickie agreed. "I'm sure that's what Mr. Hanes wanted, since he was the one who appointed you. But little brother, that takes away nothing from your smartness. Mr. Hanes may have wanted you to take his spot when he retired, but he's smart enough to know that you're smart enough for the job. No matter how much he wanted you to have the job, if you hadn't been qualified the school board and superintendent never would have signed off on you as their new principal."

"The way I see it, Sis, and I'm completely grateful. If my Godfather hadn't went to bat for me, at 24 years old with just a few years of teaching under my belt, no way I would have obtained the position of being a high school principal at Barrington Hills High School. Father told me, that there were one criteria that I didn't meet. I needed to obtain a certain certification from the state of Illinois to become a principal. But what they did were, since I had obtained straight-A all through college, they allowed me to take the job based on an equivalency test from the state," he said, smiling. "It was a three hour test of 300 questions. But guess what, Sis. I aced the test with a one hundred percent passing mark."

Vickie raised both hands. "I'm not surprised. I already know how smart you are," she said and stared into space awhile.

"You look like you're in deep thought right now," Wally observed.

"Yes, I am. I'm just thinking what a blessing that Mom and Dad knew Mr. Hanes years ago when they first got married. He lived in the house next door to them and they became close enough that he and his wife, Elizabeth, was asked to be your God parents. Plus, when they left Charleston and moved here to Barrington Hills, I was nine and you were just 8. I remember how left out I felt when they would always send you things. Then when Mom and Dad decided they wanted us to attend high school in Barrington Hills, they drove us there to live with Aunt Minnie. Mr. Hanes' wife died a year after we started school here. But he started picking you up every weekend and spending time with you. He was a well-mannered, levelheaded old man; and the principal of Barrington Hills High at that time, and had been for many years. I feel he took you under his wing and groomed you into the fine upstanding guy that you are today."

Wally nodded with a solemn look on his face. "Father is a good man and I need to adjust my schedule to spend more time with him. When we last spoke over the phone last week, he shared with me that he's ill with some kind of condition that affecting his sight and his ability to walk sturdy."

"That doesn't sound good. I know Mr. Hanes is far in his late eighties, but I thought he as in better health," Vickie said with compassionately voice.

"I thought he was in better health as well. But apparently he isn't. He told me that he now has a live-in caregiver and his condition isn't improving."

"No ill wishes toward Mr. Hanes, but it's been a common fact since you were twelve years old that your God parents had you listed in their will as their sole heir to their estate. I know he's not rich, but he's probably well off," Vickie said and waved a hand. "But that's too depressing. Therefore, let's get back on my favorite subject of how proud I am of you and the good job you are doing at Barrington Hills High. Plus, Mom and Dad brags on you all time to their neighbors and also to me when I call."

"I need to give them a call soon. I guess I haven't gotten used to the fact that they are living in Florida now," Wally said, smiling.

"I haven't gotten used to it either, but they seem to be happy there since they couldn't wait to get away from Mississippi and enjoy Florida weather they told us," Vickie reminded him. "But it didn't come as a surprise to us when they decided to sell the house and farm to move to Tallahassee. They had discussed it with us when they first made the decision. They were both just tired of the hard work I'm sure," Vickie figured.

Wally nodded. "Yes, I'm sure you are right. But their moving away didn't really affect us as much as it would have if we had both been still living at home. We would have had to relocate after they sold the house." Wally grinned. "Instead of moving to Florida, we probably would have moved up here to stay with at Aunt Minnie."

Vickie nodded. "Aunt Minnie can sometime be hard to take. But you're right. We wouldn't have moved to Florida and would have most likely ended up at Aunt Minnie's."

"I know you didn't like the idea of staying on with Aunt Minnie after college."

"That's true. But I couldn't afford to move out."

"I know you couldn't afford to move out at that time. But, I should remind you that you seemed okay at Aunt Minnie's until I said you could rent a room from me."

"Sure, staying with Aunt Minnie wasn't that bad after I moved back into her home after college. You're probably thinking about how she was when we were in high school. She was way too controlling and way too strict and way too preachy," Vickie reminded him.

Wally grinned and Vickie was pleased to see that he was smiling about something, and she wanted to continue talking about other things, anything other than Courtney to keep his mind off of how miserable he was after breaking off with Courtney.

"Aunt Minnie used to be as strict as they come. She was hell-bent on keeping you away from Kenny back then," Wally reminded her.

"Yes, I remember. She thought Kenny was the worst boy I could ever talk to. She didn't like him period." Vickie laughed, thinking of the fun old memories.

"I remember, and it was all because we had that band together," Wally remembered. "Kenny was on the drums and I was on bass." He grinned. "That was a life time ago, but we were pretty good back then, don't you think?"

"I agree, you and Kenny and the other three members were pretty good, playing at different high school events and around town at some clubs."

"I remember, when Aunt Minnie would hide my guitar and wouldn't tell me where to find it. I would have to search the entire house find it. Nobody would ever figure that she's Dad twin sister. She's completely different from him in attitude. She was mean and loud back then, but whenever we visit her now, she's easier to talk to."

"I guess so, Wally. She's much older now with a lot of health problems. That's why she has lost a lot of her fire."

Wally narrowed his eyes. "What are you doing? Why are we suddenly talking about Aunt Minnie and our high school band days? I know what you are trying to do and I appreciate it, but ignoring my problem isn't going to make it disappear. I need to talk about what transpired with Courtney and get it out of my system."

"But why concentrate on that, when we can talk about how wonderful it was when Mr. Hanes offered you that principal job after serving for all those years himself," Vickie said, smiling. "He stayed there all those years and waited to pass the reins to you, it seems. Now you can stay for many years to come and step down for your son."

"My son, let's not get ahead of ourselves," he grinned. "I think I need a wife before I can start counting my chickens."

"Aunt Minnie would always say that. Don't count your chickens before they hatch. But seriously, little brother, it warms my heart that you were offered the job, not just because you were qualified but because you were super qualified. You are a well-liked upstanding principal of a very popular school in one of the wealthiest towns in Illinois." She held up both hands. "I rest my case. You definitely do not need Courtney with her haywire behavior throwing darkness into your bright world and your above board reputation."

He shook his head. "It's not even about that."

"What do you mean?" Vickie asked.

"I mean, it's not even about what she's going through or how messed up she is in the head. It's about the fact that she never loved me."

"But she should have loved you," Vickie seriously stated. "You were the one guy who would have moved mountains for her. Some people don't know what's good for them. She doesn't want you, but she wants some guy who she'll never have."

"Maybe, but the heart wants what the heart wants. My case with her is no different than how she feels about Britain Franklin right now. The only difference is that tonight I knew how to finally walk away."

"Little brother, you are smarter and stronger than I give you credit for. Walking away from Courtney couldn't have been easy, but yet you found the courage to do it."

He nodded. "Yes, I did it; and that's what Courtney needs to do before she can put things back in perspective," Wally sadly explained.

"If you ask me, I think Courtney is too far over the edge to walk away from the Franklins, especially Britain. I do not picture a good resolution to her madness. If Kenny and his family doesn't wake up and see that she's off her rocker, the ending will not be pretty," Vickie stressed strongly.

"Do you honestly think she's that far gone?"

"Yes, I do; and it's just a matter of time before she proves my theory to everybody when she ends up hurting herself or someone else."

"If you think it's that bad, you need to talk to Kenny about alerting his family of her irrational behavior."

"Wally, believe me, when I tell you that I have talked to Kenny on more than one occasion about Courtney's odd obsessive behavior. Nevertheless, whenever I bring her up and try to get into a discussion about what I know is going on with his sister, he shuts me down. He just won't talk about Courtney's problems with me. I don't know if he's trying to ignore them or if his family is dealing with her situation in a different way," Vickie explained and paused before she continued. "That reminds me, when Kenny was over earlier, I brought Courtney weird behavior to his attention and tried to start a discussion."

"What did he say?" Wally curiously asked.

"He listened, but he didn't really say that much. It takes two to have a constructive conversation; therefore, it didn't go that far since I was doing most of the talking."

"So, you're telling me that Kenny didn't share any kind of opinion about his sister's current manners?" Wally asked.

"He didn't say much, Wally. He just seems to let whatever I say about his sister roll right off his back. He thinks I'm making too much of her high emotions, so he calls it." Vickie reached out and lifted her mug from the coffee table. She finished the last swallow of hot chocolate and then placed the mug back on the table coffee.

"I think Kenny has his head in the sand regarding Courtney. He's no help and doesn't believe she has gone off the deep end. He has always been close with his sisters and I'm sure he doesn't want to think the worse of her. Especially, since in their household, Courtney was always considered the shining star of their family according to his parents."

"Why was that?" Wally asked.

"Kenny told me his parents held Courtney up as an example for him and Trina, since Courtney was dating the heir to a billion dollar estate," Vickie said. "You have to give her credit for the past and all she achieved even if she did destroy her own future."

"You're right; the Courtney I knew wanted to make something of her life. She wanted to be a teacher and settle down and have a family. That's what she used to say to me back before she ever dated a Franklin. Now she's a mess and doesn't want anything except her next glass of vodka," Wally said regretfully.

"I'm sure Kenny knows she drinks too much, but he hasn't said anything to me about anything that is too far out about his sister," Vickie said. "I think he's probably in denial and doesn't believe she's that far gone."

"But Vickie, I witnessed her transformation tonight. I was shocked and only a blind man couldn't see that Courtney has changed," Wally stressed strongly.

"I know, and he agrees that she's different and sort of out of control, but he doesn't believe she's off her rocker. You would have been much better off with the sister who had the crush on you. Trina was crazy about you back then but you had to chase Courtney."

"What did you just say?"

"You heard me. Trina Ross, remember her? You would have been much better off with her. She's the sister who loved you."

"But being invited to her family Halloween Party didn't make for the best first date."

"I guess not, since you ended up meeting her big sister, who you fell head over heels for on the spot. Who knew back then that Trina would have been the best choice for you when we were all in high school and college?"

Wally scratched his head and smoothed his hand down his short brown waves. "Trina is an attractive young lady, but she never dawned on me as a love interest."

"I guess not, because correct me if I'm wrong. You said back then, she's not the pretty one," Vickie reminded him.

Wally lifted his left eyebrow as he stared at his sister. "I said that?"

Vickie nodded. "Yes, you said that, probably because you were so smitten with Courtney until you couldn't see how pretty her sister was. Because Trina is pretty, and even better than that, she's also sane," Vickie said jokingly.

Wally looked straight ahead with a distant look in his eyes as if his thoughts were far away. Then he looked toward Vickie and nodded. "I know you said that in a joking way, but you're right. Trina is pretty and she has a level head on her shoulders along with a good heart," he smiled. "Back when Courtney had it together, she used to tell me that whenever she wanted some solid advice, she would talk to her sister. Trina is a year younger than Courtney, but many years wiser according to Courtney. Plus, I remember how good of a sport Trina was when I told her that I was going to ask out Courtney. I had expected her to rip into me for choosing to date her sister instead of her, but she didn't yell or get upset visibly. But, I'll never forget that crushed look in her eyes. I'm sure she was deeply hurt."

"I'm sure she was. She didn't let on, to save face. But she was crazy about you back then. I think that's why she has stayed single. She has been hung up on you all this time; and you have been hung up on Courtney all this time. Things happen for a reason and you had to experience Courtney's wrath before you could accept Trina's feelings for you."

"Maybe you're right. I'm done with playing games and being Courtney's whipping boy. She's on her own. Maybe it did take all of this before I could open my eyes and take a second look at Trina. I will give her a call. Do you know if her cell number is the same?"

"Yes, it's the same," Vickie told him.

Wally narrowed his eyes toward Vickie. "Are you sure about that because the number I have in my phone contacts with her name on it, is quite ancient," he said.

"Nevertheless, it's the same number. Trina cell is the same, and I should know since we work together and I have to call or text her about her schedule sometime."

"Good, I might just surprise her with a call very soon," he said, smiling.

"Are you serious?" Vickie asked.

"Am I serious about what?"

"Are you serious about Trina?"

"What do you mean am I serious about her?"

"I mean you have been hung up on Courtney for all these years and never really had a thing for Trina. So, I'm just wondering are you serious about maybe asking Trina out."

Wally nodded. "Of course, I'm serious. You think I'm sitting here talking about her and reflecting on the good things I remember about her, just to pass the time?"

"I'm pleased to hear you're serious about asking Trina out, because that means you really have decided to move on from Courtney."

"But all this could be moot if Trina has moved on from me. After all, it's been five years since she had that crush on me, and I repaid her affections by going out with her sister. That ship has likely sailed and it's probably too late for Trina and me," he nodded.

"I don't think it's too late for you and Trina. She and I work together at the same counter remember? She isn't dating anyone."

"Are you sure about that?"

"Yes, I'm sure. Believe me; everybody at Franklin Gas knows who's dating, and who's dating who. Believe me when I say Trina is not dating anyone at the moment. She was dating some guy a few months ago, but it ended quickly."

"Does this some guy have a name? Who was he?" Wally asked.

"I never knew his name, and nobody else at work found out his name. We just all knew Trina was dating some guy from downtown."

"Are you referring to downtown here?"

"No, I mean downtown Chicago. But their courtship ended very quickly, almost before anybody knew about their relationship, it was over," Vickie explained. "So, there you have it, the coast is clear for you little brother. Why not ask her out and correct the mistake you made years ago when you chose Courtney over her," Vickie suggested.

Wally smiled. "I didn't think anything could make me smile this evening, but reflecting on the possibility of a new start with Trina is an uplifting thought. But I couldn't blame her if she told me to get lost. She knows how long I carried a torch for her sister."

Vickie nodded. "Yes, she knows all that, but she also knows nothing happened between you and Courtney romantically. You two were just friends during college."

"That's true; and you're right, I'm sure Trina knows that. She's understanding. Plus, I have always been able to talk to her about things; and I have never had that kind of a connection with Courtney. I don't know why her gentle soul hadn't dawned on me before."

"How could it, you were blinded by your misguided feelings for her sister."

"Look, I know you're upset about breaking off your friendship with Courtney, but look on the bright side. She makes it easy to forget her."

"Yes, she does; and after a few days of a cooling off period for me, I will call Trina and ask her out. Does that make you happy?"

Chapter Twenty

Sunday afternoon, the sixth day of April, right before noon. It was a cloudy and cold gray looking day, Charles Taylor, Sabrina and Starlet had just left the Taylor mansion for church when Samantha stepped outside and walked to the edge of the long porch to get some firewood for the living room fireplace. It wasn't something she would normally do but with everyone out of the house, including all the staff, she decided it was cool enough to start a fire and she wanted to relax in front of the fireplace with a cup of hot chocolate and try to read a new novel she had just purchased. She was suffering with the tail end of a cold and didn't feel much like doing anything else. She had already cancelled a morning brunch with Paris since she was doing so much coughing, sniffing and blowing her nose. She didn't want to do anything social and she didn't want any visitors to give her cold to. But she and Paris had plans to see each other that evening.

Just as she bent over to pick up a couple of logs that were stacked neatly at the edge of the porch, a warm hand touched the back of her neck. It startled her. Samantha instinctively jumped backward, dropping the two sticks of firewood. Then she swirled around and there stood Kenny Ross.

"Hi, Samantha, let me get that for you," he said, laughing slightly.

"Hi, thanks," she frowned from the smell of wine seeping through his pores.

Samantha grabbed the door as he stumbled inside with his arms full of firewood. When he bent to lay the wood on the floor, a bottle of red wine fell out of his coat pocket. Samantha was startled and her face warmed with disappointment.

She grabbed her mouth with both hands in shock. "Kenny, I can't believe you're off the wagon. But you're drinking again." She pointed toward the front door. "Therefore, I don't mean to be rude, but you need to just leave now! Okay! How many times back in college did I ask you not to come around me when you're drinking? I know we were back in college then, but the same goes. I don't want you around when you're drinking? I don't want you coming to my home intoxicated the way you are right now! So, please, Kenny, Just pick up your wine bottle and leave!" She suggested, pointing toward the front door.

Kenny roared at her with a boiling angry expression on his face. His loud mouth and the strange look in his eyes, somewhat frightened her. "If Paris Franklin came over here intoxicated would you be so quick to kick him out?"

"I'm not going to discuss Paris with you, Kenny." Samantha took a seat on the sofa and grabbed her face.

Then she looked at Kenny with surprise, compassion and disappointment in her eyes. She was so happy when he had pulled his life together and was no longer drinking. Now out of the blue he seemed to be back at it.

Kenny held up both hands. "I know this looks bad but it's not as bad as it looks. I'm not really drinking again. I'm just drinking today. I'll give it up again tomorrow. You have my word," he promised.

"But, Kenny, why today? You know you are an alcoholic and it's not safe or healthy for you to drink period."

"Samantha, please don't give me a hard time. How much harm could come out of one day of boozing? It's been so long since I had a drink, so I had a glass of wine with lunch and by the time I was finished, I had ordered four glasses. So when I left the restaurant I figured I would just buy a bottle," he explained.

"It's not okay for you to spend a day drinking thinking tomorrow will be okay. One in a hundred things could happen to you or someone else because of your drinking. You need to take your bottle and throw it away, then go home and jump in bed and sleep it off," Samantha stressed strongly. "It's not safe for you or others for you to be drinking under the influence of so much alcohol."

"I'll be just fine," he said, grinning. "Do you mind if I have a seat?" He pointed to the couch cushions next to her.

Samantha solemnly pointed toward the opposite sofa. "You can have a seat over there for a moment, and then you need to leave. I don't want you here in a drunken state."

"I can't think of anywhere I would rather be than here looking at your lovely face," he said as he took a seat across from her.

"Kenny, I'm happily dating Paris and you're in a relationship with Vickie Simpson. Therefore, it makes me uneasy when you take the liberty to talk to me in such a fresh way. If you don't know, I'll tell you that I do not find it clever or cute. So could you please not talk to me in a flirting manner?"

He stared at her for a moment and then he winked at her. "You once were okay with my flirtation toward you when we were in college together."

"That was then, and at that time I wasn't dating anyone and you weren't dating anyone. But now we are both in relationships," she reminded him.

"What if we weren't in relationships, would you mind me flirting with you then?"

"Kenny, it doesn't feel comfortable having this kind of discussion with you. So, please change the topic or just leave. Because you really need to get over this obsession you have for me." She paused and nodded toward him. "You need to start obsessing over Vickie, someone who cares about you."

"Because you don't give a damn, do you?"

"Don't put words in my mouth, Kenny."

"Well, do you give a damn?"

"Yes, I do care about you; and you know I care about you," she said seriously. "But only as a good friend. I'm forever grateful to you for the kind gesture you gave to Paris and I last fall when you came by the house and made him see you and I were not girlfriend and boyfriend back in college. If you hadn't shown up that day, Paris and I may not have made it. Therefore, we are both very grateful to you; and I have heard Paris speak kindly of you."

He shook his head. "I could care less about his thoughts of me," Kenny snapped.

"That's not true. I think you do care. That's your liquor speaking now."

"What different does it makes, he's with the woman I really want to be with."

"Kenny, I think it's your liquor talking. You know we are just friends."

"Always as a friend," he snapped. "You can keep your friendship. I don't need or want your handouts!"

"Kenny, why are you getting an attitude because I said we are just friends? You know we are just friends."

"Samantha, we could be more than friends if you would just give us a chance."

"Kenny, snap out of it. I can't talk to you while you are half drunk."

"I may be half drunk, but I still know what I'm saying and why. I'm crazy about you now and always have been and I loathe your friendship suggestion."

"Kenny, what are you getting at? You know we are never going to be more than friends. I'm committed to Paris for goodness sake," she stressed strongly.

"Of course, you are committed to the rich pretty boy," he snapped angrily.

"So, what if he's rich? If you want to mention whose rich, you can add me to that list. But we shouldn't be talking about pocketbooks; we should be talking about who cares about who. I know Vickie cares about you. Not to mention she's devoted to you and I believe she would marry you in a New York minute," she suggested.

"What part of I don't want Vickie Simpson for a wife don't you understand?" Kenny said firmly, looking straight in Samantha's eyes.

"Yes, Vickie is crazy about me, and she's a nice young woman. But she's not you, Samantha. I want to be with you and whenever I drink I can't deny my feelings for you. All the money in the world couldn't make me forget you," he said, smiling and paused. "I'm not really trying to diminish what I share with Vickie, I know she's a good woman and I could deal, but she's just missing that something that is you."

"You just said she's a good woman, so give her a chance. You could grow to love her if you just move on from thinking there could be anything between us," Samantha said.

Kenny stood up, pulled his bottle from his coat pocket and shouted. "This is the last of his bottle." He turned his bottle up to his lips and finished the last drop of wine.

The fact that he finished his booze in her face, made her blood boil and said in a very upset tone. "The nerve of you to stand here drunk; and drink in my face! You know I don't like it when you come around me drinking."

"It doesn't matter whether I'm drunk or sober; you always find something to bitch about with me. Now don't you, Miss Samantha? I think that's what your staff calls you, right? Should I call you, Miss Samantha?"

"Kenny just stop being a jerk and go home before you do or say something that you cannot take back," she urged.

"But you didn't answer my question."

"You just asked me two questions, which one was you referring to?"

"It doesn't matter whether I'm intoxicated or sober; you always find something to bitch about. That question," he said sharply.

"That's not true, so could you just please leave my house and go straight home," she strongly suggested. "Because you know, I don't purposely fuss with you. I'm offended that you just said that. However, I'm trying to give you a break because I know it's the booze. But I still don't want you around me when you're like this!" She pointed toward the door again, hoping me would leave.

"Miss Samantha, I just don't think you want me around either way!" he said in a humbly voice. "It didn't use to be this way back in college. The moment you got back home you changed and started giving me the cold shoulder, especially after you landed yourself a Franklin guy!"

"You are not being truthful, Kenny. So why do you keep ignoring my wishes for you to leave here?"

"Maybe because your wishes stinks!" he shouted angrily. "I have no intentions of leaving here until I accomplish what I came for."

"What is that supposed to mean?" she curiously, alarmingly asked.

"It simply means that I plan to give you a taste of your own medicine and show you that I have changed as well."

"Yes, Kenny, you have changed overnight," she nodded. "Right now, I feel you have changed into a bigger drinker than you were before you gave up the booze last fall."

He laughed. "You don't have a clue what I mean. Because that was the wrong answer." He held up one finger. "The correct answer is that I have changed into the man that's going to break a few rules to teach you an important lesson," he seriously stated.

Samantha grabbed her mouth with both hands. His words stunned her. It dawned on her that he was acting completely out of character as if he was totally intoxicated to the point that he probably didn't know what he was doing or saying.

"I guess that got your attention," he grinned as his eyes looked wet and red. "I meant it. I'll show you who you can use for a doormat. I worship the ground you walk on, but I'm tired of being your doormat while you treat me like your hired help and order me out of your big fancy home!"

Samantha was stunned and couldn't speak as Kenny poured hurtful words toward her. She had forgotten how different from day and night his drinking could make him.

"All the flowers and gifts I gave you back in college were just fine before you started rubbing shoulders with the rich boy. Now we're just friends and everything I do is annoying and suddenly wrong," he explained angrily.

"Kenny, we have always been just friends."

"Maybe, but you should have told me that when you were accepting my flowers and gifts for every occasion from Easter to Christmas! And the list goes on and on!"

"You were giving me those things because you wanted to. I didn't lead you on. Plus, I mostly accepted them because of our friendship and I didn't want to hurt your feelings by not accepting them," Samantha politely explained.

"Maybe you should have hurt my feelings and I would have gotten the message that we are just the friends that you think we are."

"Think about it, Kenny. We went out a couple times, but it was just as friends. We never kissed in the real sense of the word."

"And why didn't we kiss?"

"We just didn't because I don't think of you in that way," Samantha explained. "It's not personal. You can be very sweet, one of the nicest guys in the world when you're not drinking. That's why Vickie is lucky to have someone like you."

"You think Vickie Simpson is lucky to have someone like me, but you can't stomach me for yourself, I guess?"

"Vickie is nice and goodhearted."

"If she's so nice and goodhearted, you have a lot of friends that you could introduce her to," he suggested.

"Kenny, you do not mean that. Everybody knows how you are always glued to Vickie. And why would I introduce her to any of my friends when Vickie and I are not really close. Besides, she wants to be with you, Kenny," Samantha stressed. "Just stay with Vickie and give your relationship with her a chance."

"Okay, let's make a deal. I'll give my relationship with Vickie a chance if you'll give me a chance. How is that for a deal, yes or no?"

"Kenny, you're talking out of your head. I'm already in a relationship and I'm very devoted and committed to Paris. Therefore, what you just said is a moot question. So I'm asking you nicely once again, please just leave, Kenny." Samantha stood up from the sofa and pointed toward the door again.

"What part of I'm not leaving until I teach your high society rich ass a lesson! I thought I made that quite clear, didn't you understand?"

"What did you just say?" Samantha asked. His statement caught her off guard.

"No, what, I'm drunk and highly upset and I don't plan to leave this house until I give you what Paris probably hasn't." He leaped off the sofa and rushed over to her and grabbed, wrapping her in his arms.

"Kenny, let go of me. What are you doing?" she said in a panic voice.

"What does it look like I'm doing?" She scuffled and wrestled with him and tried to break free of his embrace until they ended up across the huge room against the living room wall. He pushed her against the wall and brought his face down to hers.

She pushed with all her strength but she couldn't bulge him away from her. "Kenny, please take your hands off of me. What if someone walks in and see you touching me in your drunken state?" she warned him. "Just stop while you're ahead. "You could end up in jail for this out of control drunken conduct against me. Is that what you want?"

"Maybe it is what I want if it means I get to get that real kiss that I never got from you," he said as he pushed his forceful, cold, dry lips against hers.

During her scuffle against him, she slightly bit her bottom lip. Then she screamed as he pushed his mouth against hers. Samantha thought he would cut off her breathing from the suffocating grip of his mouth against her tender lips. He was out of control and pushed her against the wall every time she tried to push him away.

When Kenny released his lips from hers and attempted to kiss her neck, she let out a loud scream. But that only made him more determined to kiss her. The thought of his behavior sent an agonizing pain through her stomach.

"Now shut up and just cooperate! You can't stop me anyway!"

"This is wrong," Samantha cried.

"You think so, do you? Well, I'll tell you what's wrong. It's wrong to treat me like a second class citizen every time I see you, always making me feel like I'm not good enough. Pushing Vickie in my face right now, when you know I have been in love with you since college. Nevertheless, you would never give me the time of day. Well, you will give it to me now, because whether you like it or not, I'm going to take that kiss that you never thought I was good enough to get from you," he said laughingly.

"Kenny you need to snap out of your mood," Samantha snapped.

"I'm not in a mood. I'm just being real. I want to kiss you and I plan to do just that. You probably want me to kiss you anyway. I don't know why you have made it seem so forbidden to me all these years."

"I'm not taking you serious because you are just out of your head drunk."

"You should take me serious, because I mean everything I'm saying. I'm going to kiss you and enjoy every minute of it, Miss Samantha Taylor. Now, who's in control? Do you still feel like the high and mighty Taylor that you are?"

Kenny gripped her tighter as he pinned her arms back against the wall and kissed her neck and the side of her face. She turned her head from side to side, trying to avoid his kiss and it made her feel intense anger for him. Then he urgently pushed his tongue down her throat, suffocating her with his out-of-control lust. At that moment, as he kissed her, she wished she had enough strength to push him away and slap his face. She tried to push him away but she couldn't move him as he held her and kissed her passionately as if he had never kissed a woman before.

A few seconds later after he released his arms from around her, she laid there against the wall, still and upset as her stomach boiled with disappointment and extreme anger for him. But he looked down at her as if he had just quickly sobered up back to reality. He had a shock look on his face as he flew across the room toward the sofa, threw his coat and hurried toward the front door. By the time Samantha walked across the living room floor to look out the window, his car was gone. She grabbed her face and cried as she slowly walked across the room and took a seat on the sofa.

Chapter Twenty-One

Monday evening Samantha sat in a side chair near the fireplace in her room. She wasn't reading or checking her social media pages. She sat with her arms folded, leaning slightly forward looking at the low flame in her fireplace. She was heartbroken and filled with confusion over her breakup with Paris. She strongly felt that the drunken kiss incident from the day before with Kenny had ruined their relationship. She and Paris had not been able to come to terms. He wanted to know who had kissed her and she chose not to confide in him. Therefore, that Sunday evening before Paris left the Taylor's mansion, he and Samantha decided to end their relationship; and breaking up with him hurt her more than anything in the world that she could have ever imagined.

She was still only working part time at her father's company downtown and she was climbing the walls thinking about Paris and wanting to be with him. But she thought to herself, what could she do? He had left that morning to take the vacation to France that the two of them had planned to take together; and on his short visit to her home that morning when he dropped over to say goodbye, he gave her no indication that the two of them would be able to work things out. Therefore, she felt she needed to throw herself into an important project to help her cope with his absence. Something that would buffer her lonesome days and nights while he vacation in another country.

While pondering what would be a worthwhile project, that's when Kenny Ross popped into her thoughts.

Although, she was highly disappointed in his indiscretion toward her on the day before, his disrespectful behavior also made him appear broken and in helpless. She thought about how much he needed help with his addiction. Her heart went out to how much he was suffering with his disease. Therefore, she decided that she wanted to make a difference in his life and be the one to help him get sober to help him be a better man. She felt his treatment toward her was beneath him and that he was a much better person than what he had displayed in his uncontrollable drunken state.

She had always liked Kenny as a friend and thought how they had been so much closer during their college days. Now their association felt strained and Kenny seemed uncomfortable in her home. She wanted that to change. She wanted to reconnect with him and help him through the process of getting back on the wagon.

She still had his phone number and after pondering over the idea for fifteen minutes, she convinced herself to call him. She knew that deep down no one could replace Paris in her heart, but she felt she needed someone in her orbit to show her attention and warmth during her lonely days without Paris. And although, Kenny had displayed very discourteous behavior when he kissed her against her will, she felt that he would be a good distraction in her life while she waited for Paris to return. Her mission would be to help him with his drinking problem.

In the looks department there was no contest that Paris was drop dead gorgeous to Kenny's above average cute looks. Kenny was tall and attractive, with short wary black hair hanging to his ear. Samantha had been fascinated with Kenny's wild ways in the past during their college days. However, now that they were both grown up she had no other interest in him other than as a friend.

She hesitated slightly as she stood from the chair and stepped over to the landline phone that sat on her bedside table. She lifted the receiver and paused down at the phone for a moment before she dialed Kenny's number. Then she took a seat on the side of her bed as she listened to the ringing in her ear. After the third ring, she contemplated on hanging up the phone. Then after the fourth ring, an older woman with a friendly voice answered the phone.

"Hello, may I help you?"

"Yes, I'm looking for Kenny, is he home?" Samantha asked.

"No, dear, I'm sorry, but Kenny isn't in at the moment."

"That's right, I have his home number. He moved, didn't he?" Samantha asked.

"That is true. He did move into his own apartment but he still stays here with us from time to time," Mildred said. "Anyway, he left home a few minutes ago and I think he's coming right back. I think he just headed to the gas station."

"Okay, thanks, I can just give him a call back."

"You have made one call. I'll have him call you when he gets back. What's your number, dear?"

"Is this his mother?"

"Yes, this is Mildred Ross."

"Hi, Mrs. Ross, my name is Samantha Taylor."

"Did you say, Samantha Taylor?"

"Yes, ma'am, I'm Samantha Taylor. Kenny and I went to college together."

"I know, you are Charles Taylor's daughter," Mildred said excitedly.

"Yes, ma'am, I am."

"It's a pleasure to hear from you Miss Taylor. Kenny talked a lot about you when you two were in college together," she friendly explained. "My son thinks a lot of you and what you stand for."

"Thanks for telling me," Samantha softly said. "Kenny is a good guy too. All the things I'm an advocate for, he cares for those causes too," Samantha said sincerely.

"Yes, he does care about many things," Mildred said. "But my son has one great flaw that's holding him down and I'm sure you know it's his drinking."

Samantha felt awkward commenting about his drinking to his mother, therefore, she didn't say anything as Mildred continued. "Just give me your number and I'll have him call you. He'll be quite thrilled to hear you called the house."

"Thanks for giving him the message. My number is 847-555-6314," she said and hung up the phone, which she carried across the room with her where she took a seat on the small white sofa in her room.

She placed her back against the cushions while holding the house phone in her lap, and less than five minutes of hanging up the phone with Mrs. Ross, the phone rang. She smiled down at the ivory phone, knowing the caller was probably Kenny. At the end of the second ring, she picked up the receiver and placed it against her ear.

"Kenny, is that you? I didn't expect a call back so soon," she said in good cheer.

"It's me and I didn't expect to hear from you period," he said humbly.

"I'm sure you didn't expect to hear from me, but I want to be the bigger person and put that kiss behind us. Besides, I've been thinking a lot about you and the fact that you kissed me against my wishes yesterday."

"I was blown away when Mom told me you had called the house and left a message for me to call you. I don't think you have ever called my house and left a message for me," he said excitedly. "But this is most likely not a social call. You're probably, and rightfully so, calling to chew me out for my indiscretion toward you yesterday," he assumed.

"Kenny, that's not why I'm calling," she said sincerely.

"It's not why you're calling?" he said with surprise in his voice. "I assumed that would have been the reason for your call, but you know I'm a million times sorry. I apologize for the drunken bastard who grabbed you and kissed you."

"I believe you are sorry and I accepts your apology," she said seriously.

"Thanks you for accepting my apology," he humbly stressed. "You know that was not me yesterday. I don't know or recognize the drunken fool that put his hands on you," he said seriously. "I don't know what swallowed up my brain. I know I had had more than enough to drink," he humbly said and then was silent on the other end of the receiver for a second. "I have gone on binges before and I have never crossed the line with you like that."

"No, you haven't."

"One time is too many and I hope you can find a way to forgive me," he humbly mumbled. "But seriously, as much as I'm thankful for your forgiveness. I don't think I deserve it. Because, Samantha, believe me when I say I'm ashamed of my conduct and can't believe you are letting me off the hook so easily."

"I don't see it like I'm letting you off the hook. I just realize you have a disease that takes control of you when you indulge in too much alcohol," she softly said.

"Only you could say something like that and not call me out on my drunken unspeakable behavior," he seriously stated. "I guess that's why I have you on a pedestal so high. There's no other female out there like you, not even your sisters would have stood still and not let me have it for such disrespectful conduct. Therefore, you are high up there on my pedestal and I seriously doubt any other female could ever reach it."

"I'm just trying to be reasonable and fair. I didn't want you to treat me that way and force a kiss on me, but I also realize that your actions were under the influence."

"Samantha, again I'm sorry. You know how much I care about you and how much I think of you."

"Yes, Kenny, I do. I'm aware of how you feel about me as a person," she acknowledged. "Plus, I know you feel just awful and you're beating yourself up. But don't. We both know what got into you yesterday."

"Yes, we do. The booze. The poison I can't seem to resist," he said regretfully.

"Yes, Kenny, you were falling down out of your head intoxicated yesterday. But no matter how we analyze it, I know you didn't mean it. The person who was talking disrespectful and took a kiss from me, that's not who you are."

"You are right, it's not who I am; and I definitely didn't mean it. I would never in good conscience do anything to disrespect or hurt you, Samantha. I hope you know that."

"I do know that. That's why I forgive you and I'm not going to hold it against you."

"Thank you, you are too good. I don't know what I have ever done to deserve the kindness of someone like you," he said gratefully.

"I'll admit that at first, after you first left the house, I was thrown and shaken and quite upset with you for your obnoxious language and that kiss," she softly admitted. "However, after I sat quietly on the sofa awhile reflecting on what had taken place, it dawned on me that you are a slave to your own addiction," she seriously stated. "Since you have a disease that is controlling you."

"That's absolutely correct. I have this damn drinking problem that runs in my family. I got on the wagon last fall and somehow I'm back at it again," he said regretfully. "It's a constant struggle to try to stay sober."

"I would like to help you do that," Samantha announced.

"You would like to help me do what?"

"I would like to help you stay sober."

"First of all, I have to get sober to stay sober," he grinned. "Is this a prank caller? It definitely doesn't sound like Miss Samantha Taylor," he said teasingly. "But let me make sure I'm hearing you correctly. You would like to help me get sober and stay that way, is that correct?" he asked.

"Yes, you heard me correctly. I want to help you get back on the wagon. It will also help me."

"The more I listen the more I think this is a prank caller. Because I don't think the real Samantha Taylor would be calling my home after I acted like such a drunken bastard at her home yesterday," he said with a voice filled with remorse.

"You know I'm not a prank caller, but I'm glad you are not taking it lightly what happened due to your drinking yesterday," she said.

"No way am I taking it lightly. I realize how blessed I am that you are even talking to me; and the fact that you are not upset with me is just icing on the cake," he said with a voice filled with gratefulness.

"You are right; I'm no longer upset with you. But make no mistake. I was initially very upset with you about what you did. But as I just said to you, I know it was all that alcohol inside of you."

"It was the alcohol, but still, there's no excuse, really. I was just a plain drunken bastard yesterday. When you told me to leave your house, I should have just left."

"Don't think about it. It wasn't completely your fault. You have a disease and I plan to help you rid yourself of it," she assured him.

"By helping you, something good will come from what you did. Plus, it will help me do something noble during the time Paris is away. Because believe me, Kenny, I desperately need something meaningful to fill my time."

"So, I'm it! Your guinea pig?" he grinned. "But I'm not complaining. "I'm pleased and willing to be whatever you need me to be. So, if you need me to be a guinea pig, one guinea pig coming up."

"I wouldn't call you a guinea pig," she softly laughed. "But seriously, you do need a lot of help with your addiction and I would like to do what I can to help you."

"This is too incredible."

"What's too incredible?" she asked.

"The fact that you called and left a message for me to call you back," he said excitedly. "Now of all things, you are telling me that you want to help me get back on the wagon and help me stay sober," he said excitedly. "You have to admit that it does make sense what I said."

"What did you say?"

"You could have written me off for my appalling behavior. Before you called, I was considering the possibility of never hearing from you again."

"You're right, it would have been completely understandable if I had decided to throw away your phone number instead of dialing it. But I wanted to be bigger than that. So here I am on the other end of the phone forgiving the bad conduct; and I'm glad we can move past what happened and continue being friends," she caringly uttered.

Silence filled the line, then he said. "I would've understood completely if you had chosen to never speak to me again. Seriously, after yesterday, why would you even want to speak to me or call me or even bother to care whether I end up getting sober of not. The rotten bastard I was to you yesterday pretty much wrote me a farewell ticket from you?"

"I know it was rotten what you did yesterday. But we really don't need to keep bringing it up. I want to move past it. The Kenny I know is inside of you somewhere and I will help you to bring him out. He surfaced last fall when Paris and I needed him the most," she said warmly. "That was your finest hour when you came to our rescue.

Therefore, I'm willing to look past the foolish mistake you made yesterday and put my energy toward helping you to stay sober so you don't make any more foolish mistakes like that again."

"Do you really mean that? This coming from the girl who blew me off at her Halloween party last fall," he said jokingly.

"I didn't blow you off."

"I know you didn't. I was just kidding. Besides, I was so mess up and wasted at your Halloween party until blowing me off is what you should have done," he seriously stated and was silent on the other end of the receiver for a moment before he continued. "You are right about one thing, Samantha."

"What's that?" she asked.

"You're right that I'm no good to be around when I have had one too many, which seems like most of the time. I'm not proud to admit this, but lately, I'm drinking pretty much ninety percent of the time."

"You were doing so well, but I'm sure you had more than a few things that could have knocked you off the wagon this time?" she said sadly.

"More than a few things are correct. I don't think I need to list them. You've heard and read all the scandalous news that's floating around about parents. My father almost murdering my mother was no small back page news, and certainly not a headline I'll be able to shake out of my mind too soon," he admitted. "The booze seems to help me to cope and that's why lately, I drink from sun up to sun down. It's more like ninety nine percent of the time instead of ninety percent of the time," he admitted.

"Kenny, I'm deeply sorry for what you and your family are going through and especially your burden of addiction. I promise, I'll do my best to help you cut that figure in half until its non-existence, how does that sound?"

He didn't comment on what she asked, line was silence until he uttered. "How time flies. That Halloween party seems like yesterday but it was almost six months ago."

"You are right, how rapidly time goes by," she agreed.

"But that was then and this is now," he said and paused as he got choked up with warmth from the thought that she cared so much about his wellbeing. "Now, by some wonderful miracle, I'm sure I don't deserve, I have the most beautiful woman in the world giving me a call after I just displayed such improper conduct with her."

"Thank you for that compliment."

"It's only true, but I have to wonder if this call is in regards to Mr. Franklin taking off to France?"

"Paris left this morning to start his vacation in France for the next two weeks, but I'm not calling you because he left town. I'm calling because Paris and I broke up last night and we didn't try to reconcile this morning when he dropped by to say goodbye."

"If he dropped by to say goodbye, it's clear you're still it for him," Kenny mumbled.

"I wouldn't go that far, since he left for France and I'm still here," she quickly replied. "Therefore, I thought it would be meaningful to focus my time to rid you of alcohol after what it made you do yesterday."

"I'm beside myself pleased with this call," he said. "Miss Samantha is going to help rid me of alcohol?" He laughed. "I'm pleased, but it makes me wonder."

"It makes you wonder about what?" she asked.

"It makes me wonder about your boyfriend or your ex-boyfriend," he said.

"I guess I don't get what you're getting at. What are you wondering about?"

"If you're going to give me all this attention to help me get sober, I'm wondering where does that leave the Prince?"

"It doesn't leave him anywhere," Samantha softly answered.

"Accept still inside of your heart, I'm sure," Kenny said.

"No comment on that. I just told you that Paris and I broke up last night, and his goodbye sealed it this morning."

"Wake up, Samantha; it doesn't sound like he's done with you or you with him."

"Then we see it differently, because as far as I can see, we are done."

"Why did you breakup?"

"I told him what happened yesterday, that I was kissed against my wishes. But I refused to share with him who kissed me. He was highly disappointed that I chose not to confide in him," she said solemnly. "I guess every time he looked at me it was a reminder of another man kissing me," Samantha explained without a detection of sadness in her voice.

"Did you ever mention…?"

"No, Kenny, I never mentioned to him that it was you who kissed me. I forgave you for your crime because I know it wasn't you. Therefore, I never would've been able to live with myself if I had confessed to Paris or my family for them to think less or hate you."

"Thank you, I'm determined to get sober and stay that way after what it made me do to you."

"Don't mention it again. I'm satisfied that you are willing to give up alcohol, which is the real crook. I know it was the alcohol that controlled you. You were so intoxicated until you could barely stand up."

"I'm grateful, and as much as I'm grateful. I don't deserve your forgiveness and silence. What I did to you was improper and in some cases it could be considered a crime."

"It only becomes a crime when the law is involved. Plus, as much as I hate what you did, I don't think you would be thrown in jail for the kiss."

"You never know. Lesser cases have been made. Therefore, I'm forever grateful that you didn't call the cops or tell your folks."

"Kenny, what kind of friend would I be if I called the cops on a friend who I knew wasn't himself," she explained. "And yes, I agree that what you did could be considered a crime, the fact that you grabbed me and kissed me against my wishes. But you didn't really hurt me. You startled and confused me. But I'm over it. Besides, as I just said, I don't think you would have gone to prison for kissing me," she said seriously. "Besides, I refuse to send a man to prison who thinks as much of me as you do," she said teasingly.

"I'm glad you can tease and find humor in it because frankly, I cannot," he admitted.

"Kenny, I'm not trying to make light of it, but I honestly do not believe you'll ever do that again, sober or not."

He interrupted. "You are hundred percent right about that."

"Kenny, I'm just trying to relay to you that I know you care about me as a friend, despite your behavior and how you treated me yesterday," Samantha explained.

"I do care about you as a friend, and I'm honored you want to be mine. However, on the serious side, I do have deeper feelings for you. But I'm not kidding myself. You have made it crystal clear to me on more than one occasion how you feel about me," he humbly explained and grinned. "I'm sure I only have your attention right now because Paris isn't around. Fortunate for me, you have set your sites to fix this broken man, and I'm grateful."

"You're right, I do miss Paris," she sadly uttered. "However, I have to be realistic."

"What do you have to be realistic about?" he asked.

"Realistic that Paris may never be able to see me in the same way as he used to."

"Because you shared with him that you were kissed by another man?"

"Not just that. I feel we could've moved on pass that. But he was just plain disappointed that I couldn't share with him who kissed me. Therefore, I know I have to be realistic and face the facts. He believes in full disclosure and complete honesty," she said.

"Samantha, I don't know what to say. You are willing to risk what you have with him because you don't want to rat me out?"

"It would make your mistake worse if I mentioned you are the person who dropped by the house and kissed me against my wishes," she seriously explained. "I don't want to share your identity with anyone, including Paris. Since you are a victim too."

"I really appreciate your efforts and your loyalty. But I think you are the only one who would see it that way."

"Maybe you are right. But I'm being logical and moving on. The only hinder is that I still don't know that many people in the area."

"That's right, most of your friends live downtown," he said.

"That's right, I have very few friends in the area. That's one reason why I'll have the spare time to help you with your drinking addiction," she explained. "I'm hopeful that doing my process of helping you through your drinking dependence that you and I can possibly rekindle the closeness we used to share with each other during our college days."

Kenny grinned through the receiver. "What closeness was that? Have you forgotten that all through college you wouldn't give me the time of day?" he said laughingly. "You know I'm right, and before you stop me and say how we went out a couple times, it really doesn't count as going out. Therefore, we didn't really have closeness between us. We were friends and I wanted to be so much more than your friend. But you only thought of me as a friend," Kenny reminded her.

"How do you really know how I felt about you Kenny?"

"I know because Miss honest Samantha told me. I didn't want to hear it, of course. Nevertheless, you told me anyway."

"What did I tell you?"

"You told me that we could only be friends because you were waiting for Mr. Right to come along, which meant you clearly didn't think of me as Mr. Right. Plus, I wasn't kidding myself. I knew I wasn't in your league at the time with nothing to offer you. Your family wasn't about to have you saddle yourself with a broke fellow like me back then, not that I have any more now," he grinned. "But, at least I'm a working man without the stigma of a rock band against me."

"Why would you describe your band as a stigma against you? I thought your band was nice back then and so did a lot of other people," Samantha seriously stated. "I liked it."

"I'm glad you liked my band at that time, but as we both know, my band went nowhere really fast. It was a pipe dream that I had to give up, so I did. But thanks, anyway. I'm glad you liked my band and thought of me as your friend back then."

"I thought you thought we were close back then as well," Samantha mumbled.

"Yeah, I guess you are right that we were sort of close back in college. But I'm not kidding myself now," he said and she listened to a moment of silence before he continued. "I know you just think of me as a friend and you think I'm a meaningful project until Paris comes home from France," he said respectfully.

She didn't comment.

"So, do you think that made sense? Do you still think of me as a friend, and are you still waiting for Mr. Right? I thought Paris Franklin was your Mr. Right."

"I would like to think that we are still friends," she said and paused for a moment. "But what do you mean by your question, if I'm still looking for Mr. Right?"

"I was just wondering since Paris left for France without you. I know it's none of my business but I heard from Courtney earlier before you phoned. She mentioned that her boss took off for France for two weeks. At first I wasn't sure which Franklin she meant until she mentioned Paris name and then I realized your guy had left town. Therefore, when you phoned, I was already abreast of Mr. Franklin's travel itinerary and wondered if there could be trouble in paradise."

"I think there's two questions wrapped up in what you are saying," Samantha stated curiously. "I believe you are asking if there's trouble in paradise and if I'm looking for another Mr. Right? Is that what you are trying to find out?"

He grinned. "I hope I'm not being too forward, but it did cross my mind," he humbly said and continued. "Although, I was under the impression that Paris was your Mr. Right. Just in case he's no longer your fair guy, I would like to be in the running," he said, teasingly.

Samantha slightly laughed. "Kenny, you are probably half teasing and half serious. However, I just want to clear something up right now."

"Clear up what?"

"What our status is to each other," she said.

He interrupted before she could explain. "There's no need to clear up anything. I was just teasing. I know we are just friends."

"You are absolutely correct. Our status with each other is strictly friendship. I don't see you in any other way other than as a friend," she said seriously.

"I'm painfully aware of the fact that you only see me as a friend," he said. "However, Samantha, things and feelings can change for two people sometime."

"Sure, things and feelings can change sometime," she agreed. "But they won't change for us. We are friends, Kenny, and that's all we'll ever be."

He grinned. "I have just received your message loud and clear. But you didn't answer my question about Mr. Right and whether you are looking for another one."

"Here's my answer. I thought Paris was Mr. Right; and whether I still think he is doesn't really matter if he doesn't share the same view."

"In other words, you don't know where you stand with the man at the moment."

"That's right; because as I told you earlier, Paris and I are not seeing eye-to-eye at the moment," Samantha reminded him. "But why are you bringing this up again? I have already discussed our breakup. It's not like I can predict the future."

"I'm just trying to make sure the Prince won't be a problem or show up gunning for me for socializing with you." He laughed, in a teasing way. "I recall that he wasn't that pleased with me for crashing your Halloween party last October."

"You two made up and connected after that and he has been one of your biggest champions since," Samantha pointed out. "Besides, that's one of the reasons why I have chosen not to disclose to him that you kissed me. It would wipe out all the progress you made with him last fall when you dropped by my house and talked to us," she stressed seriously. "Therefore, I think I can safely say that you have no worries of Paris showing up gunning for you," she assured him. "Besides, it's not who he is, but one more thing."

"What's that?" he asked.

"Please stop calling Paris a Prince."

"I'm just teasing about calling him that. I just still see him in my mind's eye in that Prince costume during Halloween. And you were dressed like the timeless Cinderella," he said laughingly. "Whose idea was it to dress like the Prince and Cinderella?"

"It wasn't our idea. Carrie suggested it."

"Who's Carrie?"

"Carrie Westwood is our maid. She suggested that Paris and I dress up as the Prince and Cinderella and she offered to make our costumes."

"Wow, your maid gets involve."

"Yes, she does. We all love Carrie," Samantha warmly uttered. "She and her husband, Sam and their son, Larry, are just like members of the family. We are all much closer to the three of them than we are the rest of the staff," Samantha admitted.

"I guess they are like members of your family, if you wear the costume she suggests and then allows her to make the outfits."

"One thing I should tell you is how much Carrie love Halloween. It's her all-time favorite day to celebrate. She also offered to host our Halloween party, and my mother was fine with that. Carrie pretty much runs our household, and all the other staff gets their instructions from her," Samantha laughed.

"Your maid sounds like a super woman who doesn't limit herself to just domestic work," Kenny said.

"Carrie is a super woman to us. We love when she participates in our family events. She loves to host parties and we love to let her host our parties."

"That brings to mind all the fun costume and wild parties we attended back in college," Kenny said laughingly. "I should rephrase that and say that I attended."

"I also attended a lot of those parties as well," Samantha corrected him.

"Of course, you attended some, but none of the wild drinking parties. If my memory serves me correctly, you would always sneak in for the event parties whenever my band was scheduled to perform," he reminded her. "Do you remember those days?"

"Kenny, of course, I remember those days. They were fun," Samantha laughed.

"They were fun, but all the fun ended for us when we graduated from the university and moved back home. I showed up at your Halloween party and you acted as if you barely knew me. But of course, you had just started dating Paris Franklin."

"Kenny, I didn't treat you as if I didn't know you. Why would you say that?"

"That's how it seemed to me at the time," he said.

"How would you know how it seemed? You were out of your head loaded and I wasn't pleased that you had shown up falling down drunk."

"Maybe I was falling down drunk, but I still felt you were sort of giving me the cold shoulder," he confessed.

"I was with my boyfriend and you were being obnoxious to both of us. Do you think we should have greeted you with open arms regardless to your vulgar mouth?" Samantha asked. "Besides, don't tell me that you are still upset about that?"

"No, of course not. I'm not upset; I'm just letting you know that I haven't forgotten how bold you were to stop talking to me on the spot after Paris Franklin asked you out."

"Okay, Kenny, enough already. We have gotten off course. Besides, that's ancient history. I called your house earlier because I was thinking of your wellbeing and I want to get back to the reason I called you," Samantha said sincerely. "What I have in mind is something that I feel is noble and I would like to hear your thoughts."

"Okay, what do you have in mind?"

"It's what I said earlier in our conversation. I'm serious about trying to help you give up alcohol. I'm also very serious about the two of us rekindles the kind of friendship we had with each other back in college."

"I believe you are serious. I just don't know how you plan to do it. That's a lot to tackle and execute. You plan to help me give up booze and in the process, rekindle the kind of friendship we had back in college?" he said with cautious optimism. "It all sounds too good to be true. But seriously, we have different viewpoints on what kind of friendship we shared back in college. I remember feeling like a lost puppy who desperately wanted to be your friend. Therefore, I grabbed every chance I could to talk to you. But to be honest, I sort of felt like you considered me an afterthought," he admitted. "I don't mean to sound rude, but I'm just trying to be honest about how I felt back then and how I thought you felt."

"Kenny, maybe you remember the past in that way because we were just friends and you wanted it to be more. Nevertheless, you and I were close friends who talked on the phone to each other every other day. Plus, we hang out in the library, the campus bookstore and the lunchroom together a lot."

"You are right. We did a lot on campus together. However, you still only considered me as a friend. You weren't dating anyone at the time. But the boy you were spending time with wasn't someone you wanted to date."

"I didn't want to date you because I didn't have those kind of feelings for you. But we were good friends. As a matter of a fact, I considered you to be one of my best friends back in college," Samantha admitted.

"I was one of your best friends? Maybe that's why it was so easy for you to breakup with me back then. You only considered me a friend," Kenny said solemnly.

"That's what you were. What else did you consider yourself to me?" she asked.

"You are right," he agreed. "I couldn't have called myself anything else but a friend, especially since you never allowed me to take you on a real date. You allowed me to take you to the movies twice and out to dinner once, but we have never consensually kissed."

"Those were some fun memories, especially when we used to meet in the college library and do some assignments together," Samantha recalled.

"Yes, those were fun memories until they weren't."

"What do you mean?"

"Well, you remember our library assignments as fun, but I recall them as bittersweet. But mostly what sticks in my brain is what happened after we studied."

"What do you mean what happened after?"

"How you would always turn me down when I asked to take you out to eat or to a movie afterward," Kenny reminded her.

"Correct me if I'm wrong," Samantha politely said. "Usually when the studying were done and the library closed, nothing nearby was still open and you didn't have a car at the time. So, really, Kenny, where could we have gone?"

"Nothing nearby was still open, but I think we could've found a café somewhere. Walking wasn't out of style and I'm pretty sure I could've sprung for public transportation," he said.

"Kenny, that was then and this is now. I don't want to focus on the sour grapes of our past friendship. We are starting a new connection. Therefore, do we really need to discuss what you didn't like about our past alliance?"

He continued as if she never asked him a question. "Of course, visiting your campus apartment at the time was out of the question. I dropped by once to leave you a notebook and I recall so well how

Sabrina and Starlet wouldn't even give us the privacy of sitting in the front room alone," he reminded her. "Therefore, visiting you at your campus apartment was out of the question."

"I guess you're right and I didn't give you much of a chance to be more than a friend," Samantha admitted.

"Thank you for acknowledging that," he said warmly. "I know you don't want to have this conversation and we really don't have to have this conversation, but I would just like to set the record straight," he said respectfully.

"Okay, I'm listening," she said. "What record would you like to set straight, Kenny?"

"I would like to set the record straight that we were only friends back in college because that's how you wanted it. I wanted to be more than just a friend, but you made sure that never happened. For one, a boyfriend takes a girl on real dates; and if my memory serves me correctly, a real date is something you and I never experienced."

"But we did go out a few times," Samantha reminded him.

"Yes, we went out a few times, three to be exact. But what you and I did together, I could have easily have done with my mother," he pointed out.

"Don't forget to include the time you just mentioned, when you visited my campus apartment."

"I know and I just mentioned how I dropped by your apartment once. But a house visit is not a real date. Besides, I have already mentioned how Sabrina and Starlet wouldn't leave the room. The three of you stuck together and beat me at cards that evening."

"My sisters and I have always been protective of each other," Samantha shared.

"That's obvious, but on the other hand, maybe I should have asked Sabrina or Starlet if it was okay with them if I took you out?" he said teasingly. "Maybe I would have had better luck with them giving me permission to take you out than I received from you."

"Do we have to keep going over and over this topic? I would like to be friends again if that's okay with you. Just as I said before, that was then and this is now. I think we've established that we were only friends in college. Not, that it should be an issue now."

"Okay, I get it," he cheery said. "You want to be friends again and if I want it to be more than friends, I still have to get off the pot and take you out on a real date," he teased.

"Kenny, I know you were just teasing. But please don't tease about being more than friends," she said firmly. "You are fully aware that friends are all we'll ever be."

"Okay, I'm honored to be your friend. What about let's start tonight," he suggested.

"Let's start what tonight, Kenny?"

"Let's start our new alliance."

"Let me be clear on what we have decided. You are okay with the idea of me helping you get and stay sober?"

"Yes, I'm more than okay with it," he said excitedly. "I'm excited about it. I'm also excited about reconnecting our friendship."

"I'm glad you're onboard with trying to stay sober. Really, Kenny. I feel you are wasting your life and harming your insides by drinking so heavy so often."

"Yes, I'm onboard," he assured her. "So, let's get started tonight?"

"What did you have in mind?" she asked.

"How would you like to go dancing? I know it's a Monday night, but I know a neat dance hall that's popular on Monday's," he suggested. "It's in the area and it's along your style. Therefore, I'm sure you'll really like it," he assured her.

"Maybe tonight isn't the best time. It is a week night and we both have to work tomorrow. Therefore, maybe we should wait until later in the week. Besides, I need to come up with some kind of strategy to use to help get you sober."

"That's not going to be an easy task. However, in the meantime, we can go out and get reacquainted at a nice dance hall," he suggested.

She softy laughed and without hesitation. She accepted. "Okay, I'll go dancing with you. Dancing sounds fun. Besides, we don't have to make it a late night," she said excitedly.

She welcomed the distraction and thought to herself how going out to a dance hall would keep her from sitting at home alone in the big house thinking of Paris.

"Great, I'll have the most beautiful date in the room," he said excitedly.

"Kenny, listen for a moment."

"Listen for what?"

"We are going dancing, but it's not a date."

"I know it's not a date, but you'll still be my date," he said teasingly.

"I know, I'll be your date, but I just want to be clear that it's not a real date and we'll never be more than friends," she firmly said, not wanting there to be a misunderstanding.

"Calm down, Samantha. I'm not dense. I get it. You have only pounded this in my head a few hundred times. I was just kidding, but there's no law against hoping for more."

"You can hope for more, but I want to be crystal clear that I'm not interested in you in any other way than as a friend. I still love Paris deeply and when he gets back home, I'm desperately hoping and praying that we'll be able to work things out."

"Of course, you are hoping for that. I'm just glad you want to hang out with me at all. So, I'll pick you up around eight o'clock if that's okay."

"Sure, eight o'clock will be fine," Samantha said excitedly. "Going out dancing is a splendid way to reconnect our friendship."

"Before I get off the phone, I want to thank you for forgiving me and wanting to help me stay sober. I'll show you that with your help I can do it," he promised.

"Kenny, I'm glad to hear you say that. I would like for you to start tonight."

"Okay, that's the plan. Starting tonight, I'll be a boy scout and give up the booze. You have my word that I won't touch a drop this evening. Your inspiration to help me is going to work wonders toward my efforts to get on the wagon and stay there."

"That's great. I'll do all I can to help keep you sober," she said and then hung up the phone and rushed out of her room.

Chapter Twenty-Two

Samantha headed straight downstairs to confide in Sabrina about her date with Kenny. But before she reached the bottom of the staircase she noticed Sabrina heading across the living room floor in the direction of the dining area.

"Sabrina, I just got off the phone with Kenny Ross. He's coming over this evening to take me to a dance, can you believe it?" Samantha said excitedly. "He'll be here soon so I need to get back upstairs and get dressed."

Sabrina stared at Samantha with a surprise expression on her face as they both headed toward the dining area, enroot to the kitchen. They met Carrie halfway to the kitchen. Carrie was carrying a serving tray with tea for one.

"Carrie, could you please make that tea for two," Sabrina asked respectfully. "Samantha will be joining me in the living room.

Carrie nodded and gracefully turned on her heels to head back toward the kitchen for another teacup and tea for two. Sabrina and Samantha turned around and headed back toward the living room to be seated next to each other on one of the sofas.

Sabrina looked at Samantha and smiled. "I know you want to get out of this house now that Paris has left to spend the next two weeks in another country. But Kenny Ross again, really?" she said disappointedly.

It was obvious in Sabrina's voice that she wasn't pleased to hear Samantha was going out with Kenny Ross. She didn't care much for Kenny because of the disrespectful drunken behavior he had displayed in the past during college; and she disliked him now even more than their college days because of the discourteous conduct he displayed at their Halloween party. She felt Kenny was an unsuitable associate for Samantha since he was such a heavy out of control drinker who didn't seem to want to make anything of his life. She was also disappointed in Paris for leaving town and taking the trip to France without Samantha, especially since he and Samantha had planned to take the trip together. She felt Paris was being thoughtless and unappreciative of what he had with Samantha.

Carrie brought in the tea and served them both before she returned to the kitchen area to finish her work. However, Sabrina and Samantha only enjoyed one cup of tea before Samantha rushed out of the living room to head up to her room to dress.

Minutes later when Samantha came back downstairs and stepped into the living room dressed in a long lavender dress with an antique white lace top, Sabrina stared hard with approving eyes. "You look beautiful," Sabrina smiled. "However, I must say, you sure did change into your outfit rather quickly," she said with disapproval in her voice.

"You said that disapprovingly that I dressed so quickly," Samantha inquired.

"I'm sorry and my intentions are not to make you feel bad. But I cannot pretend to be pleased about your date with Kenny Ross," Sabrina said as she scooted forward on the sofa, reached out, lifted the tea pot and poured hot tea into her cup as well as Samantha's.

"I don't want you to pretend." Samantha lifted her teacup and saucer from the coffee table and held it in her lap. "I understand if you do not approve. I know it's sudden, but I think you also know that Kenny and I are just friends."

"I'm sure you're just friends, but I'm sure Kenny wants to be more than friends." Sabrina lifted her cup to her mouth and took a sip of tea. "Don't get me wrong. He's not a bad guy, but he's so messed up, with his drinking and all the drama surrounding his family."

Samantha nodded. "Yes, he has a lot going on in his life that's not good."

"Including his heavy drinking," Sabrina reminded her.

"I know his drinking is a problem, but I plan to help him with that. I at least would like to try. Because without that vice, he would be a much nicer person."

"I understand your need to want to fix him," Sabrina smiled. "It's sort of like the little lost kittens and birds you used to bring into the house and nurse back to health."

Samantha smiled. "I was just a kid when I wanted to fix all those stray animals and nurse them back to health."

Sabrina nodded. "Yes, you were just about ten years old or so, but you have always had that trait in you to want to fix what's broken."

"And you think I want to fix Kenny Ross because I feel he's broken?"

"Yes, I'm a realist and I think that's how you see Kenny. I think you see him as a broken person that needs fixing; and maybe he does need fixing. But I just don't see anything worthwhile coming out of you going out with him."

"Helping him get sober is going to be a worthwhile cause," Samantha explained.

"That would be worthwhile and amazing if it happens. But one thing is sure to happen," Sabrina warned her.

"What's that?" Samantha asked.

"You're going to get his hopes up unnecessary," Sabrina pointed out.

Samantha didn't comment as she listened to Sabrina views on Kenny.

"We both know that you are still hopefully in love with Paris. Besides, you know how Paris is and how serious he takes things. He took the trip away from you to most likely put things in perspective after you refused to reveal who kissed you yesterday. Now, when he gets back, if he does want to reconcile, he'll have yet something else to deal with."

"Something else like what?" Samantha asked.

"The something else that you are about to do." Sabrina shook her head. "I don't think Paris will be very pleased about you going out with Kenny, whether you're just friends or not. It didn't sit well with him the first time and it probably will not sit well with him this time either," Sabrina pointed out.

"I don't mean to be disrespectful, but you have never had anything positive to say about Kenny. I was excited to tell you that he's taking me dancing, but I knew you were going to have something discouraging to say about him," Samantha mumbled.

Sabrina lifted her teacup to her mouth and took a small sip of tea. Her hand slightly shook because she felt Samantha was headed for trouble going out with Kenny. She stared at Samantha with concerned eyes. It was plain how disappointed she was in Samantha for accepting a date with Kenny Ross.

"Sabrina, there's no need to look at me with such disapproval. It's just a date. We're not dating or anything remotely similar to dating. It's just a date to go out dancing. Something to get me out of the house tonight," Samantha explained, wanting to make Sabrina more accepting of Kenny.

"Samantha, my opinion may seem bold, but I just feel what you're planning to do with Kenny Ross is not going to work or end well."

"It might work. I want to try at least," Samantha admitted.

"Besides, why tonight? It's not the weekend. It's a Monday night," Sabrina asked.

"This is a Monday night dance party," Samantha quickly said.

"I'm just puzzled to why you feel the need to go out with Kenny Ross the same day Paris left town," Sabrina asked. "It's almost like a slap in the face to Paris, if you ask me."

"Well, Paris and I have apparently gone our separate ways. So what difference does it makes if I go dancing with Kenny?"

"It makes a big difference. You and Paris have not officially called it quits. He's upset and you're upset, but the discontent between the two of you will not last."

"I do hope you are right."

"Of course, I'm right. You two are crazy about each other. It's almost like you were born to be with each other."

"That's a sweet sentiment to say about us," Samantha smiled, lifted her cup to her mouth and took a sip of tea. "But it's sort of messed up at the moment."

"I agree that things are out of sorts for the two of you; and I believe that's the main reason why you're going out with Kenny Ross tonight," Sabrina speculated. "I know you're upset with Paris, but you shouldn't be. He just wanted to know who had kissed you. I know you said he pressured you last night to give him a name."

"Yes, he did pressure me," Samantha admitted. "I felt he was being insensitive of my feelings and privacy. I didn't want to share it and he kept insisting on knowing who had kissed me after I had clearly told him that I didn't want to reveal the person's name."

"Don't you think you are expecting the impossible from that guy?" Sabrina asked.

"What do you mean?"

"You wanted to tell your boyfriend that another guy kissed you against your wishes, but after you told him something like that, you felt he shouldn't ask the name of the other guy? The way I see it, you shouldn't have mentioned the kiss if you were going to keep who kissed you a secret. It didn't make sense to mention it to any of us for that matter."

"You are undoubtedly correct that I shouldn't have mentioned it."

"But apparently it really bothered you; otherwise, you probably wouldn't have mentioned it. When we arrived from church and then later when Paris came over, you made a big deal about how an old friend had dropped by and kissed you against your will. Then when everybody wanted to know who kissed you, you clammed up and didn't want to talk about it or disclose the person's name," Sabrina explained. "Therefore, it was either a big deal that you were kissed or you had just overreacted and the kiss hadn't been as dramatic to you as you had originally thought."

"There is no mistake about it, the kiss did upset me. I didn't encourage it and I didn't want to be kissed by the person who kissed me," Samantha assured her.

"In that case, why won't you tell any of us who kissed you?" Sabrina asked. "The fact that you have chosen not to share it with Paris is almost like lying to him. You know how the Franklin brothers are. They do not tolerate lies from anyone."

"I know, and I feel awful about not confiding in Paris." Samantha leaned forward and placed her teacup on the coffee table. "I just felt I couldn't." She looked seriously toward Sabrina. "But I want to make it clear to you that I'm not going out tonight with Kenny to get back at Paris for not taking me to France with him. I'm going out with Kenny because I feel I can do him some great good."

"You feel you can help him with his drinking."

"Yes, I feel I can help him get back on the wagon and stay sober. I'm looking forward to trying," Samantha said hopefully.

"I'm sure I wouldn't be this concerned if Kenny wasn't such a heavy drinker."

"I know you are looking out for my best interest, but could we please not discuss Kenny anymore. I had a feeling you were going to say something negative about him. But as I said before, don't worry, it's just a simple date," Samantha said assuredly, and then stood from the sofa and gracefully strolled across the living room to look out of the window. She was anxiously awaiting Kenny.

"Samantha, you guessed right that I would say something pessimistic and unenthusiastic about Kenny Ross. Just as I knew, I'm sure you knew that everyone at college thought of Kenny as problematic. He was always in those rock bands, going to all night wild parties and doing questionable stuff."

"What kind of questionable stuff are you referring to?"

"Well, I'm sure you heard the same things that the rest of us heard, drugs, alcohol and all night parties," Sabrina firmly stated. "You know as well as I do that the students at college called him a drunken loser."

"I know they called him that, but that was an awful thing to call Kenny."

"It was an awful thing to call him. However, he brought it on himself, showing up at all the parties completely intoxicated. Besides, from our college days, I'm not a fan of his. I'm rooting for you and Paris."

"I'm rooting for me and Paris too. But Kenny can't stand in our way since he's just a friend. Besides, Paris took his vacation without taking me, after we had decided to take it together," Samantha stressed strongly. "To say the least, I'm not pleased about it."

"Put yourself in his shoes, Samantha. He comes over to see you last night and you tell him that some guy kissed you against your will and you wouldn't tell him who it was. Men need to be heroes and confront

246

men who disrespect their women. He wanted to know the name of the person so he could go confront him and tell him to stay away from you."

"Maybe you're right, but I didn't want him to confront this person. I just wanted him to know and then drop it. Since the person didn't mean any harm toward me."

"Well, as I said before, it would have been better if you hadn't mentioned the kiss since you chose not to share who kissed you. We both know how straight-laced Paris is, and how he's not going to soon forget that you told him you were kissed by someone else and that person kissed you against your will."

"You are right. He won't soon forget it."

"Can you blame him, Samantha? I think what bothered him the most is the fact that you wouldn't reveal that person's name who kissed you. I'm sure that puzzled him, because it puzzles me that you won't reveal that person's name. It feels like you are trying to protect that person after the disrespectful way that person treated you."

"I know it does sound that way, but I think you understand why I didn't tell."

Sabrina stared with confused eyes. "No, I'm sorry, but I don't understand why you couldn't tell on someone who treated you in that awful manner and showed you such little respect. Maybe, you could enlighten me. I really want to understand," Sabrina humbly said.

"It's so complicated. But I can tell you this much. The guy is someone we all know and he kissed me, but he wasn't in his right mind," Samantha explained.

"What do you mean he wasn't in his right mind?"

"He was under the influence of alcohol. You know how alcohol can affect a person's conduct," she nervously said, hoping Sabrina wouldn't figure out who she was referring to.

Sabina grabbed her face with both hands and stared toward Samantha. "Please, tell me it wasn't Kenny Ross who treated you so impolite. Please, tell me you wouldn't befriend someone who would kiss you against your will, intoxicated or not. Clearly, he cannot be trusted to keep his head on straight and his hands to himself."

Samantha didn't answer since she knew she could never reveal to anyone that Kenny had been the guy who kissed her and made her so upset.

"Samantha, you didn't answer me. Was it Kenny Ross who dropped by the house and treated you so inexcusable while we were all at church, was it?"

Samantha looked at her sister with a serious expression. "Remember what I told Paris when he dropped by on his way to the airport today?"

Sabrina nodded. "Yes, I remember what you said to Paris. I was standing right here in the living room when you told him."

"Okay, you know I said I would never reveal the man who came here and kissed me."

"It just doesn't make sense to me that you won't reveal this person."

"It's because I made too much of the kiss and I don't want to mess up that person's reputation. Even though he shouldn't have kissed me, he was sorry right afterward."

"It's too bad how you made such a big deal about it; and now talking it down."

"I'm not talking it down. It was what it was. He kissed me and I didn't want him to, but I shouldn't have mentioned it to anyone since I knew he was sorry and didn't mean it. Therefore, why destroy someone's reputation when he really didn't mean it in that way."

"I'm not suggesting that you destroy someone's reputation, but at least you don't have to be friends with someone who would turn around and disrespect you in that way. That's why I asked if it was Kenny," Sabrina paused and looked toward her sister. "But of course, it wasn't Kenny. I don't think you would be as friendly with him if he had been the one to kiss you against your wishes in a drunken state," Sabina said seriously. "Therefore, please forgive me for assuming it could have been him."

"There's nothing to forgive. I just think we should talk about something else."

"Of course, I'm sorry we got on that subject. But I'm still surprised that you are going on a date with Kenny when you know how very strict Paris is about complete devotion in a relationship."

Samantha nodded. "Yes, I know the Franklin guys expect devotion and they shouldn't expect anything less, since they are devoted. But right now, Paris and I have gone our separate ways. Therefore, I do not feel as if I'm doing anything that I shouldn't be doing. Besides, we both know that it's not a real date. Kenny and I are just friends."

Sabrina smiled. "I hope you two are just friends."

Samantha smiled. "You hope we are just friends, which sounds as if you think we could possibly be something else." Samantha held up both hands. "Never could Kenny and I be anything other than friends. I tell you like this, if Paris called me right now and said he wanted to try again, I would say yes so quick before you could blink," Samantha stressed strongly and then grabbed her face with both hands, and wiped one tear before it rolled down her cheek. "I love him so very much until it hurts to just think about him being so far away in another country right now. I just pray he will get over that incident and love me inspite of the fact that I feel I shouldn't reveal the man's name who kissed me."

"Paris loves you very much and I'm sure after his vacation in France, he'll come home anxious to see you and make up," Sabrina said encouragingly, lifted her teacup and took one last sip before placing the empty cup on the serving tray.

Samantha smiled. "I hope and pray you are right," she said in her sister's eyes. "Simply, because there's no other man in this world that could ever take his place in my heart. Without Paris, I would cease to ever look for love. No other man in this universe could ever make me completely happy as I am when I'm with Paris Franklin."

"If that's true, why not just cancel your date with Kenny. Why borrow trouble for you and Paris? Besides, there's so much negative gossip circling around Kenny. His drinking problem is one, and then there's the awful incident that happened with his father shooting his mother and her boyfriend," Sabrina explained. "I basically hate to see you get tangled up with Kenny because I feel it will hinder your reunion with Paris."

"Believe me; I don't plan to allow anything to come between me and Paris."

"My only beef with Kenny is his drinking. He seems like a decent guy when he's sober. Therefore, I hope you can help get him sober, for himself, you and his family."

"Thanks for saying that about Kenny. You are right; he really is a nice guy. What he did for me and Paris last fall was priceless. He's my friend and my other high hat friends will just have to accept that," Samantha said with conviction.

Sabrina nodded. "Well said and I guess that's my queue to be quiet and let you wait for Kenny to arrive." Sabrina headed out of the room toward the staircase.

While Samantha stood in the window waiting for Kenny, she glanced around when Starlet tapped her on the shoulder. "Have you seen Sabrina?" she asked.

"Yes, she was just here. I think she went upstairs to her room," Samantha said and then glanced back to stare out of the window.

"What are you doing?" Starlet asked. "Are you going out with some friends this evening? I know Paris left for France this morning and is out of the country."

"Yes, he left the country and I miss him like crazy."

"But you two broke up before he left, right?"

"Yes, we're allegedly not together, but I'm hopeful for his return and working it out."

"Of course, you'll work it out. But who are you going out with tonight?"

"I figured I would get out for a short while."

"That's good. No need for you to be stuck inside just because Paris left town," Starlet said teasingly. "But who's the lucky man that's taking you out tonight?"

"Kenny Ross is taking me out dancing."

"Kenny Ross is taking you out?" Starlet asked with surprise in her voice.

"Yes, he's taking me out dancing. You know Kenny and I are friends."

"Yes, I know you two were friends during college, but now, I didn't think you two were that friendly. Besides, I don't think Paris would see it as a friendly date."

"Paris isn't here and Kenny is; he wants to take me dancing and I'm excited to go."

"I guess I don't understand why you would choose to go anywhere with Kenny Ross? A lot of people call him a loser."

"But we were raised to think independently of what others says."

"That's true we were, but..."

"There is no but, Starlet. We both know being called that, doesn't make him one."

"Okay, but that's what everybody at college called him. Besides, he drinks like a fish," Starlet reminded her.

"He used to drink like a fish. He won't be drinking like that anymore. He's giving it up tonight," Samantha announced.

"He's giving it up tonight?" Starlet snapped, not pleased that Samantha was going out with Kenny. "Is that what he told you?" Starlet paused to collect herself. "Listen for a minute, Kenny Ross has a four year degree in something. But he's still throwing his life away on nowhere jobs that he doesn't seem to hang on to that long. I think it's because of his addiction to alcohol. He has no excuse for not seeking high career positions," Starlet explained. "You told me yourself that Paris offered him an executive position but Kenny has never shown up at Franklin Gas to even interview for the position."

"That's because he already has a job at that restaurant where he works."

"I'm sure he doesn't want to lose that job," Starlet said arrogantly.

"Just cut him a break. Sabrina has. He's not perfect but he's my friend."

"I don't expect him to be perfect. But you are my precious sister and I just want him to be average," Starlet politely stated. "I guess I just don't care for Kenny Ross because he's too over the top when he's drinking. He was so rude and nasty to you and Paris at the Halloween party last year," Starlet reminded her.

"I know he was, and he more than apologized and made up for that scene. Paris and I both forgave him for that."

"But is he trying for a better job, maybe the one Paris offered him?" Starlet inquired.

"I have no idea; and frankly, I'm not concerned with his choice of employment."

"I'm increasingly convinced that it's not in Kenny's desire to reach for a higher position," Starlet said. "He just seems content just throwing his life away on nowhere jobs; and if that's not reason enough to make him an unsuitable choice for a husband, what is?"

"Starlet, you do not have to paint me a picture of Kenny's life. I already know everything you are saying. Besides, I'm not getting ready to marry the guy, I just plan to go dancing and have a good time," Samantha firmly uttered. "I'm a full-grown woman. Don't you think I deserve to have some fun while Paris is on a vacation of a lifetime without me?"

Starlet stepped over to the coffee table and lifted the silver teapot and poured herself a cup of tea. "You want to share a cup of tea while we are waiting?" Starlet asked.

Samantha nodded. "Sure, I'll have a cup. I just shared a cup with Sabrina. But I thought Kenny would have arrived by now. Therefore, I would love another cup while I'm waiting. But I'm sure he'll be here soon."

Starlet glanced at her gold Gucci watch. "Sydney will be here to pick me up in about ten minutes. We're having dinner downtown in the John Hancock building. They have their best menu specials on Monday nights," Starlet said and lifted both teacups and passed one to Samantha.

Samantha took the cup and sipped it instantly. "I'm sort of excited about going dancing with Kenny. But I haven't gone out with anyone other than Paris since we started dating. So, I'm sure it's not going to feel natural being out with someone else."

"Well, Samantha, whose fault, is that? You don't have to go out with Kenny. You can change your mind if you want."

"I know you are right, but I want to go out with him and keep him sober."

"You're going to help him stay sober?"

"Yes, that's my mission with Kenny."

"Out of all the men in Barrington Hills, you needed a mission with Kenny Ross?"

"Starlet, I know you think Kenny is a questionable guy. But I know him better than you. Besides, I have heard all the things you said about him. I know Kenny isn't your favorite person. However, I'm not going to pick my friends just to please other people. We were not raised that way and you know it," Samantha stressed.

"I know we were not raised that way, but I'm just trying to look out for your best interest. It doesn't mean that I think I'm better than

252

Kenny Ross. It's not about being better; it's about using good sense. If Kenny is considered a sore spot where Paris is concerned, why would you want to push the envelope with such a nice guy like Paris?" Starlet pointed out. "I know Kenny Ross is your old college friend, but I'm only pointing out that getting yourself back associated with him might not be the best idea."

"It may not be the best idea for others, but it's the best idea for me. I don't plan to be lonely for the next two weeks while Paris is away. I have a mission with Kenny and I plan to spend my time helping him stay sober," Samantha stated firmly, annoyed that Sabrina and now Starlet was giving her a hard time about Kenny.

Starlet took the last sip of tea and placed her cup on the coffee table. She gracefully walked over to one of the many living room windows and looked out. "I don't know what's keeping Sydney," she said while looking outside and then looked around at Samantha. "The only thing I have to say, Samantha, is please be careful. We both know that Kenny is worse than ever. That's why we didn't want you to see him during college, and that's why I wish you wouldn't start seeing him again. Plus, it doesn't please me to share this with you, but the grapevine has it that he uses women for their money."

"What grapevine, Starlet?" Samantha asked, shaking her head.

"A couple of my friends mentioned it while we were in a bookstore today. While browsing in the store, we spotted Kenny Ross and Vickie Simpson."

"I hope you were not gossiping with your friends about Kenny."

"We were not gossiping. One of them wanted to know who he was. They thought he was cute and one was interested until they figured out that he was the same person who had crashed our Halloween party. Then one of my friends, Karen Scott, realized that he was the guy she had dated briefly in college and then they both exchanged looks with each other and said, "That guy uses women for their money."

Samantha didn't comment as she thought back during the time at the Halloween party when Kenny told them that Vickie was his wallet for the night.

"Karen Scott were dating Kenny when? I never heard about it," Samantha said.

"Karen said they dated for just a short time, long enough for Kenny to swindle her out of a great deal of money."

"I don't know if I believe that. Swindle is such a negative word. Maybe she spent some money on him, but he probably didn't swindle her out of it. Besides, Karen Scott is just your age. She didn't have a job and she was still in college for goodness sake. Where would she get a lot of money from for anyone to swindle from her?" Samantha asked.

"Where do you think, Samantha? She would get her money the same way we got ours, from her family. According to Karen, she was lying about what she needed the money for and she was giving it to your friend, Kenny Ross."

"Did Karen say how much he swindled out of her?" Samantha curiously asked.

"Why are you asking that question if you don't believe any of it?" Starlet asked.

"I'm just curious; and I'm also curious why Karen would even bring this up to you. This isn't something she should be proud of or want to broadcast."

"Believe me, Karen isn't proud of it. However, she brought it up after they asked about you. They were concerned when they didn't see you at church yesterday. They asked about you and I mentioned that you and Paris broke up last night and that Paris left for France this morning. Then they asked if you had plans to date anyone else."

"Why would they ask such a question?" Samantha inquired. "Paris and I just said goodbye to each other today? I'm not thinking of anyone else."

"I know, but they were mostly sort of joking when they reminded me that you and Kenny used to hang out sometime at college. They hoped he was out of your life for good and wouldn't start showing back up since Paris was out of the picture. That's when Karen mentioned that she had dated Kenny for a while during college. She said she was attractive to him because he was in a band, but he broke her heart by using her for her money."

"Well, if that was during college, it was a while ago. We have all grown up since then. Besides, it's always two sides to every story.

They have shared with you one side. I'm sure if you asked Kenny, he would have a completely different story to tell."

"That's probably true, Samantha. Kenny probably does have his own side, of course," Starlet agreed. "Nevertheless, we only have one side of the story to go by, I would much rather believe Karen Scott than Kenny Ross. Given the choice which one of them would you believe?" Starlet asked.

Samantha didn't answer as she gracefully walked across the living room floor to the window and held the curtains back, just staring out into the night.

Starlet continued. "Besides, Karen only mentioned it to warn us about Kenny so he wouldn't be able to use you the way he used her."

"But how do we know he used Karen?"

"We know it because she said so; and according to her, he swindled her out of $3000 dollars," Starlet announced, shaking her head. "I'm not trying to come down on your friend. Besides, I could care less whether he wear Saint Laurent, Givenchy, Christian Louboutin or Oscar de la Renta shoes or a pair he sewed together himself, I just care about you!" Starlet strongly stated. "If Kenny swindled Karen out of that kind of money, it's not too much of a stretch to think he could do the same to someone else or you."

"Kenny was drinking heavy in college. If he took money from girls, that's why."

"Why are you making excuses for this guy who have be so disrespectful to women?"

"I can make accuses for him because I don't think he really means to be that way. He isn't really that way. It's just when he's drinking. He has a disease called alcoholism."

"Samantha, are you sure you don't have any feelings for Kenny Ross?"

"You know how much I love Paris; why would you even ask me that?"

"I know how much you love Paris, but I know the two of you allegedly broke up last night or this morning before he left for France, all because you refused to disclose who came here and kissed you. Plus, no matter the crime you seem to find excuses for Kenny. I'm just wondering where you draw the line with this guy. You don't seem to mind that he swindled my friend out of a boatload of money," Starlet stressed irritated.

"I do mind if it's true."

"If it's true, of course, it's true. You know Karen Scott isn't the type of girl who would lie about something like that."

"I'm sure Karen didn't lie, but I just don't think he swindled her. That would mean he somehow tricked her. I believe she probably gave it to him willingly just the same as his current girlfriend. Vickie used to pay for his drinks sometime when they would go out."

"Are you okay with the fact that he allows his women to pay his way?"

"No, I'm not okay with it and he's not doing that now. He used to do that when he was drinking heavy. But he's not going to drink like that anymore."

"I know he was drinking heavy, and then after the Halloween party last year he gave it up, but a couple weeks ago he was back at it," Starlet announced.

"How do you know that?" Samantha asked.

"I know because Sydney and I saw him a couple Saturdays ago when we went out to dinner. He was in the restaurant with Vickie Simpson but he was clearly drunk out of his mind. After he knocked over the pitcher of water on their table twice, the establishment asked Vickie to take him and leave the premises and come back when he was sober enough to be served without accidentally knocking things over."

Samantha grabbed her face with both hands. She was shocked that he was out in public in a drunken state. "That's just awful. I'm glad Vickie was with him."

"I'm sure Vickie Simpson took him straight home. But if he was drinking heavy like a fish two weeks ago, when did he give it up?"

"I thought I mentioned to you that he's giving it up tonight. He won't be drinking anything while I'm out with him. He promised me."

"If he promised you that, I guess you do have a strong friendship with Kenny. But just be careful because I don't want you to get hurt by Kenny Ross. I know he's your friend and you like him as a friend, but he swindled a lot of money from Karen."

"Stop using the word swindled," Samantha suggested.

"But Samantha, he either swindled $3000 from Karen or he didn't. Besides, why would Karen lie and say he did, if he didn't?"

"Three thousand dollars is a lot of money. Karen got to be kidding about the amount." Samantha grabbed her mouth for a moment. "Starlet, do you believe that? That's a lot of money for Karen to part with. Besides, where would Karen get that kind of money to just hand off to Kenny just because he asked for it?"

"Well, let me see." Starlet tapped her forehead. Her parents are not totally deprived. They are both working people, only in their mid-fifties. Besides that, they have a boatload of money," Starlet was frustrated. "You aren't listening? I told you Karen said she got the money from her parents. She fibbed to them about what she needed it for."

Samantha nodded. "You're correct. Her family is quite well off."

"Exactly, therefore, Karen would have had no problem giving $3000 to Kenny if he pressured her and swindled it out of her," Starlet said.

"I'm sure you are right, but when we were still in middle school, I always heard that Karen Scott family was a poor associate of ours. Therefore, I never thought they would have dished out that kind of money to Karen back in college," Samantha recalled as she gracefully took a seat back on the sofa with her teacup in her hand.

"Karen told me how back then her family didn't really have any money."

"But Karen family has money now. Apparently enough to dish out $3000 at the drop of a hat to Karen," Samantha said with her eyes toward the front windows.

"Karen told me that what happened is, when her great grandfather passed away ten years ago he left her father the bulk of his estate."

"I never knew that. " Samantha hopped off the sofa and strolled back over to the window and pulled the curtains back. "But it all makes sense now. I kept remembering Karen as that little girl in middle school who we all befriended and loved so much but she was considered a poor relations." Samantha stood at the window looking out for Kenny. "Then I remember during high school how every time I saw Karen she was dressed in nice designer clothes with designer purses. I guess she's not a poor relations anymore."

"No, Samantha, she isn't a poor relations anymore. Karen hasn't been considered poor since her adulthood. She's rich," Starlet nodded.

Samantha shook her head. "No, your friend Karen Scott is not rich."

"What do you mean she's not rich?"

"I wouldn't go that far to say Karen is rich. Because Karen is not rich," Samantha stated seriously. "However, it would be correct to say that her parents are wealthy."

"What are you talking about, Samantha? What's the difference, it's all the same."

"Not according to Mother. She said Karen family was wealthy but not rich."

"Why would Mother say that to you? You just happened to hear her say Karen family was wealthy but not rich? That doesn't make any sense to me. It's not even something to mention in the first place," Starlet pointed out.

"The subject had come up for some reason when we were making a list of invitees for the Halloween party. I don't recall how the subject came up but I clearly remember how Mother made a point of saying, Karen family was wealthy but not rich, and after she said that I inquired to what was the difference and she went on to explain the difference to me."

Starlet held out both arms. "I'm waiting to hear what Mother said to you. I want to hear what she said since I don't see any difference between wealthy and rich. All my life I have been told I'm rich, but as far as I can see, my friend Karen is just as well off as we are."

Samantha shook her head. "That's not what Mother told me. Apparently, the Taylor's are more prosperous and affluent than the Scott's."

"Whether we are more affluent or prosperous or well to do or whatever, it still doesn't make any difference. Karen family is just as affluent as we are as far as I'm concerned until you tell me something different than what you have. So, where do we fall in that class, Samantha? Did Mother mention that to do?"

"I just told you that Mother told me that we are rich but Karen family is wealthy."

"What else did Mother tell you?"

Samantha smiled and then slightly laughed as she looked toward Starlet who looked like a princess in her long peach and white evening gown. "When you are curious about something you do not give up do you? But I guess it's just as well that we are discussing something that is pointless, since talking about how rich or not rich someone is, is futile senseless talk that Father would frown on for sure."

"Yes, Samantha, I agree that it's senseless but it's also harmless. I'm just curious to why Mother would refer to Karen family as wealthy but think it's less wealthy than we are."

"I know it probably sound weird to you since it sounded weird to me when Mother told me. But as I said, this conversation may be pointless but I'm glad we're spending our time waiting for Kenny and Sydney without the twenty questions about Kenny."

"I'm not sure if you were listening to what I said about him anyway," Starlet casually uttered. "Therefore, what else did Mother tell you about rich and wealthy? I have had people refer to us as rich. I have also had people refer to Paris's family as rich."

"I can answer for the Franklin's and I can answer for us. Mother told me that both the Franklins and the Taylors are considered rich."

"But Karen family is considered wealthy and not rich. So my question to you, which I'm sure you asked Mother and she explained. What's the difference in wealthy and rich or well-off for that matter? It all spells the same to me: a boatload of money."

"Okay, here's the difference that Mother explained to me. She told me that anything over ten millions is rich. Anything slightly under ten millions is wealthy; and anything slightly over two millions is well-off," Samantha explained. "So does that answer your question about the different classes of wealth?" Samantha asked, in a more relaxed mood.

Starlet smiled. "It does answer my question, but it's all a lot of money to me. Thanks for explaining what Mother told you, not that we are the wiser or any better off for our futile senseless conversation but it was interesting."

"It was interesting, but you are so right that it was pointless."

"Yes, it was pointless and I know we got off the topic for a minute, but I hope you'll think about what Karen shared with me about Kenny.

We both know if she said he conned her out of that much money, he probably did."

"Okay, Starlet, I'm not saying Kenny was right to do that if he actually swindled money from Karen. But Karen was over eighteen and I'm sure he didn't hold a gun to her head to get the money."

"What are you saying, Samantha? I know you are not blaming Karen for being used."

"No, I'm not saying Karen should be blamed."

"It sounded like that's what you were saying."

"It's not the point I'm trying to make. We both know that when someone swindle, con, steal or harm someone else, it's morally wrong and sometime criminally wrong. However, I'm just saying that I don't think the con-artist can be blamed if he's smart enough to con someone out of their stuff. People need to be smart and not let someone play them for a fool. Karen probably wanted to give him money just to be with him. Kenny is a jerk but he is also quite cute with a wild side and Karen is a smart young lady, but she was probably pulled in by Kenny's charm."

"I agree that Karen should have known better. If he asked for the first dollar, that should have been a red flag. It never should have gotten to the crazy amount we're discussing. Nevertheless, Samantha, you're smart and I have much confidence in you. So, I hope you won't let Kenny charm you out of money as he did Karen," Starlet firmly stated. "Just be careful since you're not too keen on hearing constructive advice regarding Kenny."

"Starlet, I don't mind your advice. I just want you to trust me regarding Kenny. Besides, we were raised not to always believe what we hear about others," Samantha softly said. "Most of the rumors about Kenny are true, but people can change, you know?"

Starlet nodded. "Yes, people can change, and for your sake, Samantha, I hope Kenny Ross has changed his ways from his college days. However, I'm doubtful after witnessing his conduct two weeks ago when Sydney and I saw him in that drunken state at that nice restaurant," Starlet nodded, pointing toward the guest closet. "Don't forget to throw on your coat before Kenny arrives. It's rather cold outside tonight."

Samantha looked toward Starlet and shook her head. "I was thinking about not wearing a coat to the dance tonight. This dress is made of thick cotton and has long sleeve and besides it gets warm on the dance floor when everyone is dancing."

"I know how that can be. I'm sure you don't want to dance in a coat, but you should probably take your coat. You are just getting over a cold. Besides, it's the middle of March, not the middle of summer."

"Starlet, I know it's the middle of March but it's not that cold. But just to please my little sister, I'll throw on a coat." Samantha stepped to the guest closet and grabbed a jacket.

Samantha threw on the jacket as Sydney was just pulling into the driveway. Shortly Sydney and Starlet had left for their dinner date. Five minutes later, Kenny knocked on her front door. Samantha rushed across the floor to open the door. She was pleased to see how nice he looked all dressed up in nice clothing. She remembered he was always a fine looking fellow when he was dressed well and wasn't drinking or intoxicated.

"Hi, Kenny, what have you done to make yourself look so nice?"

He rubbed his hands together and smiled as if he knew he looked well-dressed. "Thank you," he said as he lifted her right hand and kissed the back of her palm. He seemed anxious as his clear brown eyes kept smiling at her and glancing back at his Timex watch. "Samantha, are you ready? I don't think we have time to chat inside. We need to head straight to the dance. It fills up quickly on a Monday night. Besides, I'm a bit late picking you up." He glanced at his watch again.

"Sure, I'm ready," she said as they stood in the front foyer.

They left for the dance right away and enroot to the dance while seated in the car, Kenny seemed nervous but all smiles. "So, you think I look good tonight?"

"Yes, Kenny, you look very nice this evening."

"Thank you, you look nice also," he said. "You'll see; we'll have fun. I'm grateful to get this opportunity to take you out and make up to you for my lousy behavior yesterday."

"Kenny, I know you are sorry, but could we please not discuss that incident ever."

"Oh, sure, I won't mention it again."

Chapter Twenty-Three

When they arrived at the dance club, Samantha felt comfortable with the setting since it was a nice place that she was familiar with. She had gone there once before with Paris. It was a very expensive chateau and she was surprised that Kenny had chosen to take her out to such an upscale establishment. She had assumed that he would have taken her to a more affordable enterprise, considering his salary was quite average. Nevertheless, she took it as a compliment to her.

When they stepped into the foyer of the entrance, a greeter took their coats, and then a host took them to their reserved table in the middle of the establishment. The round tables were small with only walking space between them and the table where Samantha and Kenny were seated consisted of two chairs with a red ribbon tied on the back of each straight back hair and all the other fifty tables were small with just two chairs as if the dance club was set up just for couples. Each table was covered with a red draped to the floor table cloth with a shorter white lace cloth covering the red one. The carpet was wall to wall in blush red carpet and the curtains at the many windows were long red sheer curtains with long lacy white sheers in the middle showcased against snow white walls and drop ceiling that housed a large twelve light chandelier sparkling in crystal.

After they were seated, Samantha reached across the table and touched Kenny's hand. "Thank you for bringing me to such a wonderful dance club."

Kenny looked at her and smiled. "You are welcomed, but I thought you had been here before."

"Yes, I have been here, once, but I had no idea this is where you had in mind when you invited me out to dance. I love this place."

Kenny smiled. "I'm glad to hear that because I love it as well," he said as he picked up the wine menu and glanced at it.

Samantha swallowed hard because she knew he wasn't supposed to be drinking; and no way did she want him to buy a drink while she was out with him. Yet, she did not comment while he looked over the wine list.

He looked up from the wine list, smiling and shaking his head as he glanced across the table at her. "I think I'll play it safe and let you choose the wine," he grinned and passed the wine list to her. "I think we both know that you're better suited to pick a decent bottle of wine."

She took the list and immediately spotted the bottle of wine that she wanted. "This one is really smooth and sweet and this is the one Paris and I ordered when we were here." She passed him the wine list and pointed to the exclusive bottle.

Kenny looked at the bottle she had pointed it and he swallowed hard as he noticed the expensive cost of the bottle of wine. He was silent for a moment and it dawned on Samantha that it was probably out of his salary range.

Samantha quickly said. "I love that one, but I can choose something a little less expensive. I'm sorry I picked that one, I wasn't thinking for a moment."

Kenny immediately drew an attitude as he looked with a solemn face across the table at her and crossed both arms on the table, leaning toward her. But just stared at her in silence.

She discreetly took a deep breath. She could tell that something had gotten him in a heated mood. "What's the matter, you look upset all of a sudden?"

He nodded. "Yes, I am upset."

"Is it because I picked that bottle of wine? I wasn't thinking and I'm sorry I did that."

He shook his head as he stared at her. "I'm not upset that you picked the wine, I'm upset that you picked out the bottle and then politely said no because you just assumed I wouldn't be able to pay for it. Do you have any idea how that made me feel?"

"I guess not, but I'm sorry just the same. I was trying to be considerate," she apologized.

"I'm sure you were trying to be considerate, but it still was a low blow to me. It makes me feel as if you think I don't have a dime to my name."

Samantha grabbed her face with both hands and smiled. "It wasn't my intentions to offend you and I think you know that."

"Just watch it," he said. "I'm not rolling in dough but I'm not in the poverty line either. I think I can take my date out and buy a decent bottle of wine without being asked to do the dishes to pay the check," he said firmly.

"Kenny, I'm sure you can. And as I said, I was just trying to be considerate," she said.

They both looked up at the tall waiter that had just approached their table.

Kenny immediately held up the wine list and pointed to the wine of Samantha's choice. The waiter jotted it down and headed across the establishment toward the bar area to fetch their wine. When the waiter returned with the bottle, he poured wine into Samantha's glass and when he went to pour wine into Kenny's glass, Samantha instinctly placed her hand over his glass and shook her head toward the waiter. "The wine is just for me. He isn't drinking this evening."

The waiter nodded, placed the bottle on the table and walked away. She looked at Kenny and smiled as she lifted her wine glass to her lips and took a sip. "I love this wine."

"If you love it so much why didn't you let me try it so I could give my opinion?"

She smiled. "I know you are kidding."

"I'm not kidding. "I would like to try the wine." He held out both hands. "I know starting tonight I'm on the wagon and I don't plan to get off. I just want to take a sip and give you my opinion."

"Kenny, I don't think that's good idea. We have been over this conversation before. I think it's best for you to not even try it at all."

"I just want a sip of the stuff. I'm dropping over a hundred bucks on the bottle. No disrespect intended, but that kind of money do not grow on trees for me and my family."

"Kenny, I know that and I didn't pressure you into buying the bottle. I said I could have chosen something different."

"You said that, but we both know that you wanted the one you first picked," he stated seriously. "But that's fine. I'm glad I could buy you what you wanted. But I don't know why you're making such a big deal about the fact that I want to take a small sip."

Samantha immediately grew annoyed at Kenny's insistence attitude to taste the wine. "Kenny, after what you did to me yesterday, you promised you would never take another drop," she said firmly.

"I meant that. I just want to taste the wine. I don't plan to drink any of it. What harm can come from a sip of wine? I had drunk a couple bottles of wine yesterday when I lost my head and kissed you against your will. I'll be forever apologetic, deeply remorseful and repentant about my idiotic conduct."

"Kenny, I was upset with you, but I was able to get over it so quickly because I knew it wasn't you who grabbed me like that. I know it was your intoxication. I also know that you are like two different people when you drink. I want to be friends with the sober Kenny, but I cannot be around the drunken intoxicated one! I will not set myself up to go through that kind of disrespectful conduct of yours again," Samantha stressed strongly.

"Believe me; I would never put you through that pitiful shameless side of me again."

"But, that's just it, Kenny. You have no control over your behavior and conduct when you drink. It provokes an awful side of you," she said and held her stare for a moment. "You are an alcoholic and you already know that you cannot have just a sip."

"I can have one sip and it won't hurt a thing," he insisted.

"I was your sacrificial lamb yesterday when you got dead drunk and kissed me without my consent. I was deeply hurt over the incident. But the bottomline is, you were out of control and shouldn't have done what you did."

"Why are you bringing up the subject? I know I was out of line. Nevertheless, you said earlier that we didn't have to rehash or discuss it. I thought you wanted it to fade into the past," Kenny reminded her.

"Maybe I could allow it to fade into the past if you would find a way to stop lying to me. You gave me your word over the phone earlier that you would give up alcohol tonight," she stressed strongly.

"That's still my plan. One sip won't count."

"I'm not sure you are serious about giving up your booze," Samantha said irritated. "I'm praying you do. Something good needs to come from your little stunt yesterday."

"Something good will come from it. I'm giving up booze tonight just as I promised."

"I want to believe you, Kenny. I hid your identity from Paris and my family."

He shook his head. "I still don't know why you did that. So what if they know I kissed you. You are a grown woman. It was just a harmless kiss."

"That's a lie, Kenny," she said angrily. "How can you sit here and say it was just a harmless kiss? We both know that it was nothing harmless about it. You kissed me against my will which makes it a crime."

"I have never heard of a kiss being a crime and I can't think of any fellow who has ever been locked up for kissing a pretty girl," he said, smiling.

"Kenny, I don't like your attitude about what you did to me. It's not the attitude you displayed right after. I could see you were sorry."

"Look, Samantha. Of course, I was sorry and you know that. That's why you are sitting here with me now; otherwise, I'm sure you wouldn't be giving me the time of day."

"Well, don't make light of it," she snapped.

"Okay, I will not and it won't happen again. How many times do you need me to say how sorry I am? But I would like to get one thing straight."

"Okay, what's the one thing that you would like to get straight?"

"I'm sorry, yes. But I'm basically sorry for my drunken conduct. I'm not really sorry about the kiss. I would be lying if I said I was sorry that I had the opportunity to kiss you. Although, I know the manner in which it happened was questionable and over the top and I do apologize for that hundred percent."

Samantha shook her head and collected herself as she glanced about the fancy establishment. The music was slightly loud and the guests were chatting to the point that no one in the dance club could hear their conversation.

"Kenny, let's just drop this subject. I have accepted your apology. I know deep down that you never would have grabbed me like that if you hadn't been out of your head intoxicated. Therefore, we do not need to discuss it ever again. Especially if nobody else is supposed to know that you are the mystery man who kissed me."

"Before we put this topic to rest, I think you should rethink keeping my identity a secret from your family and Paris." He lifted his glass of water to his mouth and took a sip.

"Why would you want me to reveal to them that you are the one who kissed me?"

"I just don't like how keeping this secret is going to weigh on you. Paris left town and took his vacation without you because he's not pleased that you didn't reveal to him who kissed you."

"That's true, and I'm touched that you are concerned about me keeping it a secret. However, if I tell Paris and my family it was you, they will be furious with you and question my friendship with you. They already feel our friendship is staking on thin ice since it's a thorn in Paris's side. Then to find out that you are the one who kissed me and I'm still friends with you, they won't understand my reasons."

"I'm not even sure if I understand your reasons," he said, smiling.

"Well, I understand my reasons and that's what counts. But also, I was so taken aback that you kissed me, until I made too much of it; and that's how Paris and my folks visualized it." She lifted her glass and took a sip of wine. "As upset as I was with you, I wish I had kept it to myself. I wouldn't be in this pickle with Paris and my family thinking I'm foolish to stay friends with you."

"For your information, I do not care about how or what Paris Franklin and your family think of me. But clearly you do, and you have me wondering why you would protect me in such a way? I know we are friends and I appreciate your support, but in this case I just don't get it," he said curiously as he placed both elbows on the table and stared at her. "So, maybe you can enlighten me on what's really going on with you keeping my identity from your family."

"Kenny, I have told you. I just don't want them to think any less of you, and I don't want any roadblocks as far as our friendship goes."

"Our friendship means that much to you?"

Samantha nodded. "Yes, it does. You are a good person, Kenny. Deep down you are just about as good as they come. If I reveal that you kissed me, it would make you appear like some awful person and you're not. Then our friendship would just antagonize my family and friends." Samantha lifted her glass to her lips and took a sip of wine as if she needed it to calm her nerves.

"I understand what you are saying, Samantha, but I still feel very strongly that you should share with Paris and also your family that I was the one who kissed you."

"Why are you insisting that I share that with them?"

"By not telling them, it makes me feel as if I have done something that is worse than it is. I'm trying to move on and clear my conscience but it's hard to do when you're keeping a secret from your boyfriend and family about it. I just think you should tell them the truth. Tell them that I came over drunk as a skunk and grabbed you and kissed you without your consent. I know they will be angry and upset, but if need be, I'll throw myself at their mercy. I just want the nightmare that happened yesterday to be over," he said with conviction as he reached out and grabbed her glass of wine. "I won't touch it without your consent," he said as he held the glass near his mouth. "So, do you mind if I take a sip and let you know what I think?"

Samantha smiled and shook her head. "You are determined to take a sip of that wine, so go right ahead." She nodded toward him. "You are not going to be satisfied until you try it."

Kenny turned the glass up to his mouth and took a small sip of the wine and then gracefully passed the glass back over to Samantha. "You are right. It's really good."

"I told you it was great wine, but back to what you suggested. I have empathy for you and I promise that I will think about what you have said. I was raised to be open and honest and I want to be completely open with Paris, and I'm very honest and transparent with him but in this incident I didn't want to see you hurt."

"I appreciate your consideration and compassion, but I think it will hurt us more if you keep the secret. It will surely seal every chance of you and Paris Franklin getting completely past this. That is, if you two try again. Not that I want you to give him another chance. It's no secret how I feel about you, but if friendship is all I can have, then I'm happy to settle for that."

Samantha smiled. "Let's dance. I love that dance song and I would rather be on the floor dancing than just sitting here discussing what happened yesterday," she suggested. "That dance floor is huge and lit up beautifully. So, Kenny, are you ready to get on the dance floor for a while?" she asked, smiling. "Don't think I have seen you dance. No, I take that back. I recall seeing you and Vickie Simpson dance at our Halloween party. If that can be counted since you were so intoxicated."

Kenny shook his head. "It's starting to sound like I had all my fun while I was wasted," he looked toward the dance floor but didn't attempt to take her on the dance floor.

"So, Kenny, let's dance? I know it's not proper for me to ask you. But I figured I would ask since you haven't asked me. But maybe you're not interested in dancing."

He gave her a downcast look and smiled. "You are being too cute if you're trying to read my mind. That's not what you are doing, are you?" he teased.

"Nope, I'm not trying to figure out what's on your mind. But I was wondering." She smiled. "Then again, maybe you are interesting in dancing. Otherwise, why would you bring me out to a dance club?"

"Samantha, we will dance shortly," he promised.

"I like dancing from particular songs." She glanced over her shoulder toward the DJ station and then looked back at Kenny. "That song the DJ is playing now is one I really like."

"I like that song as well." He glanced at his watch. "Hopefully the DJ will play more songs that we like as the evening roll on. I just need to get warmed up before I can make my way out there on that dance floor."

"How are you supposed to get warmed up? Are you telling me you cannot dance without a little booze in you?" she laughed.

"Why are you laughing at me? I did not say that I cannot dance without a shot of booze," he said, embarrassed because he knew it was true.

"I know you didn't say it, but you are giving me that impression. I have asked you a couple of times to dance and each time you haven't been warmed up I guess."

He leaned forward and looked her in the eyes. "You are right of course. I'm embarrassed to admit it. But frankly, I can only tolerate myself on the dance floor once I have knocked back a few glasses of wine."

She looked at him and nodded. "Okay, there's my answer. I don't think I'll be dancing tonight," she said, smiling. "But listen, that's okay. You're doing the right thing by not drinking. Therefore, I'm not upset. I get it. A lot of my friends are the same way. They won't get on the dance floor until they have had a few drinks. Then they don't know how to get off the dance floor," she said laughingly.

During their time at the dance club, Samantha didn't get to dance but she enjoyed her time out with Kenny. She was just pleased to be out of the house and preoccupied on that Monday night to keep her from focusing too much on missing Paris.

Kenny glanced at his watch and it was 10:00 p.m. "I think we should probably take off. What do you think? It's starting to get late although it's still fairly early. Therefore, if you like, we could stop off somewhere else," he suggested.

Leaving the hall club was fine with Samantha, but in route to take her home, Kenny headed in the opposite direction toward his home instead of the Taylor mansion. Samantha was busy checking her text messages as he drove at a leisurely speed. Although, when he pulled into his driveway and killed the motor, she looked out the windshield and passenger's window and then she looked at him with a confused look on her face. "We're at your house? Why are you stopping here?" she asked. "You need to get me home."

"It's still fairly early and I hope you don't mind stopping here."

"But why stop here?"

"I hope you don't mind, but I just wanted a quiet place where we could talk for a while. My mother is home, so I'm not up to anything if that's what you think."

"Kenny, nothing out of the way never crossed my mind. Do you think I would be out with you in the first place, if I didn't trust you?"

"That's mighty kind of you to say after my ill behavior yesterday."

She didn't comment about his statement. She wanted to know about his home. "This is your family home, but I thought you moved into your own apartment. Did you move back home?"

"No, I haven't moved back home as of yet."

"But yet, we're in your parking lot."

"That's because I don't officially still live here, but I stay here more than I do my own apartment right now. I just feel I need to be here to be supportive to my mother."

"I know it must be hard for your mother with what she has been through, and your father incarceration. I'm sorry that you and your family are suffering right now."

"Thank you, but we are getting by," he said, glanced at her and focused out the windshield. "So, what do you think about spending a little time here visiting? We really have a lot more to talk about. It's just that I couldn't talk to you the way I wanted to in that upscale crowded establishment. I can't think straight when music is overshadowing my voice."

She glanced toward him and nodded. "I don't mind visiting for a short while. What is it that you want to talk about? It's getting late and doesn't feel quite decent to visit your home at this time of evening."

"It will be fine," he said, grabbed the door handled and pushed opened the car door and stepped out.

He walked around to the passenger's side and opened the door for Samantha. They walked softly up the front steps and across his front porch. She stood beside him feeling out of place visiting his home at such an inappropriate hour as he gently turned the key in the front door lock.

He unlocked the door and they stepped out of the cold into his warm, dark living room. He locked the door behind him and immediately clicked on the lights. The house was quiet and still. Then he heard a voice from down the hallway. "Is that you, Kenny?" Mildred asked.

"Yes, it's me, Mom," he said. "Plus, I have a friend with me who's going to visit for a while. We'll be upstairs in my room."

"Okay, Sweetheart, you two enjoy yourself. Trina is upstairs in her room, but Courtney is still out. Goodnight."

"Goodnight, Mom," Kenny said, removing his coat and placed it across the back of the sofa.

"Kenny, I'm not going upstairs to your room with you. I'll visit for a while, but not in your bedroom," she politely told him. "It's not that I don't trust you. It's just not proper."

He nodded. "I understand. We can visit here in the living room." He stepped across the floor and closed the door that connected the living room to the hallway and dining area. "Now our conversation will be in privacy," he said as he stepped over to the blue sofa and took a seat, placing both feet on the coffee table. "Please be seated and make yourself comfortable," he said, smiling.

She slowly slipped out of her coat and glanced about for a place to hang it. Kenny hopped off the sofa and grabbed her coat. "Excuse my manners. I'll put this away for you." He looked toward the guest closet but didn't care to bother walking to it to place the coat on a hunger. Therefore, he threw her coat across the back of a nearby recliner. "It'll be just fine there," he said as he watched her take a seat on the big navy chair opposite the sofa.

It was almost 10:30 p.m., but Samantha didn't say a word about going home, when she knew she should probably leave. Her father and sisters would be concerned about her whereabouts if she didn't get home at an appropriate hour. However, she didn't mind visiting with Kenny for a while to hear what was on his mind. But after a several minutes when he just sat there on the sofa looking down at the floor without saying a word, she wondered what was going on with him. Now that they were in his home, suddenly he seemed sad and withdrawn.

"Kenny, what's the matter?" she asked. "You asked me to come in and visit awhile, but it's getting seriously late and you're not talking."

He snapped his head right up and looked toward her and smiled. "I'm sorry; I just have a lot on my mind right now."

"I understand and maybe I should just leave. We can talk another time," she suggested.

"I'm fine and don't want you to leave yet," he assured her. "I know the clock is ticking and I promise not to keep you here too late."

"But you were sitting there not talking. For a moment I thought you were going to fall asleep," she told him.

"I don't know what it is, but suddenly, I just feel drained."

"What do you mean? What could have made you feel that way? We both know you're not tired from dancing," she said jokingly.

"That's true since I didn't do the honors of dancing with you once. But, Samantha, believe me when I say I wanted to. It was no use since I wasn't drinking. I'm no good at dancing without a stomach loaded with liquor to make me feel silly."

"No need to explain, Kenny. I was just kidding. I'm not trying to give you a hard time. However, you do look tired. Maybe its best if you just take me home so you can get to bed and rest," Samantha suggested. "I could just call a taxi and let you get right to bed."

"Please, do not kid with me about taking a taxi. You know I would never put you in a taxi and send you home from here."

"But if you are tired, I really wouldn't mind and I wouldn't be offended in any way."

"But I would be offended. Samantha, no way would I allow you to leave here in a taxi. You are my date for the evening. I picked you up from home and I will return you to the Taylor mansion safe and sound the same way I picked you up," he said seriously, then grabbed his stomach and appeared to be in discomfort.

"Kenny, what's the matter? Is your stomach upset?" Samantha asked concerned.

"It'll pass. It comes and goes. It's nothing to be alarmed about," he assured her.

"But you appear to be in a lot of discomfort. Therefore, you should be alarmed."

"It's my repercussions from giving up alcohol. It's hard Samantha. But I'm doing it more for you than for myself. I know it changes me into some idiot that I do not precisely care for. Therefore, I need to stay away from the stuff at all cost or pain."

"Kenny, I had no idea it was such a struggle for you to not to drink."

"It's a constant struggle," he said and glanced down and back over at her. "You were right about what you said at the dance."

"Okay, what was I right about?"

"You were right when you said I couldn't take a simple sip of alcohol."

"But you managed from that sip."

He nodded. "Do I look like I managed? I managed with a lot of struggle because I do not know how to stop at one sip. Tonight, you really saved me by being insistence that I have no more than a sip."

"So you're feeling these ramifications from your heavy drinking of yesterday?" she asked.

He shook his head as he grabbed the back of his neck with both hands. "No, it's not from yesterday, it's from tonight."

"What do you mean? You didn't drink anything tonight."

"But I wanted to drink and that's why I literally begged to take a sip of your wine."

"You're not telling me one sip has your stomach in pain, are you?"

"No, the one sip isn't what's hurting my stomach. It's the aftermath of taking the one sip. That one sip has me in pain because it lit a fire that wants more fuel added to it," he said irritated. "I just need a drink and I'll be fine. But I know I can't have a drink."

"How are you going to cope with not drinking anything tonight?" she asked.

"I just need to take a quick nap and then the discomfort will subside." He yawned. "But I really feel lousy to get you here in my home and fall asleep on you. But I know my system. It'll take thirty minutes to an hour nap, then I'll be able to function and get you home safely.

"Sure, I understand, I'll just stay seated right here and answer some social media messages while you take your nap." She glanced at her diamond Fendi watch. "It's not too late, as long as I get home before midnight, all will be good."

"Thank you, Samantha, for understanding. You are a peach of a female that I don't deserve to have in my company. But I'm still glad you want to be," he said as he slipped out of his black JC Penney's shoes and fell back on the cushions of the sofa. "I'm really glad you don't mind the fact that I'm taking a quick nap on you. I know it seems rather rude, but this alcoholic disease gets to me in this way," he drowsily uttered. "So do me a favor and step into the kitchen and grab me a bottle of water. That will help ease my stomach as well."

"Sure, I'll be right back," she said, got of her seat and headed toward the closed door.

"You can't miss the kitchen when you stepped into the hallway," he said. "It's the second door on your right."

She opened the door and stepped out of the room and pulled the door closed behind her. He listened for her footsteps and then jumped off the sofa and grabbed a bottle of vodka out of the bottom drawer of the curio stand. He stood there, twisted off the cab and turned the bottle up to his mouth and didn't lower it until it was half empty. He lowered the bottle and ingested the alcohol and then turned the bottle back up to his mouth and finished off the pint bottle and placed it back into curio drawer.

When Samantha located the kitchen around the bend, she found Kenny's mother removing a pitcher of water from the refrigerator. "Hi Mrs. Ross, I'm Kenny's friend, Samantha. I stepped in here to grab him a bottle of water."

Mildred slightly jumped by surprise as she glanced around and nodded at Samantha as if she was distracted. She was polite to others as she went through the motions of trying to live a normal life each day. However, deep down she felt the joy and real purpose of her life was over since she couldn't have a life with Antonio Armani. She also felt she had shamed her family and her children; and on top of that she felt her husband had brought a permanent stain of scandalous disgrace against their family.

"Grab a glass from the dish rack," Mildred said. "We're out of bottle water, but our tap water is filtered and just as healthy," she said as Samantha placed the tall glass on the counter.

Mildred poured cold water into the glass and smiled at Samantha. "So, you are that young lady that Kenny speaks so highly of? He told me about you and how you're the good friend who's going to help him back on the wagon." She shook her head. "My son means well, but don't get your hopes up that Kenny will ever fulfill that wish of completely giving up booze. He has been down that road too many times and failed terribly I'm sorry to say." She placed the pitcher back into the refrigerator without pouring any water for herself as if she had known Samantha would be stepping into the kitchen for a glass of water.

"Kenny is a good young man with a bad disposition of being enslaved to that poisonous booze that he can't seem to give up," Mildred said, smiling. "But he has it honest. His father is an alcoholic as well; and I have the mental scars to show for it."

Samantha felt somewhat uneasy and didn't know what to say to Mildred because of all the negative news that surrounded the Ross family.

"Don't worry, Sweetheart, about saying something to offend me," Mildred said humbly as she looked at Samantha with serious eyes. "I'm sure you have heard on the news and read online all the sorted details of the scandal that has engulfed this family," she said as she looked into space for a moment before she looked Samantha in the face. "Kenny and all my children didn't come out on the other side unscathed from all the disgraceful news surrounding our home. Therefore, it all adds to an alcoholic drive to drink," Mildred explained with her back leaned up against the kitchen counter.

Samantha stared and didn't say a word as she glanced at the glass of water in her hand knowing she needed to head back into the living room, but she didn't want to be rude and walk away while Kenny's mother was in the middle of conversing with her. Plus, she wondered why his mother stated that Kenny mentioned she would be the one to get him on the wagon, which implied he hadn't quit drinking. Then again, she thought maybe Kenny had mentioned that to her but hadn't yet mentioned to her that he had given up alcohol.

"Samantha, I know you want to head back in the living room and give Kenny that glass of water, but I would just like to say something that I hope you will take to heart."

"What is it, Mrs. Ross?"

"You are a decent young lady and I'm pleased that you have taken an interest in my son's well-being and somehow you want to get him away from alcohol. But please be careful with Kenny. You are Charles Taylor's daughter and God knows this family has enough problems right now. We don't need your father breaking down our door."

"Mrs. Ross, why would you think there would be a need for my father to break down your door?"

"Do you really think you need to ask me that question? I'm sure you know why I said that, sweetheart."

276

"Yes, Mrs. Ross, I think I do know."

"Of course, you know it's my son. He tells me that the two of you went to college together. Therefore, you most likely know about his rude out of control drunken side."

"Yes, I do, but I'm not really concerned about that because he's not drinking anymore. He gave up drinking earlier tonight before he came to my home to pick me up."

"Is that what he told you?"

"Yes, Mrs. Ross, Kenny has given up drinking. I'm a witness that he didn't take a drink tonight."

Mildred looked at the glass of water in her hand and nodded. "Yes, I'm sure he told you he had given it up and he probably meant it at the time. But I used to sleep with an alcoholic every night and their minds are never too far from their drink."

"Mrs. Ross, tonight at the dance club Kenny didn't share a glass of wine with me. He only took one small sip and that was it. I'm so proud of him that he has chosen to walk away from all that drinking."

"Samantha, just be careful and don't be fooled by what my son says, just keep your eyes on what he does. I'm not convinced that he has given up his drink and I'm sure you probably knows as well as I do that when he's drinking he become a complete jerk that's unfit to be around," Mildred seriously reminded her.

"Thanks, Mrs. Ross, I'll keep my eyes open as you suggested. It was nice meeting you," Samantha said as she headed out of the kitchen and down the short hallway toward the living room.

Kenny was lying back on the sofa against the cushions. He smiled when Samantha walked back into the room. He was feeling the effects of the Vodka he had sneaked and drank and he wanted more Vodka by the time Samantha stepped into the room. She walked in slowly and didn't close the door behind her as she noticed he was still seated.

"Here's your water," she said as she stepped over by him and passed him the tall glass of ice water.

He sprung forward in his seat and took the glass. He immediately lifted the glass to his mouth and took a small swallow almost not drinking any water at all.

"I thought you were thirsty," she said.

"I was but I only needed to wet my tongue," he lied, and then he pointed toward the door. "Please shut the door."

She turned around and stepped over to the door and pulled it closed and then took a seat back in the big blue chair. She smiled at him. "Do you feel any better? I think you look a little better."

"No, I don't feel any better. I'm drained and beat if you must know. Besides that, I have been on my feet all day at my dead-end job. You should keep in mind that I don't have an easy cushy job like you Miss Taylor," he said as he placed the glass on the coffee table and then fell back against the cushions again.

"Kenny, what are you trying to say?"

"I'm not trying to say anything. I'm just stating the facts. We both know that you come from a family where you are set for life whether you work or not," he said rudely.

"Okay, but why are you bringing that up? What does it has to do with anything, and why are you saying it as if you are pissed at me for my life?" she asked. "I work just like you do," she suspiciously uttered. "If I didn't know better I would say you're drank."

He didn't comment about the drunk remark. "I know you work, and I also know that the concept of a job and work is also of vital importance to you. However, it's not a necessity for your wellbeing, is it?" Kenny asked with a bitter edge.

Samantha braced her back against the cushions of the chair as a flood of uneasiness ripped through her from Kenny's dialogue. The conversation had suddenly turned to a tone where it seemed as if he was stating that she somehow felt he was beneath her. It seemed to her that he was purposely being rude and hurtful. She wondered if he was being rude and cold toward her because he was upset that she didn't allow him to take a drink earlier. Then she thought that maybe his dialogue and behavior was part of his pain of wanting a drink and not being able to have one.

It made Samantha even more determined to reach him. She desperately wanted their friendship to work so she could make a difference in his life. But what she didn't know was that he still wanted to keep drinking even though he had promised her that he would give it up. Deep down he wanted to give it up because he had promised her, but he had promised to quit many times but didn't seem to have the willpower to follow through. Samantha had mentioned to Starlet that if he had swindled Karen out of money, it didn't matter since he had changed from his old ways back in college. However, his present behavior and attitude wasn't giving Samantha any positive signs that he had changed. Since he was talking rude and craving alcohol. Then she wondered to herself if he really was worth her time and efforts? She wondered if her sisters could be right. She pondered the thought and realized that their rightness would prove her to be somewhat naïve and blind to Kenny's true colors. Therefore, she was determined to be right and knew she needed to be strong to get Kenny on the right track and keep him there.

Kenny said in a humble voice, "Samantha, if you're really serious about the two of us reconnecting our friendship as we were back in college, you'll be willing to help me out," he said from an intoxicated mind.

"What do you mean by help you out?" she curiously asked.

"It's just a little favor I need."

"What kind of favor?"

"A favor that you could probably handle easier than any other friend," he said.

When he said that, a signal went off in Samantha's brain regarding the conversation that she had just had earlier in the evening with Starlet about how he had charmed Starlet's friend, Karen, out of money. Samantha braced her back against the cushions waiting for the next shoe to drop as her anxious heart pounded in her ears. Her heart was in her throat. The thought of him asking for money ripped at her.

"I'm waiting for you to tell me what kind of favor you need from me."

"I'm getting to what kind of favor, but first of all I just want you to know that I'm in a serious situation at the moment."

With every word out of his mouth, it led her to believe that he was getting ready to ask her for a loan. She thought as she sat there looking toward the floor in deep thought.

He looked toward her grinning. "Why are you so quiet?" he asked. "Did you hear what I just said?"

"Yes, Kenny, I heard you." She looked over at him with a solemn look on her face. "You said you are in a serious situation. But I didn't say anything because I'm just listening to hear what kind of serious situation you are referring to?"

"Do I need to write it on the wall or spell it out to you, Samantha? I'm talking about being in bad shape," he grinned. "What don't you get about someone being in bad shape?"

"I don't get what you are talking about," she stressed. "I'm not a mindreader and have no idea what you mean when you say bad shape?"

He grinned and winked at Samantha. "I guess you are right. You couldn't imagine what kind of condition I'm in. How could you know when you stiffed me with that expensive bottle of wine tonight?" He held up both hands. "But hey, I was willing to pay it, so no need to rehash. But I want you to know I'm not trying to take you for a ride just because you're a rich." He held up one finger. "However, if you can do me this favor, then I'll know you're serious about resuming our friendship." He held up one finger again. "Providing, I'm not just someone to fill your time until the Prince takes you back."

"Kenny, I wouldn't have accepted your invitation to go dancing tonight if I wasn't serious about being friends the way we were back in college. So I certainly want you to know I'm your friend," Samantha stressed. "So, tell me, what is it that you want from me?"

"I lost my job this week and now I have no means of income," he said sadly. "If I don't find something soon I'll have to give up my apartment."

"Kenny, you lost another job. I thought you just started working there."

"How could you have thought that?" He looked at her with suspicious eyes. "How would you know how long I have worked anywhere? I haven't really discussed my employment history with you," he snapped.

"I'm sorry, you are right."

"Sorry is fine; yet you must have said what you said for some reason."

"I probably heard someone say it because of your reputation," she said.

"That's right, my reputation. The one that has me lined up with one dead-end job after the next and I can't keep any of them. It's because of my out of control drinking? Is that the reputation you are referring to?"

Samantha nodded. "Yes, that reputation, but you and I both know you're no longer that person. You're trying to improve your livelihood by staying sober."

He grinned. "That's right. I plan to stay sober for you, Miss Samantha."

"Kenny, I don't listen to gossip but I have heard rumors that nailed you as not keeping jobs for that long. Surely, I have no idea how long you worked where you worked or where you worked. I just heard the gossip that you got jobs quickly but always left each one just as quickly. Therefore, my best guess had me assuming that you had worked where you worked for only a couple months or less," she explained.

"I think I did mention to you that I was working at my father's restaurant."

"You did mention your job at the restaurant, but I didn't know your father owned it."

"No, my father doesn't own the place. It's where he worked for the past twenty years and he got me a job there, and occasionally Courtney and Trina would work there on the weekends. But after my father committed a crime, he was instantly fired and I got kicked out as well. Now my father is sitting in a penitentiary and I'm standing in the unemployment line. "

"I'm sorry you lost your job from the fallout of your father's bad deeds."

"I'm sorry also, but sorry doesn't pay the bills," Kenny said seriously. "I know I could move back home since I'm here most of the time anyway, but I still want to keep my apartment so when I feel my mother is stable to function on her own without me living here. I'll move back into my apartment. But I need to have an apartment to move back into," he explained sincerely. "Losing my job at the restaurant has hit me pretty hard. I have a few dollars in the bank, but not enough to pay my rent and the car payment for this month."

Samantha laughed when he mentioned apartment rent and car payment. He wondered why she was laughing and asked. "What's so funny?"

Samantha thought to herself but didn't reveal her thoughts to him, "I'm laughing because it seems that you are up to your same old tricks. The same tricks that Starlet had mentioned to me earlier; and it's so obvious until it's funny. Especially, if you think I'm an easy target that you plan to con out of money," she thought to herself and then had a second thought. "I'll play along with Kenny because I truly want to help him stay on the wagon. He's a decent person when he isn't drinking."

"So, are you going to tell me what's so funny?" Kenny asked again.

"I'm sorry, Kenny, but I'm not laughing at you. I'm laughing at something my sister said earlier."

"Well, you sure know how to crush a man's ego, Samantha. I poured my heart out about how lousy I feel about losing my job and you sat there and laugh," he snapped and drew an attitude.

"I'm sorry, Kenny. Please continue. What favor did you want to ask of me?"

"I need to borrow fifteen hundred dollars from you."

"That's a lot of money, Kenny. But is that how much you need for your apartment rent and car payment?"

"Yes, Samantha, that's how much I need. I'm not pulling your leg. I'm really out of work. I got laid off last Monday and my rent and car payment is due. I can show you the bill for my car payment if you want to see."

"No need to show me the bill, I believe you; and I believe you have lost your job. I'm sorry about it and I hope you find something soon."

He waved his hand. "Sure I will, I always do. I'll have another job before the end of the week, but what about the favor?"

"Sure, of course." Samantha nodded. "Drop by the house tomorrow and I'll have the money for you."

After Samantha promised him the money, he slipped on his shoes and stood. He smiled at her and glanced at his watch. "I'm feeling much better and should get you home before your father come gunning for me."

"Why would you say something like that, Kenny?" Samantha stood from the chair, stepped over to the sofa and grabbed her coat and slipped it on.

"I'm just kidding around, of course. I know your father would never do that. But it is way past the time I wanted to get you home," he said, grabbed his coat from the arm of the sofa and threw it on.

Chapter Twenty-Four

On Tuesday morning, Samantha rolled out of bed earlier than usual. She showered and dressed for work, had breakfast with her family and went into the downtown office at 9:00 o'clock. She worked until 1:30 and then headed back home. During her drive home, thoughts of Paris floated in her mind and she wondered about how his vacation was going. She hadn't heard from him and she hadn't texted or called him. Thoughts of him saturated her mind and caused her to miss him terribly. She pushed the thoughts away and tried to focus on Kenny. But a serious expression overtook her face as she thought to herself.

"I'm encouraged about my reconnection with Kenny. However, in the back of my mind for some reason I feel uneasy about him. I can't quite figure him out but he seems a great deal different from what I remember of him back in college. It seems he isn't as interested in our reconnection as he is in borrowing my money. It seems he only became serious minded and cheered up after I promised to loan him some money. Therefore, I'm on the fence about Kenny and I'm not convinced he's really being sincere with me or if he's just using me to secure loans just as he used Starlet's friend, Karen," she thought and then turned on the car radio to overshadow her thoughts.

She turned the radio off when a commercial mentioned something about being ripped off. Then her mind went back into thought. "I guess I'm so suspicious because he asked for the fifteen hundred dollars.

Maybe he did just lose his job and needed the money for his apartment rent and car payment," she thought.

She inhaled sharply and she continued to think about Kenny. "I'm going to give him the benefit of the doubt. After all, fifteen hundred dollars is not as much as three thousand dollars. Furthermore, I desperately need the distraction of helping him to stay sober. Knowing I'm helping someone else will help me concentrate on my efforts for someone else instead of focusing on my own worries and problems. It helps me cope with Paris absence. Besides, I really don't want to throw in the towel on Kenny, since there's a chance that he's sincere about staying sober and getting his life back on track. I want to do the right thing toward helping him. Maybe he has changed and I'm willing to be patient and find out."

When Samantha arrived home from work, she didn't go upstairs to her room. She slipped out of her coat and hung it in the guest closet. Then she took a seat on the living room sofa and fell back on the cushions. She felt exhausted from not much sleep from the night before. She really wanted to head upstairs and take a nap, but she tried to avoid taking naps during the day. However, thirty minutes after arriving home, Kenny showed up at the Taylor mansion. It was 3:00 o'clock in the afternoon.

Samantha was seated on the living room sofa glancing through a Reader's Digest magazine when she glanced up from the magazine at the sound of Kenny's car pulling into their driveway. His car engine couldn't be ignored since it made a loud sound as if it was falling apart. She stood up from the sofa, placed the magazine on the coffee table and hurried across the large room toward the front door. He rang the doorbell before she could reach the door, but she answered the door moments after he rang the bell. She showed him inside and they took a seat on opposite living room sofas facing each other. She smiled at him but noticed how anxious he seemed in her presence. She remembered that he always displayed that trait whenever he was drinking. The thought of him drinking after he had promised not to immediately irritated her.

"Kenny, I'm not going to beat around the bush, I'm going to ask you straight out. Have you been drinking?" she asked.

He stared at her for a few moments, but didn't bother to deny it as he nodded. "You got me, and I'm guilty," he said.

"So, you have been drinking after you promised you wouldn't," she said disappointed.

"Yes, I have been drinking," he said while looking straight in her eyes. "I know I promised and I will make good on the promise." He held up both hands. "But it's going to take some time before I can get officially on the wagon."

"But I thought you had already given it up. I told everybody including your mother that you gave up drinking alcohol last night."

He nodded. "That was my intention."

"You got through the night and you didn't drink, what triggered you to start drinking today? I wish you had contacted me so I could have encouraged you not to take a drink," he suggested. "I could have kept you from drinking just as I kept you from drinking last night."

He held up one finger. "You might as well know," he reluctantly said. "I did drink last night. I didn't drink while we were out at the dance club, but I did so later," he admitted, looking her in the face.

Samantha sat on the opposite sofa across from him with an extreme disappointed look on her face. She was shaking her head in disbelief. She pointed to her chest and then toward him. "What are we doing together if I can't help you? I was under the impression that you got through the night without drinking any alcohol, now you tell me that you did drink," she said in a defeated voice.

"Samantha, I'm deeply sorry. I know this isn't what you wanted to hear but I'm trying to be on the honest. I really need you in my corner if I'm going to shake this disease," he stressed strongly.

"Okay, Kenny. I need to know exactly when you took a drink," she said anxiously. "Right now, I'm not clear on when you had an opportunity to take a drink without my knowledge. I was watching you very close and all I remember is the one sip you took from my glass at the dance club."

"I just said it wasn't while we were out at the dance, but later," he reminded her.

"Later like after you took me home?"

He just looked at her and didn't comment. He didn't want to reveal that he had drunk while she was visiting him.

"So, when did you drink last night? I guess you hit the bottle after you got back home from dropping me off. Is that correct?"

He shook his head as he looked down toward the carpet floor for a second and then looked back toward her with a solemn look on his face. "That's not what happened," he said. "You have this strange power of me and I have the need to be on the level with you."

"I'm glad you're being on the level. So, if that's not what happened, and you didn't drink after you returned home. I'm not sure when you had an opportunity to take drink. So just tell me."

"Samantha, listen. You need to face the facts that I'm too far gone with this disease. I mean well, but I can't wish it away. I hit the bottle while you were still at my house."

"I don't recall you drinking anything."

"That's because I sneaked and did so while you went to the kitchen to fetch me a glass of water."

She nodded. "I did leave the room. I guess I shouldn't have left you alone."

"It wasn't your fault. You did everything that you could. I was determined to get my hands on a drink. I purposely sent you out of the room so I could grab my hidden bottle."

"I guess that's why your mother had that talk with me while I was in your kitchen."

"What did she say?"

"She was just warning me about you and made a statement that referred to you as still drinking. She didn't come right out and say it. But when I told her that you had given it up, she didn't appear moved or convinced by my statement."

"My mother knows me so well and knows how I struggle with my addiction. But, listen. Hang in there with me. I promise I'll get on the wagon somehow with your help."

Samantha didn't comment as she looked at Kenny wondering if her mission to help him stay sober was hopeless, since he was starting off so rocky.

Kenny glanced at his watch and looked at her and shook his head. "I'm sorry, Samantha, but I don't have a lot time to visit right now. I have an interview to get to," he said. "So do you have the money you promised me last night? I'm pressed for time, but if you're free tomorrow evening, I would love to drop by and chat some more, if that's okay with you?" He stood up from the sofa.

Samantha nodded as she stood up from the sofa. She had the money in her dress pocket as she stepped toward him. She pulled the money from her pocket and handed it to him. He took the money and quickly stuck it in his jacket pocket.

"Thank you, I'll call or text you later," he said as he headed across the living room floor toward the front door.

He was walking quickly toward the door and Samantha walked gracefully behind him. When he reached the front door, he grabbed the doorknob and glanced around and smiled at her.

"Kenny, what's your hurry? Can't you stay and visit for a little while longer? If you're chatting with me, it helps me to keep you from drinking. One thing for sure, I don't think you'll drink in my presence anymore."

He nodded and smiled. "That's true. I will not."

"So, what's so urgent? You said you have an interview somewhere, but what time is it for?" she glanced at the clock above the fireplace and it was 3:15. Are you sure you can't spare more time to visit with me?"

He glanced at his watch. The interview in at 4:30."

"Where about?"

"Just some restaurant in town."

"Kenny, you have a four year degree, so why are you seeking out these restaurant jobs, and doing what?"

"Cooking positions. You know my father is a chef."

"I know your father is a chef. But you went to school for business management, not to cook in restaurants," Samantha reminded him.

"I know, but with my disease I wouldn't pass the substance clearance for the kind of job I went to college for," he admitted and stepped away from the door. "I have some time to spare before I need to get to the interview. So, I'll stay a little while longer." He glanced at his watch again. "But I can only stay a short while." He propped his back against the wall of the foyer, making no attempts to head back into the living room.

"You want to talk right here?" she asked.

"Yes, I'm sorry. I'm nervous and feel out of sorts not having any alcohol in my stomach. I'm too anxious to sit and visit. So, let's converse quickly so I can get to my pressing business that I need to take care of," he slightly snapped.

Samantha held up both hands. "Kenny, I think you should leave. You're in a bad way and need a drink and I don't seem to be able to help you. So, please go. My efforts seems hopeless."

"No, they're not hopeless, but it's useless to try and sit and talk the way I feel right now," he said irritated. "I'll see you tomorrow evening, if that's okay! But right now I'll take off and take care of my business," he said and rushed out of the door.

When he started up his loud engine and drove out of her driveway, she felt confused and wondered if she was ever going to really get through to him to make a real positive difference in his life. He seemed so absorbed in securing financial support until it appeared to be his main focus toward their connection.

Chapter Twenty-Five

Wednesday evening, Kenny and Samantha spent more time at the Taylor mansion talking and discussing ways he could give up drinking. They were seated in the Taylor's living room along with Starlet. As they conversed, Kenny agreed with everything Starlet said or suggested and by the end of the evening, Starlet had gotten off of Samantha's back about seeing Kenny. Therefore, Samantha retired for bed feeling more convinced of Kenny's sincerity. However, that confidence faded when Kenny dropped by on Thursday evening and asked for another loan. He borrowed the money and rushed off to the nearest bar. Then later Thursday evening, right before 10:30 p.m., he showed up in Samantha's driveway again. However, Samantha was already in bed having a restless night with thoughts of Paris. Every time she closed her eyes she would see Paris's smooth handsome face saying he loved her. She missed him desperately and couldn't forget the disappointed look in his eyes toward her the last time she saw him on Monday before he left for France.

She laid in her bed saturated in thoughts of Paris when she was startled by a flashing light at her bedroom window. She sprung up in bed and glanced about her moonlit room and noticed nothing. But as she sat still listening, she noticed a flashing light against her bedroom window. She threw the covers off of her and gracefully stepped out of bed to investigate the flashing light against her window. She grabbed her long white satin robe from a nearby chair and slipped into the robe as she headed across her room toward the side window. She pulled the long lavender curtains apart and looked out of the window and to her surprise she saw Kenny leaning against the hood of his old black Pontiac. He smiled up at her clicking on and off the flash light pointed toward her window. Samantha grabbed both cheeks and shook her head. She was well aware of the late hour, but she was hopeful that he hadn't indulged himself in alcoholic beverages and now had shown up to lie and tell her how well he was coping without consuming alcohol. She pushed back the negative thought as a positive thought danced in her mind that maybe he had good news. She hurried out of her bedroom and rushed down the staircase to the front door to let him in. She opened the door with a smile on her face. But when she looked in his eyes, sad disappointment immediately dashed through her stomach. Instinctly, she sensed that he hadn't come back to discuss his efforts to stay away from booze. He seemed drunk and probably needed more drinking money. Nevertheless, thinking idealistic, Samantha didn't give him a chance to say a word. She took his hand and led him directly across the living room to be seated on one of the two sofas where she sat beside him.

Kenny seemed nervous and shaky with both hands covering his face. She wasn't pleased that he had shown up at a late hour. But she was pleased that they were not too verbal as to wake others in the big house. But as he sat there with both hands covering his face, looking toward the carpet, it was obvious that he was intoxicated and he was at her home for no good reason. She felt uneasy because she could sense that there was something on his mind. She wondered but hoped he wasn't trying to figure out how to ask her for another loan.

He uncovered his face and glanced about the room. Then he glanced at his watch, but didn't look at her, who was seated beside him. "I guess everybody in this huge place is either in bed or out," he mumbled.

Samantha stared at the side of his face as he looked straight ahead toward the front door. "What's the matter, Kenny? It's quite late and not really a proper time for you to show up at my home. You already know this isn't proper."

"You could have fooled me," he snapped and leaped off the sofa. "You were smiling when you opened the damn door just now. You didn't appear as if you were bothered about the time." He raised both arms. "But before I get comfortable I can just leave right back out of here if that would please you."

Samantha discreetly shook her head as he paced about in front of the fireplace ranting. She knew he was talking through a stomach filled with alcohol. She had the urge to tell him to get out. But she desperately wanted to help him if she could. But first she needed to calm him down.

"Kenny, just calm down, I'm not asking you to leave. However, we are friends and friends are supposed to respect each other. Coming here this time of night is not showing me much respect. Besides, it gives my family more reason not to encourage our alliance, which they do not understand in the first place," she explained.

"I just told you I can leave," he snapped bitterly.

"I know you told me that, but what would that solve? You are already here. Just make sure in the future not to show up here this late again."

"You have my word that I will not show up here at your home this late in the evening unannounced ever again," he assured her. "I just lost track of time."

"Kenny, I can see you have been drinking again."

He nodded. "Yes, just a couple drinks."

"I'm sure it was more than a couple, since you certainly look like you have had more than a couple of drinking," she said disappointedly.

"Why is that the first thing that crosses your high society mind, Miss Samantha?"

She swallowed hard and allowed his insult to roll right off her back. "Kenny, you're an alcoholic who's trying to give up alcohol. Is that correct?" She firmly asked.

"So what if it is?" he snapped.

"Well, my understanding is that my connection with you is about helping you to break the habit," she stressed. "However, if you have no intentions of giving up booze I wish you would level with me so I can stop trying to help you when you don't want to be helped."

"Lighten up, Miss Samantha."

292

"Kenny, please do not call me, Miss Samantha. It makes me nerves when you do so. You are usually quite drunk when you call me that."

"Okay, I won't call you Miss Samantha. But you are correct. Damn right, I have been drinking." He held up one finger. "But as you know, I'm trying to give it up."

"You keep saying you're trying to give it up. But what efforts are you making?"

"I'm making efforts by just not drinking as much. Just tonight, I left the bar and came straight to your house. I know it's late, but if I hadn't driven over here I would still be out drinking somewhere."

"I see, so you are telling me that coming here is your safe haven, your refuge from drinking?"

"Yes, that's exactly what I'm saying."

"I get it and I want to help you. But the idea is to come chat with me when you get the urge to drink and before you take a drink. I cannot help you after you are already intoxicated as you are now. Besides, you can't run to my home this time of night whenever you feel you need a safe haven from your drinking. You need to quit drinking and just go home," Samantha suggested. "I know I said I would be your friend and help you give up drinking, but I'm helping you against my family wishes and at the risk of my own lovelife," she softly stated. "I know that deep down you are a good guy; and I truly wished you weren't trapped with such a horrible disease called alcoholism."

"It runs in my family," he quickly added.

"I know it does, and that's why I don't blame you for what you did."

"You don't?" He narrowed his eyes at her.

"No, Kenny, I do not," she said seriously. "I was very angry when you caught me by surprised and grabbed me in your arms like that, displaying improper behavior with me. But I was more upset with your vulgar dialogue and the rude way you spoke to me," she politely explained. "Of course, I was shocked by the unwelcome kiss and your audacity to grab me as you did. Nevertheless, your words were more hurtful," she admitted.

"Look, I'm sure I shocked you with my actions and my words, but grateful that you know I didn't mean any of it. Just like I didn't mean any of it at your Halloween party."

"Kenny, I know and believe you didn't mean it."

"It didn't cross your mind that I got drunk and decided to take advantage of you?"

She slowly shook her head. "That never crossed my mind. I know you have some feelings for me, but I don't feel you grabbed and kissed me out of an urge to be romantic with me. I believed the only reason it happened is because you were intoxicated."

He nodded. "You are right. As much as I'm attracted to you, it wouldn't have happened if I had been sober," he admitted.

"Nevertheless, Kenny; and knowing all of that," Samantha said, and then looked at him in silence as she dreaded her next words. "I'm not sure if I can continue to lend my support to you."

"Why not?" he asked.

"My aspiration to help you will not be of any use to you, if you're not willing to try to break free of alcohol and stay sober," she said seriously.

Kenny looked at Samantha and gave her a tight smile. What she had just said made him feel uneasy because he didn't want to run her away. Even though, he wasn't hundred percent interested in putting forth the efforts to stay sober, he wanted her to think so. He realized that her desire to help him stay sober was the glue keeping her by his side.

Samantha wondered if he believed she was being serious about walking away from their connection if he didn't show more interest in staying sober. However, he didn't comment about what she had said.

Moments later after Kenny took a seat on the sofa opposite where she was seated, they both looked toward the stairs when they heard footsteps on the staircase. They spotted Starlet headed down the staircase. She was wrapped in a long silk sapphire robe and gown set designed by Oscar de la Renta. Kenny and Samantha were both silent and kept their eyes on her as she stepped into the living room. Starlet was surprised to find Kenny sitting there with Samantha at such an inappropriate hour.

"Hi Kenny, I didn't know you were here. I just got home from a movie with Sydney about thirty minutes ago. I don't think I recall seeing your car in the driveway when Sydney brought me home," Starlet said in wonder.

Samantha crossed her fingers and spoke before Kenny could say a word. "His car was parked around the back. He was here when you got home, but we were in the family room playing a board game," Samantha quickly said.

Samantha didn't want Starlet to know the truth that Kenny had just shown up at such a late hour. It would prove to Starlet how disrespectful he is toward Samantha. That would give Starlet more of a reason to discourage Samantha's friendship with Kenny.

"I see," Starlet yawned. "Nevermind me, I'm heading toward the kitchen for water." Starlet headed across the living room floor in the direction of the kitchen.

After Starlet grabbed a glass of water from the kitchen and headed back upstairs, Kenny laid back against the cushions and looking up toward the ceiling. Samantha couldn't help but notice the sad expression on his face.

"Kenny, why are you looking so defeated? Is it your desperate need for a drink that has you this way?" she asked.

Kenny didn't comment or look toward Samantha as he continued to look toward the ceiling.

"Can you answer me? Did you pay the bills you needed to pay with the loans you got from me? I sort of thought my financial help would have you in better spirits. Tell me what's wrong? Come on! Cheer up, Kenny. Don't act like a sourpuss?"

"Knock it off, Samantha," he snapped craving a drink. "I don't feel much like conversing at the moment."

"What do you mean you don't feel like conversing at the moment? I thought that's why you showed up over here in the first place."

"It is, but I have a terrible headache that's making me feel sick in the stomach."

"Do you think you might throw up?" she curiously asked and pointed to her left. "The guess bathroom is straight down that hallway to your left if you need to go."

He shook his head and looked at here with a slight smile on his face. "Thanks, but I don't need the use of your guess bathroom. I just need to share something with you."

She nodded. "Okay, what is it?"

"The silliest thing happened to me earlier today when I left your house. I was planning to go online and pay my car payment, but when I got home Trina was there. I have owed her some money for a long time. She cornered me and I had to pay her. Now you see why I'm so disheartened. I didn't expect Trina to corner me in the kitchen about the debt I owed her," he explained. "But it was my fault for standing in there counting it. I should have taken it to my room to count," he explained with sad eyes. "You know my sister, Trina, don't you?"

"Yes, I know of your sister, Trina," Samantha said. "She works at Franklin Gas."

He stumbled with his words. "Yes, that's true. But I had no idea she would see me counting the money," he explained. "After she saw me, I had no other choice but to pay her what I owed her. Doing so, put me right back in the same predicament since I was depending on that money for catch up on my car note. I always seem to have more bad luck than anything. I certainly resent asking you for more money. But if you can grant me another loan, I would greatly appreciate it."

Samantha let his lies deceive her. His confession about Trina seeing him counting the money sounded plausible. She really wanted to believe him. Therefore, without hesitation she stood up from the sofa. "Wait right here. I'll be right back." She hurried out of the living room and up the staircase to her bedroom.

Ten minutes later when she entered the living room, Kenny was waiting there on the sofa with his legs crossed and one arm propped on the arm of the sofa. His distress expression appeared calmer as Samantha walked up to him and didn't say one word. She opened her purse and pulled out fifteen hundred dollars in cash and handed it to him.

"Okay, here you are, now you should be able to take care of your bills. I'm not sure how much you owed Trina, but here's the entire amount that you originally needed to square away your bills."

He stood from the sofa, took the money and pushed it in his back pocket and then dropped back down on the sofa. He was stunned since he didn't expect to receive fifteen hundred more from her. He was surprised that she had that much cash lying around. "Thank you, but why would you have this much cash lying around?"

"Don't worry about that," he said politely, smiling. "Just take it and do what you need to do with it."

"I'll take care of my debts right thing tomorrow. I just surprised you would have this much money lying around in your home. It's almost as if you knew I would need it."

"Well, Kenny, I wouldn't go that far. It wasn't in the house because I expected to loan it to you. I'm offended that you would even say such a thing," Samantha said irritated.

"I didn't mean to tick you off, but you have to admit that most people don't have fifteen hundred dollars in cash at their fingertips to loan out."

"Of course not, Kenny, but just drop it. I just gave you the money you needed."

"Yes, you did," he said looking up at her as she stood before him.

"Now you can take that miserable gloomy look off your face?" she said took a seat back on the opposite sofa facing him.

Kenny thought about the money for a moment and smiled. He thought of how he could go out and buy his favorite expensive Vodka. He was so happy to have the money in his pocket until he couldn't control his excitement. He stood up from the sofa and glanced at his watch. "It's getting really late. I should leave your house before another one of your family member catch me here at this indecent hour, Samantha."

"You have only been here for fifteen minutes. Why are you so anxious to leave now? It was late when you arrived," Samantha said sharply. "Now that you have the loan in your pocket, it's suddenly too late to visit? Did you drop by just for the loan and then leave?"

He had really upset her off. "Kenny, I have taken as much of your sincerity as I can take," she said crossly and stood to her feet.

"Okay, what's the problem? I just think I should take off before someone else in your family or your father comes downstairs and throw me out."

"That's a lie, Kenny. That's not why you are leaving."

"I don't get you. You're pissed that I'm leaving after you made a big deal about me showing up over here this time of night?"

"Yes, Kenny, I'm making a big deal because you are already here and you have already interrupted my evening. Therefore, it seems you are only ready to take off because you have what you came for, which is the loan. You don't seem to be interesting in sitting and brainstorming about ways to get you back on the wagon."

"You're blowing smoke," he said and grinned.

"I'm blowing smoke? What kind of thing is that to say to me? Besides, it doesn't take a rocket scientist to put two and two together to realize that you dropped over this time of night just to squeeze more money out of me for your drinks. I'm sure you have those bills to pay as well, but I'm sure you're going to waste a lot of that loan on booze."

"You're right, I was bone broke the reason I dropped by. And yes, I do want to leave to get a drink, but that shouldn't surprise you. I'm an alcoholic and I need it badly. But still trying to cut back and eventually give it up," he stressed strongly.

"What year do you plan to give up your Vodka?" Samantha asked rudely.

"What do you mean what year? I'm trying to give it up in the next few days."

Samantha nodded. "You told me this same thing on Monday, the day after you got falling down drunk and behaved so inappropriate toward me. You seemed quite sincere when you promised to try to get back on the wagon."

"I was very sincere," he interrupted.

"Kenny, talk is easy. Although you appeared sincere and promised to give up drinking with my help. But honestly, I don't think you were sincere!"

"I'm telling you, I was sincere," he stressed. "I meant what I said, Samantha. I will give it up, but I do need your help."

"No, you are lying, Kenny." She shook her head. "You don't need my help. You don't even want my help. You have just been stringing me along with a lie, pretending to want to quit drinking."

"No, Samantha, you have it wrong."

"I don't I have it wrong. I was willing to give you the benefit of the doubt. But you have pushed me too far!" Samantha raised both hands with a determined look in her eyes.

"What do you mean I have pushed you too far?" He asked as if he was clueless.

298

"I'm referring to your lies about giving up drinking. I never should have tried to reconnect with you after you kissed me in that drunken state. That's on me to have fallen for your lies, Kenny. I put my own relationship with Paris in jeopardy thinking I was doing the right thing by trying to help you stay sober."

"Don't put that on me. I never told you to keep my identity from Paris Franklin. Hell, I was against that idea. Keeping it from him only made it appear worse than it was," Kenny stressed. "So, that one is on you!"

"Okay, I'll accept that I should have been on the level with Paris," she admitted. "But believe me, when he gets back home I will tell him everything and will not keep secrets from him ever again. Frankly, I didn't want to face it, but I just don't think you're ready to be sober. You're not the man that you could be and I don't want to wait around for you to find yourself."

"So, you're giving up on your project to help me, just like that?" he asked. "Plus, I guess you're also giving up on our friendship just like that as well?"

"Kenny, it's not just like that. I have tried to help you and be a supportive friend all this week. But it's just not working. I can't help or befriend someone who lies to me."

"So, you stuck with me for a week," he solemnly said. "By the way, the week isn't over yet. Nevertheless, you're done?"

She nodded with a solemn look on her face. "Yes, Kenny, I'm done."

"What happened to the honorable Samantha Taylor who sticks to her word," he snapped irritated. "So much for your word to do right by me," Kenny said disappointment.

"Kenny, it's no need going over this. I'm convinced that you were never serious in the first place. I wanted you to be serious because I wanted so much to help you sober up, but from Monday night up until this evening, you have given me no sign that you're onboard with letting go of your liquor," she said firmly.

"I told you it would take time."

"Maybe it will take time, but I don't plan to hang around and help you on the wagon when you're finally ready. I have too much to lose to hang around hoping to help someone who's not even ready to be helped at the present."

"Since I can't quit cold turkey, you figure I'm worth throwing to the wolves."

"No Kenny, I don't feel that way, and I figured it wouldn't be easy, but you're not even trying and I don't want to deal with your alcoholic issues and money problems any longer. If I could trust that you were actually onboard with trying to get sober, I would stand firm and stick by you. But honestly, I can't do this when I know your heart isn't in it," she softly explained.

"You surprise me, Samantha."

"Why do I surprise you? Did you expect for me to continue to turn a blind eye to what appears to be deception on your part?" She touched her chest. "I consider myself a good person, but one thing I'm not, and that is stupid."

"Samantha, I would never use that word in the same sentence with you."

"Maybe you wouldn't, but look where we are? You're still drinking and I'm still hoping you'll give it up. Therefore, I have decided I'm not going to continue racking my brain trying to help you when clearly you don't want to be helped." She raised both hands. "But I guess it wasn't a complete waste of time for you."

"Why do you say that?"

"You are three thousand dollars richer," she reminded him.

"I plan to repay you every dime you have lend out to me," he assured her.

"Kenny, the money you owe me is my least concern. I have just allowed you to take this lie far enough."

"What lie?"

"The lie you told me that you're ready to give up your bottle. You haven't tried to quit from the night you told me you would."

"Whatever, do what you think is best," he snapped. "Walk away from our deal if that's what you feel you need to do. However, I think a real devoted advocate and friend would stick with me through thick and thin."

"Maybe you are right, but I can't stick with you, Kenny, when you're not ready to give up your Vodka," she said irritated. "Therefore, the way I see it, so much for your word that you would."

"But I meant it, Samantha."

"Maybe you did mean it at that moment, but not a second after." She shook her head. "You might as well admit that you lied to me from the beginning. You had no real intentions of trying to sober up. Now did you, Kenny?"

Kenny stared at her but did not comment.

"Therefore, Kenny, this alliance that we have is serving no purpose for either of us." She pointed to herself and then to him.

"It is serving a purpose as far as I'm concerned. I need you in my corner."

"No, you don't need me in your corner. I'm not helping you, but you're upsetting me," she politely explained. "If I continue down this road with you, I'm afraid it we'll end up severing all ties; and that's not what I want, Kenny."

"Samantha, don't be so serious." He held out both arms. "It will all work out."

"Maybe it will work out, but I'm sorry. I can't do this anymore. I can't deal with or help someone who lies to me. You are truthful with me about many things, but you also lie to me about many more."

"The same way you are lying to Paris?"

"I didn't lie to Paris. I just didn't reveal your identity to him."

"It's the same difference. You were not completely honest with him the same thing you are accusing me of right now."

"There's a big difference between my choice to withhold information from Paris and your deliberate deception," she pointed out.

"You can split hairs, but a lie is a lie," he said, staring her in the eyes. "So, tell me Samantha, why didn't you tell Prince Charming that I kissed you?"

She turned her back to her and stared up at the ceiling, and then faced him to speak, but he interrupted her by speaking instead.

"It shouldn't be that difficult. You had your reasons for not telling him it was me."

"Of course, I had my reasons, and I have already shared those reasons with you."

He grinned and his last pint of vodka before he arrived at her house was completely kicking into his system. "Let me guess. You liked the kiss, didn't you?" He said rudely with booze filled eyes. "Yes, that's it. I'm sure you didn't tell him because you liked the kiss and probably liked who kissed you just as much," Kenny whispered and winked at her, then glanced about the large room to make sure no one was stirring.

His words shocked her, but she kept her composure, knowing he was talking through his liquor. "Kenny, don't expect me to comment on what you just said."

"You don't have to comment. Like you, Samantha, I'm not stupid either. Why else would you bother trying to sober me up in the first place? You have been fussing with me all week. Why else would a rich, Neiman Marcus shopper who drinks wine that's worth ten thousand dollars a bottle bother with an average class drunk like me if it wasn't for the reasons I just said. I think you're into me and just won't admit it."

"Kenny, how can you be so full of yourself?" she kept her composure against his crude drunken behavior.

"I'm not trying to be full of myself. I'm just trying to get to the truth."

"What truth? Clearly you know there's no truth to what you just said regarding the fact that you feel I wanted to be kissed by you. For the millionth time, I have never had those kinds of feelings for you. We are strictly friends. Nothing more and nothing less."

"The compassionate and caring seems to be more than that of a friend," Kenny said.

"It's who I am. The compassionate and caring I show to you is the same kind of compassionate I show to all of my friends," Samantha shared.

"That may be so, but you still had your reasons for not being on the level with Prince Charming."

"That's true and here are those reasons," she humbly stated, looking him in the eyes. "Mainly, I had made too much of the kiss and didn't want Paris or my family to think the worse of you for your transgression against me. Secondly, I was upset with Paris. I felt he had somewhat pressured me about revealing the person's identity.

When I wouldn't tell him, he grew an attitude and felt it wasn't a good idea for us to take our vacation together and he left for France without me."

Kenny nodded. "So, you figured you would get back at him by reconnecting with me, someone Paris has a problem with where you are concerned."

She nodded. "I'm not proud of it, but I was quite upset with him for taking our vacation without me. Therefore, I admit that I wanted to get back at him for leaving me behind. But I'm well aware how wrong I was in my thinking; and I don't plan to deal with our differences in that manner again."

"If you wanted to get back at Paris by hanging out with me, that means you were not serious about helping me off the wagon."

"That's not true," Samantha quickly offended herself. "I was hundred percent invested in helping you get sober. It was my mission to help you after your indiscretion against me. I didn't want to condemn you for your drunken behavior. I wanted something good to come out of it, by doing what I could to help you rid yourself of that disease."

"But now, you have had a change of heart and you are throwing me to the wolves to fend for myself and deal with my addiction on my own."

"Yes, Kenny, I have had a change of heart. I have had time to reflect and I realize that Paris had a right to be upset that I was upset that someone had kissed me against my wishes. Plus, I was wrong to try to reconnect our friendship after your indiscretion against me in that drunken state. Doing so, I gave you the wrong message."

"What are you getting at now, Samantha?"

"I'm getting at the fact that my actions gave you the wrong message."

"Okay, I'll bite. What wrong message did you give me?" he asked.

"I gave you the message that it was okay to treat me that way when I went and swept it under the rug and continued to be your friend."

"But you know it was the booze and that I really didn't mean to do it. You told me that you don't think I would have behaved that way if I had been sober."

"It's true, I did say that, but what you did was clearly inappropriate. Bottomline, you and I cannot be friends anymore."

"Damn, Samantha. You can turn on a dime. I thought we were having a serious visit conversing about your efforts to help me get sober wasn't working. Now, this, you don't even want to be friends anymore?"

She shook her head. "No, it's not smart on my part to maintain a friendship with you. I'm not getting anything out of our connection. I'm not getting the satisfaction of knowing I'm helping you stay sober. Plus, I'm lying to my family. No disrespect intended, but you are not a good influence in my life."

"What do you mean you are lying to your family?"

"I mean I'm lying to members of my family because of you. I just lied to Starlet when she came downstairs."

Kenny held up both hands. "Again, that lie is on you. I didn't ask you to lie on my behalf."

"I know you didn't ask me to lie, but I'm lying to protect you or myself from the truth surrounding you. Friendship shouldn't be hard work where you have to lie about things."

"I agree it shouldn't be," he agreed, sitting there on the opposite sofa looking straight at her face as if their conversation had somewhat sobered him up.

"Do you also agree that you have used me and made me look like a fool?" she asked.

He smiled at her. "You know I think a lot of you, Samantha. I think you are the most honorable, near perfect individual in this world."

"But you just like to treat me like an airhead?"

"Come on, where is this coming from?" he asked, glancing at his watch.

"It's coming from the way you have treated me this week. You have borrowed money from me and put me in compromising positions, all while lying every step of the way about staying sober. From the first night when we went dancing, you have been hitting the bottle and you haven't once put it down."

"But I told you I will."

"Maybe you will or maybe you won't. I just don't care anymore. You can call up someone else to help you get on the wagon. I'm done," she calmly said and pointed toward the front door. "So, Kenny, take care of yourself and I wish you all the best."

His eyes widen with surprise. "Now, you're kicking me out as well?"

"I'm not kicking you out. I just think it's time for you to leave. It's getting quite late as mentioned earlier. Plus, not long ago you made it seem you couldn't spare a minute. So, I think you should go home. Besides, our alleged friendship is over. I tried to befriend and help you. But I'm in the shadow of something else! Your true friend seems to be alcohol."

"I'm going to give it up," I promise.

"Well, I hope you do, but it won't be with my help. Maybe Vickie Simpson, your girlfriend can help you," Samantha suggested.

"Vickie is a good woman, but we are not as close as you think."

"Have you thought that maybe you're not as close to Vickie as you could be because of your drinking? You have given it up before. I'm sure you can do it again. Just make up your mind and do it," Samantha strongly suggested. "I really hope you get back on the wagon because you are wasting a decent guy by drinking."

"So, you think I'm a decent guy?"

"What do you think my efforts and this past week have been about? Yes, you can be a decent guy. Nevertheless, you're not a decent guy in the state you're in. In the state you're in, I prefer not to deal with you anymore. So, I'm taking myself out of this situation."

He nodded. "I guess you're right. I'm pretty rotten company when I'm drinking. And I haven't been sober since we reconnected. If I'm honest, I don't know when I'll ever end up on the wagon again," he admitted. "I guess I have pretty much used you."

"Yes, you have, but it's not all your fault. I'm also to blame for allowing you to use me, but I did it in hope of helping you," she caringly stated. "But we both realize now that I'm not equipped to give you the kind of help you really need," she sadly admitted.

He nodded with sad eyes. "I'm grateful for all you have done and I'll pay you back as soon as I'm working steady again."

"That's fine, Kenny. Just leave here and think about what I said. Maybe you'll give Vickie a chance to help you with your addiction."

He glanced down toward the floor and then looked her in the eyes. "I told you that Vickie and I are not seeing eye-to-eye lately."

"All I know is what I witnessed at the Halloween party last year," Samantha reminded him. "Vickie Simpson was glued to your side and seemed crazy about you."

He shook his head. "Maybe once, but I think she's fed up as well."

"Can you blame her? Of course, you cannot. But look, I'm sure she cares for you. You just need to straighten up and let her know that you are serious about being with her."

"I'll consider that, but no matter what, no other female will ever measure up to you in my eyes. You are the walking angel that I cannot have," he said with conviction.

"You say that about me, but look how you have treated me. You borrowed and lie," she said and stopped herself. "All of that is behind us and beside the point now. We're on the topic of Vickie Simpson, and you need to let her know real soon how you really feel about her. Let her know you're not just using her to be a designated driver or for her money to buy your liquor."

He stared at Samantha as he stood from the sofa. Samantha stood from the sofa as well with a solemn look on her face. She watched as he slightly staggered. But he didn't look toward her. He looked toward the front door in thought. He was crushed about Samantha ending their alliance. She had informed him that she was no longer interested in being the kind of friend he was using her for.

"Okay, I'll think about what you said and give Vickie a call," he said as he headed out of the room. "She may hang up on me, but I'll still dial the number," he said as he slowly headed across the living room toward the front door.

Samantha followed him to the front door and opened it for him. "Kenny, you're a good person. But you need to take stock of yourself. The best thing you can do for yourself and your family is to get back on the wagon before it's too late. You have a good future ahead of you and you need to take advantage of it. Alcohol have a way of destroying lives. Take a page from your father's life. Alcohol took control of him and destroyed his life and now he's serving time in some penitentiary. You and I can no longer be friends but I will always wish the best for you," she respectfully said.

Chapter Twenty-Six

That Friday afternoon shortly after Samantha arrived home from the downtown office, she was beside herself wallowing in loneliness for Paris, sitting mid-way the staircase looking at pictures of the two of them on her phone. Engrossed in the pictures, she didn't notice Starlet standing at the bottom of the staircase until she was already standing there tapping her fingers on the railing. Samantha glanced up and smiled. She scooted out of the way as she thought Starlet was headed upstairs but Starlet just stood there staring at her. She had a big smile on her face with one hand behind her back.

"I have something for you," Starlet said, smiling with happiness in her eyes.

"What is it?" Samantha asked curious.

"Here it is," she held up a pink lace envelope.

A feeling of excitement dashed through Samantha's stomach when Starlet waved the envelope in the air. "This refine envelope is addressed to you from Paris," Starlet smiled.

Samantha flew down the staircase and grabbed Starlet and hugged her.

"I thought this letter would bring a smile to your face," Starlet kept smiling.

"I'm sure he still loves you and the two of you will work things out," Starlet hopefully encouraged her. "It's very clear how deeply you love him."

Samantha nodded. "You are right. I'm just miserable without him. I love him more than anything and plan to let him know just how much as soon as he returns." She held the letter to her chest. "I promise I'll never make him doubt me again. I'll tell him who kissed me and I'll never keep anything else from him," Samantha said with conviction. "Just for the record, you might as well know it was Kenny who kissed me."

"Kenny Ross kissed you and made you so upset, and you rewarded him by trying to connect as friends and sober him up?"

"I know it wasn't a smart thing. But I thought I was doing something noble. But believe me, I have learned my lesson and I'm sorry I upset Paris by not telling him it was Kenny when he first asked me."

Starlet nodded. "Yes, Paris was upset, but you were also upset. The two of you needed this time a part and I know things will work out," Starlet assured her.

"You really think so?"

"Yes, I do think so," Starlet said with confidence in her eyes. "I have watched you suffer, Samantha. I know how miserable you have been since Paris left town," Starlet said warmly. "He took the time to write a letter. Therefore, I'm sure the letter is good news."

"Thanks, Starlet, but before you walk away I need to apologize to you."

"What do you need to apologize to me about?"

"I lied to you last night."

"You lied to me about what?"

"When you came downstairs for water, I lied and said Kenny hadn't just arrived. But he had just arrived. I just didn't want you to know he had been so ill-mannered by dropping over at such an inappropriate hour."

"I'm sorry he put you in that position where you felt you needed to lie for him." Starlet shook her head as disappointment showed in her eyes. "But why did he feel the need to come by so late?" Starlet asked.

"It's not important anymore. Just know that Kenny Ross and I are no longer trying to reconnect as friends. I'll just say this and let it be. The help he needs I can't give it to him," Samantha explained.

Starlet nodded. "It means so much to hear you say that. I know he was a friend of yours in college, but Kenny Ross is a heavy drinker and he used my friend for money," Starlet seriously stated. "But, I have heard by you that he can be a pretty decent guy when he's sober, but I guess he's always drunk. Therefore, his association isn't what you need."

Samantha nodded. "You're right, it's not and that's exactly what I told him. I also told him to try to patch things up with his girlfriend. I suggested that maybe she could help him with his addiction."

"Who is his girlfriend?" Starlet curiously asked.

"Remember, Vickie Simpson? You saw them together at some restaurant and Kenny was drunk. Plus, you saw them together at a bookstore," Samantha reminded her.

"That's right, and they were also together the night of our Halloween party. Plus, I have seen Vickie behind the counter with Sabrina," Starlet recalled. "She seems nice."

"She is nice, and besides from that Vickie Simpson is a pretty leveled headed person from what I have gathered from Kenny," Samantha shared. "However, according to Kenny she's not too pleased with him right now. But he plans to try to fix that."

"That's good. I hope things work out for her and Kenny Ross," Starlet said as she headed out of the living room and toward the kitchen area.

Samantha watched Starlet vanish into the hallway, then she took a seat back on the staircase and carefully with great ease opened Paris's letter. Then it dawned on her how lucky she was to have Paris in her life and how much it would destroy her if his letter was saying goodbye. She was almost too anxious to open it. Therefore, after unsealing the envelope she stared at the letter for a moment before she gathered her nerves to pull the letter out. The parchment pink lace housed the same stationary inside:

My Dearest Samantha,

After I mail this letter I'm boarding the plane to head to Milan. This trip is beautiful but so unsatisfying without you to enjoy it with me.

I have only myself to blame and I'm ashamed of my behavior of insisting to take the trip without you.

I paid top dollar to overnight this letter to you. It should arrive in your mailbox on Friday afternoon, which means I'll see you in two days. I have decided to shorten my vacation. One week abroad is long enough without you. Besides, I'm somewhat exhausted from this whirlwind trip of trying to include too much into the time I allowed myself. But I have made the most of it. In the short time, I had an opportunity to visit the cities in France we talked about, Nice, Marseille as well as Paris. I'm headed to Milan shortly and will leave for home from there.

I have enjoyed the sites but not as much as I would have enjoyed them with you at my side. That's why I scratched the other Italy cities: Venice, Florence, Naples, and Rome off the list and cut my vacation short.

I don't really know why we broke up in the first place, if we can really call it a break up? But I guess we can. However, breaking up with you certainly isn't what I wanted. I know we left things up in the air. I chose to take the vacation that we had planned without you. We were not in a good place when I left for the airport but I wanted to give us some time a part. However, one week seems like just yesterday and it's still fresh in my mind that you chose not to tell me who kissed you without your consent. I didn't mean to come on too strong insisting who, but it greatly bothered me because it seemed to have greatly bothered you, which made it appear dramatic. I think you know this much about me. I cannot in good faith have a relationship with someone who chooses not to be on the level with me.

I do care deeply for you and you're the most special woman I have ever known. But I need loyalty and honesty from you. In order for us to move forward you need to do two things for me. I need to know the identity of the person who kissed you and I need to know why you chose not to tell me.

I didn't' call or text, but it's not because you were not on my mind, it's because you were and I needed time to put things in perspective. I have just traveled the world over, been a lot of places and seen a lot of things. But it didn't matter where I ended up, my thoughts were always on you. It's absolute clear to me. You're the only woman I want in my life. Now I'm hoping fate will allow you to be the one I end up with.

I'll see you on Sunday and I'm confident that we will get through this rough patch!
Love Paris

When Samantha finished reading Paris's letter, it was covered with her tears. Just the idea that he still loved and wanted to be with her, made her world perfect again.

Chapter Twenty-Seven

Charles Taylor's chauffeur drove out of the driveway slowly that Sunday morning, on the 13th of April. Samantha stood in the living room window looking out as her father, Sabrina and Starlet headed church. She stayed home to wait for Paris. He was arriving home from his trip and she wanted to be home just in case he decided to visit her. However, she stood in the living room window for an hour after her family left for church and she received no call or text from Paris about his whereabouts. He had said in his letter that he would be arriving home on Sunday, but she wasn't sure of the time. Yet, she continued standing in the window hoping to see his car when he pulled into the driveway. She was so anxious and excited to see him. She knew her task ahead of telling him everything. She prayed he would understand and be forgiving of what she would share with him. She stood there almost trembling as she held the curtains apart. Looking out, it was a clear, calm afternoon unlike the Sunday before when Kenny came into her home and disrupted her life with Paris. She was determined to make it right.

She glanced down at her watch and it was straight up noon. She smiled at the round face diamond Gucci watch because it was a Christmas gift from Paris. She touched the face of the watch and reflected on how blessed she was to have Paris in her life and when she glanced up and looked out of the window again, she noticed Paris stepping out of his car and heading toward the front door.

She swallowed hard and grabbed her stomach with both hands and then rushed across the room to the front door. She stretched the door open and he smiled at her. He couldn't get into the foyer quicker enough and barely gave her a chance to close the door before he grabbed her in his arms and kissed her. They kissed for several minutes and then his back landed up against the living room wall with Samantha in his arms. When he released her, he folded his arms as he stood propped against the wall. They just stood smiling at each other.

"I'm so happy to see you and I owe you an apology," she quickly said as she couldn't stop smiling. "I never should have allowed you to leave my house last Sunday night without being completely open with you. I hope you can forgive me for my poor inconsiderate behavior. I should have known better," Samantha stressed.

He smiled at her. "I think we both share in our moment of going astray. We both could have been more understanding of each other," Paris said. "But what counts is how happy I am right now and how good it feels to just look in your eyes," he whispered. "I have been away and I have done nothing but think of you and my life with you. Frankly, I can't think of my future without you being a part of it." He reached out and caressed her face. "You are the woman that makes me completely happy and no one else does that for me."

"Paris, no one else does it for me, either. I have missed you desperately; and I'm so ashamed of how I behaved before you left for France."

"Don't give it another thought. All is well now," he assured her. "I know we don't always see eye to eye, but that's life and we have to cope with the bitter and the sweet when it comes to true love. Because true love is what I feel for you, Samantha. You are it for me, now and forever."

"Paris, I feel the same for you and before this conversation go any further, I want to come clean with you and let you know who, what and why regarding the kiss that pushed us away from each other."

"Let me correct you," he said as he smoothed one hanging curls from near her left eye. "For the record, I never felt that we had separated. I know I was many miles away in another country and we had supposedly ended things. But it was in my head and not in my heart. When I walked out of your door that Sunday night, I was just sore and disappointed that you chose not to confide in me. I walked out because I was upset and not because I wanted to walk away from you." He touched the side her face again. "In my heart I always knew we would work things out," he said, smiling.

"In my heart I always knew we would work things out as well," she said and quickly wiped a tear from her left eye. "I'm so blessed to have you in my life. You are true blue and so respectful. I never want to lose sight of that," she said.

He looked toward the living room and glanced about the large room. "Is anyone else here?" he asked.

She shook her head. "Everyone is at church."

He downcast his eyes at her and smiled. "I guess this is perfect timing on my part. I get a rare opportunity at the Taylor mansion to be alone with beautiful you." He pulled her in his arms and kissed her.

When he pulled away and looked down at her face, he noticed water in her eyes. "Maybe I should take trips abroad more often if they are going to have such happy effects on you," he said, smiling. "I'm assuming these are tears of joy," he said.

Samantha didn't comment as she looked up at him as if she was looking at him for the first time and she didn't want to miss anything.

"So, beautiful, you said you wanted to come clean about the kiss. However, let me be clear. You'll get no pressure from me on that topic anymore. I have reflected on the matter and all that really matters is the fact that you didn't want the kiss. It was out of your control that you were grabbed and kissed. Besides, you mentioned that the perpetrator was sorry right afterward, is that correct?" he asked.

She nodded. "Yes, that's correct."

He nodded. "I'm not pleased with that image in my head about some guy getting out of line like that with you, but I have to face facts how life isn't perfect. Mistakes and unpleasant things will happen."

"Did I just hear Paris Franklin say life isn't perfect and mistakes happen?" she teased.

"Yes, I said it," he nodded. "Besides, the incident was out of your control. A drunk friend dropped by and got out of line. He probably has a crush on you, but he was clearly out of line regardless of his stomach full of booze. He saw a pretty girl and thought it was okay to kiss her whether she wanted it or not." He shook his head. "It hurts me deeply that he violated you in that way. But whoever this family friend is, I'm assuming he's no longer allowed at the Taylor mansion when he's intoxicated."

"No, he isn't allowed here in that state."

"Okay, that's good," Paris smiled, looking in her eyes. "Therefore, we can end that chapter in our relationship right now and move on. I'm satisfied the guy is no longer welcomed in your home in a drunken state. Therefore, that incident is not likely to happen again," he said and brought his face down to cover her lips with his.

Paris passionately kissed her for at least three minutes before me pulled away. Then he held her face with both hands and smiled down at her. Her bright eyes were shining back at his, but she was only slightly smiling.

"Is something else the matter?" he asked. "I know I have a lot to make up to you for taking the trip without you. We can plan another trip to France as soon as our schedules permit," he assured her.

"It's not that," she softly uttered as she took his hand and led him over to the sofa where they were seated side by side.

He turned her face toward his and gave her a quick kiss on the lips. "Okay, if you're not sore at me about taking the trip without you, I'm at a loss for your nerves."

"I want you to know his name," she said in his eyes.

He held both of her hands in his and looked her straight in the eyes. "Sweetheart, let's be clear. I would like to know his name, but I don't need to know his name since it was an uninvited advance motivated by too much booze and it's never going to happen again. Besides, you probably won't see this family friend too soon."

She shook her head. "That's the thing, I might see him again."

"But he's not welcome here, so he probably won't make another appearance too soon," Paris suggested.

"I'm sure he won't be back here too soon, but I might bump into him in the streets and he may visit one day when he's no longer drinking. He's genuinely sorry about his mistake and it'll never happen again," she said assuredly. "It was Kenny who kissed me."

"Kenny Ross did that?"

"Yes, it was Kenny. He's beside himself sorry. He was out of his head intoxicated when he grabbed me like that." She held up both hands. "Remember how disrespectful he was at the Halloween party? We both know deep down that he isn't really like that."

Paris stared at Samantha speechless, and then he looked straight ahead and stood up from the sofa. He walked across the living room to one of the many windows and stood there, looking out in silence awhile before he walked back over to the sofa to be seated. He looked at Samantha and nodded. "Okay, the fact that it was Kenny Ross who kissed you sort of changes things," he calmly told her. "I stand by everything I said to you, and realize he was intoxicated, but I'm also aware of your history with Kenny and I just need you to tell me everything by starting with why you didn't tell me it was Kenny from the start."

She nodded. "I'm ashamed of myself for not telling you. But I simply held back because I didn't want to destroy your connection with Kenny," she wiped another tear.

"There's no need to cry," he assured her as he kissed the side of her face. "I just want you to tell me everything and then we can move on from this subject."

"That's it; I just didn't want you to think the worst of Kenny. He's a fairly decent guy with a drinking problem who got out of line, absolutely. But it has never happened before."

"But he probably wanted it to happen. I'm not going to make too much of this, but I also do not think your friend, Kenny, is all too innocent in this incident. He probably still have feelings for you," he suspected. "Nevertheless, the thing that saves him is how he has always shown you great respect. Plus, he had completely over indulged; and I'm convinced, given his respect level for you, he wouldn't have attempted such an indiscretion toward you if he hadn't been falling down drunk."

Samantha threw her arms around Paris's neck. "Thank you for not hating me for what happened; and thank you for not hating Kenny. He's in a really bad way because of all the turmoil his family is going through. I tried to help him, but I couldn't."

"What do you mean, you tried to help him?" he asked.

"I was getting to that part. I had decided to help him get sober and stay sober. I figured if I could help him then some good would come from all of this."

"I know your heart was in the right place, but considering his drunken actions toward you, I don't think it's wise for you to be around him while he's drinking."

She nodded. "I came to that conclusion as well and told him that I couldn't help him. I told him to talk to Vickie Simpson about helping him back on the wagon."

"That was good advice considering Vickie cares a lot for the guy. Plus, she's a rather level headed young lady who will probably try to keep him on the right track. Although, it hasn't really worked so far," Paris reminded her. "But in all fairness, he was on the wagon holding his own until all the sensational news hit the airways about his father and mother."

Samantha touched Paris's hand. "I'm not finished with what I have to tell you about Kenny."

"Okay, what else is there?" he asked. "We need to drop this subject and spend the rest of our time enjoying our visit instead of discussing Kenny Ross. Your family will arrive from church soon, and we have a lot of lost time to make up for," he smiled.

"This is important. You need to know I went out with Kenny while you were away."

"You went out on a date with Kenny Ross?"

She shook her head. "It wasn't a date, but I went out to a dance with him that Monday you left for your trip; and not just that, I also allowed him to visit me here at home a few times during the week," she said with her heart in her throat.

"Samantha, I'm surprised beyond words, because it doesn't make smart sense to spent time alone with Kenny after his indiscretion?" he said irritated.

She nodded and wiped a teardrop. "Of course, you are right. I realize now that it wasn't smart, but my intentions were good. I just wanted to help him instead of condemn him. The heavy drinking is destroying his life and his health. I was doing those things to try to help him if I could."

"What kind of help could you give to Kenny Ross at a dance?"

"I talked to him about ways to rid himself of the bottle."

"I assume he picked you up and drove you to the dance in his car."

"Yes, Paris, he did; and to be completely honest, although, my intentions were to help him get sober, I accepted his invitation to the dance in part because I was so deeply hurt and upset with you."

Paris inhaled sharply eyes as sorrow and deep regret ripped through his stomach. "I know you were upset, but I wasn't aware that you were deeply hurt as well?"

"Yes, I was deeply hurt that you allowed our disagreement to cause you to take the vacation that we had planned to take together without me," she explained.

"I'm ashamed of myself for that and I will make it up to you," he assured her.

"I know you will, but it was a big deal to me. The good news is, I got over it because you mean more to me than any trip we could ever take together," she gently touched the side of his face with the back of her palm. "You handsome, most wonderful man in the world, I want you to know that I'm not proud that I went to a dance with Kenny. I had the option of not telling you, but I chose to tell you. Because from his day moving forward I just want to be completely open with you. If we are completely open with each other, nothing will be able to come between us."

"The fact that you were kissed by a guy one night and went to a dance with him the next, I could take offense with that. But given your sincerity and openness about the whole ordeal, I feel this is a subject that we can put behind us. I have never been more proud of you. Because at this very moment, I know one thing for sure."

"What's that, Paris?"

"I want you to be the woman I marry."

Chapter Twenty-Eight

Straight up 4:00 o'clock that Tuesday afternoon on April 15th, Sabrina had just gotten home from a three hour shift at Franklin Gas when Courtney knocked on her front door and when no one answered her knock, she rang the doorbell. Carrie Westwood hurried down the lower level hallway from the kitchen area to answer the door.

"May I help you?" Carrie asked as she pulled the front door open to Courtney's smiling face.

"Yes, I'm here to see Sabrina," Courtney replied with a brazen look in her eyes.

Just as Courtney finished her sentence, Carrie glanced out the door toward Courtney's car. "I'm sorry, but I was expecting someone else and at first glance I thought you were from the florist," Carrie explained and then glanced at her Seiko watch, noticing it was straight up 4:00 o'clock. She had hurried down the lower level hallway from the kitchen to answer the door, assuming it was the regular Tuesday afternoon floral delivery. Unlimited Florist usually delivered right at 4:00 o'clock every Tuesday.

Courtney glanced over her shoulder and gave a quick survey of the driveway and then looked back at Carrie. "I'm sorry I'm not who you were expecting, but when I drove up I didn't see a florist vehicle."

Carrie nodded. "I'm sure they will be here soon. You wanted to see Sabrina?"

"Yes, I'm here to see Sabrina," Courtney said keenly, but smiled. "And I can assure you that I'm definitely not a delivery person," Courtney pointed to the Franklin Gas name tag that hung on her green work jacket."

"You work at Franklin Gas?"

"Yes, I work with Courtney."

Carrie wasn't sure if Sabrina was home and Courtney's unexpected arrival had thrown her for a moment. She felt a little out of sorts. Therefore, when Carrie didn't immediately respond, Courtney glanced around and looked over her left shoulder, pointing toward Sabrina's car. "Her car is parked outside."

"That doesn't always mean that she's here," Carrie politely uttered.

Courtney nodded, feeling more anxious. "I understand, but when she left work about an hour ago I heard her mention that she was headed straight home."

Carrie nodded and slightly smiled realizing that since Courtney was a coworker from Franklin Gas that she may needed to see Sabrina on business, "I think she's home. Who may I tell her is calling?"

"Tell her Courtney is here to speak with her."

"Please come in Courtney, I'll see if she's upstairs in her room," Carrie said and politely waved Courtney inside. Then she slowly closed the front door and casually headed across the room toward the staircase.

Courtney stood near the front entrance with a rushed look on her face as she anxiously squeezed her hands together. She swallowed hard when she glanced at the long staircase, wondering if Carrie was about to make the trip upstairs. Then her second thought figured Carrie would probably ring Sabrina's room. She restlessly glanced at her Timex watch. Then she glanced over at Carrie again, irritated that Carrie didn't appear to be in a rush to check if Sabrina was home.

"Mrs. Westwood, I don't mean to be rude but this is an emergency; and I'm hoping to see Sabrina as soon as possible!" she snapped, "If that can be managed."

Carrie swallowed hard, stunned at Courtney's rudeness but as the maid she knew to keep her cool with the Taylor's guest. Therefore, she bit down hard on her bottom lip and ignored Courtney's rudeness. "I understand, Miss Courtney." She glanced over her shoulder at

Courtney. I'm trying to let Miss Sabrina know that you're here. I just buzzed her room and I'm standing here waiting to see if I'll get an answer."

"Oh, you already buzzed her room?"

"Yes, Miss Courtney. I buzzed her room the moment you asked to see her."

"But I didn't see you buzz her," Courtney said coldly.

"It's quite simple." Carrie reached in her apron pocket and pulled out her cell phone. "This phone is programmed just for reaching the Taylors. The pink button rings Miss Sabrina's room, the white button is for Miss Samantha, the gray button is for Miss Starlet and the burgundy button is for Mr. Taylor's room," Carrie explained, placing the phone back into her apron pocket.

Courtney stood there with her mouth open since the device was totally foreign to her; and then quickly said. "Okay, that's good. I'm in a hurry and really need to see her."

"I'll buzz her room again," Carrie said as she stood at the bottom of the staircase with her back propped against the railing.

"Thank you," Courtney said, looking as Carrie reached into her apron pocket and pulled out her phone again and pushed the pink button.

Immediately, Sabrina buzzed back. "Yes, Carrie. Did you need me for something?"

"Yes, Miss Sabrina, you have a visitor waiting to see you. It's an emergency."

"Who is it, Carrie?"

"It's one of your coworkers, a Miss Courtney."

"Thanks, Carrie, I'll be right down."

Courtney stood in the living room window looking out, until she glanced around and saw Sabrina heading down the staircase. She called out to Courtney.

"What's the matter?" she asked curiously.

Courtney didn't answer as she stood there smiling, waiting for Sabrina to reach the end of the staircase and across the room where she stood.

When Sabrina made it across the room where Courtney stood, she had an anxious look on her face expecting to hear about an emergency.

"Carrie said you were here to see me regards to an emergency. What's the emergency?" Sabrina asked with concern.

Courtney stared up at the ceiling and then looked Sabrina in the face. "It's an emergency for sure. But there's no need for that concerned look in your eyes. It's nothing like you think," Courtney assured her and quickly grabbed her by the arm. "I can show you better than I can tell you." Courtney pulled Sabrina out on the porch before Sabrina could utter another word. Courtney's hand was sweaty and she had a bizarre expression on her face. She seemed fretful about something and the engine of her car was left running.

"Courtney, wait a minute. What's your big emergency?" Sabrina asked as Courtney hurried her outside onto the front porch.

Courtney hadn't answered, but she was still pulling Sabrina across the porch.

"Courtney, I asked you, what's the matter?" Sabrina firmly asked as she jerked her arm away. "You better tell me what's going on if you expect me to leave here with you."

"I don't have time to explain. I'll tell you in the car." Courtney stopped in her tracks and stared at Sabrina. "Just come with me." She grabbed Sabrina's arm again. "I urgently need you to help me with something!"

"But you haven't told me what."

"I know I haven't told you what it is, but it's something important. Do you think I would be here dragging you out of your house like this if it wasn't imperative that you come with me?" she explained, but was vague with the details of what she needed help with.

"Courtney, slow down and stop pulling me by the arm. Your situation may be vital but you're not getting any help from me until you tell me what it's all about. Right now, pulling my arm and rushing me out of my home is bizarre behavior. Seriously, you're behaving a little peculiar and you haven't shared any details about your urgent matter," Sabrina firmly stated.

Courtney threw both arms in the air just like a teenager without any patience. "I'll tell you everything in the car. Just come with me and stop wasting time asking me about it. I'll tell you everything you want to know when we're in the car heading to our destination. Is that agreeable with you?"

Sabrina shook her head, but mumbled. "I guess so, but I know you don't expect me to leave home without my purse," Sabrina announced.

"Just come with me," Courtney grabbed her arm again, pulling her. "You don't need your purse. This will not take much time and you'll be back home before you know it," she assured Sabrina.

Reluctantly, Sabrina agreed, pulled her arm away again and followed Courtney across the large porch and down the steps. Courtney had parked near the edge of the driveway since Starlet, Samantha and Charles were all parked along the driveway.

"Okay, I'll go without my purse, but I expect to hear all about whatever you're referring to the very instant we are seated in your car."

"It's a deal. I'll spill everything when we're in my car," Courtney promised, smiling.

Courtney swiftly headed across the huge lawn and down the driveway toward her little green Ford Fiesta as Sabrina followed behind her at a casual pace. Courtney had reached the car and was sitting inside tapping her fingernails on the steering wheel by the time Sabrina opened the passenger's door and gracefully took a seat inside. Courtney was suddenly boiling inside as she threw Sabrina an irritated look for taking her time after she had mentioned it was an emergency. However, Courtney kept her cool and didn't comment since she was quite pleased that Sabrina was at her disposal. But Sabrina was curious about what was going on with Courtney and what was so critical that she had to drag her out of the house soon after she arrived home from work. The moment Sabrina bucked up; she looked over at Courtney with serious eyes.

"Okay, start explaining yourself. If you can come drag me out of my house right after work before I had a chance to change out of my work clothes, I deserve an explanation and it better be a good one," Sabrina firmly stated as she stared at Courtney with intense annoyance. "When I agreed to go shopping with you sometime it didn't give you a standing invitation to drop by my house and interrupt my life at the drop of a hat," Sabrina explained, not pleased with Courtney's odd behavior. "I don't mean to be rude but you're acting rather peculiar."

"What do you mean about peculiar?" Courtney asked, backing out of the driveway.

"I can't put my finger on it, but you just seem a bit different than before," Sabrina calmly observed.

"What do you mean about I seem a bit different, than before what?" Courtney slightly snapped but caught herself not to come off too hostile.

"I just mean, I recall back when we first met during the time you were dating Rome. You just seemed more reserve and quieter. I don't mean any disrespect, but you almost seem like a different person now."

Courtney shifted in her seat nervously because she was a different person. She had gone through a transition for the worse from the moment Britain rejected her and Rome broke off with her. "It's not disrespectful to say that, but I'm curious to know if you mean different for the better or for the worse?" Courtney asked, anxious to hear her remark.

Courtney life flashed before her face, as she remembered a time when she was quiet and respectful, but that time seemed ancient to her. She was very aware of how her behavior had changed for the worse. She wasn't her regular self and she had nearly slipped over the edge since her breakup with Rome. Plus her torture was twofold since Britain had also pushed her completely out of his life. She couldn't seem to get a grip or reclaim her sanity. She was secretly drinking heavy and her family wasn't aware. She had lost interest in things that usually meant importance to her. She was wind up and focused only on her love and need to be with Britain Franklin and the agony of knowing he didn't want to be with her, because he preferred Sabrina. She had built up hostility toward Sabrina and her mind could only entertain dreadful things that she wished would befallen Sabrina.

"You just seem different. We can leave it at that, because we need to change the subject to why you have pulled me away from home. What is so pressing that you couldn't give me a moment to grab my purse?" Sabrina asked seriously.

Courtney laughed. "No way was I going to let you go back inside for your purse. It would have taken you ten minutes or better to get through that big house and upstairs to your room; and this emergency couldn't spare that time."

"What emergency? You still haven't told me what's so urgent?" Sabrina reminded her, starting to regret her choice to go along.

"Just calm down, I'm getting to that," Courtney told her.

"I am calm. I just want to know what is this all about."

"I'm sorry if I excited you. It's vital, but nothing to explain," she said and threw a quick glance at Sabrina.

Sabrina sat there with a confused look on her face waiting for Courtney to explain herself and the supposedly emergency. Sabrina stared at Courtney and said firmly. "What do you mean it's nothing to explain? We're headed somewhere. You can either explain where we're headed or you can turn this car right back around and take me back home."

"I actually have something to show you, Sabrina. It's easier to show you than to tell you about."

"You have something to show me?"

"Yes, I have something to show you that you won't believe."

"Okay, what do you have to show me that I won't believe? Where are we headed to see this something that I won't believe?" Sabrina asked irritated.

"It's in the cemetery," Courtney mumbled in a low voice.

"Did you say it's in the cemetery?" Sabrina asked surprised.

Courtney nodded and spoke in a louder voice. "Yes, I said cemetery. We are headed to Blue Angels Cemetery."

Sabrina stared at Courtney speechless for a moment, and then she said as Courtney drove at a regular speed down the highway. "Blue Angels is where my mother is buried."

Courtney nodded. "That I know since I visit your mother's grave from time to time," Courtney said, but she was not being truthful since she had never visited Candace's grave out of compassion. She had only visited it today in order to execute her plan.

Sabrina looked at Courtney with disbelief in her eyes. "My goodness, you mean you sometime drive out to Blue Angels Cemetery just to visit my mother's grave?" Sabrina asked. "I had no idea. You have never mentioned it before."

"I know I never mentioned it, but I drove out today right after work to visit your mother's grave."

"You drove out to Blue Angels today to visit my mother's grave?" Sabrina asked with surprise in her voice and on her face. "It's considerate and a compassionate thing to do, but I don't understand why you would go out of your way to visit my mother's grave? You didn't even know my mother."

"I didn't know your mother, but I know you; and I know how much grief you went through over losing her. I just thought it would be a nice thing to do and leave some flowers from time to time, which I did today," Courtney said.

"So, today, not long ago, you just visited my mother's grave and left some flowers?"

"That's correct." Courtney nodded.

"I don't know what to say. That was so thoughtful of you. You have caught me off guard with your thoughtfulness. I paid her grave a visit yesterday and left some red roses," Sabrina smiled. "Thank you so much for thinking of my mother."

"You are welcomed, but my visit to your mother's grave didn't end well and that's why I'm driving you there now."

"That's right, your emergency and the something you have to show me involves Blue Angels Cemetery," Sabrina recalled. "So what's the emergency at Blue Angles?"

"It's what I saw in the cemetery when I was visiting your mother's grave that has me out of sorts," Courtney anxiously explained.

"What did you see, just tell me already," Sabrina urged. "We are almost there anyway." She waved one hand. "Besides, you promised to tell me once we were seated and headed to our destination. So tell me already."

"Okay, listen; I saw a brown paper bag overflowing with money," Courtney told her.

"You saw a bag of money?"

"Yes, a bag of money in the cemetery next to your mother's grave."

"Courtney, you need to stop fooling around. You did not see a bag of money next to my mother's grave. I do not believe that."

"I'm not lying. Why would I drag you out of your house to see it, if it's not true?" Courtney fussed.

"I don't know why you do what you do, Courtney. Nevertheless, you will not convince me that there's a bag of money sitting next to my mother's grave. If you saw a bag of money it was all in your imagination."

"I'm not pulling your leg, Sabrina. I didn't imagine seeing that money. But when I saw it sitting there, it startled me, and I figured it couldn't be real. I stood still for a moment and gathered my nerve. Then I walked closer to examine it and upon closer inspection it was clear it was actually a bag of money."

"I'm not saying you have convinced me, but just for argument sake if you were that close to the bag and could see it was real, why didn't you grab it?"

Courtney didn't comment right away as she considered what she would say. "I wanted to grab it, but I was too scared. Therefore, I ran and jumped in the car instead. I grabbed my face for a moment and sat in the car wondering if my eyes were playing tricks on me. I couldn't believe what I had just seen," Courtney explained convincingly.

"You had a right to think your eyes were playing tricks on you, since they most definitely were. I'm not convinced there's a bag of money in that cemetery."

"You don't have to be convinced, but I know what I saw and to prove my eyes were not playing tricks on me, I got out of my car and ran back over to your mother's grave and there sat that bag of money."

"The more you talk the less I believe you. You were so afraid the first time, but yet you got out of your car again and walked over to the same spot, saw the money and still didn't grab it." Sabrina shook her head. "So, why didn't you take it that time? Why would you leave a bag of money sitting there if you could see it was real money?"

Courtney stumbled with her words, raking her brain to come up with a good explanation. "I thought about taking it and I wanted to, but as I said before I was too scared to reach down and touch it. It gave me the creeps."

"Okay, it gave you the creeps, but not enough to keep you from examining it twice?"

"What do you want me to say? I was just too terrified to touch that money. Plus the thought of being in a graveyard overwhelmed me and made me panicky. But absolutely, I wanted to see if the money was real so I could take it. But I was too scared to touch it since I was alone. After my second examination and I was convinced it was real, I just wanted to get in my car and get away from there as quick as I could," Courtney explained.

"You and I are not best friends, but you come to my home and grab me instead of another friend?" Sabrina held up one finger. "I'm still not convinced we'll discover a bag of money in the cemetery, but for argument sake, why would you want to share that kind of information with me? It didn't occur to you that you would either have to turn the money in, and if nobody claimed it, you would have to share it with whomever found it with you?"

"I thought of that," Courtney said. "But I don't mind sharing with you. Plus, I came to you because the money was sitting next to your mother's grave," she paused. "I thought maybe someone left it there for your family."

"Courtney, do you hear yourself talking? Do you honestly believe that someone would leave a bag of money in a graveyard in hope that my family would get it, or do you think they would bring it to our home? I'm just wondering which way makes more sense to you?" Sabrina asked.

"Of course, bringing it to your home makes more sense. But apparently we are not dealing with someone who is using their senses. They have more than a few screws loose to leave a bag of cash in a graveyard for anyone to grab," Courtney stressed convincingly.

Sabrina shook her head. She wasn't buying Courtney's story because it sounded too far-fetched to be true. She felt Courtney was the victim of her own imagination. However, she sat there speechless for a while, thinking to herself about all the angles of Courtney's story. She figured as incredible as it sounded, it was a very slim chance that it could be true; and that slim chance weighed heavy on her thoughts as she wondered, "Why would a bag of money be left in a graveyard? And if so, it meant trouble."

Courtney drove at a legal speed most of the way to the cemetery and the last five minutes before they were to arrive at the cemetery, she drove over the speed limit straight down the highway toward Blue Angels Cemetery. It was around 4:15 when they pulled into the large peaceful looking cemetery. Courtney quickly killed the motor and dropped her head on the steering wheel for a second, and then she looked over at Sabrina without commenting as she pushed the driver's door open and quickly stepped out of her car. She left the driver's door open as she stood near the hood of the car and glanced curiously about the enormous, spooky burial grounds. She had just been there earlier but other visitors were roaming around, visiting other grave sites. Now, no other bodies were walking about and it felt eerie and spine-chilling to Courtney at the thought of being in the huge graveyard. Sabrina sat glued to her seat, staring out of the passenger's window with aggravation of being there. Then she rolled down the window and calmly uttered.

"Courtney, I would like for you to know right now that I'm not pleased at the thought of being out here on the hunch of some bag of money you thought you saw. I'm not convinced, you saw anything near my mother's grave site."

Courtney waved her hand without looking toward Sabrina. "You don't have to believe it. In a few minutes you'll be able to see it for yourself. So you might as well get out and come face the music. I'll show you the money and you'll know once and for all that I'm not lying about what I saw," Courtney said over her shoulder and beckoned for her, but Sabrina didn't make a move to get out of the car.

"You can forget it. I have no intentions of getting out of this car to follow you on some ridiculous hunch. It's too preposterous and outlandish to be true," Sabrina firmly stated. "Nobody in their right mind would leave a bag of money in a cemetery or anywhere else. It's hard to even spot a nickel on the ground, but you expect for me to believe you spotted a whole bag of cash?" Sabrina firmly stated, shaking her head. "I'm sorry, Courtney, but I just don't believe it. But you can go ahead and check it out. I'll wait right here until you go and retrieve the bag you spotted," she said seriously. "The sooner you go and check it out, the sooner you can get me back home," Sabrina said irritated. She felt Courtney had pulled from home for something absurd.

Chapter Twenty-Nine

Courtney was anxious as she kept glancing at her watch. Nearly ten minutes had gone by since she and Sabrina had pulled into the cemetery. Nevertheless, she couldn't get Sabrina to exit the car. Her plan wouldn't work if she couldn't persuade Sabrina to leave the car and follow her. She swallowed hard and conjured up a sad face as she stepped over to the passage window and rested both arms on the lowered window.

"I thought you would have gotten out of the car by now. Why are you still sitting there? We're out here and I want to show you that bag of money I saw sitting next to your mother's grave," Courtney humbly said.

Sabrina shook her head. "Why don't you just go on and do what you need to do. I'm out here with you, so you're not alone. However, I have no plans of getting out of this car."

"Come with me, why not?" Courtney asked politely.

"I don't care about seeing the money that you're convinced you saw. Just get me out of this creepy cemetery," Sabrina firmly suggested. "I don't want to be here."

"I thought you were just out here yesterday to visit your mother's grave?"

"Yes, I was just out here yesterday. However, whenever I come visit my mother's grave, I'm with my entire family. I do not come out here alone. This cemetery disturbs me. So, can we please leave?"

"We'll leave as soon as you get out and see that money. You have made it quite clear that you don't believe there's a bag filled with money out here, so come see for yourself," Courtney urged her.

"Look, Courtney, you're right. I have made it clear that I don't believe there's any money lying freely in this cemetery. But you seem to believe it's real. So by all means run along and grab it, and then we can go," Sabrina suggested.

"It's too creepy out here. I don't want to go over to that grave site alone," Courtney mumbled, hoping Sabrina would get out of the car and accompany her.

"Courtney, what part of I'm not getting out of this car you do not understand? I'm irritated and quite annoyed that you would drag me out here at the whim of your imagination, since we both know there's no bag of money sitting out there," Sabrina firmly stated and then glanced at her watch. "So, please! Just do it already!" Sabrina raised both hands. "Run and get the money that you think is over there so you can get me back home, please! I have plans with Britain and I need to do my hair."

Courtney swallowed hard at Sabrina's announcement as her heart raced with contempt. "What kind of plans could be that important on a dull Tuesday night?"

Sabrina stared with bewildered eyes. "I beg your pardon. What did you just say?"

Courtney waved one hand over her shoulder as she stepped away from the window. "It was nothing. I just want you to get out and accompany me to that grave site. I want the money and I want to prove it's there, but I'm too scared to attempt getting it on my own." Courtney stepped to the passenger's door and pulled it open. "So, please, get out and walk over there with me. I'll grab the bag and then we can leave this creepy place," she begged.

Sabrina stared at her, frustrated with herself that she left home with Courtney in the first place. She noticed that Courtney seemed jumpy and more anxious than usual as she stood there at the open car door. Courtney was holding her breath for Sabrina to step out of the car. Her behavior appeared as if her life depended on Sabrina getting out of the car to accompany her to that grave site. Then after about three minutes of standing there and anxiously waiting to get out, Sabrina inhaled sharply and calmed herself down from the frustration, annoyance and irritation that she felt toward Courtney; and then slowly stepped out of the car.

"Since I'm out here, I might as well see this through so you can get me back home," she said. "So, lead the way to your riches that has fallen from the sky," Sabrina joked.

Courtney boiled inside at her dislike for Sabrina. In her mind, Sabrina made her world unhappy and everything she didn't want it to be. She felt if Sabrina was out of the picture, then she would be happy and she would have a chance with the man she loved, Britain Franklin. But she kept her cool to deceive and delude Sabrina into following along with her little scheme to trick her; and although, Sabrina was one hundred percent certain that Courtney did not see a bag of money in the cemetery, she followed along so Courtney could get to the bottom of what she thought she saw.

Courtney had walked a short distant a head of Sabrina, but as Sabrina trailed gradually behind her; Courtney looked around, stood still and waited for her. When Sabrina caught up with her, Courtney grabbed Sabrina by the arm.

"Please keep up. We need to stick right by each other's side," she suggested. "As you can see, this place is enormous and it's easy to get turned around or lost out here," Courtney anxiously stated as if she was almost out of breath. "You have to see what I saw. Then I'll know my mind isn't playing tricks on me."

"Courtney, I'm doing this to humor you, because clearly your mind is playing tricks on you. You can't honestly believe you are going to find a treasure of money out here," Sabrina uttered and glanced about. "This just isn't a good idea, being out here alone in this isolated place."

"But you're not alone. We're together," Courtney mumbled.

"It just doesn't feel right. Besides, how far do we have to walk to get to that spot? I don't recall my mother's grave site being in this direction," Sabrina observed.

"Just a few steps more," Courtney said and then pointed toward a small brown bag sitting near a freshly covered grave that was nowhere near Sabrina mother's grave. They stood still as Courtney pointed both hands. "Can you see that little bag sitting over there?"

"I cannot see a bag, but what I can see is, where you're pointing is nowhere near my mother's grave site." Sabrina suspiciously stared Courtney in the face. "Why did you say it was near my mother's grave?"

Courtney didn't comment as Sabrina continued. "What's the matter? You can't answer that question?" Sabrina annoyed and infuriated. "I'm sorry to say this, Courtney."

"You're sorry to say what?"

"What I'm about to say to you, but it's for your own good."

"What's for my own good?"

"Being forthright. You need to say what you mean and mean what you say."

"Are you calling me a liar?" Courtney snapped.

"I'm not calling you anything. I just know you have turned into someone whose word isn't that reliable," Sabrina said sharply. "So, I'm waiting to hear why you lied and said the bag was sitting near my mother's grave! I want the truth and not another fabrication from you, please!"

"Okay, I'll tell you. I told a little white lie because I needed to convince you to come with me. I figured if I told you it was near your mother's grave, it would encourage you to come out here with me to see for yourself."

"What is it that I'm supposed to see for myself? Is it the money? I'm sure that's another piece of fiction," Sabrina said crossly.

"I'm sorry I lied about it being near your mother's grave, but it's still out there." Courtney pointed. "Can you see that bag over there?"

Sabrina focused her sights straight ahead in the direction that Courtney pointed, and then she stared hard to make out the object in the distant. From a distance, it appeared to be a small brown paper bag with money leaking out of it.

"So, do you see it or not?" Courtney asked, figuring they were close enough that Sabrina should be able to see the bag.

"Okay, it does look like money, but I'm still not convinced. This feels odd."

"It might feel odd, but you have to admit that it looks real."

"So, what if it looks real? If it is, it means trouble and we need to get out of this cemetery and head home. Whoever left the bag is up to no good and could be hiding in the bushes. This is too creepy for my blood; and I'm heading back to the car right now," Sabrina turned on the heels of her blue Givenchy flats and headed back toward the car.

Courtney rushed up behind her and grabbed her by the arm and literally pulled her back toward the direction of the bag of money. "You're coming with me. We're out here together and we'll get that bag together."

"Okay, let go of my arm," Sabrina tussled her arm from Courtney's grip and lagged along behind her.

Courtney glanced over shoulder and waited, then grabbed Sabrina's arm again as they walked closer; and the closer they walked toward the freshly covered grave, the more Sabrina could see that it appeared to be real money. And all while they were walking toward the bag, Courtney had Sabrina by the arm.

"I guess you're right, Courtney," Sabrina said shocked. "It does appear to be a bag of money." She grabbed her face with both hands. "I can't believe someone would cash out here or anywhere!" She froze in her tracks. "We'll have to turn it in, of course. I can give it to my father to take care of. He'll get to the bottom of it," Sabrina suggested. "If that's okay with you or you can take it and turn it in."

Courtney nodded with dazed eyes. "I don't care about that. You can give it to your father to handle."

"Okay, I will, but of course, we'll count it first." Sabrina continued to hold her face in astonishing bafflement. She couldn't believe Courtney's anecdote had turned out to be true. However, seeing was proof, and she was looking straight at a bag filled with money sitting on the ground near the freshly covered grave site.

Courtney looked at Sabrina. "Well, don't just stand here. Go grab the money so you can give it to your father to turn in," Courtney suggested.

"You want me to walk over there and pick up that bag?" Sabrina stared at Courtney with anxiety in her eyes. "I don't think so. You discovered it. You should walk over there and grab the bag yourself," Sabrina suggested.

"You said your father would handle it and get the money turned in. Therefore, you should grab the bag. Besides, I have a confession to make."

Sabrina glanced toward the sky and then at Courtney. "What's your confession?"

"I'm a coward and too scared to walk over there and grab that bag."

"What are you afraid of, Courtney? I'm standing right here."

"You just mentioned that someone could be hiding in the bushes."

"I know I said that, but I'm sure nobody is lurking out here. So just walk over there and grab the bag so we can take off."

Courtney was anxious. She knew her plan wouldn't work without Sabrina's cooperation of stepping over to grab the bag. "Please, Sabrina, just do it already. Can't you see how scared I am to step over there? Besides, you're taking it home with you anyway."

Sabrina shook her head. "You act like a kid sometime the way you behave." Sabrina held up both hands. "However, just to move this along so we can get out of this cemetery, I'll walk over and grab the bag so we can finally get out of this creepy cemetery."

Courtney nodded and held her mouth tight to keep from laughing. She said bingo under her breath. She had just tricked Sabrina right into the trap she wanted her to fall into. Therefore, as Sabrina walked toward the bag, just inches away, she fell into a deep dark hole. She was hanging on by her hands and when she looked down into the pit it scared her terribly. She knew instantly that the bag of money had been a trap for someone to fall into the hole that she had fallen into. She screamed out for Courtney.

"Courtney! Courtney! That was a trap! Come help me out of this hole! I can't hold on much longer. If I fall to the bottom I could injure myself or even break my neck!"

Chapter Thirty

Moments later, Courtney was standing over Sabrina, bending over laughing to the point of almost crying. She held her face in merriment.

"Excuse me, if you think this is funny," Sabrina snapped angrily. "I don't think you would be laughing if it was you hanging over in here!"

"But it is funny, Sabrina!"

"Okay, it's funny. I'm glad you find it amusing, just pull me out of this hole. I can't hold on much longer," Sabrina urged. "So, please stop playing around and help me out of here," Sabrina demanded.

Courtney didn't reply and through Sabrina's water filled eyes, she noticed Courtney backing away. She couldn't figure out what was going on with her and why she was backing away and not helping her out of the hole. Then Courtney yelled out.

"I'm leaving now! Sabrina. Did you really think I would help pull you out? Get real Miss Sabrina Taylor! It was my idea. I set you up. You knew it was too incredible to be true and you were right, but you still fell in my web. You could probably kick yourself for being so stupid!" Courtney kept laughing.

"Courtney, what are you trying to say?"

"I'm not trying to say anything. I have said it! I played a trick on you so you could fall over in that deep hole."

"Why would you do something so cruel and dangerous? It's not a bit funny and once everybody knows what you have done, I don't think you'll have the last laugh. Your family and my family will not be pleased with your behavior! What you have done raises several red flags, one being that you are unstable and the other being you really have changed, and not for the better," Sabrina seriously said as tears rolled down her face. "You have a serious issue going on in your head that you need professional help for."

"So, I need a shrink because I tricked you in that hole?"

"Yes, I think you do. Normal sane people don't do things like this," Sabrina cried. "I knew you were odd of late but I didn't think you would go this far to do something so dreadful."

"Now, you know. I'm not lying down to be walked on for any of you rich bitches anymore!" Courtney yelled angrily.

"I have no idea what you are referring to, but it's not too late for you to come to your senses and help me out of this hole."

"You can rot in there for all I care. Why should I go through all the trouble of getting you in there, just to pull you out? That whole money tale was just a ploy to get you out here. I covered that hole with sticks and dried weeds to make sure you wouldn't notice it. I wanted you to try to get that bag that I filled with play money so you could fall in. And now that you have, I'm satisfied!" She laughed. "From a short distant the money appeared real, but only the ten singles on top were real money. All the rest was play money from my monopoly board game. Pretty clever, don't you think? I pulled that off and tricked you without breaking a sweat!"

"But, Courtney, why are you doing such a despicable thing? The fact that you finds pleasure in this really bothers me. Besides, I thought we had buried the hatchet and developed some kind of alliance with each other. I know we'll never be best friends, but I thought we had some kind of viable connection with each other. Now you play a dirty trick on me like this! What gives! Why are you doing this? What did I ever do to you?" Sabrina asked tearfully.

"That's a good one. What did you ever do to me? I don't have to answer that. I'm sure you can put two and two together and come up with four!"

"Courtney, just tell me what's your beef?"

"Well, just in case it hasn't dawned on you, I'll tell you! You little perfect witch! You took Britain from me! We were getting along just fine until you moved to town."

Sabrina shook her head in shock. "You can't be serious! You went out of your way and played this dangerous trick on me because of your feelings for Britain? I thought you had moved on and were over him."

"That's where you are wrong! I'll never be over him, never!" Courtney shouted. "And I dare you to stroll into my workplace and take all of Britain's attention."

"That's not what happened."

"It is what happened." Courtney yelled angrily. "You moved to town, strolled into Franklin Gas and now he won't give me the time of day! It's your entire fault. I never knew I could hate someone as much as I hate your guts, Sabrina Taylor. I detest you! I wish you were dead!" She screamed.

"Don't say that, Courtney. You have to know deep down that I didn't take Britain from you. You and Britain were not dating or anything. He told me months ago that the two of you were just friends."

"Yes! We were just friends. But I was hoping for more. I'm sure you get that."

"Yes, I get it. And in the very beginning when Britain and I started dating the first time, I had a hunch that you had feelings for him."

"See, you had a hunch! Why didn't you follow your hunch and stay out of his face?"

"Courtney, give me a break here! It's not like he was dating you, okay? You were never more than a lunch partner to him. You know that and I know that and everybody else knows that. So, no matter how you put a spin on it, whether we got together or not, he probably wouldn't have asked you out; but he did ask me out."

"You should have said no!"

"Okay, maybe you are right. But I had no idea that you were so into him."

"Now you are lying! You just said you had a hunch!"

"Yes, I had a hunch, but..."

"So which is it? You had a hunch or you didn't know? Or you just didn't care? I'm sure it's the latter! You should have stayed your distant!" She stared in silence for a moment. "Britain and I were starting to get real close, but guess what? You and your filthy rich family had to move to town and mess up everything!"

"It's not logical to blame me for your problems, Courtney," Sabrina stressed.

"It is logical and a very rational statement because it's true. I lived it and it was beautiful just like a dream come true for me. It was right before you moved into the area." Courtney wiped her tears. "Britain liked me. I know he did. Why else would he have made a long list of plans for my birthday? It was going to be my chance of a lifetime, and our chance to finally be together and alone." Courtney grabbed her face and stared toward the sky for a moment. Then her eyes turned stone cold toward Sabrina. "You know what? None of the things on his precious list never happened for me because of you! If you hadn't moved to town Britain and I would be together! I know we would!"

"Courtney, you need to wake up! You can't blame me that Britain didn't ask you out! Whether I moved here or started working at Franklin Gas has nothing to do with your non-relationship with the man! You're not making any sense!"

"From where I'm standing, I'm making a lot of sense! It lifts my spirits to see you off in that deep hole! If you rot there I'll have another chance with him! Do you get me now?"

"Yes, I get you loud and clear! That's what I mean. If you're getting some kind of kick out of treating me like this, something is seriously off with your behavior and actions! Something has gone very wrong here, Courtney!"

"Yes, something is wrong here. You're wrong to be dating Britain!"

"No, Courtney. Something is wrong with you to be carrying on like this! What you're doing is dangerous and appalling. You're acting like you're off your rocker!"

"Shut up, Sabrina! Don't say that to me. I'm not off my rocker. I'm just teaching your emaciated frame a lesson so you'll stay away from Britain! You know what you'll get if you don't! Besides, I had no other choice after Britain said so long!"

"What are you talking about now?" Sabrina asked.

"Britain told me to get lost the other day."

"He wouldn't talk to you or anyone like that. I'm sure he didn't say get lost."

"He might as well have said get lost. That's why I had to teach you this lesson. Britain ended our friendship," she cried. "We're not even friends anymore. We are nothing! He told me he's in love with you, and said it wouldn't be too cool for him and me to associate too closely on a non-professional level." She raised both arms. "So, there you have it, Sabrina! Britain spelled it out loud and clear when he said he loves you."

"He said that to you and now you're carrying on like this!" Sabrina cried, feeling helpless. "You need a reality check! The man is not into you! Sane people don't go around doing dangerous stuff like this when they don't get asked out. You need to see a shrink if you think what you're doing right now is sane behavior!" She angrily fussed. "Besides, he may have just told you that he's in love with me. But he made it clear last December when you made that scene at his house that there could never be anything between the two of you. Granted, you got your job back and now you are working on site again and he's polite to you. But Courtney, Britain isn't into you and could never be. You were once with his brother. That's the beginning and end of the story!" Sabrina reminded her.

"Shut up, Sabrina! I hate your guts. You don't know what you're talking about. It's not because I was with his brother, it's because you're in the way. It's you that's keeping me and Britain apart!" Courtney angrily shouted. "Therefore, as far as I'm concerned, you can rot in that hole. That's exactly what will happen because once I drive out of here, nobody is driving out here to look for you? Nobody! It was not nice knowing you! So long sucker!" Courtney laughed.

Sabrina cried. "No! Wait! Please come to your senses and do the right thing!"

"I have come to my senses! I'm doing the right thing right now! This is what you call payback, you little rich bitch! You took Britain from me and now I'm taking him from you! Not to mention how you all use to laugh at me behind my back."

"Courtney, you really have gone off the deep end. I have no idea what you are talking about. But I know I have never laughed at you and I don't know of anyone that have laughed at you. Where are you getting these ideas? More and more you are proving my point that you are not yourself and you seriously need some professional help to help you work through the distorted ideas that are floating around in your head."

"There's nothing distorted about my ideas except thinking this hole is good enough punishment for the hell you put me through! You can thank your marbles I'm having some mercy on you!"

"What is that supposed to mean, Courtney? How can anything be worse than this?"

Courtney laughed. "I can think of a few more things that I wanted to do but I settled on this! Being out here in this isolated scary place off in that deep hole, you'll suffer harder and longer." Courtney glanced about at the deep woods surrounding the cemetery and wrapped her arms around herself. "Yes, this punishment will fit you just fine. You'll barely survive out here in the cold and dark with no food or water or protection from whatever might be lurking around."

Sabrina was so choked up with fright and disbelief of what Courtney was doing until she could no longer speak. She felt hopeless as if her words would make no difference.

"What's the matter? You can't talk now?" Courtney asked. "You better speak now because when I leave, you won't have anyone to talk to except for those around you who can no longer talk."

Sabrina finally found her voice again, took a deep breath and was desperate to try to get through to Courtney. She realized that she needed to keep a cool and calm head to try to reason with someone who was unreasonable. She needed to desperately plead to get Courtney to come to her senses. She realized she was dealing with someone who was obviously mentally unstable as well as intoxicated on top of the madness. She realized that she needed to reach deep within herself to try to pull Courtney back to reality. She also realized that she needed to think quickly and try every angle that she could think of. First of all, she decided to try to make Courtney feel that she felt that Courtney had been playing a trick or a game; and that no harm was done and that maybe Courtney would help her out of the hole since Sabrina didn't think she had really meant her any harm.

"Courtney, don't you think it's time to let me out of here?"

"What are you talking about?"

"Don't you think this little game has lasted long enough? I'm tired of hanging on like this and this is not what I consider a fun game," Sabrina said hopeful that Courtney's mind would follow along and help her out of the hole.

"I think you are the one that's losing it if you think this is just a game," Courtney said in a dazed manner. "This is not a game. This is your punishment for taking Britain away from me. You need to keep that in mind."

"I know you are just kidding around and it's time to stop the foolishness and let me out of this hole so we can get back home. It's getting close to dinner time at my house and Carrie will wonder what's keeping us so long," Sabrina mentioned Carrie to alert Courtney to the fact that Carrie is aware that she left with Courtney.

"That's right, thanks for reminding me that your housekeeper knows that I dropped by your house to pick you up. I'll pay her another visit when I leave you out here. I'll go and tell her that we went to the Mall and somehow we separated from each other," Courtney informed her and shook her head. "You may think this is a silly little game but this is really happening. This is my day in court with you and you lose."

Sabrina was drained and didn't know what else to say to get through to Courtney. She was afraid for her life and realized it was useless trying to reason with Courtney. Now she was just plain angry and frustrated and determined to say whatever came to her mind that she thought would help her talk some sense into Courtney to do the right thing.

"So, you plan to leave me out here and lie to my family that you left me at the Mall?"

"That's exactly what I plan to do."

"And you think Britain will want to be with you if I'm not around?"

"That's exactly what I think. Whether he admits it or not, I know that guy wants me. He will be my man one day. I'll make sure that happens if it's the last thing I do!"

"Courtney, he doesn't love you. You need to move on from Britain and get some help. You are really sick out of your head right now."

"The only one sick is you, Sabrina, if you think I will ever move on from Britain. I just told you that I will make him my man or die trying! If it's the last thing I do! If you're smart you'll take me at my word.

You shouldn't under estimate me. That's why you're down in that hole right now! You under estimated me!"

"Okay, maybe you're right and maybe you and Britain will be together one day. But right now, you need to help me out of this hole. We need to get out of this cemetery and back home," she pleaded.

"Thanks for reminding me, I think I'll leave right now. Because I can't stomach your lies. Telling me how maybe Britain and I will be together when you know you don't believe that. You're just trying to throw me off balance! You can't beat me at my own game!" Courtney shouted down at her.

"I'm not trying to beat you at anything, I just want you to help me get out of this hole. Can you please do that, Courtney?"

Courtney glanced over her shoulder as if she had heard a noise, and then she looked down at Sabrina and shook her head.

"Courtney, you can't leave me hanging in this hole like this. Help me out of here, please!" Sabrina cried out.

"No way, I'm not lifting a finger to help you get out. You might as well save your breath and stop begging me to help you. Frankly, you're wasting your time trying to convince me to help you!"

"You are not a murderer, Courtney."

"Who said anything about murder?"

"I'm saying it because anything could happen to me if you just leave me out here in this isolated cemetery off in this big hole."

"You probably won't die," Courtney laughed.

"What sort of thing is that to say, that I probably won't die? Courtney, I'm appalled at your behavior. If anyone had told me that you were this far gone off the deep end from reality, I wouldn't have believed them!"

"Well, believe it and just shut up about! You probably won't die anyway! I couldn't be that lucky, but I can hope!" Courtney laughed and then pulled a bottle of vodka from her jacket pocket, twisted off the cap and turned it up to her mouth for a long swallow before lowering the bottle, placing the cap back on and tucking it back inside her pocket.

"Courtney, seriously if you don't stop this madness, you could end up a murderer. This is no joke. It's a dangerous game and if you leave me out here to die, that's what you'll be. You'll be a murderer. Is that what you want? Do you really hate me that much that you want to see me dead and all because of Britain? Don't be foolish, Courtney. Don't turn yourself into a killer," Sabrina desperately pleaded.

"Get real! You're not going to die! I couldn't be that lucky! Somebody will find you first. But if I'm lucky, by the time someone does find you in that hole, you'll wish you were dead," Courtney laughed. "In the meantime, I'll be there to comfort Britain."

Courtney stood silent for a few minutes with both hands on her head, looking down at Sabrina. Her face was covered with tears and just as Sabrina thought Courtney was considering pulling her out of the hole, Courtney walked closer to the edge of the hole and stepped on Sabrina's fingers, causing Sabrina to fall to the bottom of the deep, dark cold pit.

Courtney turned and ran away from the hole, leaving Sabrina at the bottom of the pit. She was laughing with tears falling from her eyes as she ran like something was after her. She took her hands and covered both ears to fade out Sabrina's cry for help as she ran through the cemetery toward her car.

CPSIA information can be obtained at www.ICGtesting.com
Printed in the USA
LVOW11s0706281115

464478LV00001B/1/P